Nawlins

DERIC AUGUSTINE

First Edition 2025

Illustrations by Frida "fridouw" Lundqvist

Map Art by Brittany Petrone

Jacket design by Jeff Manning

NAWLINS
OASIS
THE GARDENS
CLASSROOMS
CLASSROOMS
SENIOR DORMS
GYM
AUDITORIUM
11TH GRADE GIRLS DORM
11TH GRADE BOYS DORM
10TH GRADE GIRLS DORM
10TH GRADE BOYS DORM
9TH GRADE GIRLS DORM
9TH GRADE BOYS DORM
LIBRARY
COMMON CENTER
COURT YARD
BOOK STORE
CALL CENTER
6, 7, 8TH GRADE DORMS
CLASSROOMS
HISTORY VILLA
STORE

Dedication

To my late mother, Donna Marie Augustine:

I miss you more than words can ever express. Thank you for shaping me into the man I am today. I will always cherish our conversations, the values, morals, and principles you instilled in me, and, most of all, the love and strength you poured into being my mother.

Raising twin boys wasn't easy, but you gave us your best, and I want you to know how deeply my brother and I love you. We carry your lessons and your love with us every day. I hope you are looking down on us with pride, knowing that your sacrifices and guidance continue to guide our steps and inspire our dreams.

Rest In Peace
Forever your son,
Deric Augustine

Dedication

To my late father, Deric Augustine:

I promise to become the father you were destined to be but never had the chance to become. Carrying your name is an honor, and I hope that one day, through my accomplishments and acts of service, it will stand as a beacon for future generations.

I will strive every day to build a legacy that makes you proud—a legacy of love, resilience, and purpose. Thank you for being the foundation of the person I am today.

Rest In Peace
With all my heart,
Deric Augustine II

Dear Young Wizards,

The magic you are searching for already lives within you, waiting to blossom into the powerful person you are destined to become. Until that day comes, be strong, be fearless, and embrace every moment of this incredible journey we call life.

Much love
Your big bro,
Deric Augustine

Prologue

The monstrous beast barreled down the snowy highway, its massive frame charging through the blizzard with terrifying speed. Its dense, white fur blended into the storm, making it nearly invisible except for its fiery red eyes that pierced the night like twin beacons. With each bound, its claws scraped the icy pavement, relentlessly pursuing the speeding truck.

Three-year-old Link gripped the seatbelt strap in the backseat, his hands slick with sweat as tears stung his eyes.

The beast lunged, saber-toothed fangs flashing, its hot breath fogging the rear window. Link screamed, but the creature's thunderous roar drowned him out as it slammed into the side of the truck, lifting the right wheels clean off the ground.

Tilting sharply, the truck balanced on two wheels before crashing back down with a bone-jarring thud, jolting sideways on impact. Tires squealed as Sammy fought the wheel, yanking it left, then right, struggling to regain control. Once the truck leveled out, he reached into the console and pulled out a black wand with a glimmering crystal handle.

"Get down, son!" Sammy shouted.

He aimed the wand and fired. A bright blue beam shattered the rear window and struck the beast in the snout. It let out a piercing shriek, tumbling across the road before disappearing into the swirling snowstorm.

As the gap widened between them and the beast, Sammy pressed harder on the gas. Link wiped the tears from his eyes and met his father's glance.

"Son, you are a Deslondes. We are strong and brave. I need you to stay strong. Can you do that for me?"

"Yes, Pop," Link replied, his voice small yet firm.

"Good," Sammy responded, unclipping a gold necklace from around his neck. "I'm going to put this chain on you. It will keep you safe."

The chain held a bar-shaped gold pendant with a diamond encased at its center.

As they crossed onto the steel bridge, Sammy hit the brakes. The truck slid, tires grinding over the icy surface until it finally skidded to a stop. Through the fractured windshield, a cloaked silhouette stood motionless in the middle of the bridge.

"Not good," Sammy muttered, his knuckles tightening on the steering wheel.

He slammed the truck into reverse but froze as a flash of red reflected in the rearview mirror.

Link turned, his heart sinking as the beast reappeared, its red eyes glowing ominously in the darkness.

Sammy shifted back into drive and floored the gas pedal, hurling the truck directly toward the cloaked figure.

The figure raised an arm, clutching a gold wand.

"Brace yourself," Sammy instructed.

Link gripped his seatbelt tighter as Sammy slammed on the brakes and yanked the wheel, sending the truck spinning across the slick bridge.

A crimson beam erupted from the figure's wand, striking the side of the truck. Glass shattered, airbags burst open, and the vehicle crashed through the guardrails.

The truck teetered, its back half dangling precariously over the raging river below.

"Are you okay, son?" Sammy called out.

"Yes, Pop," Link croaked, clinging desperately to the seatbelt strap holding him in place.

The truck jerked as Sammy reached for his wand. "Hold on, Link!"

Link screamed as his grip slipped, sending him plummeting into the dark abyss below.

"Link!" Sammy dove after him, his voice cutting through the howling wind.

As Link plummeted, the biting cold air lashed against his skin, but it was the sight of the raging river below that truly froze his heart with fear.

A blinding white light burst from Sammy's palm. It curled around Link like a ribbon of energy before hardening into a crystal-like, egg-shaped shield.

"I love you, son," Sammy's voice echoed faintly as the shield plunged into the river.

The last thing Link saw was his father silhouetted against the storm. And then there was only darkness.

Chapter One

Donna woke from the dream, gasping for air. Her heart pounded, her head throbbed, and her skin itched. As if the nightmare wasn't bad enough, she now had to deal with the anxiety it left behind. She tried to ignore the crowded subway and focused on taking slow, steady breaths. When that didn't help, she pressed her index and middle fingers to her temples, massaging in slow, deliberate circles.

The massage remedy usually helped with her throbbing migraines, but it wasn't working. The high-pitched squeals from the train's wheels reminded her of the creature's screech. She reached under her seat and grabbed her backpack. Her small brown hand moved around pencils, erasers, and notebooks until she felt the cap of the medicine bottle.

What she hated most about her anxiety medication wasn't the bitter taste but the stupid orange cap. She could never get the damn thing open. It took all her might to push the lid down and twist it loose.

A few minutes passed, and she was feeling better with the help of her pills. She hadn't expected to fall asleep on the subway; she just wanted to rest her eyes a bit, but exhaustion got the best of her. She'd picked up more hours at her restaurant job this week to pay for a trip to the movies tonight. Honestly, the extra hours of work on top of her first year of high school were burning her out, but luckily, today was the last day of school.

Donna yanked up the strap of her denim overalls, which kept hanging over her slender shoulder, and sank into her seat. She hated that her anxiety had such a grasp on her life.

She rested her head against the window and stared outside. Nothing special caught her eyes—just the usual graffiti on the walls as the subway entered another tunnel. When she finally sat up, the moisturizer in her kinky, curly hair had left a stain on the glass. She tried to wipe it away with her hand, but that only made it worse. Donna looked around, but no one was paying attention to her. Everyone on the train was in their own little world—typical New Yorkers.

She pulled out her favorite composition notebook and a pencil from her backpack and started to write:

Hay, Notebook,

I had that crazy dream again. Well, really, it's a nightmare. About the accident. But this time it felt so real, as if I could see everything through my brother's eyes.

In this dream, they didn't die because of a car crash. There was a scary creature and someone in a cloak with a wand.

My dad had a wand, too, and some kind of magic coming from his hands. What is this dream trying to tell me?

Dad also told Link he was a Deslondes. What is a Deslondes?

Donna dug into her backpack again and pulled out her outdated iPhone with a cracked screen. She typed *Deslondes* in Google, and a musical group from New Orleans popped up.

This can't be right. Dad wasn't in a band.

The sound of the announcement, "Tremont Station," interrupted her thoughts.

The dry afternoon heat hit Donna like a freight truck as she exited the subway station. But she wouldn't let the heat take away the joy of being done with the school year. She untied the bandana from her thick hair and shook her curls loose.

You would have thought that Donna was some celebrity, the way folks were waving and smiling at her, but in reality, this neighborhood was like an extended family—everyone knew everyone. And on a Friday afternoon, most locals were hanging out on the stoops of their brownstones.

Two old-timers were playing cards at the first brownstone Donna passed. One of the guys looked upset, as if someone had just taken all of his lunch money.

A group of middle-school girls showed off their double Dutch skills on the sidewalk with two turners, one jumper, and a set of ropes.

"Hey, Donna Marie," the girls said as Donna politely walked out of their way.

Most of the families had lived here for generations, fostering the camaraderie that made this block a community. The most famous landmark in the area was a bodega. Donna had to make a quick stop there to pick up some milk for her oatmeal in the morning before work.

Donna looked up at the big yellow sign above the entrance that read *Angie's*.

Angie, the owner and the heart of the bodega, greeted her with a warm, full smile as Donna walked through the door. Her pearl earrings dangled as she perched on a stool by the register.

"Hola, Donna. Last day of school?"

"Yep. Finally, summer break!"

"How's your mom?" Angie asked. "She's doin' fine?"

"She's well. Thanks. We're going to my favorite place tonight."

"Let me guess... The movies?"

"How did you know?" Donna asked.

"Do you know how often I witnessed you begging your mom to take you to the movies, while she used to drag you in here to carry the groceries?"

"I guess you're right," Donna said, chuckling.

"Let me make some fresh cannoli for you two to sneak into the theater."

Angie stepped to a pastry station, and Donna walked to the back of the bodega toward a refrigerator where the last half-gallon milk carton sat on the top shelf. She pulled hard on the fridge handle. Tippy-toeing, she pressed her body closer to the fridge to grab it.

As she shut the door, a black cat walked up to her and pranced over her feet, leaving black hair on her white tube socks. Donna gave the cat a side-eye.

"Um… Excuse you, cat. Dingy Chucks are acceptable, but dirty socks aren't."

The cat continued brushing against her legs, leaving more hair on her socks. Donna gave up, reaching down to pet the handsome feline.

"When did you get a cat?" Donna asked as she walked to the register.

"What cat?" Angie responded.

The black cat walked between Donna's legs, presenting itself to Angie. It sat on its bottom, flicked its tail, and looked up at her.

"I've never seen this cat a day in my life, but it can stay to keep out the rodents."

Angie demoed the homemade cannoli to Donna, the mouthwatering cream filling oozed from the two pastries. She placed the plastic container in a brown bag, which crunched as she closed it, handing it to Donna. Donna attempted to pay for her milk, but Angie insisted it was on her tab—something she did quite often.

Donna started to walk down the street to her brownstone, but stopped when she caught a glimpse of the black cat in her peripheral vision. When she turned her head, the cat looked around as if trying to avoid eye contact with her.

I know you're following me.

Donna picked up the pace as she crossed the street, refusing to look back because she didn't want to encourage the cat. But curiosity got the best of her once she reached the other side. She glanced over her shoulder. Luckily, the cat was nowhere in sight.

Bye, you stinky cat. Her pace quickened as her brownstone came into view.

And there it was—perched right on her front steps like it lived there. Or like it had always known this was her home.

"You're kidding, right?" she exclaimed, as if the animal could understand. "How did you beat me here?"

She sighed, giving it a pat on the head. The feline elongated its neck to show its approval. Or was it showing off the red collar she now saw around its neck?

There was a gold-colored name tag hanging from the collar. *How the heck did I not see this earlier?*

Donna crouched and took the pendant between her fingers, tilting it closer to read the bold lettering etched across the front.

"Well, hello, Mr. Whiskers. It's good to meet you. Though what you're doing here, I don't know."

She flipped the tag. An engraved fleur-de-lis caught her eye—one with a horizontal line beneath it. She recognized the symbol immediately because it was part of her mother's favorite football team's logo, the New Orleans Saints.

No phone number. No address.

Mr. Whiskers pawed at the brown paper bag in her hand, eyeing it like it held his next meal.

Donna sat on the steps, opened the bag, and pulled out a cannoli. She broke off a piece and placed it beside him. He dove in without hesitation.

"Slow down, buddy."

He licked his paws, clearly satisfied with the ricotta filling, then hopped off the step and strutted away without so much as a meow.

"Oh, great. You just wanted my food."

She watched him disappear around the corner, then turned and headed inside.

The wooden stairs creaked beneath her as she climbed to the second floor. At the black door with chipped white paint, she gave a firm nudge with her shoulder to get it open.

Inside, the cramped studio apartment barely fit a twin bed and an oversized blue beanbag. The refrigerator buzzed incessantly—a broken compressor that got louder by the day. She gave it a gentle kick, and the noise faded.

From beneath the sink, she retrieved a white bucket catching drips from a leaking pipe and emptied it into the toilet. After setting it back in place, she opened the fridge, took a gulp from a milk carton, and spilled some on her dingy Chuck Taylors.

The microwave clock caught her eye. She capped the milk, stuffed it back in the fridge, and hurried to her bed.

Kneeling down, she reached beneath the frame and slid out a small metal security box. Duct-taped to the top was a laminated piece of paper: Mom's Physical Therapy Money. She pulled out an envelope, tucked it under her arm, and slipped back out the door.

Chapter Two

D onna stood motionless in front of the entrance of Eunice Manor, which was a few blocks away from her brownstone.

It was happening again like clockwork: the heaviness in her chest, the itch crawling across her skin. But what bothered her most were the heightened sounds—taxis blaring at the red light, birds chirping nonstop, and a baby's cry from across the street pounded her ears like a speaker pressed against her eardrum.

"Breathe, Donna. Breathe," she said as she closed her eyes and massaged her temples.

The massage managed to keep her anxiety at bay this time. After a few deep breaths, she looked up at the gloomy sky.

The nursing home was a gray place, filled with gray people who looked forward to so little these days. There were no paintings on the walls, flowers, or anything bright—as if the place liked being gray. Despite the setting, the person Donna visited here always lightened her mood.

The woman at the informational desk waved at Donna as she entered. Donna waved back and continued down one of the long bland halls.

She stopped at the last door. A square glass panel allowed her to see inside the room. Unlike the rest of the nursing home, this room had vibrant colors and green potted plants by the windows. Donna pressed her forehead against the glass and smiled as she looked at her mother.

Catherine sat in a wheelchair, reading a novel. Her right hand held the book steady while her left arm rested stiffly against her chest—awkward and unmoving. A stroke two years ago had left her partially paralyzed on that side.

Donna's breath fogged up the panel as she watched. She quickly wiped away a tear. *Come on, Donna, pull yourself together. Mom can't see you like this.*

After her pep talk, she walked into the room.

Hey, Ma," she said.

"Baby girl," Catherine replied, her voice stretching the vowels in that familiar New Orleans drawl that always warmed Donna's heart.

Donna loved the way her mother said *baby*. It wasn't just a word; it was a melody, pronounced in a sing-song manner unique to those from New Orleans, the *a* and *y* were drawn out and dancing. She wrapped her arms around her mother, sinking into the comfort of Catherine's embrace. The creamy brown skin of her mother carried a faint scent of vanilla from her favorite lotion—a scent that whisked Donna back to her childhood, to times when Catherine would wrap her up in her arms and hold her close to her chest.

Donna pulled back and kissed her mom's head. Catherine now wore her hair short and natural—since she had to cut all her hair off for the operation that left a hook-shaped scar on the left side of her head.

"How was your last day?"

Donna handed her the report card.

"All A's. Good job, my 'sha," Catherine said, her voice carrying the warm cadence of her New Orleans roots. "But then, I knew you would."

Perhaps even more than *baby*, Donna cherished when her mother called her *sha*. It was a Louisiana term of endearment, embodying a sense of love.

"Angie sent you something." Donna pulled the cannoli from her bag. "But first, you have to do twenty arm raises."

"Oh shucks. You little sneaky thing."

There was a knock at the door. Excited to see her favorite nurse through the panel, Donna walked over.

"Can I talk to you for a second?" Donna asked Nurse Rose.

They moved to the hallway.

"Any update on the speech rehab and physical therapy?" Donna asked.

"Unfortunately, her government assistance denied the request."

Donna sighed and took a deep breath. "I just want things back to how they were."

She looked back at her mother and pulled out the crinkled white envelope from her pocket.

"Is this enough to pay for physical therapy this month, at least?" Donna asked, handing over the envelope.

Nurse Rose counted the bills.

"This will cover it. I'm sorry I can't do anything else," she said, rubbing Donna's arm.

Donna's phone rang.

It was Mr. Walks, her boss from Walks Way Deli. She hesitated to answer—a call at this hour was probably bad news.

Sure enough...

"Donna," he began, "I hope you're not busy."

"Well, I... I am. I'm with my mother at the nursing home. We are going to the—"

"I need you at the restaurant. Your coworker bailed on his shift and I fired him. Get here in thirty minutes."

"But I have a special day planned with my mother."

"You see, Donna, I really thought you wanted this job. But if I'm wrong, just tell me now."

Mr. Walks waited, no doubt knowing the silence was killing Donna.

Finally, he said, "Come in right now, or you're fired. What will it be?"

She wanted to say, *screw you and that restaurant*, but she couldn't because she needed the job to help pay rent. Plus, Mr. Walks paid her in cash and was going to let her work more hours this summer.

"All right," she said and hung up.

"Everything okay?" asked Nurse Rose.

"I have to go to work."

"Your mom has been looking forward to your trip to the movies."

"I know," Donna replied, unable to say more without crying.

When she went back into the room, Catherine was standing up with a small gift bag in her hand.

A group of nurses entered with a birthday cake.

"Mom, look at you! Standing with no cane."

"Happy fifteenth birthday! You thought I forgot, didn't you?" Catherine said.

Catherine and the nurses sang "Happy Birthday" to her.

"Make a wish, my 'sha," her mom said.

I wish you were a hundred percent healthy again so you could leave this place.

Donna blew out the candles and gave her mom a hug.

"I got something for you," Catherine said, presenting Donna with a small jewelry box.

Donna carefully lifted the lid of the dark blue velvet jewelry box. Inside, nestled against the plush fabric, lay a gold necklace with a small, bar-shaped ruby pendant.

"Mom, this is beautiful."

"Your father gave me this necklace. The ruby represents his birthday," Catherine said.

"July fourteenth," Donna recalled.

"It was a pair. Your father's necklace had a diamond pendant."

"What happened to it?"

"It was lost in the accident," Catherine said, her gaze drifting away for a moment.

"Let me help you put it on, Donna," Nurse Rose offered.

Donna lifted her hair as Nurse Rose clipped the necklace around her neck.

"I'm never taking it off," Donna vowed.

As she caressed the ruby in her hand, a vivid memory from her dream flashed before her—it was the exact style as the diamond pendant her father had draped around Link's neck. *How did I dream about that diamond pendant when I've never seen it or heard about it until now?* Despite her urge to share this bewildering coincidence with her mother, Donna hesitated. Catherine was radiating joy, and Donna didn't want to cloud the moment with the shadows of their tragic past. Instead, she simply embraced her mother, burying her face in the comforting scent of vanilla, holding tightly to the warmth of the present.

Chapter Three

It was almost midnight. Exhausted, Donna trudged up the stairs to her apartment, her apron stained with the remnants of her shift. As she reached the second floor, her neighbor's door swung open.

"How dare Mr. Walks make you work on your birthday! You should've called me. I would've taken a train there and told him to kiss my Black ass," Jacquie said.

Jacquie was Donna's godmother. She and Catherine were great friends and used to work together before Catherine's stroke. Catherine and Jacquie weren't sisters, but Donna still called her "Auntie," even though she was now old enough to use her first name.

"Chill, Auntie. It's not a big deal. I made some money to help you out with the bills, and I didn't want to stress you out while you were working."

"Hunny, real estate can wait. Nobody messes with my niece and gets away with it."

Donna couldn't help but laugh as she imagined Jacquie showing up to her job and cursing at Mr. Walks. Jacquie wasn't a fan of holding her tongue, no matter who she was talking to.

"It's not funny. You know I will always have your back."

Jacquie opened her arms wide and smiled. Donna walked into her embrace, and Jacquie hugged her tightly while patting her back. At five foot seven, Donna now towered over her godmother, which always made them laugh.

"Happy birthday, Donna Marie."

"Thanks, Auntie."

"Your mom told me she gave you the necklace. Let me see."

"You knew she had it all this time?" Donna said, untucking the chain from under her shirt.

"It's stunning! And of course, I knew; I'm her best friend. She was waiting for the right time to give it to you. Oh, that reminds me—"

Jacquie went into her apartment and returned with a small box wrapped in polka-dot paper.

"One of my houses closed in the Bronx, and I got a nice commission. So, I got you a much-needed birthday gift."

Donna swiftly tore away the wrapping paper, revealing a new iPhone.

"Thank you, Auntie!" she said, jumping up and down.

"You're welcome. It's not the newest one, but I figured it's better than that busted phone you have now."

Donna's temporary excitement quickly faded. She was grateful for her new phone but would've rather had a movie day with her mom.

"Auntie... I'm tired of seeing my mother in a nursing home. I wish I had the money to give her the best medical care in the world."

"God won't give you adversity you can't handle. Keep your head high. Your mother's blood runs in you. She's a fighter, and she's resilient."

"I wish I could be strong like her," Donna said.

"That's where you're wrong. Look at me."

Jacquie held Donna's chin while she stroked her cheek.

"Hunny, you are just like your mother."

"Thank you, Auntie." It was all she could manage to say. But at this moment, she didn't feel at all like her mom.

Donna peeled off her grimy work shoes the moment she stepped into her apartment, resting the back of her head against the door as she let out a deep sigh—finally, a moment to herself.

With every step towards her bed, it felt as though bricks were strapped to her feet. She retrieved the security box, fished the crumpled bills from her pocket, and tucked the money inside. Unfolding her work apron, she reached into the large front pocket. Her face lit up with a smile as she drew out the birthday card from her mother. Holding it to her lips, she planted a gentle kiss on the card before placing it carefully in the box.

After sliding the box back under the bed, she collapsed onto the floor, pausing for a few heavy breaths.

Though she knew a shower was necessary before sleep, the weight of her eyelids and the sheer exhaustion in her bones begged to differ. With a flick of her wrist, she flung the apron across the room and clambered onto the bed. Just then, rain began to tap against the windowpane, soon accompanied by a flash of lightning and the distant rumble of thunder, lulling her into a much-needed slumber.

All night, rain pattered the pavement outside in a chaotic symphony. It wasn't anywhere near morning, but Donna, a light sleeper, was jolted awake by the rolling thunder a few minutes earlier.

Taking advantage of the unexpected wakefulness, she busied herself setting up her new phone—a welcome distraction, perhaps the real reason she couldn't sleep.

While the phone updated, she lit a honey-scented candle on the windowsill and gazed at her reflection mirrored in the glass. The flickering candlelight cast dramatic shadows across her sharp features, reminiscent of her mother's high cheekbones and full lips. Yet, as she studied her image, she wondered if she inherited her mother's inner strength as well.

Her introspection was abruptly cut short by a loud meow. Peering out the window, she spotted Mr. Whiskers standing under a streetlamp.

"Dude... What are you doing out there? Hungry again?" she called out.

The cat's responding meow seemed to affirm her guess.

"Taking that as a yes," she muttered, spooning tuna into a bowl.

Slipping on her favorite black hoodie, she stepped outside, carefully balancing the bowl as she tiptoed past Jacquie's door, avoiding the creaky floorboards.

Descending the stoop, the fresh, rain-cleansed air greeted her, along with Mr. Whiskers, who affectionately rubbed against her leg. She set the bowl down on the sidewalk, her voice soft but laced with irony.

"So, you're just using me for food... it's fine. I could use a friend right now. I had to work on my birthday. Because I'm poor. My father and brother died before I even got a chance to meet them. I have no friends because there's no time; I'm always working, studying, or worrying that my mom might have another stroke. And if my life falls apart, I have no one to take care of me. Do you know how that feels?"

She paused, gasping for breath as Mr. Whiskers stopped eating and looked up at her.

"I guess you do. Your cat parents abandoned you too?"

As she connected with Mr. Whiskers' mesmerizing eyes, glowing amber and gold in the streetlight, a voice shattered the moment.

"Hey, kid."

A disheveled man clutching a beer bottle stumbled toward her. Heart pounding, Donna raced up the steps. The man gave chase, grabbing her arm and yanking her back down, causing her to slam onto the concrete.

Her right wrist absorbed most of the fall, but that pain was nothing compared to the feeling building in her chest. Her heart felt like it was about to explode. An unbearable heat rushed through her skin. She squeezed her eyes shut, desperately trying to ease her anxiety, but it was no use.

"Your hands! Why are they glowing? What are you?" the man said.

Donna's eardrums throbbed. She kept her eyes tightly closed and took deep breaths as if she were about to drown, gasping for the last available air.

She couldn't take the excruciating pain in her chest anymore. She opened her eyes and screamed at the top of her lungs. First-floor windows shattered, car alarms blared, and nearby streetlights burst in a torrent of sparks.

The man fled into the shadows.

As the pain in Donna's chest began to ease, the red glow emanating from her hands also faded.

What is happening to me?

Taking deep, slow breaths, Donna worked to steady her heart rate. She reached up to massage her temples with her index and middle fingers, only then realizing the extent of the damage to her wrist. A sharp moan escaped her lips as the pain intensified.

Mr. Whiskers approached Donna, rubbing gently against her side as if trying to soothe her. Jacquie stormed out the front door, and the cat scampered away, disappearing into the darkness of the night.

Donna pressed her ear against the cold door of the hospital room where she waited, listening to Jacquie speaking with a police officer outside.

"Her mother's disabled and in a nursing home. Has been for some time."

"What about her father?" the officer asked.

"Unfortunately, he passed away in a car accident before she was born. I'm her legal guardian."

"Why was she outside alone this late?"

"She snuck outside to feed a cat."

"The Bronx isn't a place where a fifteen-year-old girl should be wandering at night. I'm sure you don't need me to tell you that."

"So, a man attacked her, and it's somehow her fault? It looks like you're more concerned about why Donna was outside than trying to find the person who attacked her."

"Ma'am, I'm just doing my job."

Jacquie sighed loudly. "You know what? I understand. It won't happen again. Thank you, officer."

Donna hurried back to the exam table. The white paper covering the blue cushion ruffled as she took a seat.

Jacquie entered the room and sat next to Donna.

"You have to be more careful, hunny. If you'd gotten seriously hurt, the state could legally take you from me. No more going outside at night without my permission. Is that clear?"

"Yes, Auntie."

"I don't know how I'm going to tell your mother about this."

"No! Please don't tell her. I don't want to stress her out. Please, Auntie."

"I don't want to stress her out either, but she's your mom and she has to know you were at the emergency room."

"Okay. But... Please, let's just tell her I fell rollerblading or something and that's why I had to go to the hospital. I don't want her to worry about me. It may cause another stroke. Please. I'll never go outside again without your permission."

"You don't even own a pair of rollerblades... But okay, I understand. I'll tell her you borrowed them from a friend."

"Thanks, Auntie."

"I'm sorry this happened to you," Jacquie said, rubbing Donna's shoulder.

A knock sounded at the door before it opened to reveal a doctor—an elegant Black woman with locs pulled back into a neat ponytail.

"Hey there, I'm Dr. DuVernay."

She pulled a stool from the corner, rolled it beside Donna, and sat down.

"I heard about what happened and it's not your fault," she said.

Donna, who hadn't often seen Black female doctors, felt an unexpected comfort in her presence.

"I will do everything I can to make you feel better. First, let's check out your wrist."

Dr. DuVernay gently examined Donna's swollen wrist. She winced slightly as the doctor probed the tender spots.

"Okay. The good news is your X-rays show no broken bones. But there is significant swelling, so it will be sore for a couple of weeks. Ice will help it heal faster."

She wrapped Donna's wrist in a cooling compression bandage and handed Jacquie a brace.

"And you're Donna's aunt?"

"I'm her godmother and legal guardian," replied Jacquie. "So, you could say I'm a jack-of-all-trades. Or Jill."

Dr. DuVernay chuckled. "Keep the compression pack on for about an hour. After the swelling goes down, you can put on the brace."

"Thanks. I'll make sure she wears it," Jacquie said.

"Donna, you also suffered an anxiety attack tonight?" Dr. DuVernay asked.

"Yes. They started after my mother got sick a couple of years ago. But tonight... I've never felt this kind of pain. Like my heart was beating out of my chest. And my hands... I could have sworn I saw..."

Donna stopped herself before she mentioned the glow. She didn't want to sound crazy or worse—she didn't want Jacquie to think she was on some sort of drugs.

"I saw glass everywhere when I opened my eyes. I don't know how that happened."

"It was raining tonight, and the police said the glass could've broken from a lightning strike of some sort," Jacquie explained.

Dr. DuVernay removed the stethoscope from her neck and placed the cold gauge on Donna's chest.

"Hmm... Hmm," she murmured as she listened.

"Everything okay?" Jacquie asked.

"Yes," she replied, looping the stethoscope around her neck again. "I'm going to take a blood sample and run some tests. Nothing to worry about; just want to see if there's an underlying cause for those anxiety attacks."

She prepared Donna's arm for the needle. Donna nervously looked away.

"I've been told on many occasions that my needles don't hurt, not one bit. I promise."

She smiled at Donna, who cracked a tiny smile in return.

The needle went in, and Donna barely noticed.

"See, I told you it wouldn't hurt," Dr. DuVernay said as she removed the needle.

She placed a brown bandage on Donna's arm.

"You are great with kids. Do you have any of your own?" Jacquie asked.

"I do. I have a seventeen-year-old son. I've cleaned up many scrapes and other war wounds throughout the years. Luckily, no broken bones."

"Does he go to school here in the Bronx?" Donna asked.

"No, my family and I live in New Orleans. That's where I'm from. I've been in New York for two months, training surgeons. I was supposed to return home last week, but, um... my visit got extended."

"Well, I'm glad you stayed because you're the best doctor I've ever had."

"That's sweet of you to say, Donna."

"You know, my mom is originally from New Orleans. I've never been, but I want to visit badly."

"Ah, that's why you're so special; you have roots in NOLA."

"Oh, I'm nothing special," Donna said, dropping her head.

"We're all done here. I'll call you if I find anything. It was a pleasure meeting you both," she said.

Dr. DuVernay touched Donna's hand for a moment, staring at her eyes as if she was studying her. It didn't feel weird—it felt as if she'd known this woman her whole life.

"I think you're more special than you give yourself credit for, Donna Marie."

Chapter Four

Lil Wayne's "Tha Block Is Hot" was blasting over Lincoln's headphones as he sat on the garage floor of his parents' mega two-story home, shining the exhaust pipes of his Scout Bobber motorcycle with a rag.

He had received the motorcycle as a birthday gift last year. His parents were skeptical before buying it because of the safety hazards, but they eventually gave in—his outstanding school achievements helped persuade them.

When Lincoln was younger, he had dirt bikes that he would ride around the three acres of land in his backyard and throughout their gated community, Eastover, in New Orleans East.

When he wanted more space, his parents would drive him to his grandparents' home in Opelousas, Louisiana, where his family had a farm and plenty of land for him to ride. It seemed like every year in high school he would get a new toy to ride—his first big boy dirt bike at fifteen, a racing four-wheeler at sixteen, and an expensive motorcycle at seventeen. He'd be eighteen soon, and he was expecting a car.

His parents were well-off, but he wasn't a spoiled kid. He was aware of his privilege and didn't take anything for granted.

The garage door lifted, and a matte-black Range Rover pulled into its usual spot in the four-car garage next to the matte-black G-Wagon.

"Wassam, Ma. How was your trip?" Lincoln asked as Rima stepped out of the SUV.

"It's midnight, son. What are you doing up?" she asked, holding her briefcase in her hand.

"I couldn't sleep."

"Well, I'm glad you're up because you can grab my luggage from the trunk… My trip was good. I'll tell you more about it inside. I'll make us a midnight snack."

Lincoln opened the SUV's liftgate and grabbed the spinner suitcase.

"Ma? Did you bring a body back with you? This bag is heavy as crap."

"Watch your mouth. And since I stayed in New York an extra week, I had to do some shopping."

"Did you buy me anything?" he asked.

"We give you an allowance. You can buy your own stuff."

He placed the suitcase down and tried to roll it, but one of the wheels was stuck. He pushed and pulled the bag, but the wheel wouldn't budge. When he kneeled down to inspect it, he found the culprit—a pebble jammed inside. He tried to pry the rock loose with his finger but failed.

He stood up and removed a black wand from the front pocket of his hoodie.

"Levite," Lincoln said, pointing his wand toward the suitcase.

The suitcase slowly lifted in the air and floated in front of him, moving in the direction of his wand.

"That's more like it," he said, walking from the garage into the kitchen.

"Is your father up? Should I make three sandwiches?" Rima asked, stationed in front of the massive refrigerator.

Lincoln lowered the suitcase by the stairs leading to his parents' room.

"I think Dad is upstairs sleeping. Did you know the wheels weren't working?" he inquired.

"That's why I needed you to lift it for me with your huge muscles. I didn't know you were going to cheat," Rima said.

They both laughed.

"I had to stand on business."

"Child, I wish you would stop saying that. I hope you stood on business with your chores."

"I did my thang: washed the dishes, cut the grass, took out the trash, organized the garage, washed the cars and all that. But you know who did not stand on business? Dad."

"Is that right? What did he do?"

"Ma, we both know he can't cook... I still don't know why you had to stay in New York for an extra week. You made me suffer even longer," Lincoln said, hopping up and taking a seat on the kitchen counter.

"Boy, if you don't get down from my countertop, I'll make you suffer even more."

"My bad, Ma," Lincoln said quickly, hopping back down.

"The night I was supposed to come back home, I was packing my bags when a cat started making noise on my balcony. I don't know how it got up there because I was on the tenth floor."

"Um, what does this cat have to do with anything?" Lincoln asked.

"This cat is the reason I stayed an extra week."

Lincoln laughed but then recognized his mom was serious. She didn't smirk or chuckle. She remained stern as she layered the sandwiches with lettuce and tomatoes.

"The cat looked identical to the one De— To the one that my friend used to have when we were in college. I mean, it was just an alley cat, but my friend used to feed it and call it his cat."

"Come on, Ma. That was probably just a random cat that wanted some food and climbed up to your balcony."

"I thought the same thing until I opened the window and took a closer look. It had the same collar that I remember."

"Okay, that's kinda cray-cray."

"I missed my flight looking for that cat. And the next day, the hospital called and begged me to stay a few more days to help out in the ER and I agreed."

"So, this cat was the reason I had to order takeout for another week behind Dad's back. You know how hard it is to sneak food in here without him knowing. I swear he checks the trash cans."

"This cat led me to something… extraordinary. Last night, a fifteen-year-old girl came into the ER with a sprained wrist and a panic attack. Something nudged me to run a blood test on her… and what I discovered… well, you won't believe it."

Rima opened her briefcase on the kitchen island and removed a test tube.

"What are you doing?" Lincoln asked.

Without answering, Rima delved back into her case, retrieving a sleek black wand. A dark red vine twisted around its handle, spiraling down to the base, its texture pulsating as if alive, fused into the wand itself.

"Onyesha," she said.

A beam of blue light erupted from the wand's tip, striking the test tube, which then levitated between them. The blood inside began to swirl, gaining speed until the cap popped open. A spiral vortex of blood formed, floating in the air before stabilizing.

"Donna Marie Guillory is a wizard, and she doesn't even know it," Rima declared.

"Wait, she has no idea?" Lincoln was astonished, his eyes drawn to the purple sparks glistening within the blood.

Recalling his sixth-grade lessons at Nawlins School of the Gifted, he remembered learning that wizard blood possessed a distinctive purple sparkle invisible to Norms.

"No, she's completely in the dark about it. It's likely why she suffers from anxiety attacks, much like you did a few years back."

"Yeah, but I always knew I was a wizard."

"But you didn't understand how to control the immense power within you, which led to your anxiety," Rima explained.

Lincoln vividly remembered the overwhelming anxiety he faced starting at thirteen—the throbbing headaches that felt as if his skull might split, the searing sensation crawling across his skin, and the excruciating pressure around his heart, as if it were being squeezed from within. Just thinking about those times sent shivers down his spine.

"How does she not know? Has something like this ever happened before?"

"No. Every wizard born is archived in our registry, and I've checked the database; there's no record of Donna Marie or her parents."

"What are you going to do?" Lincoln asked.

"I've spoken with the Chancellor. She wants Donna in New Orleans to tour the school as soon as possible. Admissions has already sent out an invitation. If she accepts, I'll be the one to break the news to her."

"This is wild. I can't believe she doesn't know she's a wizard... You know, she probably won't even believe you; might think you're just cappin."

"Cappin? What's that?" Rima asked, discarding the tube in the trash.

"Come on, Ma, I thought you was up to date. It means she might think you're lying about the wizard thing."

"If that's the case, I'm sure she'll change her mind once she visits Nawlins and learns about the gifts hidden inside her."

"Yeah, you're right."

"Here's your sandwich," Rima said, offering him a plate laden with his favorite: turkey, avocado, lettuce, tomatoes, and pickles, all perfectly assembled on olive oil-coated wheat bread.

"Thanks, you're the best," Lincoln said, planting a kiss on her cheek.

Lincoln lingered in his room for half an hour before he made his way to the garage. It wasn't insomnia that kept him up past midnight—it was the allure of his clandestine retreat by the lake.

He silently opened the garage door, shifted his motorcycle into neutral, and carefully rolled it out onto the street. Once he had pushed it far enough from the house, he donned his helmet, started the engine, and melted into the night.

Fifteen minutes later, he parked along the curb facing Lake Pontchartrain—Louisiana's vast expanse of water that seemed to hold secrets as deep as its depths. Lincoln descended the seawall steps and sat at his favorite spot near the solitary light pole, the salty air mingling with the tang of seaweed embracing him.

Externally, Lincoln's life appeared flawless—a loving family, affluence, and endless opportunities. Yet, beneath the surface, he grappled with the truth of his identity. Rima and Charles DuVernay, who lovingly raised him, were not his biological parents. They had adopted him after rogue wizards claimed the lives of his real parents. His birth father, Deedy Deslondes, had been the intended target, and his mother, a Norm, was merely collateral damage. As the last of the Deslondes lineage, Lincoln's true heritage was a secret that could endanger his life if ever revealed.

He reached into his black leather jacket and pulled out a weathered Polaroid. The back scrawled with a message in black sharpie:

"To my best friend,

My family says hello."

—Deedy

He resisted the urge to flip the photo over, knowing it would only fuel his anger—an anger he had worked tirelessly to master. Anger that could lead to uncontrollable rage, unlocking a formidable power he dared not to unleash again.

He stuffed the photo back into his pocket and headed home.

Chapter Five

Donna was reluctant to return to work today. The threat of termination loomed over her, a constant reminder from Mr. Walks. He had excused her absence the day before, thanks to the doctor's note, but her wrist still throbbed with a dull ache. The swelling had lessened, but the brace scratched and irritated her skin—a relentless annoyance, especially since her job demanded so much of her hands. When curious customers asked, she claimed it was a rollerblading accident in Central Park, though she didn't even like rollerblading.

The trauma of Friday night's ordeal lingered vividly in her mind. She accidentally spilled coffee on a tabletop, which splashed on a customer's suit. The gentleman was understanding and gracious, contrasting sharply with Mr. Walks' furious reaction. His face turned a fiery red as he stormed over and hurled a towel at Donna.

As the disgruntled customer departed, he left Donna a generous tip, no doubt a silent protest against Mr. Walks' harshness.

Donna had always thought Mr. Walks had it in for her. He seemed to hate everything about her. It was all wrong—what she wore, how she spoke, how she carried a tray, how she served or didn't serve a table.

"You only got this job because your aunt Jacquie gave me a good deal on this building years ago, and I owe her," Mr. Walks would often snarl.

One day, Donna wore her hair in braids, sparking immediate backlash.

"Too urban," Mr. Walks had scorned, sending her home without a day's wage.

Yet, when her white coworker styled her hair similarly, Donna watched and waited for a rebuke that never came. Instead, Mr. Walks praised her colleague, "You wear your hair very nicely, you do, young lady. Very neat and practical."

And his glance at Donna carried an unspoken challenge: *What will you do about it?*

Midway through her shift, the restaurant had slowed down a bit into a quiet afternoon. Mr. Walks had assigned Donna the task of rolling silverware. As she lined up napkins and polished utensils, an older woman dressed in worn clothes entered. She approached Donna with a gentle, hesitant gait, dragging a battered spinner suitcase behind her.

"Hello, I was wondering if you have any spare food?"

"I'm so sorry, but we don't," Donna replied.

The woman's face drowned in disappointment. She reached into her pocket and pulled out a few coins.

"I'll have a cup of coffee. Is this enough?"

"I'll tell you what," Donna said. "I'll buy you a slice of cheese pizza to go with that coffee. It's the only thing good at this restaurant," she whispered. "How does that sound?"

The lady smiled.

"Thank you. Thank you so much, child. God bless you."

Mr. Walks was standing by the double doors leading into the kitchen. He placed his arm across the doorway so Donna couldn't get past.

"What do you think you're doing?" he asked.

"What do you mean?"

He pointed to the woman.

"She ordered a slice of pizza," Donna explained.

"I don't want her kind in here."

"And what kind is that?"

"The kind that looks dirty and doesn't have any money."

"She has money, and I won't refuse service to her," Donna responded.

"Hurry up and get her out of here," Mr. Walks said, lowering his arm so Donna could walk by.

She slowly walked into the kitchen and took her time pouring a cup of coffee.

As she walked out, she overheard Mr. Walks talking to the cook.

"That Black bum is always outside my restaurant, begging for food. And now that stupid girl's gone and let her inside."

Donna was pissed, but she kept her composure. She placed the coffee next to the woman.

After the lady finished her meal and walked out, Donna reached into her tip pocket, pulled out some bills, and paid for the dinner.

As Mr. Walks burst through the double doors, she started to take off her work apron.

"Where do you think you're going?"

Donna flung her apron at him. "I quit, you racist asshole! That's where I'm going."

The apron landed comically on his bald head. He yanked it off, fixing her with a furious glare.

A strange tingling sensation buzzed through Donna's hands, and she glanced down to see a faint red glow emitting from her palms. Quickly, she stuffed her hands into her pockets.

Mr. Walks tossed the apron to the floor and stepped menacingly closer.

"What did you say to me, little girl?"

As the tension mounted, Donna felt the tingling intensify. Suddenly, Mr. Walks clutched at his throat, gasping for air as if an invisible force constricted him. He staggered about the restaurant, his movements erratic and desperate. The cook rushed out and wrapped his arms around Mr. Walks' big belly, performing a forceful Heimlich maneuver. After several vigorous thrusts, Mr. Walks expelled a deep breath and, shockingly, coughed up a small, live toad.

"What the hell have you been eating?" asked the cook.

Mr. Walks stood frozen, staring at the toad as it let out a loud, echoing croak.

A fit of giggles overtook Donna. Someone possibly choking shouldn't have been funny, but she couldn't help herself as she strutted out the door. The crisp air hit her face as she made her way toward the subway station.

While on the train, she carefully inspected each of her fingers—there was no glow or sign of anything out of the ordinary. *This must just be more symptoms of my anxiety. Like the flashing lights I see with a migraine?*

Donna spotted Mr. Whiskers on the steps as she approached her brownstone. She gave him a few pets before he jumped onto her leg.

"What are you doing, cat?"

Mr. Whiskers looked at her as he dangled from her jeans.

Donna picked him up. He then lifted his front paws toward the door and started to meow.

"Okay. I guess I can bring you inside, but you're getting a bath first. You stink."

Jacquie was waiting for her at the top of the stairs.

"You quit your job?" she asked. "Mr. Walks called and told me you pitched your apron at him and called him a derogatory term before quitting."

"He called a woman a 'Black bum.' I couldn't take working there anymore." Donna didn't even try to explain the toad incident.

"He said that? I oughta go to that restaurant right now and talk some sense into that man. I didn't like you working there anyway. I think a front-desk job at my office just opened up. I'll ask my boss if the company can hire a minor for the summer."

"That would be cool. I would love to work with you."

"What derogatory term did you call Mr. Walks?" Jacquie asked.

"A racist asshole," Donna said shyly.

"He is a racist asshole... But you can't call grown-ups that. And what are you doing with that nasty cat?"

"I'm just going to keep him inside for a little while."

"If he comes in, he's your responsibility. Get yourself cleaned up, and let's go see your mom," Jacquie said.

Once again, Donna felt the familiar oppressive weight in her chest, followed by heart palpitations. These symptoms always surfaced during visits to her mother.

Pausing at the entrance, she took a moment to collect herself, leaning against the hot brick wall. She pressed her fingers against her temples, hoping to alleviate the mounting pressure, but the massage brought no relief. She fished a pill from her pocket and swallowed it dry, grimacing at the lingering bitter taste. She longed for a glass of water or even a can of soda—anything to wash away the unpleasantness.

Jacquie placed a hand on her shoulder.

"I'm fine," Donna said. "Thanks, Auntie."

They walked through the sliding doors and went to Catherine's room, where she was sitting in her wheelchair, watching a soap opera on the television.

"I don't know why you like watching those boring shows," Jacquie muttered as they walked into the room.

"Oh, what a pleasant surprise. I get to see both of my favorite people today," Catherine said, smiling.

"Your daughter quit her job today," Jacquie announced.

Donna flopped onto the couch and waited for her mother to chew her out.

Catherine sat in silence for a moment, then smiled again. Donna smiled back, and they both burst into laughter.

"Like mother, like daughter, huh?" Jacquie said to Catherine. "I remember when you told me you used to get fired from your summer jobs in high school too."

The two friends giggled.

"Oh, Donna, I forgot to tell you something came in the mail for you today." Jacquie reached into her purse and handed Donna an express mail envelope.

"'Nawlins. School of the Gifted,'" Donna read.

She opened the envelope and pulled out a brochure and a letter. She read the letter aloud.

"Dear Donna Marie Guillory,

We are delighted to inform you that we are formally inviting you to attend Nawlins School of the Gifted for the fall term.

Every year, each school district submits its top five students for evaluation for enrollment to Nawlins. Our admissions board and prestigious alumni carefully review each student's academic and personal accomplishments, offering enrollment to a handful of lucky students.

If you accept our admissions offer, you will join Nawlins' rich history.

Nawlins is the oldest historically Black institution in the world, dating back to 1811. Specializing in training and developing academic skills in minority students, we are proud to report a 100% placement rate in college and a 100% graduation rate from graduate school.

Donna Marie, we would like you to tour our campus this summer in New Orleans. A legal guardian will have to accompany you as a chaperone. We will pay for all expenses, including flight, hotel, car services, and per diem for food.

Please review our brochure for details and contact us with any questions.

Seek knowledge. Knowledge is power. And whoever has the power controls the world.

Nicole Decken,

Chancellor of Nawlins."

"Donnie Marie, this is an amazing opportunity. Nawlins is the best school in Louisiana and nearly impossible to get into," Catherine said.

Donna opened the elegant brochure. Glossy photos of the campus stretched across the first two pages.

"It's huge," Jacquie said, peering over her shoulder. "Oh, no wonder. See, it's a college as well."

Donna stood and handed the brochure to her mom. Catherine studied it for a moment, eyes scanning each page.

"You should go," she said firmly.

"But how did they even find out about me?" Donna asked.

"Someone from the school district must've submitted you," Jacquie said. "You've got a 4.3 GPA!"

"Go on the tour. See what they have to say," Catherine added.

"They're paying for a trip to New Orleans. We're going." Jacquie grinned.

Donna tried to hide the massive smile creeping across her face.

Chapter Six

Welcome to New Orleans! Donna read the white and black sign hanging in the airport's baggage claim area while waiting for Jacquie's duffel bag. Blue, red, yellow, and orange Mardi Gras beads wrapped around each cursive letter.

She flipped her curly hair out of her face as she approached Jacquie at the infotainment screen near the welcome booth, where her aunt was engrossed in the local attractions.

"Auntie, this bag is kinda heavy. We're only here for a day. Did you bring your entire closet?"

"Oh, let me carry that, hunny. I don't want you to aggravate your wrist," Jacquie said. "And I may have packed a few outfit changes. I might find my future husband in New Orleans. I love Southern gentlemen." She winked.

A tall man in a black suit stood by the exit, holding a small sign with Donna's name.

"Looks like we are getting the VIP treatment on Nawlins' dime," Jacquie said.

"Why does he have my name on a sign, and why does he have on a suit?"

"Because he works for a private chauffeur company, and we are his clients. He's kinda cute too."

Donna pulled her eyebrows down and wrinkled her nose.

The man politely carried their bags to the black SUV parked in the pickup area.

Donna rolled down the window, and the humid air struck her face as they headed east on the I-10 interstate toward downtown.

The driver pulled into the valet section of a fancy hotel in the French Quarter.

"Welcome to Hotel Monteleone," greeted a staff member, opening Donna's door with a flourish. Donna caught Jacquie slipping her phone number to the driver on a napkin. Shaking her head, Donna pretended not to notice as they were escorted to the check-in desk.

After they checked in and freshened up, they began their walk to Nawlins.

Much like a New York afternoon, the French Quarter buzzed with people crowding both sides of the sidewalk. Folks here seemed more patient. Cars waited quietly for traffic to move, and pedestrians strolled instead of rushing.

Not used to Louisiana's summer heat and humidity, which made New York's feel like a breeze, Donna was already sweating as they walked past the old French and Spanish-style buildings the hotel concierge had mentioned in their directions.

Jacquie was in her element, stopping frequently to capture various architecture with her camera, and engaging with fellow tourists.

Donna, trailing behind and stifling a yawn from the early flight, grew impatient. Jacquie's bubbly enthusiasm, usually infectious, now only heightened Donna's desire to reach their destination swiftly.

They turned a corner, and Donna's eyes widened as she beheld the iconic sight of Nawlins. Its buildings were grand and stately, reminiscent of imposing elegant castles. A tall black iron fence surrounded the expansive grounds, enhancing its regal appearance.

A young woman in a crisp white shirt and khaki pants awaited them at the wooden door at the school's entrance.

"Wow…" Donna murmured, her fatigue momentarily forgotten as she took in the grandeur of her new surroundings.

"You must be Donna Marie. I'm Zina, your official Nawlins tour guide. It's a pleasure to meet you, luv."

Donna was mesmerized by her New Orleans accent. It reminded her of her mother.

"Hi. This is my aunt, Jacquie," Donna said.

"You look so young. Are you a student here?" Jacquie asked, shaking Zina's hand.

"Yes, ma'am. I'm starting my first semester of college here at Nawlins this fall. For now, I'm working a summer job through the school's Peer Pilot Program. I get paid to give campus tours and also earn internship credit."

"I like your accent," Donna blurted.

"Some people from this city have thick accents and some don't. I do because I'm from the seventh ward. Oh, and we New Orleans folks sometimes end our sentences with 'baby' and 'luv.' So, don't take it personally, it's just our lingo."

"Oh, my mom is from New Orleans and she says baby all the time. I love it." Donna said, trying her best to mimic Zina's accent.

"You have to elongate the A sound… BAAABAY. Now, try again."

"*Baaa*by," Donna said, opening her mouth a little wider as she tried to stretch out the A sound.

"We will keep working on that." Zina smiled.

The tour began in the main lobby, which was as spacious as the cafeteria at Donna's high school. The windows were gigantic, stretching as wide as the double doors they had just entered through. The glossy black floors gave Donna the sensation of walking on black ice.

"These floors are trippy," she said.

"Some of the finest architects designed this school, and they were all Black. We take great pride in employing people of color," Zina explained with a note of pride. "The floor is new. Absolute black marble."

Donna had never seen anything like this outside of television dramas about affluent schools that seemed too luxurious to be real.

The campus was deserted, likely because everyone was away for summer break, leaving a silence that was only broken by Jacquie's rumbling about how fancy everything looked.

"Check out that amaaaaazing antique chandelier, Donna," Jacquie said as they passed through a library.

"I see it, Auntie," said Donna, cringing, secretly glad no one else was around to overhear Jacquie's enthusiasm.

While the chandelier failed to stir much excitement in Donna, the next room captivated her completely. The walls were adorned with black-and-white photographs that pulled her in. Though Donna never had a thing for photography, and her only camera was on her iPhone, the images in this room were striking—crisp, clear, and filled with joyful expressions of Black people smiling and laughing.

The tour was almost over. They had made the rounds of all the major academic departments, and Zina was now leading them on a stroll around a courtyard. Various bike trails and walking paths winded their way through the groomed grass.

Donna saw a familiar face walking in their direction.

"Hello, ladies. Good to see you again, Donna."

"Dr. DuVernay! What are you doing here?" Donna stared at her.

"You can call me Rima now." She chuckled. "And I volunteer here. Who do you think pulled your grades and showed them to our staff? Very impressive academics, by the way."

"Ah, that's how the school found me!"

"I attended grade school at Nawlins and continued my education here at the medical school. I loved it, and still do, which is why I'm a member of the admissions committee and the Prestigious Alumni group. I want to take you and Jacquie to dinner. You deserve an authentic New Orleans dish before you leave tomorrow, and you can meet my husband too. He's a professor here."

"That would be amazing," Donna said.

Unfortunately, Auntie had a different idea.

"I'm so sorry, Rima, but I think I officially have a date tonight. It's our driver who picked us up from the airport." Jacquie grinned.

Donna raised an eyebrow. "Auntie, I'd really like to go. I can find out more about the school."

"Jacquie, what if you go on your date, and I'll take Donna to dinner and bring her back to the hotel after?" suggested Rima.

Donna offered Jacquie her best, sweetest smile.

"Okay, okay." Jacquie laughed.

Rima and Donna had dinner at Dragos, a restaurant where Donna fell in love with their signature charbroiled oysters topped with a buttery garlic sauce. After dinner, Rima took Donna on a tour of the French Quarter.

The hot, humid air flowed through Donna's hair like a blow-dryer set to low heat as they sat in the back of a horse-drawn carriage.

The smell of beignets sparked Donna's sweet tooth as they passed Café du Monde, where many tourists savored the restaurant's famous powdered beignets. Street performers lit up the sidewalks with musical performances and dance tricks. Donna chuckled as it reminded her of New York as far as the hustle and bustle of it all.

The tour guide operating the two-person carriage slowed the horse down with the reins as they turned the next corner, where the surroundings were quieter.

He rambled with a Cajun country accent.

"Over there to our right is the Old Ursuline Convent. It's where the vampires known as the Casket Girls were laid to rest after their killing spree. They slaughtered hundreds of townsfolk before they were finally stopped."

"Casket Girls? What's that? They really murdered hundreds of people?" Donna asked, fully invested.

"The girls arrived from France in the 1700s carrying trunks that looked like caskets as they exited the boats, hence their nickname."

"And they were vampires?" Donna asked.

"Yes. The Casket Girls rampaged the city, killing the men they were meant to marry, sucking the blood from their bodies until they were all shriveled up like prunes... But don't worry, those vampires have been resting for hundreds of years. The Ursuline nuns sealed the attic with over eight thousand silver screws blessed by the Pope to make sure they couldn't escape."

Donna looked beyond the iron gates toward the white building, and sure enough, the windows to the attic on the third floor were shuttered and sealed.

"That's just some folklore," Rima said.

"Maybe, maybe not," the guide responded with a creepy laugh.

"We will get out right here, thank you," Rima said as the carriage approached Nawlins.

Donna and Rima walked along the sidewalk opposite Nawlins, where the school's tall white towers expanded toward the sky.

"So, what do you think about the school? The opportunity to be a student here?" Rima's eyes sparkled, waiting for Donna's response.

Donna's mind was in overdrive. She hardly believed this was true. *A prestigious private school wants me? Why? I'm not special. I'm just Donna Marie.*

"Why me?" she asked. "There are probably millions of people my age who are just as good at school as I am."

"Because you're special, that's why. You deserve to be here. Nawlins is the oldest historically Black school in the world and the only school devoted to gifted students with unique abilities. Like yours."

"I don't think I have special abilities. I pay attention in class and study hard to get good grades," Donna said.

"I'm not talking about your academic performance, as exquisite as that is."

"Then what are you talking about?"

"What if I told you that your anxiety attacks are happening because there's power inside of you?"

"What kind of power?" Donna asked.

"Wizard power."

Donna stood motionless. "You can't be serious?"

"I am," Rima responded.

"Sorry, but I don't understand any of this."

"You're a wizard, Donna," Rima said gently.

Donna blinked. "What the hell are you talking about?"

Is this lady insane? She can't be serious.

Her heart sank. Even though she desperately wanted this opportunity to be real, Donna knew it was too good to be true. Why would she deserve to be in a prestigious school? She didn't come from a classy wealthy family, and the school she currently attended was one of the most underfunded public schools in the Bronx.

The doubt hit hard, louder than reason. Donna's chest tightened as her breath quickened. She stepped back, then turned and broke into a run.

"Have you ever felt it?" Rima called after her. "The magical powers inside of you... something you couldn't explain?"

A familiar tingling sensation sparked in Donna's hands. *The glow... is it real?* But to her, it felt more bizarre than magical. *Wait, am I really considering this?*

Halting, she examined her hands, turning them over with a heavy sigh before walking back to Rima.

"Place your hand on the door and see what happens," Rima instructed gently.

Donna pressed her left hand against the aged wooden door. A tingling surged through her palm, and she could feel her heartbeat throbbing in her forearms. She clenched her eyes shut, bracing for an anxiety attack.

"Open your eyes," Rima said.

A fleur-de-lis symbol with a wand below it burned into the middle of the door like a giant tattoo. Holographic cursive letters began to appear below the crest.

Donna read the letters under her breath.

"'Nawlins. School for Wizards.'"

As the door swung open, releasing a burst of chilly air, Donna staggered back and looked at Rima, who nodded as though this was an ordinary event.

Is she trying to kidnap me or something? I gotta get out of here. The thought flashed through her mind as Rima reached into her jacket.

Is she pulling out a weapon? But instead of fleeing, curiosity rooted her to the spot.

Rima removed a black wand from her pocket and aimed it at the streetlights.

"Onyesha," she said.

Onya what?

A beam burst from Rima's wand and struck the streetlights, illuminating them with vibrant colors. The scenery around them shifted dramatically—the street stretched, the buildings skewed and grew as if the world itself was reshaping.

"You can run away and return to the Bronx or give me a chance to prove this is real. Let me show you the school, and then you can choose. Deal?"

Rima extended her hand for Donna to grasp.

Donna hesitated. The vampire tales from earlier hadn't scared her, but this display of magic was different—it was real, and frighteningly so. A part of her wanted to return to the hotel and tell Jacquie everything. No doubt Jacquie would've had the SWAT team there in a heartbeat. But a part of Donna, a daring, curious part, wanted to see more. Magic was real, and apparently it was within her. Ignoring it felt like denying a part of herself. Tentatively, she reached out and took Rima's hand, stepping into a world she never imagined could exist.

Chapter Seven

As they entered the grand entrance hall, Donna was immediately drawn to five striking paintings that dominated the length of the hallway. She paused, captivated by the artistry.

"These wizards are the original members of the Coven," Rima said. "They were the first five wizards to be blessed with powers."

"What's the Coven?" Donna asked.

"The Coven is comprised of all wizards who are descendants of the ones you see here."

The first painting featured a tall, slender man with vanilla skin and long, flowing black hair. He wore an elegant coat and bowtie, with a vintage monocle perched precariously on his right eye. His arms were folded, and his left hand clutched a gold wand.

"This is Jean Pierre Dubois. He was the fifth and last original Coven member, thus making him a Five. Don't let his Creole good looks fool you; he was a force to be reckoned with."

Donna was at a loss for words. How does one respond to tales of ancient wizards? "I like his glasses. They're very swaggy," she managed.

Rima laughed. "You sound like my son."

"What is a Five?" Donna asked.

"In the wizard community, you will find that some of us take pride in the bloodline's ranking system. A Five means his powers aren't as strong as the other four ahead of him."

A broad mahogany man stood tall in the next painting, dressed in brown trousers and a fitted shirt that showed off his brooding physique.

"He looks kinda scary," Donna said, eyeing the deep frown across his face.

"That's Cane Hargis," Rima explained. "He was a champion prizefighter back in his days and a skilled carpenter, too. The Hargis family make up the Fours. You're the same age as one of his descendants, Chike."

Each portrait unfolded a layer of history, transporting Donna into a new world, rich with legacy and lore.

The next painting depicted a dark-skinned man in refined 1800s attire, a top hat completing his distinguished ensemble, hands resting atop a gold walking cane.

"That's Philmore DuVernay, the third Coven original," Rima introduced.

"He looks like my old principal," Donna blurted out. "He was short and with a thick beard too. And he walked with a cane."

"I bet his cane wasn't a wand like Philmore's," Rima said. "He's my husband's ancestor."

The fourth painting captured a woman with caramel skin and bright green eyes, her hair styled in two braids, a gold wand peeking from her skirt's waistband. Donna read the placard underneath.

"Augustin Decken. That's a dope name."

"I'm sure she'd appreciate the compliment." Rima smiled.

"She's stunning," Donna said.

"Yes, she truly was. She was a Two. The chancellor of Nawlins, Nicole Decken, is a descendant of Augustin. And you'll have classes with her twins, Casie and Jay, who will also be sophomores in the fall. If you decide to attend school here. But I would watch yourself around Casie…" Rima paused. "I shouldn't have said that. Please don't repeat it to anyone."

"Your secret is safe with me," Donna said.

Donna took a step back to study the first four paintings. Each one shared a distinct, striking detail.

"They all have golden wands?" Donna observed.

"Yes, each original Coven member's wand was pure gold, except for Solomon's." Rima pointed to the final painting.

"Solomon Deslondes, of the first bloodline. He is the founder of Nawlins and the most powerful wizard that ever lived."

The painting of Solomon showed him barefooted, levitating above the ground, and his right hand reached for a diamond wand that traveled toward him from above. His eyes were completely black, and protruding dark veins traveled down his eyelids toward his cheeks.

Deslondes?

Donna's temples began to throb as she noticed a faint red light traveling from his left palm.

"The light coming from his hand, can other wizards do that?" Donna asked.

"No. Only Solomon had that gift."

"So, there's no way lights can surround my hands if I tried?"

Rima paused for a second and tilted her head.

"No, that's not possible. Wizards need wands to use their powers… Solomon could use his powers without a wand because he was the only one who could transform into pure-wizard form."

"What does that mean… pure-wizard form?"

"I don't know much about it, but our history books say his powers were 'immaculate' when he was in pure-wizard form. As you see in the painting, his eyes are pitch-black, and he's using his powers with his hands. The only way you could do the same is if you were a descendant of his bloodline. But that's not possible because Solomon didn't have any children."

Donna walked closer to the painting and looked down at her hands.

"This way," Rima said, walking toward the black sliding doors.

Donna took a deep breath as she heard various voices emanating from the other side.

Everything is about to change.

She had always known she deserved a better life—not in an entitled or snobbish way, but an easier life. She thought of her mother's words, after she put on the birthday pendant: "Donna Marie, life challenges us for a reason. God sends these tests your way so you will feel truly blessed when everything turns around. Because believe me, it will. When it turns, magic will happen for you."

No doubt, her mom didn't mean *magic* in the way things were turning out. *Man, if she could see this now.*

Maybe a better life waited for her beyond the sliding doors. Perhaps this opportunity, this school, would ease her hardships. More than that, she could learn enough to get a wonderful career and enough money to help her mother one day. Maybe, maybe. So many maybes.

She wished she could let go of any fear and doubt, but she would have to take them with her for now.

Taking a deep breath, Donna stepped through the sliding doors, ready to face whatever awaited her on the other side.

Donna and Rima entered a circular courtyard surrounded by several buildings, including the school's library and bookstore, their white-pillared balconies boastfully displayed. Antique lanterns with flames inside floated effortlessly above, casting a warm glow over the area. In the center of the courtyard stood a juice bar where small glass spheres hovered up and down the paths, serving drinks. One of the spheres stopped in front of Donna, slushing around oranges inside before gently compressing them. Just as she reached out, it zipped away toward a student lounging nearby, poured the fresh juice into a cup, and vanished.

"Welcome to Nawlins!" Rima exclaimed. "The campus is nearly as large as the entire French Quarter. It's concealed within a traditional-looking five-block radius but harbors this secret world within."

"So, non-wizards can't enter?" Donna asked, her eyes scanning the enchanting scene.

"The doors will only open for wizards. When we get visits from Norms, we use the small portion of the campus that serves as a regular school, just like the tour you and Jacquie experienced earlier today."

"A Norm is normal?"

"See, you're catching on already!" Rima said.

At that moment, Donna wasn't sure what amazed her more: the revelation of wizard powers or the faces around her in the courtyard—a stunning mosaic of black and brown skin tones, more beautiful and diverse than anything she'd ever seen. It felt like magic in itself.

"The students, they're all Black," Donna said.

"Yes, and these are only the students choosing to attend summer school. Wait until you see our entire enrollment."

Magic seemed to be everywhere. Some students floated on levitating hoverboards that resembled high-tech skateboards without wheels. Other students walked while book bags with robotic legs trailed closely behind. On a grassy field near the juice bar, a group was playing a game similar to basketball but with no backboard—just a rim and a green ball that floated between the students, who were each using a wand of a different shape, size, and color.

"Will I get a wand?" Donna asked excitedly.

"Yes, you will. *Wand* to see mine?" Rima grinned. "Sorry, that was a mom joke."

Donna nodded as Rima pulled the wand from her pocket, holding it delicately with both hands as she presented it.

It was sleek and black, the polished surface almost too perfect, as if it had been carved from obsidian. A dark red vine coiled tightly around the handle, twisting down to the base like it had grown naturally into the wood. The vine shimmered faintly in the light, almost as though it pulsed with life, its crimson hue deepening at the tips.

"You can touch it if you want to," Rima said.

Donna hesitated, then gently placed her fingers on the base. A chill shot through her fingertips, sending a shiver down her spine.

"Wow, it's cold… but I like it," Donna said, a small smile playing at her lips.

"Wands are catered to each wizard's strengths and weaknesses. We will find the perfect one for you," Rima said. "If you choose to attend Nawlins," she added.

A buzz went off in Donna's pocket with a text:

Jacquie: Hey, how's everything going? Are you safe? I'm tracking you on your phone and it looks like you're back at the school.

Donna: Hey, Auntie. Yes, everything is cool. Rima is showing me more things around the campus :)

Jacquie: Okay, hunny. I should be back at the hotel in about an hour. Make sure you're back by then. By the way, this guy is dreamy. I think I found my husband.

Donna: Eww, bye, Auntie.

A girl walked over to them. She had on a gray hijab that covered her hair and neck, making her model-like cheekbones and perfectly shaped eyebrows stand out. The best way to describe her style was *poised*.

"Hey, Noor. I'm surprised you didn't go back home for the break," said Rima.

"I decided to take a music class only offered during the summer. I'm glad I did because I love Professor Osborne."

"Noor, this is Donna. I'm taking her on a tour," Rima said. "She's from the Big Apple too."

"You're from New York?" Donna asked.

"Yes, Harlem."

"I'm from the Bronx."

"No way! That's why you got so much swag. Who else but us New Yorkers wear Timbs in the summer?" Noor said, sticking her foot out and pointing to Donna's shoes.

They both had on the classic butter Timberland boots. Pretty much every New Yorker had a pair, but Noor's were in better shape.

"I see you, girl, with the drip!" Donna said.

"I have to get back to my dorm to study. But I'll see you around," Noor said.

Rima took Donna on a proper campus tour to see what life at Nawlins could really offer her. Their initial stop was the Department of Spells—a striking building where each classroom boasted pristine white marble floors, alabaster walls, and matching desks.

In an empty classroom, a life-sized dummy stood at the front. Curious, Donna stepped closer and gently pressed her finger against its chest. The soft black material gave beneath her touch, leaving a faint impression that slowly faded as she pulled her hand away.

"What is this thing?" she inquired.

"It's a training dummy that students use to practice their spells," Rima replied. "They have to be replaced often."

"Why is the classroom so white?"

"Every department was uniquely built for a purpose. These classrooms are white so that students can see the remnants of a failed spell. A single mark on the floor or wall can be traced back, forcing the student to learn how to correct their mistakes."

The next stop was the Dawa building. These classrooms had rustic log cabin designs.

"What does dawa mean?" Donna asked as she walked onto the shiny wooden floor.

"Dawas are concoctions that we brew."

"Like, love potions and stuff?"

"You watch too many movies. Love dawas aren't a thing. Wizards can't make someone fall in love with them. Now, there are dawas that can make you more enticing to a person, but we can't create organic love. Oh, and don't say the P word; that's a Hollywood thing."

"What P word? Potions?" Donna asked.

"Yes. That P word." Rima shook her head. "Dawa is the correct term."

"This classroom looks like an expensive ski trip," Donna said, walking around the room.

Giant wooden pillars held up the tall ceiling. There were granite tables scattered around and a green chalkboard on the main wall. Two shelves stretching to the ceiling housed hundreds of glass jars labeled with ingredients such as snake venom, bat fangs, bee stingers, and spiderwebs. Cabinets on the side of the room stored black pots in all sizes.

"These cabins were designed to give that exact feeling: a winter escape. The room is kept cold so the ingredients stay fresh. Whenever I'm here I get the urge to use one of those pots to make some gumbo."

"I've never had gumbo," Donna said.

"Just you wait."

The last visit was to the Ancient Magic building.

A black double door automatically opened as Donna walked into the classroom. Everything was ultramodern and black—from the walls and the L-shaped desks to the wall-mounted glass board. Two training dummies stood in the front, but unlike in the Spells classroom, they had some kind of transparent barriers around them.

Donna touched one of the barriers with her index finger. She felt a pulse shudder at the spot where her finger touched.

"The sahani protects the classroom and students from the energy beams," Rima said.

"What kind of energy beams?"

"They are a wizard's primary form of defense. Ancient Magic is taught from *The Book of Giza*. When the first wizards were blessed with powers, they were given *The Book of Knowledge* and the *Book of Giza*. *The Book of Knowledge* contains rituals, spells, dawas, chants, and other information that doesn't cause physical harm. But *The Book of Giza* has entities that could harm and even kill. Students must be sophomores to take Ancient Magic."

They exited the building through a vast oval-shaped path between tall trees with white flowers and thick, dark red rosebushes.

"This place is called the Gardens. The roses and magnolias bloom in all seasons here at Nawlins. The Gardens separate the high school from the college campus," Rima explained.

Donna drank in the fabulous aroma. Even though it was all so strange and new, she felt calm and at peace with everything she'd seen and heard of Nawlins.

"Let's sit down in private and chat," Rima said. "Since I'm on the alumni board and the admissions committee, they gave me a fancy office to use when I'm not working my little doctor job."

"But being a doctor is a huge accomplishment," Donna said.

"I know. I was trying to be sarcastic. I'm still working on my jokes. As my son tells me all the time." Rima laughed.

Rima's office was high up on the top floor of the administration building in the center of the campus, which offered a spectacular view of the city from the large windows.

A man wearing a navy suit was sitting with his legs crossed on a levitating couch.

"Sweetheart, what are you doing here?" Rima asked.

The black leather couch lowered to the ground, and the man stood up. He was an inch taller than Rima, who was about five foot seven. He hugged Rima and gave her a gentle kiss on her cheek.

"Sorry I couldn't make it to dinner with you ladies. I got caught up with some lesson plans. But I wanted to talk to Donna and give her my opinion of Nawlins from a professor's perspective."

"Donna, this is my husband, Charles. He's a professor of Spells," Rima said.

He shook Donna's hand with a firm grip. "It's a pleasure meeting you, Donna. My students call me Professor DuVernay."

"Nice to meet you, Professor DuVernay," she replied.

"Please take a seat, Donna," Rima said as she walked to her desk.

On one side of her desk were academic awards and framed diplomas in a glass enclosure. On the other side was a circular photo collage. Each photo contained Rima, her husband, and a boy who appeared to be about seventeen now. He had light brown eyes and a chiseled jawline.

"Is that your son?" Donna asked.

"Yes, that's Lincoln. He'll be a senior. You might not see much of him because the juniors and seniors have classes on the opposite side of campus."

As Donna sat, her chair lifted off the ground until her feet dangled.

Rima smiled at her.

"So, Donna, you must have so many questions for us. This experience must be overwhelming for you."

Donna paused, not sure where to start. "How did you know I was a wizard?" she asked.

"When you came into the emergency room that night in New York, I drew your blood. It contained wizard properties that Norms cannot see."

"I don't know anything about wizards. I don't even know how to work my... powers? I'll be so behind if I attend school here. Can I catch up fast enough? And do Norms know we exist? Does my mom know what I am? Is she a wizard?"

Donna stopped to catch her breath.

"The wizard community is private," Rima said. "We keep our powers a secret from the world."

"Your mother is not a wizard," Professor DuVernay added. "We read your school file, which had some information about your father. I'm sorry to ask this, but did your father pass away not knowing that your mom was pregnant with you?"

"Yes," Donna said, looking down, fidgeting with her hands.

"More than likely, your father didn't tell your mother he was a wizard," Rima said.

They all sat silently for a moment as Donna took this in. She sank down in her chair, twiddling her thumbs together.

"Wizards start their studies at Nawlins in the sixth grade. So yes, you will be behind, but you can catch up with hard work and dedication. You have powers just like the other students here," Professor DuVernay said.

"Even the Coven members?" Donna asked. "Rima told me I'd be taking classes with some of them."

"Their powers are naturally stronger than other wizards, but that doesn't particularly mean they have an advantage. I personally know wizards who aren't in the Coven and worked really hard to outperform them," Professor DuVernay said proudly, placing his hand on Rima's shoulder. "My wife and I were in the same classes at Nawlins. I am a member of the Coven, and she constantly beat my test scores."

This brought a smile to Donna's face. She was no stranger to hard work. The thought of a new challenge intrigued her.

"This school is incredible. It is. But I can't afford the cost. And my mother... I can't leave her alone in New York. I work a lot to help pay for her stroke rehabilitation and other stuff. My mom needs me."

"We give all our students free enrollment, books, and room and board," Rima said. "I'm very sorry to hear about your troubles with your mom. I wish there was something I could do. Unfortunately, wizards can't use their powers to produce money. I'm sure we would all be rich if that were possible."

"We understand how big of a transition this would be. Being away from family is one of the most difficult challenges for our students. But we do have a call center where you can video chat, and we provide tablets that you can use to send emails anytime," Professor DuVernay said.

"And you'll be able to go home during the winter break," Rima added.

Donna had never been away from her mother, not even when Catherine underwent brain surgery after the stroke. She'd stayed by her bedside the entire time. So, the thought of being this far from her for so long felt overwhelming.

What if something happens to Mom while I'm away?

Someone knocked at Rima's door.

"Come in," she said.

A woman walked into the room. She wore black dress pants, a black and white blazer, and high heels. She looked at Donna with piercing dark eyes.

"Donna, this is Nicole Decken, chancellor of Nawlins," Rima said.

Donna thought of the painting of Augustin Decken in the entrance hall. The Chancellor didn't have Augustin's bright green eyes or long hair, but there was still a striking resemblance.

Donna got up to shake her hand. She was expecting to feel warmth, but the Chancellor's cold touch radiated through Donna's body as they grasped hands.

She gave Donna three firm shakes and then let go.

This lady means business.

"Donna Marie. I've heard so much about you. The child who didn't know she was a wizard amongst Norms.

"I was just telling Donna what we could offer to enroll her here," said Rima. "Chancellor, can I talk to you in private?"

The two women conversed in the corner of the room. Donna saw the Chancellor looking troubled, shaking her head. Then shortly after, Rima shook her head.

Professor DuVernay whispered to Donna, "My wife likes you. She's going to find a way to get you into Nawlins."

The Chancellor returned and gently rested her hand on Donna's shoulder. "Rima has kindly filled me in on everything. My, the hardships you and your mom have had to face. I'm deeply sorry to hear about it. We want to cover all your expenses to attend Nawlins."

"The school cannot pay for your mom's care, but I want to cover that part personally. We'll get her the rehab she needs," Rima added.

"You'll do that for me? I... I don't know what to say." Donna's voice tailed off into an embarrassing squeak she wished she could take back.

Then the tears came fast and furious, unstoppable.

"I... I can't accept that. It's too much," she said softly. "I never thought anyone would help me... us. But I can't."

"We would love to have you here," Rima said.

"I know. I need time to think it over," Donna replied.

"We understand."

Professor DuVernay rose from his seat and placed his arm around Rima. "Donna, take as much time as necessary. But you are a wizard. You do belong here," he said, giving her a warm smile.

"Yes. We will be waiting for your answer," the Chancellor said. "Rima, you should take Donna to our history villa before she leaves to show her why she belongs here."

A white picket fence surrounded the historic villa. Rima waved her wand over the lock, and the gate creaked open, revealing a white, two-story building. Six stone columns supported the balcony.

A man who looked a little older than Rima was mopping the porch, dressed in a dark blue jumpsuit with a worn white towel draped over his shoulder. Two other mops floated beside him, gliding rhythmically across the floor as if enchanted.

When he paused, they did too—standing upright like obedient pets. He removed his cap and gave a wave.

"Hello, Rima. What brings you here?" he asked in a deep voice as he leaned on his mop.

"Hello, Mr. Espree. I'm showing around a potential new student."

"New student? These sixth graders are getting taller, huh?" he said, rubbing his bald head.

"Donna will be a sophomore in the fall."

"What? What school was she at before?"

"I just found out I am a wizard," Donna said.

Letting go of the mop, Mr. Espree stood upright and squinted at her.

"What's your last name, kid?" he asked, walking closer.

"Guillory."

"I don't think I know any Guillorys that went to this school."

"Come on, Mr. Espree, you couldn't possibly know everyone that went here," Rima said.

Mr. Espree lifted his eyebrow.

"It's good to meet you, Donna. I just made my rounds in there, so keep it clean."

Rima removed a bronze skeleton key from her pocket and inserted it into the keyhole of the front door. They entered the main room, which was filled with historical artifacts, antique furniture, and paintings.

"All of the artifacts in the house were built or used by our ancestors," Rima said.

Donna glanced into the open bedroom to her left.

"Paul Broyard built that bed himself, and back in those days, they had so few of the woodworking tools we would use today. He was the best carpenter and craftsman of his time. He and his workers helped build Nawlins in the early 1800s," explained Rima.

Donna walked up to a violin in a display case. Its plaque read, *Sol Northup*. She was taken aback by the delicate furnishings, jewelry, pottery, and craftsmanship around the room.

"Our people did all this back then?" she asked.

"Yes, and the way you say *our people* speaks volumes," Rima replied.

Donna shivered as she stepped into a dimly lit room lined with historical artifacts of punishment and control.

Nooses and rusted blades were encased behind thick glass. In the center stood plexiglass compartments containing old restraints such as iron neck collars and cuffs, accompanied by haunting images that captured generations of suffering. A wave of unease washed over her.

"This is awful," Donna murmured, her voice low.

"I know," Rima said gently. "And I'm sorry to show you something so heavy. But it's part of our past, and it's important context for the next room."

Donna spotted a staircase as they walked to another room.

"What's up there?"

"Nothing important, just some rooms containing old documents, yearbooks, and other paperwork. There were no computers back then, so we have to save their information somewhere."

They entered a large, empty room, the walls draped in thick black fabric. An iridescent crystal ball floated near the ceiling, casting a faint glow.

"It's necessary for you to see this to understand the source of our powers," Rima explained as they stood in the mysterious, quiet room.

"But this room is empty?" Donna said.

Rima took out her wand and pointed it at the crystal ball.

"Onyesha," she said, blasting the ball with a dim stream of light.

The ball began to spin, picking up speed and scattering colorful light across the room, soon projecting a 4D hologram around them. Suddenly, Donna felt as though she was standing in a green pasture, the ground moving beneath her feet as the scene zipped towards a hill crowned by a giant magnolia tree. Rima grasped her hand, and Donna clung to it tightly.

A tall Black man ascended the hill, his muscles flexing with each step, stopping beneath the magnolia. Donna watched, transfixed, as Rima began to narrate.

"Solomon Deslondes. Leader of the Uprising of 1811. A Louisiana native slave, born at the Woodland Plantation not too far from here. He grew tired of the physical and psychological trauma of slavery and decided it was time to rebel against the oppressors of his people. Solomon gathered four of his most trusted friends: Augustin Decken, Philmore DuVernay, Cane Hargis, and Jean Pierre Dubois. Together they took over their plantation."

The holograms of Philmore, Cane, and Jean Pierre were walking up the hill to Solomon.

A light flashed over Donna's body as a hologram walked through her. She flinched when the hologram looked back at her. It was Augustin Decken. Donna heard intense breathing behind her. When she turned around, she realized Augustin wasn't looking back at her—she was looking at hundreds of holograms of enslaved people spread throughout the grassy pasture below the hill.

"They planned to take control of New Orleans because it was the primary site for slave trading in the nation. They gathered five hundred slaves to help them revolt. The night they ventured out to start the Uprising, the original five friends went to a sacred site to conduct prayer, asking for strength, wisdom, and courage. Their hearts were pure and set on one goal: to free their people from bondage."

The five holograms on the hill kneeled before the magnolia tree, grasping each other's hands as Solomon looked up to the sky.

"The Creator granted them a blessing, bestowing them wizard powers."

A bright light illuminated the darkness, and a violent wind swept up Solomon toward the sky. He slowly descended toward his friends. He was now wearing a black cloak, and a wand made of diamonds glowed in his hand. Two large books resembling well-preserved antique Bibles hovered before Solomon. One was black, bound in bronze iron straps with *The Book of Giza* etched across its cover. The other was light brown, its black iron straps holding together pages marked *The Book of Knowledge*. The same wind swept up the other four friends, and they reappeared on the hill wearing the same cloaks but carrying gold wands.

The light intensified, cascading toward the back of the room where hundreds of others stood down the hill. Donna shielded her eyes with her hands as a mighty wind surged through the space, whipping against her skin and tossing her hair.

"When the five friends walked down the hill to meet the other members of the revolt, they found the others were blessed with wizard gifts as well, but they were holding long wooden wands and wearing burgundy cloaks."

The crystal ball stopped spinning, and the room went pitch-black. An eerie silence took over the darkness.

The ball started to spin again, changing the hologram terrain into a battlefield.

"The oppressors fought with guns, knives, and swords, while the wizards wielded energy beams from their wands and cast spells they had learned from *The Book of Giza*. Many of the oppressors died, and after each battle, the remaining would all beg the wizards for mercy. Solomon spared their lives, and to prevent retaliation, the wizards wiped their knowledge of the events. The oppressors' only recollection of the revolt was that enslaved people freed themselves, set their plantations on fire, and escaped to free territory in the North."

The hologram terrain changed into Nawlins' first building site in the French Quarter.

"When the revolt was over, the wizards built Nawlins to nourish and develop their gifts and to provide an education for the wizard community. All of our students are descendants of those original revolt members. So, Donna Marie, this is why you belong here. It's in your roots," Rima said.

Donna thought of her nightmare. *You are a Deslondes...* What did it mean? Was she ready to find out?

Chapter Eight

N ew Beginnings," Donna mumbled to herself as the driver from the airport dropped her off in front of Nawlins' main entrance. When she walked through those doors a couple of months ago, she was a visitor—now she was a full-time student.

The summer had flown by quicker than she expected. She saved enough money to buy new clothes for her new school—well, slightly worn from her favorite thrift shop in Brooklyn. But she did treat herself to something new: a pair of Nike Air Force 1s. She always wanted a pair but couldn't afford it. But with the help of Rima and her job at Jacquie's office, she was able to buy her favorite crispy white kicks.

Throughout the summer nights, Donna often found herself lying awake, excited about the magical spells she would learn and the dawas she might create. She had tried several times to make her hands glow by holding her breath and tensing her muscles, though all she got from her efforts was a flushed face and a light-headed feeling.

The good news was that her anxiety seemed to have vanished. Rima had told her that knowing she was a wizard would help release the tension in her body, allowing it to flow freely.

"No need to be nervous," Donna muttered to herself, watching parents drop off their kids. Yet a nagging worry lingered: just how far behind was she compared to all the other sophomores?

She didn't want to be the odd one out, but she had to start somewhere. Luckily, she had a secret weapon to give her a much-needed confidence boost.

Nawlins forbade pets of all types, but Chancellor Decken made an exception for Donna, knowing the new transition would be hard for her.

Donna lifted the small blanket covering the pet carrier resting on top of her spinner suitcase. Mr. Whiskers looked up at her and seemed to smile, reassuring her that everything would be okay.

She grabbed her bags and walked through the door, passing the paintings in the entrance hall. She paused in front of Solomon's portrait, her eyes drawn to the diamond wand in his hand.

A girl collided with Donna in the bustling hallway. She sported a yellow and black letterman jacket, a bold "C" emblazoned on the left side.

"Watch where you're going!" the girl shouted as she brushed off her jacket and walked away.

"Hey, that was rude. You bumped into me," Donna said as she stared at the large white number *2* stitched on the back of the jacket.

Donna glanced back at Solomon and walked through the sliding doors.

In the courtyard, there were folding tables surrounded by a group of students wearing collared shirts.

"Hello, welcome to Nawlins! My name is Monique. I'm a college senior and part of the work-study program, along with my classmates here assigned as high school monitors. Here is your school-provided tablet where you can find a map to the living quarters." Monique handed the tablet to Donna.

"Thanks," Donna said, doing her best to juggle her luggage and the tablet.

"Remember you have to be at the welcome ceremony this afternoon. Don't be late," Monique said.

A rush of students met Donna head-on, scurrying and shoving their way in every direction, wearing stylish outfits, including the latest Air Jordans and other brands that Donna couldn't afford.

Zooming in and out on the map, she realized finding her dorm room would be harder than she thought. Carefully reading the fine print on the buildings, she finally located the sophomore dormitories, which were nowhere near her current location.

Stepping into her dorm building, Donna was immediately met by the sight of two chandeliers floating elegantly near the ceiling. Black butterflies fluttered whimsically between them, adding a touch of magic to the room. At the far end of the lobby, a tall vintage grandfather clock stood imposingly. Beside it, Zina waited, dressed in a collared shirt like the other monitors.

"Hi, Zina," Donna called out.

"Donna, I've been on the lookout for you, luv. Today is very different from the tour I took you on in the summer, huh? Sorry, I couldn't reveal that you were a wizard then; I had to wait for Rima to break the news. Anyway, I'm the monitor for your dorm, but I think of myself as your big sister in this."

Zina scanned her tablet. "You're in room 305."

Donna's eyes widened at the sight of the long staircase. She looked back at her heavy suitcase and sighed.

The pet carrier on top of her suitcase moved. Zina came over and slowly raised the fabric layer. Mr. Whiskers stood, stretched his body, and then pressed his face against the mesh breathing holes.

Donna handed her a letter signed by the Chancellor herself.

"Wow, but make sure to keep an eye on him; we can't have house pets running wild on campus," said Zina. "Anyway, that suitcase is massive. What did you pack?"

"I don't suppose there's an elevator..."

"You guessed right. But I can do better than that. You did come to Nawlins, you know."

Donna raised a brow as Zina lifted her wand and Donna's bags disappeared.

"Don't worry. They're in your room."

"I can get used to this magic stuff," Donna said.

"You have about an hour to unpack, then you need to get to the auditorium."

"Thanks, Zina," Donna said, walking toward the staircase.

Framed photos of previous sophomores neatly adorned the walls along the broad wooden staircase. Donna stepped back toward the sturdy railing, taking a moment to admire the images of wizards from the past. Students whispered as they passed, stealing glances.

When she reached the third floor, she was puffing and panting.

Why haven't they built an elevator in this place? she wondered. *It's huge.*

As she approached room 305, Donna heard her favorite song. A girl was rapping the words to "Big Poppa" by the Notorious B.I.G.

She knocked timidly, and no one opened up. The music must have been too loud to hear her pathetic knocks, so she inserted the key.

"'I love it when you call me Big Poppa,'" the girl rapped from one of the rooms.

"'Throw your hands in the air, if youse a true player,'" Donna rapped as she walked through the door.

The music volume decreased, and the girl peeped her head out.

"Donna."

"OMG, Noor!"

"Give me a hug, new roommate!"

Donna embraced Noor, who looked as poised as she had that summer. Her chocolate complexion and wide brown eyes gave her a magnetic, radiant presence.

It was scary to have to enter a dorm room after someone else, wondering who would be in there, what she'd be like, and whether they would get along. But it seemed that Noor and Donna would get along just fine.

The bedrooms were located across from each other, with a moderate-sized living room in the center.

"Hope you don't mind. I took this room. Want to see it?" Noor asked.

"I would love to," Donna responded.

Noor opened the door to her room, showcasing a Knicks banner above her neat bed. In the corner were a keyboard, guitar, mixing table, and a microphone.

"You make music?" Donna asked.

"Sure do. I will be the next Lauryn Hill, with some Sade vibes," Noor replied confidently.

"I like that." Donna paused. "Um, are you allergic to cats?"

"Girl, I love cats!"

Donna sighed with relief. She unzipped the carrier and carefully picked up Mr. Whiskers.

"She's beautiful," Noor said.

"He's a boy. His name is Mr. Whiskers."

"Sorry. Well, Mr. Whiskers is a handsome cat." Noor gave him a few pets. "You better not let the other students see him, or our dorm will be filled with people begging to pet him. Everyone will already want to know who you are because we never get new sophomores."

She was especially grateful for the ensuite bathroom and the spacious closet with sliding doors, where she neatly tucked the litter box on the right side.

"This is your side of the closet, Mr. Whiskers. I'll keep it open so you can come and go as you please."

Mr. Whiskers seemed to approve, darting around the room before leaping onto the bed. That's when Donna noticed a small rectangular box waiting for her. Tied with a simple string, a note rested on top, addressed to her in flowing script:

Donna Marie,

I hope you enjoy your new school. The first few days might be overwhelming for you like they were for me, but always remind yourself that you belong here, because you really do.

Rima

She opened the box, revealing a sleek black wand with a dark red vine spiraling around the handle—just like Rima's. Donna picked it up, surprised by the texture. The vine looked rigid, but it felt soft and warm, molding gently to her hand as she found her grip, as if it had been waiting for her all along. The crimson tendrils pulsed faintly, radiating an unsettling energy.

I really am a wizard.

She lifted the wand and moved it around like she was a Jedi battling a Stormtrooper.

"Donna Marie," Noor said behind the door.

"Come in."

"That's a cool wand."

"Thanks, it was a gift," Donna said.

"Whoever gave it to you must be important. That thing is expensive. I'm about to head to the auditorium. Want to join me?"

"I'll meet you there. I still have to put some things away."

"Okay, cool. What class do you have first?"

"Spells," Donna replied.

"Me too. I'll find you in the auditorium, and we can walk to class together."

After Donna unpacked and tidied the room, she stepped back and observed her work. Posters of Biggie and Aaliyah hung on the walls, a new white down comforter from Jacquie styled the bed, a small New York City rug brightened the dull floor, and Mr. Whiskers' toys lay in the open closet.

"Oh, the last touch," Donna said, digging into her bag.

She pulled out a framed photo of her and her mother, placing it carefully on the desk. Her new space now felt complete—a bridge between her past and the hopeful future awaiting her at Nawlins.

Chapter Nine

L incoln thrived on the freedom of his motorcycle rides. On the road, there was no room for distraction. Every turn and shift demanded his full attention, allowing him to escape from the constant buzz of everyday life.

He pulled into Nawlins' garage and parked in his usual spot in the corner on the second level. Draping his leather jacket over the seat, he placed his helmet on the handlebar and fished a pair of headphones from his backpack. Slipping them over his ears, he started playing Lil Wayne's first *Carter* album as he prepared to face the campus.

As he strolled toward the auditorium, several students greeted him, throwing up peace signs. Lincoln, ever the introvert, acknowledged them with a nod but kept his headphones on, cocooned in his music.

Despite his reserved nature, Lincoln couldn't escape his popularity. Part of the prestigious Coven and son of a well-respected professor, he was well-known throughout the wizard community, whether he liked it or not. The weight of the DuVernay legacy was heavy, often more than he wanted to bear. He sometimes held back his magic at school to blend in. Yet he excelled academically, holding the highest GPA in his class for four consecutive years—a feat his peers often attributed to favoritism. However, they didn't see how strictly his father, Professor DuVernay, graded him, constantly pushing him toward greatness.

Lincoln entered the dome-shaped auditorium, a vast space that could comfortably host Nawlins' entire student body and then some. Used primarily for receptions, recitals, and other significant events, it was a familiar setting to him.

For Lincoln, the welcome ceremony was an old routine. He felt little enthusiasm for the predictable speeches about school policies and achievements that he had heard year after year. Opting for solitude, he found a seat in the last pew of the junior/senior section. The room hushed as Chancellor Decken stepped onto the stage, ready to address the assembly.

"Welcome, students of Nawlins. We are thrilled to have you here for another year. I would also like to warmly welcome our new sixth graders, who will follow in their ancestors' footsteps by joining our prestigious school. This year, our mission is to inspire positive change in every way we can. A change in our academics, a change in our magical gifts, and a change in our personal lives. And by change, I mean we must aspire to be better than in previous years."

A girl walked in at the last minute and sat in the back of the 9th- and 10th-grade section. She had big curly hair and was wearing a black Biggie Smalls T-shirt. When she looked his way, Lincoln's head suddenly throbbed. He shut his eyes and pressed his index and middle fingers to his temples. When he peeked again, the girl was massaging her temples too, as if she was going through the same pain. Their eyes met again as they both took deep breaths. *Who is this girl?* Lincoln wondered, forcing his focus back to the Chancellor.

"Finally, I want to remind you that students must not use magic outside Nawlins. And cell phones and other unapproved electronics are restricted. So, there will be no TikTok or Instagram at Nawlins. We must keep our wizard identity hidden at all costs. All high schoolers may not leave campus on the weekdays and have a strict 8 p.m. curfew on the weekends, except seniors. And most importantly, brooms are now prohibited on campus, which means no broom racing. The only brooms I see around here should be used for sweeping.

"Let's have a great fall term and remember why we are here: to gain knowledge, because knowledge is power. And whoever has the power controls the world."

As the crowd rose to applaud, Lincoln and the curly-haired newcomer remained seated, their gaze locked in a silent exchange. Lincoln squinted, trying to place her familiar face, though he was certain they had never met.

As students began to file out, Lincoln's view was obstructed. He navigated through the dispersing crowd, searching for her, but the chaos at the exits thwarted his efforts. Feeling overwhelmed, he retreated.

Spotting his father exiting with fellow professors, Lincoln called out, "Hey, Dad!"

"Son, what's wrong?" He placed a hand on Lincoln's shoulder.

"I think I saw the new sophomore that Mom told me about."

"Yes, Donna Marie is going to be in my first class today. You should get to class yourself, young man."

"It would've sounded better if you'd said 'handsome young man.'"

Professor DuVernay laughed. "You and your mother with your bad jokes. Just get to class," he said, walking away.

"Our jokes are better than your cooking!" Lincoln grinned, bidding his father goodbye.

As he turned to leave, a familiar soft voice stopped him.

"Lincoln," Tamia said gently.

He stood still for a second, closing his eyes and thinking about what to say. His mind went blank.

"Lincoln, look at me," Tamia said, even softer.

Turning slowly, he faced Tamia, the girl he had once loved more than anything. Her silky black hair cascaded over her shoulders, highlighting her delicate features. Her brown sweatshirt almost matched her creamy skin.

And just like that, the feelings of love, guilt, and heartbreak struck him.

"I saw you sitting in the back. Did you do that so you could avoid me?" Tamia asked.

"I don't want it to be awkward between us."

"You're making it awkward. You didn't talk to me all summer. No text. No call. Nothing."

"I'm sorry, Tamia," he said. "The breakup wasn't easy for me."

"You think it was easy for me?"

"No," Lincoln said, holding his head down.

He and Tamia had met at their first welcome ceremony. He was sitting in the last row of the sixth-grade section, and just before the ceremony started, she sat next to him. Lincoln looked over to see a nervous Tamia rubbing her hands. She looked his way, and he smiled at her, trying to ease her mind. She smiled back and brushed her long, fine hair over her ears.

Tamia was beautiful inside and out, something Lincoln could always see.

As they spent more time together, they started to open up more.

They understood each other—both burdened by expectations they never asked for. Tamia was the eldest daughter of Chancellor Decken, with two younger siblings, Casie and Jay, whose narcissistic and bratty behavior she often vented about to Lincoln. But it wasn't just them. Her mom constantly pushed her to become someone she wasn't, pressuring her to follow the Coven's path and turn her back on anyone outside the top bloodlines.

"Everyone should be treated equally," Tamia would tell her mom whenever they argued.

After their fights, she would call Lincoln and talk for hours. "Hypocrites. That's what they are. The Coven is no better than the oppressors our ancestors fought against," Tamia said.

Lincoln felt the same way. He thought the Coven should be dismantled and the bloodline-ranking system shouldn't exist.

Tamia eventually confessed to Lincoln that she sensed how unique he was. Almost nonchalantly, he performed the most difficult spells in one try. His dawas were flawless. And even though he showed these signs of greatness, she knew he was still holding back his abilities.

He considered telling her the truth about his powers, but never did.

She was so special to him. He loved her so much that he broke up with her last year to avoid exposing his biggest secret to her.

"I know it wasn't easy for you either. I just need time. I can't be friends with you right now," Lincoln said.

He walked away, his heart heavy with unresolved feelings and the burden of secrets he still carried.

Chapter Ten

Donna thought her anxiety attacks were behind her, but when she laid eyes on the boy in the auditorium, it felt as if something was clawing at her skin all over her body. He looked so familiar to her, not just because she recognized him from Rima's photos, but as if she'd met him before.

Lincoln DuVernay. I know those light brown eyes from somewhere, Donna thought as she waited around the corner from the Spells classroom.

Shake it off. It's the first class of the day. You can do this, Donna Marie.

Noor was waiting for her at the door.

"Hey, girl. I was looking for you in the auditorium."

"It took me longer than expected to unpack, so I just sat at the back."

"Let's hurry in. Professor DuVernay doesn't tolerate tardiness," Noor said.

A nervous flutter stirred in Donna's chest as she stepped into her first class at Nawlins. Whispers died down, and eyes turned her way, making her stomach twist. In the front row, she met the gaze of a handsome boy with a crisp taper-fade.

Wow, he's hot.

As she and Noor climbed the steps to a pair of empty seats, Donna clocked the letterman jacket he wore, a bold *C* stitched on the left. It matched the one worn by the girl who had rudely bumped into her earlier.

Silence fell over the room as Professor DuVernay stepped in. He extracted a wand from his briefcase, and with a graceful motion, a blue beam shot from the tip towards the whiteboard. His name began to materialize in elegant cursive, as though he were drawing each letter in the air with a marker.

"Hello, class. My name is Professor DuVernay, and welcome to Spells 501. Today, for your placement exam, you will turn your lizards into baby alligators. You've had all summer to prepare for the spell, so it shouldn't be too hard."

Professor DuVernay looked at Donna.

"As you all have noticed by now, we have a new student. Please introduce yourself."

Donna awkwardly banged her leg on the desk as she stood.

"Hello, my name is Donna Marie Guillory. I'm from the Bronx, and this is my first term at Nawlins."

A girl sitting two rows in front of her turned around and looked her up and down. It was the same girl who bumped into her in the entrance hall. She had long hair, tiny freckles, and hazel eyes.

"First term? Where have you been all this time?" the girl said, smirking.

Donna hesitated, the weight of the room's stares pressing into her.

"I just discovered I was a wizard a few months ago."

The classroom went silent.

"Let's get you caught up, then," Professor DuVernay said.

"Looks like you have years of catching up to do," the girl said.

Some of the students laughed.

"Excuse me, Ms. Casie Decken, but I distinctly remember when you were in the sixth grade. Would you like me to discuss all the difficulties you encountered using your powers back then?" Professor DuVernay asked.

"Please tell us, sir!" a student shouted.

"I'm sure those humble beginnings will inspire you to be patient as Ms. Donna Marie learns to master her powers," he said, still watching Casie closely. "Now, open your textbooks to chapter one, and let's begin."

Donna sat and took a deep breath as the tiny lizard before her tried to crawl out of the plastic bin on top of the desk. The lizard slid down the sides of the bin every time it tried to escape—a resilient little reptile.

Donna sighed when she opened the thick brown book to the transformation spells. *I'll never get the hang of this.*

She glanced over to Casie, who effortlessly moved her wand in crisp motions as she said, "Badilisha."

A red smoke surrounded Casie's lizard. Once the smoke evaporated, a baby alligator occupied the long plastic bin on her desk. She proudly called out to Professor DuVernay, who inspected the alligator.

"Well done, Casie."

He pointed his wand toward the board, and Casie's name wrote itself in cursive below the header *Class Rankings* at number one.

Casie looked back to roll her eyes at Donna.

She would be even cuter if she didn't have that stank-ass attitude, Donna thought as she gripped her wand.

"Don't worry about Casie. She thinks she's better than everyone because she's in the Coven. And because her mom is the chancellor. And because her grandfather is the president of the Wizard High Council... But I'll show you the ropes. We New Yorkers have to stick together," Noor said.

"What's the Wizard High Council?" Donna asked.

"It's like the government for wizards."

"Oh."

The handsome boy sitting in the front had the number 2 on the back of his letterman jacket, just like Casie.

"Does that jacket mean he's in the Coven?" Donna asked Noor, gesturing to the boy.

"That's Jay, Casie's brother. And yes, the C is for Coven, and the two is their bloodline's rank. Their older sister, Tamia, is a senior, so you probably won't see much of her."

"Why is Casie so mean?" Donna asked, remembering Rima's warning.

"Casie hates anyone who poses a threat to her," Noor replied matter-of-factly.

"How am I a threat?"

"Because you're beautiful, and most importantly, new meat on campus."

"Meat? Gross."

"Shh," Professor DuVernay said as he inspected an alligator.

Noor and Donna were the last two to perform the placement test.

"Watch my movements and pronunciation," Noor whispered to Donna.

Noor grabbed her brown wand and made a Z motion with her wrist while chanting, "Badilisha."

A blue smoke wrapped around the lizard, then expanded as the lizard grew. After a few seconds, the smoke evaporated, revealing a baby alligator.

Professor DuVernay approached the desk. He raised his eyebrow at Noor when the alligator snapped at him.

"Your gator has a little attitude, but you completed your task," he said.

He waved his wand toward the board, and Noor's name appeared at number ten.

Donna was up next. She was so nervous her palms were sweating. It felt like the entire class was watching, silently waiting to judge her first attempt at showcasing her powers.

"Can you feel the magic inside you?" Professor DuVernay asked.

Donna closed her eyes. She felt lighter, as if her wizard gifts were freely flowing through her, finally unblocked.

"Yes," Donna replied.

"Harness it. And channel it to your wand. Chant the spell as your power flows with your movements. Concentration and confidence are the keys to a successful spell," he said.

Donna opened her eyes as her power fluttered through her body. A tingling feeling flowed from her heart to her arm. She lifted her wand and made a Z motion.

"Badilisha!"

A red smoke engulfed the tiny lizard on the desk. Donna and Noor leapt back as the smoke expanded, consuming their entire workspace. A full-grown alligator's foot, followed by its massive, scaly body, emerged from the dissipating cloud. The creature snapped its jaws menacingly at Donna.

"Don't panic!" Professor DuVernay commanded.

Why not? Donna thought frantically, ducking behind her desk. *An alligator nearly just took my head off!*

Chaos ensued as some students scrambled towards the door, hurdling over desks and backpacks in a frantic bid for safety. Professor DuVernay fired a red beam from his wand, striking the alligator, which froze in place before transforming back into a harmless lizard.

"I'm so sorry," Donna stammered, rising from behind her desk with trembling hands and unsteady knees. Heat rushed to her face, burning her cheeks with embarrassment that outweighed her fear.

"It's okay. It was your first time performing a spell. You'll improve."

Professor DuVernay pointed his wand at the board, and Donna's name appeared at number thirty—last place.

The school bell rang, sparing Donna from further humiliation. As she exited class with her head hung low, she became the subject of whispers. Casie passed by with a disdainful eye roll. Donna recalled her mother's words, *"Don't mind the haters; they're just intimidated by your potential."* But the sting of the moment was hard to shake off.

"It wasn't that bad," Noor said, smiling.

"That alligator almost chewed off our arms. It was bad," Donna replied.

"Okay. It was kinda bad."

"I'm last in class. I've never had a failing grade in my life," Donna said.

"The placement test wasn't a real test. It was just an exercise to see what we needed to improve on. And it gives bragging rights to the top students, which unfortunately boosted Casie's already enormous ego."

The two girls shared a laugh. Jay walked by and caught Donna's gaze. She blushed as she looked into his hazel eyes, then quickly looked away.

"You hungry? Let's grab food at the CC," Noor suggested.

"The CC? What's that?"

"It's the common center. The food is delicious, and it's a chill vibe."

"I could use both right now," Donna said.

Donna was surprised that the CC had so many amenities. The lounge area on the second floor had an art studio, a theater, and a large game room filled with arcade machines and the latest video game sets. Some students in the arcade were yelling at the large TVs as they played *Madden* and *Call of Duty*.

In the center of the building was the main cafeteria, known for its authentic Cajun dishes. According to Noor, the chef's favorites were the Creole red beans, jambalaya, and the fried catfish and shrimp po'boys.

The cafeteria quieted as Donna stepped inside, balancing her tray of jambalaya. Whispers rippled through the room, and curious eyes followed her every move.

"Who is that?"

"What's her bloodline rank?"

"I've never seen her before."

Donna sat beside Noor at a circular high-top table and took a spoonful of jambalaya. The spices hit instantly—her eyes watered, and her mouth felt like it was on fire. She reached for her water and took a deep gulp.

"Wow, that's spicy," she gasped.

Noor giggled. "That's New Orleans food for ya."

Donna laughed through the burn, nodding.

"It reminds me of how my mom used to cook," Donna said softly. "She's originally from New Orleans... but she hasn't cooked in a long time."

Noor's smile turned gentle. "Then you'll fit right in."

Donna took in the different cliques at the tables. Casie and Jay sat in a section with other students wearing black and yellow lettermen jackets bearing numbers on their backs. Donna shook her head in disapproval.

"Of course, the popular kids," she said.

"You already know the twins. That light-skinned pretty boy is Ryan Dubois. He's a Five. They always wear those jackets to remind us that they're better," Noor explained.

"Hey, beautiful," a boy said, walking up to Noor. He picked her up from her stool and spun her around as he hugged her.

"Donna, this is Chike, my boyfriend. If you can't tell." Noor chuckled.

"Pleasure meeting you, Donna. You're the new girl the streets are talking about."

"I was just telling Donna about your cocky Coven friends," Noor said.

"Don't listen to her. We aren't all cocky," Chike responded.

Noor pinched him on the cheek, and he lowered his face to her eye level. He was tall, so he had to bend over awkwardly.

"That's because you're different, right?" Noor didn't ask; it was a statement.

"Yes, ma'am. I'm one of the nice ones," Chike hurried to respond with a full grin.

"Good boy," Noor said, kissing him on the other cheek. "But I still hate when you wear that jacket."

"I'll see you later. I have to hit the weight room for football," he said.

"Do your thing," Noor replied.

"So... You have a boyfriend?" Donna said, nudging Noor on her side as she sat back down.

"I do. That's my baby," Noor said, looking back at Chike as he and Jay exited the CC.

"He's a Four?"

"Yeah, Cane Hargis is his ancestor. He and Jia are my only real friends here besides you. Yes, you're my friend now."

Donna smiled. *OMG! I have a friend! I have a friend! I have an actual friend!*

"Who's Jia?" Donna asked, trying to control her excitement.

"She's the spicy one, with a spicy French accent, too," Noor said. "Here she comes now."

A girl strutted into the CC as if she were walking in a fashion show. She wore a white blouse tucked in her high-waisted denim jeans. Her silk-pressed hair flowed down her back. Donna knew her designer purse was Louis Vuitton because Jacquie had a knockoff version. Even the robotic legs of her backpack pranced with a snobby walk beside her, matching the girl's every step. Left foot. Right foot. Of course, it was Louis Vuitton too.

Does Louis Vuitton have a wizard department? What's next? A Gucci broom? Wait, that would actually be kinda cool.

"So, you're the new girl everyone is talking about," the girl said, sliding off her sunglasses and popping a chewing gum.

"This is Donna Marie. She's a New Yorker, so she's cool like me," Noor said.

"Bonjour, Donna Marie. That's a beautiful name. I'm Jia."

"Thanks. Um, where are you from?" Donna inquired.

"France. Bordeaux, to be exact. Have you been?"

"Ah, no. I haven't been anywhere other than New York and now New Orleans."

"Of course, you Americans don't like to travel much. Such a pity."

"Hey, be nice," Noor said.

"Ma chérie, I am being nice," Jia replied. "So, Donna, how was regular high school?"

"It's pretty much like what you see in movies—a big popularity contest. There isn't much real interaction since everyone's too busy on their phones, and some teachers are just there to collect a paycheck. Well, that's how schools are in my neighborhood, anyway. I wasn't privileged enough to attend a fancy private school where they prioritize education."

"Sorry," Noor said.

"Don't be. Students who really wanted to excel academically, like me, found ways to get ahead… But we had some cool stuff too, like clubs and sports. We had prom too, but that's only for the seniors."

"We have sports here, too. But the athletes can't use their powers while competing," Noor said.

"We have prom. Anyone in high school can attend," Jia replied.

"Really?" Donna said.

"It's called the Winter Formal, and the college students chaperone us that night, not the professors, so it's popping," Noor explained.

"You have plenty of time to find a date by then, Donna. Don't worry, I have to find one too," Jia said, taking out a comb from her purse and running it through her straight hair.

A date?

"Unless you have a boyfriend back in New York. Which would be a total bummer because long-distance relationships suck. I just broke up with my boyfriend yesterday," Jia confessed.

"You broke up with Jason? He seemed so nice the times you two were hanging out and you FaceTimed me," Noor commented.

"Yeah, he was okay. More like a summer fling. My parents really didn't want me with a Norm."

"Hey, you know my dad's a Norm. What's wrong with dating one?" Noor asked.

"Yeah, but didn't your parents meet in their twenties? It was probably easier for your mom to break the news to him that she was a wizard. Now imagine a teenage boy accidentally finding out I'm a wizard—he'd probably hop on IG Live and broadcast it to the world."

"Good point," Noor said.

"So I guess I have to wait until my twenties to find true love with a Norm like your mom did. Because the wizard boys here? Ew…"

Donna had never had a real boyfriend. She'd never even kissed a boy before. She wasn't sure she even knew how to talk to a boy in that way.

"No. I don't have a boyfriend," Donna shrugged.

"Donna, you're a baddie. I bet the boys will be fighting over you," Jia said.

"Facts!" Noor added.

Chapter Eleven

The white number two was perfectly stitched on the back of the letterman jacket in front of Donna. Jay turned his head, exposing his sharp jawline and a small gold hoop earring. But his long eyelashes were his best feature, Donna decided.

His hazel eyes turned in her direction, and she quickly diverted her attention to the professor as she came into the classroom.

"Good afternoon, class."

What a beautiful voice, Donna thought.

"It's an honor being in your presence, Professor Hunt. I've been to many of your performances," Noor said.

"She's a singer?" Donna whispered to Noor.

"When Professor Hunt was in the school choir, it was the best we've ever had. They won many competitions. A lot of famous rappers and singers sampled their music, and she was the lead singer. I have to get her on one of my tracks."

"Thank you, and welcome sophomores. It's a pleasure to be your educator as we explore the magical world of dawas. Dawas has always been my favorite subject because any wizard can create a unique concoction by merely manipulating its properties."

Professor Hunt walked to the board and grabbed a piece of white chalk.

"Though I am the youngest professor here at Nawlins, I sometimes prefer old-school teaching methods."

The plain green chalkboard rasped as she wrote the students' names in groups of two.

"Your deskmate will be your official partner for the remainder of the term. So, go on. Find your partner and get acquainted."

Donna scanned the list on the board until her eyes landed on her name, right next to Jay. As if on cue, he turned around.

"I'll grab my stuff and come up there," he said.

Jia looked at Donna and smirked as she made her way to her deskmate, who happened to be Noor. Donna scooted her chair to create more space for Jay, who sat and smiled.

Professor Hunt waved her wand toward the tall cabinets on the side of the room. The doors opened, and black pots levitated to the students' desks along with a plethora of ingredients, including flower petals, four-leaf clovers, pinecones, insects, animal drool, and jars of water.

Is that a stink bug? Donna thought as another jar landed on her desk.

"For your placement exam, you will create scented dawas," the professor said. "By mixing a variety of ingredients and using the corresponding chant, it is possible to create various scents from all over the world, such as fresh coffee beans from Kilimanjaro's slopes, frangipani flowers along the Perfume River in Vietnam, or even the crisp, clean scent of the icebergs in the Arctic. I will determine the group's rank based on creativity and uniqueness."

Donna didn't know what to create or where to start. She picked up a jar of lion's drool and almost gagged as the saliva dripped down to the bottom of the glass.

Jay opened the black book in the center of the desk. "What is your favorite scent in the world?" he asked Donna.

"My brownstone had a small bee farm on the roof. A farmer would extract the honey sometimes as I watched. The smell was so yummy." Donna sighed.

He grabbed a jar of bee stingers and another of fresh honeycomb.

"What's your favorite scent?" she asked.

"Fresh rainwater," Jay responded. "Every year my family vacations in Mombasa, on the coast in Kenya. It has the most beautiful views I've ever seen, overlooking the Indian Ocean. My favorite part of the trip is when it rains."

Donna was impressed. She thought he was going to say the smell of an old football.

"Let's do rainwater from Mombasa with a hint of honey," Jay suggested.

"Let's do it," she replied.

He carefully heated the cauldron pot.

Using the textbook, Donna found the ingredients for rainwater.

She grabbed a jar containing cloud particles and a jar of mint and placed them by the pot.

"Those are the right ingredients. Good job," Jay said as he placed a temperature gauge in the pot.

I'm pulling my own weight. Yes! Donna thought.

As they waited for the pot to heat, Donna overheard Chike and Ryan, who were sitting in front of her, bickering about what scent they should create.

"These two are homies, but they are always arguing," Jay explained.

"Let's make the smell of a burning oak tree," Chike demanded.

"Man, no. Let's do steamed eucalyptus," Ryan replied.

"Bro, that's lame."

"You're lame."

"Let's take this outside so I can show you how lame I am."

"Okay. Okay. Chill, Hercules... What if we use burning oak to steam the eucalyptus?" Ryan suggested.

"Ah, I like that. Fuse the two together. I knew we'd figure it out."

Chike added oak pieces to the iron pot, waved his wand, and a small fire ignited at the bottom.

"Yo, don't let it get too hot," Ryan said, tapping Chike on his shoulder.

Chike lifted his wand, and the flame slowly burned out, leaving a smoky oak. Ryan added a few ingredients to the pot, and then they both lifted their wands and chanted together.

"Kuja Pamoja."

Donna looked on as a green smoke hovered over the pot, followed by a popping sound at the base, which grew louder as the vapor increased in size.

"Something's wrong," Ryan exclaimed.

"Stop being a wuss," Chike replied.

The vapor thickened into dark green smoke, followed by a loud firecracker-like pop that echoed through the room, making Donna flinch.

"I think it's going to explode!" Ryan shouted.

The dawa erupted. Before it could splash on the students, Professor Hunt pointed her wand at the particles, which froze in the air.

She lowered her wand as the ingredients fell back into the pot.

"Your flame was too hot, causing an imbalance," Professor Hunt explained.

She walked to the board and wrote their names at number fifteen.

"Homie, we're in last place. The Coven will be pissed," Ryan expressed to Chike.

"Okay, the pot is ready," Jay announced to Donna with a smile.

He began by adding sand, honeycomb, bee stingers, and strips of coconut tree bark into the mix. Donna then attentively dropped five mint leaves into the swirling concoction.

She fumbled with the lid of the last jar, her fingers slipping.

"Here, let me help," Jay offered, reaching over. His hands brushed against hers as he took the jar, sending a warm rush through her. *Stay focused, Donna Marie!*

Jay loosened the cap slightly and handed it back. "This is the cool part. Just make sure you open it right over the pot."

Donna held the jar close to the pot's rim and gently lifted the cap. A small cloud burst forth, swirling with miniature lightning and soft rumbles of thunder—an encapsulated storm.

As the cloud descended into the pot, Jay glanced at the textbook, then raised his dark red wand.

"Ready?" he asked, his eyes twinkling with excitement.

"I think so," Donna replied, her voice steadier than she felt.

Together, they intoned the chant, "Kuja Pamoja."

Immediately, a yellow vapor enveloped the pot, punctuated by bursts of bright light. Donna instinctively stepped back, haunted by her previous magical mishaps.

Jay, however, remained calm and collected, casually stretching his arms as the vapor began to stabilize. A plume of blue and yellow steam soon rose gracefully from the pot, filling the air with a fresh, honeyed scent. Professor Hunt stepped forward and took a slow inhale of the fragrant steam.

"Wow, good job, you two. Rainwater with a hint of honey. Perfect temperature control and an impeccable mix of ingredients."

Donna let out a relieved sigh, grateful that nothing had gone awry this time—no explosions, no fires.

Professor Hunt then proceeded to write their names at the top of the leaderboard. Jay turned to Donna with a victorious grin and offered his fist. Donna met it with her own, their knuckles touching in a celebratory dap.

A flutter of butterflies danced in her chest as Jay began tidying up their workspace. As Donna reached for an empty glass jar, her hand brushed his again. They shared a fleeting, charged glance before looking away.

"We make a good team," Jay said before catching up with Chike and Ryan outside the classroom.

"You're trying to get on Casie's bad side by flirting with her brother?" Jia asked, walking up to Donna.

"We were not flirting," Donna replied.

"Y'all had little goo-goo eyes everywhere," Noor added.

"They sure did. It's giving... future husband and wife vibes," Jia said.

Donna rolled her eyes as Jia and Noor laughed.

The truth was, she did find him handsome and charming.

Although she'd never had a boyfriend, there was one boy whose hand she used to hold in middle school. But he ended up holding hands with another girl one day, and Donna "broke up" with him, devastated.

She cried to her mom, who told her stories about her father and how she fell in love with him. Catherine was a freshman at Xavier University studying business. One weekend, she went to Café du Monde to study and enjoy a cup of hot chocolate. As she got up to leave, Sammy bumped into her and spilled chocolate over her dress. He was so embarrassed, but Catherine was so fascinated with his beautiful smile that she didn't care about the accident. They ended up spending that entire day enjoying each other's company, strolling around the French Quarter.

By the end of the day, Donna was exhausted. She didn't have a magical backpack that followed her around to take the load off like some of the other students. Nawlins was enormous, and she had walked from one side to the other and back again. She dragged her feet as she headed to her dorm. A breeze hit her face, and she untied her bandana and shook her head to loosen her curls. "Ahh, much better," she said, using her fingernails to give herself a scalp massage.

When Donna opened the door to her room, Mr. Whiskers jumped into her arms. She placed him on the bed and prepared his food.

"Did you miss me?"

Mr. Whiskers let out a loud meow.

After she fed and played with the cat, Donna sat at her desk and did her homework. When she finished, she wrote an email to her mother.

Hey Mom,

The first day of class went pretty well. I'm in the top three in my core classes after my placement exams. I didn't place too high in...

Donna pondered on the right choice of words for Spells class. She felt terrible for lying to her mom, but what else could she do? Even if she wanted to tell her the truth about being a wizard, an email wouldn't exactly be the best way to say it.

Science Laboratory. But I'm optimistic. Perhaps I'll consider getting a tutor. I hope you're doing well, Mama. I miss you so much.

Love and kisses,

Donna Marie.

P.S. Mr. Whiskers says hello to you and Jacquie.

As if he knew he'd been mentioned, Mr. Whiskers jumped on the desk, rubbing himself on Donna.

"Wait a minute," she said, looking at his collar.

She unclipped the collar and brought the tag closer to the desk lamp. The mark at the bottom of the fleur-de-lis symbol wasn't a line as she had thought—it was a wand. Donna scurried around the room and grabbed a textbook from her backpack. The school's crest on the cover was identical to the symbol on the tag.

"Oh, my God," Donna said, staring at Mr. Whiskers.

Chapter Twelve

Donna was up early Friday morning, rereading the first chapter of Ancient Magic. Professor Dean Decken was the instructor, and class started today. She'd heard the course was challenging, and the last thing she wanted was to make a lousy impression on the Chancellor's husband.

It had been a challenging first week, but she was almost through it. Core classes were a walk in the park, but wizard classes were kicking her butt. She was constantly playing catch-up, not to mention she was used to being a top student. But being a top student in a regular school was easy. Here, everyone was super bright and had been practicing wizardry for years. To keep up, she was reading ahead and had signed up for tutoring with the best student in Spells class.

As Donna was packing her books in her backpack, Mr. Whiskers jumped on the desk, startling her.

"Um, sir, I thought you were sleeping," Donna said, touching his name tag. "Sorry, I have to leave early. I left food in your bowl... I still don't know how you have the Nawlins crest on your collar. Did you belong to a student here or something?"

Mr. Whiskers laid down and purred at Donna.

"But then, how did you end up in New York? Whatever it is, I'm going to figure it out…"

Noor was sleeping on the couch in the living room when Donna left for tutoring.

I didn't know our couch could float. And it's rocking? No wonder she's snoring.

Donna yawned.

"*No.* I'm not tired. It's time to go grind for the worm,*"* she said under her breath.

"The early bird grinds for the worm," Catherine used to tell Donna as she woke her up for school. Before her mom got sick, she would walk her to school every morning and kiss her on the cheek before Donna headed into the building. She was initially embarrassed by the kisses, but she missed her mother's soft touch when she had to do the walk alone.

This morning, she yearned for her mother's hand wrapped in hers as she walked across campus. Maybe it was just the way a teen girl missed her mom, but still, a pang of compunction lingered. While Donna was beginning a new life here, Catherine was alone in a New York nursing home.

"You're that kid who toured the school this summer," Mr. Espree said, aiming a spray bottle at the large library window and wiping it clean with a squeegee. Around him, three other spray bottles and squeegees hovered in midair, tending to different panes.

"Hello, Mr. Espree," Donna replied.

"Just out of curiosity, do you know your family's bloodline rank?"

"No."

"It's important. It tracks our roots all the way back to the revolt. You don't care to know?"

"Not really. A wizard is a wizard, right?" Donna tried to hide her annoyance.

"Some are more powerful than others," he said, the window squeaking under his squeegee.

"How would I find out?" Donna asked.

"Your last name should be in the registry. And if it's not there, the only other place would be *The Book of Knowledge*, where all our ancestors' bloodlines were originally ranked. But that book hasn't been seen in over a hundred years."

"Well, I guess if I'm not in the registry, I'll have to remain a mystery," Donna said proudly.

Mr. Espree chuckled. "One thing about mysteries... someday, they have to be solved."

"Welp, um, good seeing you," Donna said, scurrying to the revolving door of the library.

She approached a small study booth where a boy sat across the table, writing in a notebook. He had messy, braided hair to his shoulders and was wearing a black T-shirt that looked a little too big for him.

"Hello. Are you Chad?" Donna asked.

"Yeah... Woaaa, wassam with ya, baby?" he said in a heavy New Orleans accent.

"Um... What? I'm sorry, I didn't understand anything you just said except baby."

"My bad, I forgot you're not from here. *Wassam* means, what's up," Chad replied.

"Oh, okay. Well, hey, what's up? I'm Donna."

She slid into the seat across from him, pulling her wand from her pocket and placing it gently on the table.

An awkward silence followed. Chad tapped his fingers on the table, his eyes flicking between her and the wand.

"So..." Donna cleared her throat, breaking the tension.

"You don't recognize me, huh? I'm in your Spells class," Chad said.

"You are?"

"I was the one who beat Casie's score on the placement exam," he said.

Donna felt a little ashamed that she didn't recognize him.

"It's all good. I'm not tripping. I'm somewhat quiet, so I'm easily unnoticeable... You turned that baby lizard into a big gator, which means your powers are strong, but you need to learn how to control them. I believe any wizard can be stronger than a Coven member if they work hard at mastering their magic." He paused. "I had to work my ass off. The Coven is just a group of cocky wannabes. At the end of the day, they're just like the rest of us."

"Good speech," Donna said.

"Thank you." Chad grinned. "Nice wand, by the way" he said, leaning in for a better look. "The vine wrap. That's a serious perk."

Donna raised an eyebrow. "Perk?"

"Yeah. The vine isn't just for looks. It adds grip, especially when you're casting high-energy spells. Keeps it steady in your hand so it won't fly out or misfire. Pretty handy when things get intense."

Donna turned the wand in her hand. The red vine's texture was rough yet sturdy beneath her fingertips, grounding her with a much-needed sense of confidence.

"Huh. I didn't realize it had perks."

Chad grinned. "Trust me, with a tough spell? That grip could be a game-changer. When I get my bread up, I'm gonna get one of those wands too, ya heard me."

"Ah, yeah. Sure. Um, I heard you."

"Let's get to work!" Chad said, removing a matte-white wand from his bag. "My grandma always told me: 'To become great at something, you must master the basics.' So, this first lesson is related to breathing and movement techniques. Since the source of our powers comes from the heart and flows through our bodies, proper breathing is the key to a spell. My ancestors learned this from Solomon himself."

He grasped his wand in his left hand, then closed his eyes as he took a deep breath. He exhaled three short breaths and then opened his eyes and slowly inhaled another deep breath through his nostrils. A small blue beam permeated from the tip of his wand and quickly changed to red. The red beam twirled in the air and changed to blue, then back to red, creating a small spinning vortex of colors.

The vortex thinned and stretched to the top of the ceiling.

Chad calmed his breathing, and the beam slowly retreated into his wand.

"Wow," Donna said.

"You can control your powers like this, too, or even better. Just have to learn the basics, ya heard me."

Chad smiled, and Donna caught a glimpse of his softness underneath.

"What part of New Orleans are you from?" she asked.

"I'm from the gutta," Chad said.

"What's the gutta?"

"The trenches... The hood."

"And what part of New Orleans is that?"

"My grandparents raised me in Hollygrove," he explained. "The sixth ward. It's not the best neighborhood. Lil Wayne is from there, too. He talks about it in his songs."

"I'm from the Bronx. My neighborhood wasn't the best either. I used to live in Manhattan, but when my dad died, my mom couldn't afford our place anymore, so we had to move."

"Sorry to hear about your dad. Both of my parents passed away. That's why my grandparents had to raise me."

"I'm sorry too," Donna said.

"'Don't be fooled by the rocks that you got. You still, you still Donna from the block,'" Chad rapped.

Donna busted out laughing. "What was that?"

"I bet that's your favorite song, huh? For you to rep your city," Chad replied.

"No... Ja Rule made the best song for us New Yorkers to rep our city." Donna put her fist up to her mouth as she sang, "'I'm from New York, New York.'"

"Okay. Okay. You know your music... Sorry, just didn't want to continue with the sad mood about our parents."

"It's cool. I needed that laugh."

"I know what it feels like to be an outsider, ya heard me. When I first came to Nawlins, people stereotyped me as the kid from the slums," Chad said. "Some of the spoiled rich kids thought I was too hood for this school. I wanted to be the best wizard that ever lived. And as my powers got better, so did my confidence. My powers filled that void I had from being an outsider."

Donna smiled. *There's a vulnerable guy under that hard façade*, she thought.

She knew that façade all too well. Letting down the wall that guarded her vulnerability meant risking collapse. And if she crumbled, who would be there to catch her? Maybe that's why she often didn't feel special. It was also the real reason she chose to attend Nawlins—a hope that her wizard gifts could fill a void.

The void of a father.

The void of a traditional family.

The void of happiness.

The void of confidence.

For the first time in her life, Donna felt truly seen—someone her age finally understood the weight of losing a parent.

Chad squinted. "Um, why are you staring at me? Do I have something in my nose?"

Donna laughed. "Sorry, I was just thinking about how much I have to get caught up on."

"Let's get to work, baby," Chad said.

The two hours of tutoring evidently paid off. In Spells class, Donna managed to transform a caterpillar into a magnificent blue butterfly, its wings spanning eight inches. The class erupted in applause as they marveled at the butterfly's iridescent sheen, fluttering gracefully through the air.

Casie, who performed before Donna, watched with a scowl, probably because her demonstration garnered only a fraction of the attention. Her glare towards

Donna could cut glass, but Donna remained focused on her achievement, feeling a surge of pride as Professor DuVernay advanced her two places in the class rankings. Chad caught her eye from across the room and winked, his approval sending a warm flush through her.

She was still relishing her new victory as she sat in the front row of Ancient Magic next to Noor.

"Tutoring was a good call for you. Chad is the smartest boy in our grade. Maybe I should join too," Noor said, chuckling.

Donna turned around and looked at Chad a few rows behind her. He smiled at her. She couldn't help but blush, but their moment was short-lived. From the back of the room, Jia crumpled a piece of paper and launched it towards them, disrupting their exchange.

"Hey, Noor," Jia called out.

The ball stopped midair as a man wearing a well-fitted gray suit entered the classroom. With his shiny platinum wand raised, he levitated the paper toward him. The ball unfolded and expanded to about ten times its size, large enough so everyone could read it.

Let's hit the streets tonight!

The classroom erupted into laughter. Donna covered her mouth to hide her laugh as Noor slouched down in her seat.

With another flick of his wand, the giant paper turned to ash and disintegrated in the air.

The room quickly silenced.

"I am Professor Dean Thibodeaux-Decken. You will address me as Professor Decken. Welcome to Ancient Magic. Open your books to chapter one."

Everything about Professor Decken said *professional*.

"Ancient Magic is the base of our gifts. The spells from *The Book of Giza* helped the revolt members of 1811 successfully carry out their plan to free their brothers and sisters from bondage. And from that same book came hundreds of other materials here today to help you be the best wizards you can be. And you will. All of you," he announced.

Donna caught Casie at the end of the row, giving her the side-eye.

"Maybe not all of us," Casie said.

Donna sank into her seat. Professor Decken walked up to Casie.

"There will be no interruptions in my classroom. Do you understand, Ms. Decken?"

"Okay, Dad," Casie replied.

"Okay, Professor," he said. "Now, pay attention, class."

With his platinum wand in hand, he stepped into the center of the classroom and widened his stance.

"Moto," he said with a deep voice.

A beam of fire ignited from his wand, yet it produced no heat. *Oohs* and *ahhs* were heard throughout the classroom. The beam transformed into a long fire bullwhip as he changed his stance yet again, the soles of his shoes squeaking on the floor.

Donna was on the edge of her seat as he swung the whip around his body, putting on a show for his audience. The flame detached from his wand and morphed into a massive bat made of fire. As it soared overhead, each flap of its wings stirred a gust that swept through the room, sending students' papers flying in all directions.

The bat inhaled and let out a loud screech as sparks of fire dropped from its mouth.

Some students ducked and dove toward the floor; others jumped from their seats and backed away. With a quick Z motion from his wand, Professor Decken vanished the bat.

"The ability to control your spells is the key component in this class. I will help you, but I will not baby you."

Donna returned to her seat. Noor looked at her with eyes wide.

"What's wrong, ladies? You scared?" Casie smirked.

A covered cage on the side of the professor's desk started to shake violently.

"What is that?" Jia said from the back of the classroom.

"That is your placement exam."

Professor Decken approached the cage and yanked off the black cover, revealing a sinister black wolf. It expanded its elongated jaws, showing off long golden fangs. It growled at the students and tried to bite through its cage, denting the thick metal bars.

"Magnificent, isn't she? She's a Loyal," he said.

Noor raised her hand and the professor nodded at her.

"What's a Loyal?" Noor asked.

"A Loyal is a companion bestowed on some of the original revolt members in 1811," he responded. "Her name is Fang, and she's over two hundred years old."

Fang sniffed the air, ears twitching, as her piercing amber eyes scanned the room with quiet intensity.

"Some Loyals passed in time, and others were put to sleep after the revolt due to their innately vicious behavior. Some Loyals disguised themselves as house pets or as wild animals. This wolf is suspected to be one of the last living Loyals. Your exam will consist of taming this Loyal into its hiding form."

The Chancellor entered the classroom alongside an older man dressed sharply in a black suit. He looked to be in his late sixties, with a well-groomed gray beard, polished eyeglasses, and a flat herringbone hat that he removed with a nod to Professor Decken. His presence commanded respect, and Professor Decken introduced him with reverence.

"Please welcome the president of the Wizard High Council, my father, William Thibodeaux."

The students stood in unison, greeting the esteemed visitor warmly.

"Hello, President Thibodeaux," they said except Casie, who said "Hello, Grandfather," in a cocky tone, raising her eyebrows up and down at Donna. The Chancellor remained near the door as he walked forward.

"Good day, students. I stopped by Nawlins to wish you all a good term and to see how much progress we have made as wizards. I'm proud to say that I'm impressed by what I've seen so far. Keep up the good work."

"Thank you, President Thibodeaux," the students said, taking their seats.

He joined the Chancellor on the side of the classroom near the door.

Professor Decken waved his wand, and the cage slowly raised, freeing the beast. Fang growled as she ran toward the students before a thick gold leash and collar around her neck restrained her. The chain clanked as she jumped and paced around the desk.

Donna tried her best to mask her fear.

"I'll go first," Chad announced.

He walked down the steps to the front of the classroom, placing himself in front of the Loyal, who growled at him.

Fang yanked on her chain and stood on her hind legs, exhibiting her massive frame.

He walked closer to the wolf while raising his wand. Fang jumped and snagged even harder on her restraints.

"Nidhamu," Chad said.

A blue vapor circled the Loyal as she snapped her jaws. Chad leaned forward, and Fang jumped and scratched his left arm with her sharp claws. Chad fell to the ground, and the blue vapor evaporated from his wand. Donna gasped, but he quickly recovered and got to his feet.

"Nidhamu," he chanted again, louder this time.

A blue beam pushed the wolf away, then metamorphosed into a dark blue vapor as Chad held his wand with both hands.

The wolf silenced as the vapor covered her body.

The vapor slowly subsided, revealing a tiny black puppy. The Chancellor walked over to Chad.

"Your arm, let me see it," she said.

He winced as the Chancellor inspected the cut. She removed a liquid paste from her pocket and placed it on the wound. The wound healed immediately.

"You have tamed the Loyal. A full ten points for a successful spell but minus three for the first failed attempt," Professor Decken said.

Chad walked back to his seat as the Chancellor approached the puppy. She snapped her finger, and the puppy became a wolf again. Fang sniffed the

Chancellor, then sat on her hind legs. Fang remained docile as the Chancellor circled her, dragging her hand through the thick black fur.

She stopped in front of the wolf and stared into her large eyes. Donna tensed up, seeing her so close to the Loyal.

Fang licked the Chancellor on the cheek.

"Only their owner can command a Loyal. Luckily, Fang has been in my family for generations," she said.

She snapped her fingers again, and Fang lay down, stretching her eight-foot body on the floor. The Chancellor reached into a brown paper bag behind the cage and pulled out a large rodent.

"Is that a giant rat?" Donna whispered to Noor.

"It's a nutria."

The nutria shrieked as the Chancellor hung it from its tail. Fang started to drool as she stared at the nutria in front of her.

Disgusting, thought Donna.

"A snack for you, my darling," the Chancellor said, as if offering a dog biscuit.

She threw the rodent into the air, and Fang leaped and grabbed it in her mouth. Blood dripped as she carried her snack back into the cage.

"I hope you sophomores have a good term," the Chancellor said before leaving the room with President Thibodeaux.

"Don't you wish your moms were a boss like mine?" Casie said to Noor and Donna as she sat back in her chair, popping her gum.

Donna's nervousness grew stronger after every student successfully performed their placement exam. Her chance to volunteer was dwindling.

"Looks like we're down to our last two students. Donna and Raine. Who will come up first?" Professor Decken asked.

Donna looked over to Raine, who was wearing a black turtleneck and bell bottoms. A beige fedora with a black feather finished her look. Raine stood up and slapped her hands on the sides of her body.

"Loyals should be free and not confined to a cage. So, I won't be taking the placement exam," she said with a soft voice.

"Please see me after class, Raine," the professor said. "Donna Marie, it seems you're the last one up."

Donna's heart fluttered with every step toward the beast.

Fang sniffed at Donna, and the beast's calm demeanor shifted instantly. Donna stumbled back as the beast snapped her jaws and yanked violently on her chain. Fang's growls deepened into something primal, so loud and ferocious that a crowd of students gathered at the doorway. She clawed at the floor, dragging deep gashes into the wood as if imagining Donna's flesh beneath her paws.

Professor Decken lifted his wand. A red vapor shot from the tip, wrapping around the Loyal's body and freezing her in place. But even paralyzed, Fang's glowing yellow eyes stayed locked on Donna, shifting with every slight movement she made.

The red vapor dissipated and Fang roared.

Professor Decken rushed forward, but Fang grabbed the metal cage in her jaws and flung it at him, knocking him to the ground.

Fang charged.

The chain snapped as she lunged, her sharp teeth bared. Students screamed as the massive wolf soared through the air, aiming straight for Donna.

The Chancellor burst through the bystanders at the door.

"Kupooza!" she shouted, flicking her wand toward the beast.

Fang froze midair, claws inches from Donna's face.

The Chancellor lowered her gently to the ground. The wolf let out a low snarl before shifting back into a puppy, now motionless on the floor, still trapped in the Chancellor's spell.

The Chancellor scooped Fang into her arms, her gaze cutting sharply to Donna. Suspicion flickered in her eyes, as if she believed Donna had somehow provoked the Loyal on purpose. A school nurse rushed in moments later, kneeling beside Professor Decken. He winced but waved her off, signaling he was okay. The classroom buzzed with stunned silence, eyes darting between Donna and the Loyal.

"I... I'm so sorry," Donna said. "I don't know what happened."

The Chancellor seemed more interested in Fang than her husband's health or the students' well-being.

"Is Fang okay?" Casie asked.

The Chancellor finally broke her stare at Donna.

"She's fine. You all may leave class."

The students didn't make a move. They all stood in silence.

"I said class dismissed," the Chancellor reiterated in a serious tone.

Why did I have to be the one to make the Loyal snap? Donna thought as she exited the classroom.

Casie bumped into her, knocking her backpack to the floor. "Way to ruin class, Ms. Frizzy Hair," she said, laughing as she walked away.

Donna took a deep breath and picked up her bag as Noor and Jia came over.

"Don't worry about her. She only ranked first today because the Loyal comes from her family," Noor said.

"Yeah, and it's not your fault her family's pet has rabies," Jia said. "After this week, we deserve some fun this weekend. Especially you, Donna."

"Can we all hang out tomorrow instead?" Noor asked. "I promised Chike we would hang out tonight."

"Chike and Jia watching Netflix, k i s s i n g," Jia sang.

Donna giggled.

"Can you chill out? Before I tell Donna I saw you kissing Ryan yesterday," Noor said.

"Hey, I have no shame. I have a weak spot for boys with curly hair... Okay, let's do something tomorrow, then," Jia agreed.

After finishing her dinner in the CC, Donna returned to her dorm. Zina was sitting in the lobby near the grandfather clock doing homework.

"How was your first week?" Zina asked.

Chaos. "I don't know," she said, head low, annoyed with herself.

"My first week was rough too. It gets better. I promise."

"I hope so," Donna said, walking up the staircase.

She could hear Mr. Whiskers purring through her door as she jiggled the handle.

As she walked in, he rubbed on her leg, trying to cheer her up—well, either that or he was eyeing the new box of treats up on the high bookshelf.

The moon felt closer tonight. Donna lay in her bed and stared at the dark spots on its surface as she caressed the ruby pendant on her necklace.

Mr. Whiskers jumped on her bed and swatted at her pendant as if it were a cat toy.

"Isn't it beautiful? My father gave this necklace to my mom. It means a lot to me. So you definitely can't play with it."

She put Mr. Whiskers on the floor and lay back down, facing the moon. Her eyes started to close, and she drifted off to sleep.

Donna was in the backseat of her father's red pickup again. Snow blanketed the rural land, the surface dimly lit by the truck's headlights. Sammy had stepped out onto the wet road. A wizard in a black cloak flew low on a broomstick, slowly circling him like a predator toying with its prey. Link crouched behind the front passenger seat.

"Pop," he cried out.

The cloaked wizard flew straight toward the truck. Sammy drew his wand and fired a blue beam of energy. It hit its mark, knocking the wizard from the broom. As the wizard hit the pavement, the hood of the cloak slipped back.

Donna leaned toward the window, straining to catch a glimpse of the wizard's face, but the darkness of night concealed it. What she did see was the gold wand that clattered across the road.

"That's an original Coven wand," she murmured.

Then came the deep, eerie howl of the red-eyed beast. Sammy spun around, casting light from the tip of his wand across the murky night.

The wizard rose from the ground, picked up the gold wand, and pulled the hood back over their head.

Sammy fired a blue beam, but it was met head-on by a red beam from the cloaked wizard. The collision sent him flying into the truck's windshield, cracking the glass into a spiderweb. He fell to the ground, staggered to his feet, climbed back into the truck, and yanked the gear into drive.

"Hold on, son!" Sammy yelled, driving away from the wolflike creature that was running toward them.

Donna woke up, trembling like a butterfly trapped in a glass jar.

She steadied herself, taking deep breaths through her nose and exhaling through her mouth. She looked up at the clock above her desk. It was midnight, and she was now wide awake.

She glanced around the room. No sign of Mr. Whiskers. Donna checked the closet and then the bathroom. Still nothing. Her eyes landed on the window she'd forgotten to close, and her heart sank.

"Oh, no."

She put on her slippers and crept down the stairs. When she made it to the last step, she peeped her head around the corner. With everyone checked in for curfew, Zina was in her room, leaving the lobby empty.

The campus was so quiet at night, Donna only heard her slides hitting the bottom of her feet.

Slap-slap, slap-slap, they seemed to yell at her as she walked.

"Mr. Whiskers," she whispered.

As her search continued, she began to lose hope.

She wandered farther than expected. It was all too easy to keep on walking, thinking just one more turn, without tracking her path. Inside the school was a maze, but outside, in the dark, it was easy to get lost. And that's what she was: lost.

She was relieved when she finally found a place she recognized—the Gardens near the college campus. She saw someone sitting on one of the benches near a magnolia tree. She tried to hide but paused when she heard a familiar meow. Mr. Whiskers was lying on a boy's lap.

"I saw your shadow," he said.

"Sorry. I was just looking—"

"You snuck out of your dorm to look for your cat."

Donna walked closer, realizing who it was.

"Do you know me?" she asked.

"The new sophomore with the only pet on campus? You're pretty famous around here."

"And you're Lincoln. I saw your photos in your mom's office. She's done a lot for me. She's the main reason I'm able to attend Nawlins."

"Yeah, my mother is great, always helping others," Lincoln replied. "That's why she became a doctor."

Donna's mind was suddenly flooded with new questions. "Does she ever use her powers when she's helping patients?"

"Wizardry is forbidden around the Norms. So, no, she doesn't."

"I couldn't be a doctor. I would try to save everyone's life with my powers," Donna said, sitting on the bench beside Lincoln. "I'm glad this bench is on the ground. Those floating couches and chairs feel like someone is rocking me to sleep."

Lincoln didn't say anything. He continued to pet Mr. Whiskers, who was arching his head for more pets from his new friend.

"Why were you staring at me at the welcome ceremony?" Donna asked.

"I wasn't staring at you. You were staring at me," he replied.

"Because you were staring at me."

They both side-eyed each other.

"Your cat has been keeping me company all night," Lincoln said, breaking the silence.

"Why are you still up?" she asked.

"Can't sleep, so I decided to take a walk." Lincoln pointed to the cat. "So, you want this back...?"

Donna nodded. "This, as you call him, is Mr. Whiskers."

A slight breeze entered the area, and leaves from the magnolia trees fell around them.

"What do you think of my father's class?" Lincoln asked.

"Well, on my first day, I bombed my placement exam. I turned a small lizard into an alligator that almost killed me."

Lincoln burst out laughing, which scared Mr. Whiskers. He leaped away and landed on Donna's chest.

"Ow, Mr. Whiskers! It's time to trim those nails."

Donna repositioned her hoodie and untucked her necklace.

Lincoln leaned forward.

"Where did you get that?" he asked, pointing at the pendant.

"My mother gave it to me. It was a gift to her from my father. He passed away in a car accident."

"Oh. I'm sorry for your loss." He kept staring at it. "Are you sure that was from your father? Do you know where he got it from? That's a unique pendant."

"What's up with all the questions, 50 Cent? Yeah, it was from my father. His birthday was in July, hence the ruby birthstone," Donna explained.

Lincoln got up in a hurry to leave.

"Good night, Donna Marie. Take care of that cat of yours."

He walked away, leaving Donna on the bench, confused.

"Well, good night to you, too," she said.

Chapter Thirteen

Lincoln sat on his motorcycle in the garage. Surely his parents had heard him pull up, triggering them to light the candles on his birthday cake. His real birthday was a month away, but this was the date his parents chose to hide his identity. It felt normal to him now; in fact, he sometimes forgot his real date of birth. Maybe it was better to forget since recollecting the past was sometimes overwhelming. His parents loved holidays and celebrations. Family time was essential to them, and keeping the family together was even more important. Lincoln knew he was lucky to have them. Growing up, many of his friends weren't fortunate enough to have a loving and supporting family or even a two-parent household. His parents loved each other so much and perfectly represented Black love. A love that he hoped to have one day in the future.

When he turned off the garage light, he giggled when he heard his mother's faint voice behind the door.

"Shh, he's about to walk in," she said, trying her best to whisper.

He opened the door that led into the kitchen, and sure enough, his parents were holding a cookie cake with eighteen birthday candles spread throughout. Lincoln hated regular cake, but cookie cake was his favorite.

"Happy birthday, Lincoln!"

"Good afternoon, and thank you. I appreciate y'all so much."

"We appreciate you, and we love you," his dad said.

"Love you too."

His mom's silver gumbo pot was on top of the kitchen counter, surrounded by the ingredients for her famous recipe, including Cajun spices, smoked meat, chicken, sausages, and peeled shrimp. His parents put on their matching black aprons and began to cook.

"Since we agreed that you will get a car for your graduation gift, which will also be your birthday gift, we decided to cook your favorite food today," his mom said.

"Some hot gumbo and time with my folks. I can dig that," Lincoln said, rubbing his hands together.

He sat at the kitchen table and watched his parents work as a team. His dad chopped the vegetables while his mom poured flour and oil into a cast-iron pan and made the roux. His dad played some Luther Vandross on his phone, and his mom used a wooden spoon as a microphone and started to sing. Charles rushed to the cabinet, grabbed a big spoon too, and started to sing along, putting his hand around Rima's hips.

"Can y'all chill?" Lincoln asked, shaking his head.

"You chill. You know we love this song," Rima replied, singing louder.

Lincoln grabbed a spoon out of the cabinet and started to sing along with his parents.

"'Take time to tell me, youuuuuu really care

And we'll share tomorrow...

Together,'" they sang.

When the gumbo was ready, they all ate at the kitchen table. Lincoln stuffed his face with cookie cake for dessert.

Lincoln didn't care too much about his birthday, even though he was eighteen now. For him, it was just another day. His phone on the counter rang as he put away the dishes. He knew who it was.

"Tamia's calling you," his mom said, glancing down at the phone.

"She's been calling all day," Lincoln replied.

His parents had always liked Tamia and approved of their relationship. But they were always firm about one thing: no wizard, not even Tamia, could ever know his true bloodline. That was why he ended things with her. Not because he wanted to but because protecting her meant keeping her in the dark. If anyone ever came for him, she'd be the perfect target.

The voicemail tab lit up on his screen. He hesitated, staring at it for a moment before heading into the living room and lifting the phone to his ear.

"Hey, Lincoln, it's Tamia."

Her soft voice brought a smile to his face. The butterflies crept up in his stomach as he tried his best not to miss her.

"Happy birthday. I wish I could be there eating gumbo with you and your family, because I bet that's what you're doing today."

She knows me so well.

"I was thinking about your birthday last year, how you randomly wanted to sneak away and go to New York, and I was down. And at the last minute, your mom found out and stopped us. That was pretty silly of us to buy those plane tickets with her credit card. Good times... I am here for you if you want to talk. Hopefully, I will see you at the Raceway tonight. Love you... Bye."

That failed trip to New York wasn't random—Lincoln wanted to visit his birth parents' graves. He had never been before, and the urge was too great to resist. Lincoln didn't like birthdays because it meant another year removed from his birth parents. He didn't want to forget them, but every year it was getting harder to remember the small details. So last year, he planned that trip to feel their presence again. But when Rima found out, she canned the trip and forbade him to ever seek their gravesite because it was too dangerous.

Lincoln ran up the steps to his room. A small jewelry box lay on the nightstand by his bed. Inside was a gold necklace with a bar-shaped diamond pendant. Engraved on the clasp was a tiny inscription: *Jenkins Jewelry.*

He searched the name on his phone, and an address for a local jewelry store came up.

"Hey, Ma, Dad?" Lincoln called out, coming down the stairs.

"Yes, son. We are in my office," his dad answered.

Lincoln always enjoyed going into his father's office, particularly because there was a picture on the wall of Deedy.

Charles and Deedy met as dorm mates in the sixth grade and became brothers. Their championship broom-racing plaque hung on the wall next to Deedy's photo. Deedy wore a black leather jacket with BANDITS stitched in white letters on the left side. He had light brown eyes and his mini-Afro was well shaped.

When Lincoln entered the office, his mom was sitting in the expensive massage chair, and his dad was at his desk.

"Dad, how does she get to use your new massage chair, and I don't?"

"*Happy wife, happy life*, remember that for when you get married."

"What he said," his mom added.

"I was just talking to your mom about Donna Marie. She conjured a full-grown alligator in my class. No sophomore has ever done that, let alone a student who has never used her gifts before. Her innate power is strong. But how strong?"

"Her last name isn't in the wizard registry. And we definitely know she isn't a part of the Coven. All of the descendants are intricately documented and tracked," his mom said.

"We will find out who her father is and solve this mystery," his dad said.

Lincoln hesitated, then held out the gold necklace dangling from his hand. "You told me this necklace belonged to Deedy, and the diamond represented Cathy's birthday. You also told me the jeweler only made two of them, and hers was lost the day they died. So, how can it be that last night I saw Donna Marie wearing the matching ruby necklace?"

His parents were silent for a moment.

"Maybe the jeweler made more of them," his father finally said.

"Yeah, maybe," Lincoln said.

Lincoln wasn't convinced, but let the conversation drop, his mind racing with questions as he headed towards the garage.

"Where are you going, son?" his mom asked.

"Going for a ride on the bike to clear my head. Eighteen is a big year. I feel like I'm a grown man now."

"Alright, calm your little grown tail down. You're still a teenager in high school," she said with a chuckle.

"Hey, son, you better not be involved in any underground broom racing. Rumors are going around campus that students have created some secret racing society. Remember, if you get caught riding a broom, you will get expelled from school, and your mother and I can't help you if that happens."

"You know what, Dad? It's not fair that y'all got to race when y'all were at Nawlins, but the current students can't."

"Don't say *y'all* because I wasn't riding those death machines," his mom said.

"She has a point. Brooms were banned because someone died at the races. I was there. I saw it," his dad said.

"I know, I know. Don't worry, I'm not racing brooms," Lincoln said, closing the door behind him with a smirk.

In 2005, during Hurricane Katrina, the floodwall on the industrial canal gave way, sending a twenty-foot wall of water surging into the community.

The low-lying area flooded up to twelve feet in water.

The devastation destroyed homes, vacated businesses, and displaced many families.

Some sites were rebuilt in the lower ninth ward, but overgrown lots, torn-up streets, gutted houses, and lack of businesses still plagued the area.

Lincoln crossed the St. Claude Avenue Bridge. The loud pipes on his motorcycle created a deafening roar that ricocheted off the open steel covering.

The evening sky slowly lost its light as Lincoln parked his bike down an alley near St. Claude Ave. Once a thriving Black-owned shopping center, the space now stood in ruin, its silence creepy, its charm faded. Still, something about it stirred a quiet nostalgia. Rima used to shop here, and Lincoln would often tag along, back when the place still had life.

The only store intact was a small shotgun-style house at the end of the lot.

A light pole illuminated the dull green home with white trimming along its two big windows. A red sign swayed gently above the door: *Jenkins Jewelry*.

Lincoln placed his helmet on the handlebars. He checked his surroundings, then walked up the small white steps in front of the store. A blinking "closed" sign was in front of the security bars on the window. The front porch creaked as he tried to peek into the house.

He stepped back as a deep voice shouted from inside. "Get off my porch! Can't you read the sign? We are closed."

"Sorry, I was looking for the jeweler. I need to ask him about a birthstone pendant he made a long time ago," Lincoln stated.

There was a brief moment of silence, then Lincoln turned away and started to walk down the steps.

He heard multiple deadbolt locks clicking as he reached his motorcycle. An old man opened the door. He looked Lincoln up and down with his big oval eyes.

"I'm the jeweler, Mr. Jenkins... Ya just going to stand there or come inside?" the man demanded, waving Lincoln in.

Inside the shop was a narrow corridor of sparkling wonders. Glass cases lined the walls, filled with twinkling gold and silver jewelry under soft cabinet lighting. Mr. Jenkins led the way to a display of necklaces and pendants.

Lincoln stood near the front door, studying the jeweler. His receding hairline caused his thin gray hair to grow in patches on the side of his shiny brown-toned head. He wore a tan shirt and dark brown overalls that appeared too small for his big frame.

"What's your name, young man?" Mr. Jenkins asked.

"Lincoln."

"Lincoln what?"

"Lincoln DuVernay."

"DuVernay, huh? Interesting," the old man said, curling the sides of his thick gray mustache. "You want to take a seat, or you plan on standing there all evening?"

Lincoln moved closer, the wooden floorboards groaning under his weight. The room was dense with the scent of metal polish and something faintly musky, like old cigar smoke.

"Your pieces are phenomenal," Lincoln said. "I never expected this."

"What, you didn't think this old man could craft such masterpieces?"

"No, sorry, I didn't mean it like that."

The old man grinned, revealing yellowish teeth. "Relax, kid, can't you take a joke?" snapped Mr. Jenkins.

Lincoln didn't know what to say, so he looked around the shop. There were various impressive paintings. A portrait of a Black woman holding a baby in white garments hung on the wall closest to him. The name *Jenkins* was signed at the bottom.

"You're a painter too?" asked Lincoln. "That's amazing."

"Are you here to scold me, young man?"

Lincoln shook his head.

"Yes, I painted all these. Anything else you think I'm not capable of?" Mr. Jenkins scratched his head as he looked at Lincoln. "I know you from somewhere, kid?"

Lincoln shook his head, a smile tugging at his lips. "I doubt it, sir."

Shrugging, Mr. Jenkins turned back to his workbench, the array of lights above him casting a halo around his busy hands. "Well, show me this necklace of yours then, young DuVernay. Let's see what's got you so curious."

Lincoln took a seat on a stool in front of Mr. Jenkins. He unclipped his necklace and hesitated before placing the chain in the man's worn hands. Mr.

Jenkins opened a drawer, removed a small magnifying glass, and carefully studied the necklace.

He switched the magnifying glass for a pair of glasses with a light attached to the side. He lifted the pendant above his head, and the diamond shone as the light entered its core.

"I only made two of these pendants. I performed delicate cuts to the stone to achieve its rectangle shape. I guarantee there are no off-dimensions. Perfectly measured. A fourteen-karat gold bezel holds this precious diamond stone in place. The other necklace had a ruby stone. I made them years ago, for a young man who wanted to surprise his fiancée with matching necklaces for her birthday. I forget his name."

"Sammy," Lincoln said.

"Yes, that's right. I remember he had a well-groomed Afro. That was the style back then. Hold the chain up for me again, young man."

Mr. Jenkins gave Lincoln the necklace and walked to an old desk in the back of the store, pulling something from the drawer. Mr. Jenkins came back holding a square lockbox. He placed the box on the counter and began to turn the numbers on its dial.

"Hey, don't look at my code," he said, frowning at Lincoln.

Lincoln turned his head until he heard the box unlock. His mouth dropped as Mr. Jenkins removed a dusty wand.

"Yes, I'm a wizard. I know you are, too. Not too many Norms walking around New Orleans with the last name DuVernay," Mr. Jenkins said, blowing the dust off his gray wand.

He lifted his wand toward the pendant. A cloudy vapor filled the birthstone. When the vapor cleared, a realistic image of a woman appeared in the stone.

"Who is she?" Lincoln asked.

"That's the woman for whom Sammy bought the necklace."

Lincoln's heart instantly melted. He brought the pendant closer to his eyes. A warm smile flashed across the woman's elegant brown face.

"I forgot her name, too," Mr. Jenkins said.

"Cathy," Lincoln quickly responded.

Mr. Jenkins scratched his head. "My memory isn't what it used to be... Anyway, we Black folks age well. She hasn't changed a bit from the photo I saw of her when Sammy ordered the piece."

"What do you mean?" Lincoln said.

"The hologram inside the stone shows the person how they look now."

"That's impossible. Sammy and Cathy both died years ago," Lincoln said.

"According to the birthstone, she's very much alive."

Without a word, Lincoln put the pendant into his pocket and headed toward the exit. He stopped at the door and took a deep breath before looking back at Mr. Jenkins.

"You're sure you didn't make more than two of these necklaces?" he asked.

"I only made two."

Lincoln put his head down and clenched his fists. His parents told him that Deedy and Cathy died the night wizards attacked them on a camping trip in New York.

Why would they lie to me?

Chapter Fourteen

Is my mother really alive? The words circled Lincoln's head as he sat on his motorcycle back in the garage. *And Donna Marie... who is she, really?*

Charles was on the computer as Lincoln approached the office door. Rima was standing over his shoulder.

"Hey, son, how was your ride?" she asked.

He didn't know where to begin.

"The roads were clear... Did a lot of thinking. What are you guys doing?"

"We are searching the web for Donna's father," Charles said, sipping coffee from his New Orleans Saints mug.

"Was Cathy my mother's real name?" Lincoln asked.

Charles sat down with his coffee cup and turned his chair toward Lincoln. Rima walked up to him.

"What? Where is this coming from, son?" Rima replied, gently grabbing his hand.

"Ma, don't lie to me. What was my mother's real name?"

"Hey, watch your tone when you're talking to your mother."

"Then tell me the truth."

"We are telling you the truth. Cathy was her name. Deedy introduced her as such," Rima replied.

"Why are you asking us this? What's wrong, son?" Charles asked.

"What is Donna's mom's name?"

Rima paused. "Catherine... Catherine Guillory."

Lincoln's heart felt like it was being pushed down into his stomach.

"She's alive," he said.

"Who's alive?"

"My mother. And Donna is my sister."

"That's impossible," Charles said.

"How do you know? Have you met Donna's mom? Have you ever seen a picture of her?"

Charles turned back to his computer. Lincoln walked over to get a look at the screen.

"Cathy was going to Xavier University when she and Deedy met, right?" Charles asked.

"Yes," Rima replied.

"Top graduate from Xavier University, Catherine Guillory, receives full scholarship to NYU's MBA program," was the first article to pop up in his search.

"This article doesn't show her picture," Charles said.

"Search 'Catherine Guillory's husband,'" Rima suggested.

He clicked the header "Tragic accident in Upstate New York."

An article popped up on the screen with a photo of Deedy. Charles knocked over his mug, spilling coffee over his desk.

"My God," Rima said. "Sammy Guillory. Deedy took her last name."

"How is my mother still alive? You told me she died," Lincoln said.

An abrupt knock at the front door broke the tension in the room. Charles went to answer it, with Lincoln following close behind. Awkwardly standing there was Mr. Jenkins.

"Ah, good to see you again, Lincoln," he said.

"How do you know this man?" Charles asked, looking back at Lincoln.

"I didn't just go for a ride. I went to see the jeweler who made my necklace. This is him, Mr. Jenkins," Lincoln explained.

"Can I help you, Mr. Jenkins?"

The old man took a step closer. "Professor Charles DuVernay. You still look like that young kid who won all those broom races. Until your friend Sammy beat you."

"Excuse me, but how do you know me?"

"Before broom racing was banned, alumni could watch the sport. I won a few championships in my day too. Before you were born, of course."

"What do you want?" Charles exclaimed.

"Do you mind if I come in? This might take a minute."

Rima placed a cup of tea before Mr. Jenkins as they sat at the kitchen table. Lincoln leaned against the counter.

Mr. Jenkins poured a little sugar into his tea and took a sip.

"That's good tea," he complimented, nodding towards Rima, who raised an eyebrow in response.

"I opened my jewelry store shortly after graduating from Nawlins, where I studied art. Some of my paintings are still hanging on those walls. Would you believe it? Anyway, birthstones are my specialty. I sometimes use my powers to craft unique pieces, like the one your boy has. It shows the person it was made for, in real time. Your son here was surprised when he learned that the woman in the birthstone was still alive. I didn't tell him that he looked so similar to the person who purchased it, your friend Sammy. Or should I call him Deedy?"

Mr. Jenkins took another sip of his tea and stared at Lincoln for a few seconds.

"I know who your boy really is. And if the Elders find out, he will be in danger."

"We don't know what you're talking about. Lincoln is a DuVernay, and the Elders are all gone," Rima said.

"What's an Elder?" Lincoln asked.

"You didn't tell him?" Mr. Jenkins asked, looking at Charles.

"Tell me what?"

"The Elders killed your father, Lincoln," Mr. Jenkins blurted.

Charles turned to Lincoln. "The night of the accident, Deedy called me. He was in his truck, and he said it looked like a huge werewolf was chasing him. We jumped on my brooms and flew to New York as fast as we could. But we were too late. I saw the footprints and claw marks all over the bridge—"

"It was no werewolf. It was the swamp beast... the Rougarou," Mr. Jenkins interjected.

"The Rougarou is just a myth from wizard folklore," Rima said.

"I heard the stories since I was a child. The Rougarou was once a Loyal that escaped from its owners and fled to the swamps, evolving into a wolflike beast. But it was never seen," Charles added.

"The Rougarou was *not* a Loyal. It was once a wizard who drank a dawa made from the blood of a wizard who took his own life. A sacrifice made to give the beast its strength. But that strength would come with the curse of becoming a Rougarou," Mr. Jenkins said, taking another sip of his tea.

"Why would anyone do that?" Rima asked.

"You would be surprised at what wizards have done for Augustin. She was the one who ordered the Rougarou to kill Deedy. The Elders needed his blood but lost his body in the water."

"The Elders... Who are they, and what did they want to do with my father's blood?" Lincoln asked. He knew his bloodline was powerful, but Charles and Rima had never explained the details to him. He turned to them. "I'm old enough now. I need to know."

"The Elders are those who joined Augustin's cult when the wizards were once at war with each other. They are still alive today," Mr. Jenkins said.

Charles raised his eyebrows. "You're saying that wizards from the revolt that happened over two hundred years ago are still alive today?"

"Yes. That's exactly what I'm saying."

"Do you understand how silly that sounds? That's exactly why we never mentioned the Elders to Lincoln; it's not true. Augustin and the Elders are dead. It was a group of savage wizards who killed my friend Deedy with the help of a Loyal or whatever it was. They confessed and were convicted and are rotting in the prison of the High Council."

"Or maybe they were part of Augustin's cult and took the blame to protect her and the Elders."

"Get out of my house. NOW!" Charles demanded, standing up and pointing to the door.

Mr. Jenkins reached into his wrinkled tote bag and pulled out a wand, gently and quietly placing it on the table. Lincoln immediately recognized the long wooden wand from the many paintings and textbooks at school. It was one of the wands that had been gifted to the five hundred revolt members the night they were blessed with wizard powers—an Ancient wand.

Rima and Charles both stood back with their wands drawn. Mr. Jenkins put his hands up.

"Easy now. I'm one of the good ones," he pleaded.

They slowly sat back down, staring at the precious piece of history before them. Ancient wands disintegrated at the time of death of their owners. The only remnants were the memories and paintings passed down.

"You're an... an... an Elder," Charles whispered.

"Yes." Mr. Jenkins nodded. "That I am."

"You used a different wand at the jewelry shop," Lincoln said.

"I can't just flash my Ancient wand around at everyone," Mr. Jenkins said, showing his stained teeth as he laughed.

Mr. Jenkins paused, and for a moment, Lincoln could see the weight of all his years.

"Over two hundred years ago, I was beaten, battered, and abused by my oppressors. Solomon, Augustin, Philmore, Cane, and Jean Pierre saved my life by risking theirs, entering my plantation and freeing me. I joined their revolt after. I still remember the night we were blessed with wizard gifts. First, a strong wind lifted Solomon into the air. Then the wind swept through us all. Hurt like hell, but it filled our bodies with this majestic power."

Mr. Jenkins took a long sip of his tea, slurping the last bit. He raised his glass. Lincoln grabbed the teapot from the stove and poured him more. The old man calmly added sugar to the tea and stirred it.

"Hmm, this was made with a bit of dawa. Is that lavender? Just the way I like it," he said, smacking his lips.

"If other Elders are alive, why haven't they revealed themselves?" Rima asked.

"Because we were outnumbered for so long. We couldn't just pop up and start a war with the entire wizard community. We had to wait to grow our army. We used a youth dawa to stay alive all this time. The dawa froze me at age nineteen for a long time. I stopped taking it many years ago—the day I left Augustin's cult. That's why I'm the raggedy eighty-year-old man you see now. I guess Black does crack after all," he said, grabbing his big belly as he laughed at his own joke.

"So, these Elders killed my father? But it seems that my mom is still alive?" Lincoln said, lifting the birthstone.

"Yes, son. I'm so sorry we lied to you, but we had to protect you," Rima said.

"Catherine wasn't present the night the Elders attacked you and Deedy," Charles added, putting his hand around Rima's shoulder as she started to cry.

"You told me my mom died! You made me change my name and suppress my powers because you said evil wizards would harm me if they knew who I was."

"You are in danger. That wasn't a lie," Mr. Jenkins said. "After we built Nawlins, some revolt members believed that our gifts were meant for something greater than just being free from bondage. These wizards thought the Creator gave us powers to retaliate against our oppressors. Augustin was our leader. We wanted to harm the Norms the same way we'd been harmed: an eye for an eye. But Solomon forbade it.

"Our civil war almost destroyed Nawlins. Some wizards perished during the battle. In the end, Augustin was forced to surrender. Solomon was just too strong. As the first wizard blessed with powers, he possessed abilities that no other wizard had. And there were spells and dawas that couldn't affect him. I saw the magnitude of his power; his eyes would turn pitch-black, and he could use magic without his wand, bursting energy beams from his hands. It was truly remarkable. Augustin knew she could never take over Nawlins with Solomon alive.

"She and her followers were sent to the holding cells at Nawlins. One night, we broke out and snuck into Solomon's sleeping chamber. We ambushed him, and Augustin stabbed him in the heart with a dagger and drained his blood to use for the youth dawa."

"Did y'all know about this?" Lincoln asked, looking at his parents.

"No," Rima whispered.

Charles remained silent. He looked away when Lincoln locked eyes with him.

"Dad... You knew, didn't you?"

"Charles?" Rima prompted.

"Only a few wizards know. Nawlins covered it up by ruling Solomon's death as a heart attack to prevent more fighting in the wizard community," Charles explained. He looked at Rima. "I'm sorry. I swore an oath to the High Council."

"What happened after Solomon's murder?" Lincoln asked.

"We fled New Orleans and hid, waiting for the wizard population to grow with each generation until we could recruit a new army. I finally left the Elders when I realized that Augustin would never be satisfied until she took over the world. The lust for power changed her completely."

"Why didn't you come forward before now?" Rima asked.

"I didn't know who to trust. I have a family to protect too."

"So, what do we do?" Lincoln asked.

"We have to stop them. I think Augustin and the Elders have waited long enough. I'm sure they are planning something big. I'm an old fart now, but I want to help before I'm useless. I don't think they have much of Solomon's blood left, but they will do whatever it takes to build their army." He turned to Lincoln. "If they find out about you, they'll drain you of your blood, and who knows what they could do with it. They will be unstoppable." Mr. Jenkins said.

"We need to talk in private now," Rima said. "We will contact you soon."

"Don't wait too long." Mr. Jenkins grabbed his belongings and walked out the door.

"Do you think he's telling the truth?" Lincoln asked.

"I put truth dawa in his tea. He most definitely is," Rima replied.

"Which means Augustin is still alive," Charles said.

"If you trust him, why didn't you tell him about Donna Marie?" Lincoln said.

There was a brief silence as they stared at each other.

"We didn't know Cathy was pregnant. I don't even think Deedy knew. I would've been the first person he told," Charles said.

"Why? Because you and my father were best friends? If you were his real best friend, you wouldn't have lied to Cathy about her child being dead and then adopted him."

"It's what we had to do to keep you and Cathy safe. We had to make it look like you died that night, too, or those wizards would have kept hunting you," Rima said.

"She's right, son. We had to hide you, or the Elders would have killed you both. Cathy couldn't have protected you. She didn't even know that wizards existed. Deedy didn't want her involved in this life. We had to cut all ties with her."

Lincoln headed for the door.

"Now I know why you never took me to see their gravesites. It's because my MOTHER never had a damn grave."

"Where are you going, son?" Rima asked.

"I'm not your son," Lincoln said, slamming the door behind him.

Chapter Fifteen

It was Donna's first weekend of the fall term. Finally, a day off to enjoy the beautiful city of New Orleans. She looked through her closet. Her style was usually very casual—as in sweatpants, oversized shirts, and a pair of Chuck Taylors to seal the deal. The only flashy items were her accessories, like her fake gold hoop earrings, bracelets, and rings, and her mother's birthstone necklace, which she rarely took off.

She put on a pair of black jeans and a gray T-shirt and tied a red-and-black checkered button-down shirt around her waist.

"What shoes should I wear?" Donna queried, eyeing Mr. Whiskers as he lounged on the bed in a solitary patch of sunlight filtering through the curtains.

Mr. Whiskers ambled over to Donna's Air Force 1s, giving them a gentle tap with his paw.

"Good choice... Wait! Did you actually understand me?" Donna chuckled, half in disbelief.

With a leisurely stretch, Mr. Whiskers retreated back to his sunny sanctuary on the bed. He yawned before curling himself up in a bundle.

Donna slipped on her sneakers then hurried to knock on Noor's door.

"Noor, are you ready?"

"One second. I'm fixing my hijab."

There was a knock on the front door. Donna opened it widely to find Jia standing there with a big grin on her face.

"Let's go have some fun!" she said.

Their first destination was the iconic Café Du Monde. They sat at the outside dining area where the table was just big enough to host their powdered pastries and three steaming cups of creamy hot chocolate.

"Can't believe this is your first time trying a beignet," Jia said.

"In her defense, New Yorkers don't have beignets. We have cannoli and croissants," Noor said.

She took a bite of the beignet, and a shower of powdered sugar fell onto her shirt. The crisp exterior gave way to a soft, delightful sweetness.

"This is sensational," she declared, complementing the treat with a sip of hot chocolate.

"Better than cannoli?" asked Noor.

"This is probably the only thing that comes close," Donna replied.

After they finished their tasty treats, they continued to walk in the French Quarter.

Donna ran her hand over the cast-iron fence around one of the most famous landmarks in the area, Jackson Square's historic park.

Inside the fence was an open-air artist colony that gathered painters, portraitists, musicians, magicians, and fortune tellers.

"Who's the guy on the statue on the horse in the center of the park?" Donna asked.

"This pretty little park is named after President Andrew Jackson," Jia said. "He's remembered as the general who won the Battle of New Orleans. However, what the history books often leave out is that people of color also fought in that war, contributing to the victory in 1815. I don't see any statues of them on a horse."

Donna was surprised at how informed Jia was on the history of New Orleans. She spoke about it passionately, as if she lived through it.

Donna stopped and stared at a church overlooking the park.

"Beautiful church, isn't it? But just to the left of that church were auction blocks," Jia said. "Before the Civil War, the biggest hotel in New Orleans was St. Louis Palace, where thousands of people were sold against their will. And it happened right near that church."

"Sad but true," said Noor.

"What's sad is that Norm schools want to remove the facts about slavery from their history books."

"Can we talk about something happier?" Noor asked.

"You sound like the Norms," said Jia.

Donna spotted a band on a corner near Bourbon Street. They were playing trumpets, trombones, tubas, and drums, and singing to create music she had never heard before.

"What kind of music is that?" she asked.

"It's a second-line band. It's a New Orleans thing," Noor answered.

"Second-line music goes way back to 1724," Jia said.

A giant smile filled Jia's face as she grabbed Donna's arm and pulled her toward the band.

"Back in those days, many people of color met up in small places for social activities, even though it was against the law. They created music like this to express themselves. Sorry, I know so much about New Orleans's history; my grandparents on my father's side are from here, and they told me all these things."

Jia and Donna were now in the middle of the dancing crowd. Jia demonstrated how to properly second-line dance, shuffling her feet and occasionally tiptoeing and balancing on her heels. Her upper body flowed with confidence as her feet led the way.

Other participants danced in unique styles as horns and drums filled the air. One gentleman waved a handkerchief as his body twisted and swirled.

Donna was initially shy, but eventually let her feet move to the beat. She tried her best to mimic Jia's footwork.

"Are we going to the races tonight?" Noor yelled out as she danced near them.

"What races?" Donna asked.

Jia hushed Noor, who looked as though she'd just told a big secret.

"She was going to find out eventually," Noor said.

Jia grabbed their hands and led them away from the dancing crowd.

"You can't tell anyone," she said to Donna.

"I promise I won't."

"Broom racing," Jia confessed.

Donna's face lit up with excitement.

"Wait, broom racing is a real thing?"

"Shh, lower your voice," Noor replied.

"It's getting late. Shouldn't you ladies be headed back to the dorms?" someone shouted at them.

They turned and saw Casie walking with Chike, Jay, and Ryan on Bourbon Street.

"Last time I checked, you had a curfew too!" Jia snapped.

Donna had never hated anyone before, but she despised Casie's attitude.

Chike gave Noor a kiss on the cheek. "Hey, bae. Y'all should come to the Raceway. It will be popping."

"We are coming. It's the first one of the fall term. Should be fun," Jia meddled in.

"Let's do it," Noor said.

"The Raceway? Sounds cool…" Donna glanced at the clock displayed in one of the storefront windows. Two hours until curfew. This was her chance to make new friends, to just be a teenager and have a little fun. "Lead the way!"

Chapter Sixteen

The city bus dropped them off a couple of blocks from the so-called entrance to the Raceway. There was nothing but overgrown trees, abandoned buildings, and torn-down amusement park rides.

"This place looks like Jurassic Park. Where is the Raceway?" Donna asked.

"Hard to imagine that this used to be an amazing amusement park, huh?" Noor said.

"Now it's one of the most prominent reminders of how Hurricane Katrina devastated the area," Jia added.

Donna looked over the wasteland filled with weeds, swamps, and debris. An eight-foot waterline was still visible on all of the remaining buildings.

"A couple years ago, students cleaned up a portion of this area and built a racetrack in the sky," Jia said.

"I still don't see anything. Where is it?" Donna questioned, peering around in confusion.

"It's protected by a hiding spell to safeguard it from the Norms. And the faculty," Noor said.

"Najua nenosiri," Jia chanted, moving her wand in a circular motion.

Before them, a misty portal began to form, revealing a passageway just wide enough for Jia to slip through.

"See you on the other side," Jia grinned, disappearing into the opening which snapped shut behind her.

"It's easy," Noor assured Donna. "Follow my hand motion as we chant the words."

Donna nodded and lifted her wand.

"Najua nenosiri," they chanted together, their wands mimicking the earlier motion.

As the misty gateway reappeared, Donna could hear the distant sounds of cheering and applause. Stepping through, she felt as if she was crossing into another world.

The floating racetrack featured white dividers outlining eight lanes around a sweeping one-mile oval. The stands, built like those of a stadium, were speckled with students, while a few wizards flew around the track on their brooms.

"Welcome to the Raceway!" Jia said.

"Dope, huh?" Noor said.

"This is beyond dope... Wait, why were brooms banned in the first place?" Donna asked.

Noor and Jia looked at each other as if they didn't want to tell her.

"If everyone else knows, I'd like to know too," Donna said.

"I don't know all the details, but I heard someone fell off their broom and died," Noor said.

Donna's heart sank.

"It was a *long* time ago. Don't worry. People say it was a freak accident," Jia added.

"I don't know about this," Donna said.

"I promise you it's safe."

"When I first found out what happened, I was skeptical about coming here too, but after I saw the races, I was hooked," Noor said. "If someone falls off their broom, the broom always flies underneath and catches them. It's pretty chill."

That didn't sound chill to Donna. The thought of someone dying spooked her out, no matter how long ago it was. But she was here now and didn't want to be a party pooper.

"Come on, let's go to the racing salon," Jia said, grabbing their hands and pulling them toward the only building in the Raceway.

Inside the building was like a makeshift clubhouse. In the center stood a weathered pool table, surrounded by an assortment of worn couches, their fabric torn and tattered. Along the walls, lockers and seating areas were sectioned off beneath banners of varying colors, each representing a different group: *The Upscales* under red, *The Bandits* draped in black, *The Vibes* marked by white, and *The Coven* in yellow. The decor gave the space a rugged, lived-in charm, something like a frat house. As the main event neared, the clubhouse buzzed with the energy of spectators and competitors congregating in anticipation.

"Not only do I have to worry about winning the race, but now I have to worry about making sure you guys meet your curfew," Zina said, approaching them by the lounge area.

"Don't worry... we'll make it on time," Jia said.

"Donna, I'm counting on you to keep this place a secret. Not many students even know about the Raceway, and if the professors find out... we could all get expelled," Zina said, her voice low and serious.

"I won't tell a soul," Donna replied.

She stared at the broom Zina was holding. It was jet black with a gold tail and *Bandits* was engraved across its center in gold letters.

"That's a cool broom," Donna said.

"Thanks. I'm captain of the Bandits' college team. We won the champion relay race last year. The Bandits' high school team is pretty good too. You should root for them."

"I will," Donna said.

"Unfortunately, the Coven won last year's high school relays, so they have bragging rights on your side of campus," Zina said, shaking her head in disapproval.

Zina walked to her team's section to prepare for the race.

"I cheer for the Bandits too. But don't tell Chike because he's on the Coven team," Noor said.

"I cheer for the Bandits because of Lincoln. He refused to be on the Coven team," Jia said. "Chad is on the Bandits too, and a junior named Mya."

Jia pointed to the Bandits' lounge section, where Chad and Mya were polishing their brooms.

"OMG, I know Mya from *Teen Vogue*. She's even more beautiful in person. Can't believe she's a wizard like me," said Donna.

Mya had a skin condition called vitiligo, causing depigmentation of her skin. Her chocolate and vanilla coloring created a unique symmetrical pattern on her face and hands.

Chad had on a black hoodie, and Mya wore a black leather jacket. Lincoln approached his teammates, wearing a black tactical-style vest, showcasing his toned arms. They all had *Bandits* stitched on the back.

Lincoln looked over at Donna, and their eyes met. Her head started to throb, just like when she first saw him at the welcome ceremony. *What is wrong with me?*

Noor touched Donna's shoulder.

"Hey, are you okay? You look a bit, like, off."

"Yes, I'm good," Donna responded.

She glanced back at Lincoln, now huddled up with his fellow racers, probably strategizing.

The Coven walked by the Bandits and stared them down.

"That's Chike's older brother, Nnamdi. He's a senior." Noor nodded toward a stocky boy. Chike and Casie walked behind him. They all wore their lettermen jackets.

"Why doesn't Lincoln like the Coven if he's one of them?" Donna asked.

"I heard he despises them. He got suspended last term because he got into a scuffle with a Coven member."

"Which one?"

"Ryan's cousin, Darius. He's a freshman in college now," Noor replied.

"Yep. It happened in the CC because Darius tried to talk to Lincoln's ex. It was mostly pushing, but they both suffered the consequences," Jia added.

"I heard it happened because Tamia rejected Darius and then he went around campus bad-mouthing her," said Noor.

"Tamia is Lincoln's ex?" Donna asked.

Noor and Jia both gave big nods as if there was major drama there.

"Shall we play some ping-pong, ladies, before the relay starts?" Noor smirked.

"Yes, we need a rematch," Jia quickly responded, pulling Noor by her hand toward the ping-pong table on the side of the room.

Donna trailed behind, watching Raine as she stood on a ladder painting a mural on the wall. The way she painted looked effortless as she delicately dipped her brush in a palette hanging from the ladder.

"You like anime?" Raine asked as she added red paint to some sort of blast coming from the male character's hands.

"It's the only thing I enjoy watching," replied Donna. "But I don't recognize this character."

Raine put down her brush and jumped down from the ladder. She took a couple of steps back and placed her hands on her hips.

"It's Solomon; anime version, but it's him... Can you believe he was the only wizard who could use his powers without a wand? Straight super Saiyan mode." Raine jumped and landed with her feet spread and her arms extended together in front of her as if she'd just created some type of energy blast.

Donna couldn't help but giggle.

"Imagine having all that power. I bet it was incredible to witness."

"I bet," Donna said, looking down at her hands. "What happened to him? He was the most powerful wizard, but I feel like we don't talk much about him or his legacy."

"My pawpaw always says it's hard to have a legacy when you don't have kids to carry on your name."

"Why didn't he have kids? Like, what happened to him?"

"Some say he died before he could have any kids. Some say he lived a long happy life without being married, devoting himself to better the wizard community."

"That's what we were told," Jia shouted out, as she was about to serve.

"Yeah," Noor added.

"Some say he was murdered," Raine mumbled.

"By who?" Donna whispered.

Raine walked closer to Donna.

"Not sure. But think about it, someone with all that power might have been envied by many. Maybe even some of his closest friends."

Raine stared at Donna for a few seconds, squinting.

"Some rumors even say he ran away with a Norm and vanished without a trace. That he might indeed have descendants out there... somewhere."

"Looks like they're letting anybody in the racing society these days," Casie said, walking up to them and sneering at Donna. "It's the goth girl who got in on legacy, and Noor and her friends who are only here because her boyfriend is on my team."

"Actually, I'm not goth; it's more afro punk," Raine said.

"Same thing," Casie responded.

"Don't you have a race to prepare for?" Donna said.

"Don't you have a placement test to bomb?" Casie snapped. "After that alligator and Fang almost took your head off, I thought you would've cried all the way back to New York."

"Hey, can we all just get along?" Jia asked from the ping-pong table.

"Yeah, we are all wizards here," Noor added.

"Some are better than others." Casie folded her arms and looked at Donna.

"The race will be starting soon!" the speaker on the wall blasted.

"Have fun *watching* me race. Bye, lames," Casie said, walking off.

"Raine, you come from a family of racers?" Donna asked, trying to forget Casie.

"Yep, my mom was on the Bandits. Y'all have fun out there. I'm going to finish this mural."

The girls picked the perfect viewing spot in the middle of the raised bleachers. Donna listened intently as her friends gave her a crash course on broom racing.

The four-mile relay consisted of each teammate doing a lap around the track. Each racer started in their assigned lane in a stagger position to ensure everyone covered an equal distance. After the first lap, the racers could then merge lanes. The teams that came in first and second place would qualify for the top two playoff spots, while the other two teams would have to continue in wild-card races to determine who raced the second-place team.

The announcer, a short girl with wavy hair, mounted her broom and flew toward the middle of the track with a small microphone fitted to her ear.

"What's up, Secret Racing Society. I'm Lacey and welcome to the first relay race of the fall term. The first heat is ready, and in lane one, we have the Upscales."

"The Upscales are some of the richest students on campus. Some call them bougie, but I think they're classy," Noor said to Donna.

"If I raced, I would be an Upscale. It's giving... rich and fabulous," Jia proudly said, applying lip gloss as she held up a compact mirror.

"Yeah, we know," Noor replied.

The Upscales' three racers were wearing classy uniforms, including matching red collar shirts and khaki trousers. The final piece of their ensemble was a pair of eye-catching tall brown boots that laced up to the calves.

"In lane two, we have the Bandits, led by last year's solo race winner, Lincoln," Lacey continued. "In lane three, we have last year's reigning champs, the Coven. Led by Nnamdi, who will surely give Lincoln a run for his money in the second leg."

Casie stood up on her broom and bowed as the crowd clapped.

"What is she doing? The announcer didn't even mention her name," Jia said.

"She wants attention so bad," Noor said.

"Right! Like, girl, sit down somewhere," Jia replied.

Donna couldn't help but laugh. She was happy that her friends felt the same way about Casie as she did.

"In the fourth lane, we have the Vibes."

The Vibes didn't have matching uniforms or even color coordination. They looked like they were just wearing their regular clothes.

"The Vibes consider themselves the cool crew. I think they are just here for the vibe," Noor said, covering her mouth as she giggled.

"Yeah, they kinda suck," Jia said.

"Racers, take your positions!"

The racers straddled their brooms. Donna's excitement was through the roof, if there was a roof.

"On your mark... Get set... GO!"

A bright green light flashed from the announcer's wand with a loud bang as the green flames in two floating signal posts ignited.

The racers took off, and Jay and Chad were immediately caught in a fierce battle for first place, followed by the Vibes in third. The Upscales trailed in the back.

"Chad positions himself lower on his broom to avoid the ricocheting air," Lacey noted.

Chad moved past Jay by a foot before they entered the curve. Donna gasped when they both leaned simultaneously, but they managed to avoid a midair collision. Jay pulled ahead by a couple of feet when they approached the last straightaway.

Noor pointed to Lincoln and Nnamdi, who were floating side by side at the exchange point.

"They have to wait for their partners to cross the exchange line, which will trigger the floating signal to flare a green light to take off," Noor explained to Donna.

"And here it is, folks, the second exchange with Jay leading by a broomstick. The showdown between Lincoln and Nnamdi is seconds away!" Lacey shouted into the mic as the crowd rallied in the stands.

Jay crossed the exchange line first, triggering Nnamdi's green signal.

Nnamdi hurried out of the curve, but Lincoln was right on his tail after Chad crossed the exchange line.

Donna clapped and cheered with Noor as Jia jumped up and down, shouting Lincoln's name.

Lincoln flew close to the inner lane as he threaded the air. He leaned to the left as he approached the broad turn, but Nnamdi was right behind him.

The Vibes and the Upscales continued to battle for third place.

As Lincoln leveled out of the curve into a straightaway, the crowd noise increased. Some cheered for Lincoln, others for Nnamdi, but Lincoln was the fan favorite.

"Side by side, neck and neck. This is the race we wanted to see!" Lacey said.

Nnamdi pressed a button on the left side of his broom.

"What's that button that Nnamdi pressed?" Donna asked.

"It's his broom's special ability. An air hole expands through its core, funneling air to the back of the broom," Noor explained.

He gained more speed, pulling him away from Lincoln.

Casie and Mya floated next to each other in the exchange zone, awaiting their chance to finish the last leg of the race.

Donna's heart began to beat rapidly as she watched Lincoln. She put her hand on her chest and took a deep breath. *I can't have an anxiety attack now. I'm having fun. What's wrong with me?* She took another deep breath to calm down.

Nnamdi and Lincoln entered the last straightaway, inches from each other.

Two grip handles opened from the sides of Lincoln's broom. He tucked in his feet, positioned himself lower, and picked up speed. He swiftly pulled away from Nnamdi.

"That was a neat trick," Donna said to Jia, desperately trying to be heard over the crowd.

"Yeah, every broom has a little trick. Bells and whistles, you can say."

It looked like Lincoln was now at least two broomsticks ahead and could possibly pull away even farther as they got closer to the exchange line.

Suddenly, Donna thought she saw Lincoln slow down, as if he was allowing Nnamdi to gain ground.

"Lincoln crosses first, one broomstick ahead of Nnamdi," Lacey said.

Mya's green flame sparked, and she flew off. Casie joined her shortly after.

"And they are off. Let's see who will race their way to victory!"

Casie exited the first turn behind Mya. She lowered herself on her broom to gain speed and closed the gap by about a broomstick as the two racers entered the last turn.

"It's the final straightaway. Who will take first place? The Coven or the Bandits?"

The Vibes passed the Upscales by a broomstick as they traveled a few meters behind Casie and Mya. Casie managed to close in on Mya by half a broom as they flattened out of the turn.

Suddenly it looked like Mya lost control as she sharply veered right. Casie maneuvered herself out of the way as Mya frantically tried to straighten her broom.

"Oh no, Mya is headed toward the lane post!" cried the announcer.

Mya crashed into the post and catapulted off her broom, which snapped in half.

Lincoln appeared out of nowhere on his broom and lifted his wand. A red beam shot toward Mya, immobilizing her in the air.

"Mya's safe, and the racers have crossed the finish line with the Coven in first place, the Vibes in second, and the Upscales in third," Lacey declared.

"I think Casie knocked Mya off her broom," Donna said.

"What? I know Casie can be a real you-know-what, but I don't think she would put someone's life in danger," Noor said.

"I wouldn't put it past her," Jia muttered.

The Raceway got quieter as Lincoln lowered Mya onto the grass field below the track. Some older students gathered around Mya, who was cradling her arm and moaning in pain.

"Hey, girls," Zina said as they made their way onto the turn from the stands. "Get home by curfew. I'm going to take Mya to the medical bay on campus. I think her arm's broken."

"Yes, ma'am," they replied.

"Don't call me ma'am," Zina said with a quick smile before leaving.

"I want to fly," Donna said.

"With what broom? None of us have one," Jia said.

"You can use my broom," offered a voice.

Donna turned to see a girl striding toward them with effortless confidence. "That's Tamia," Jia whispered in Donna's ear.

A Black goddess.

That was the only thought Donna could muster as Tamia approached. Silky curls bounced on her shoulders, and her radiant smile revealed a perfect set of pearly white teeth.

"I don't think that's a good idea. I don't even know how to control my powers yet," Donna replied.

"Everyone starts somewhere," Tamia encouraged with a gentle smile.

"What if I accidentally break your broom?" Donna asked.

"I have another one. It's not as fast as this one, but I don't care; I'm not a racer... So, what do you say? Let's see what you got, new girl."

Donna wanted to say yes, but she definitely didn't have the money to buy Tamia a new broom if she broke it. And she'd just witnessed what happened to Mya, who was an experienced racer.

"Donna Marie, what are you waiting for? Say yes!" Jia told her.

"Yeah, give it a shot, Donna," Noor said.

"Donna Marie, you got this," Tamia said, smiling.

"Okay. I'll try," Donna replied, trying to suppress her excitement.

Tamia reached into her bag and pulled out a small round black tube. She tossed it in the air, and it transformed into a broomstick that levitated into her hand. Tamia thrust the broom in Donna's direction, and it slowly floated to her.

"Not too many wizards have the honor of owning a broom. After brooms were banished, many were confiscated, and all broom shops shut down," Tamia explained. "So, the Racing Society rarely sees new racers because of a lack of brooms."

"And you're trusting me with yours?" Donna asked.

"If I were a new girl on campus, I would want to try flying too," Tamia said.

Donna walked around the masterpiece, studying its craftsmanship. Her reflection bounced off the black glossy paint.

"The foot pegs provide extra handling and control, and the tail is composed of molded twigs from a magnolia tree," Tamia said. "You have to be one with the broom. It will act as an extension of your body. The slightest movements trigger its direction, speed, and altitude. Have fun!" Tamia called out as she walked away.

"Tamia is like the coolest girl on campus," Noor said. "Even though she's the Chancellor's daughter."

"Wait, that's Casie's sister?"

Jia and Noor nodded.

"How is she so nice?"

"Maybe because she's a mature senior," Jia said.

"I doubt Casie will be a mature senior," Donna said.

"Speaking of immature sophomores, we can't stay for long. Most of them are already leaving," Noor said.

"We'll be fine," Jia replied.

Donna carefully straddled the broom with her long legs.

A rush filled her body. She'd never ridden a broom, yet it felt like second nature. She placed her feet on the pegs, grasped the front of the broom, and found her balance with ease.

Her friends looked surprised.

Be one with the broom, Donna repeated to herself.

With a gentle tug of the broom, Donna rose into the air, hovering above the center of the Raceway. The wind brushed against her face, and a memory from many years ago surfaced. It was Halloween, and her mom had dressed her as

Wonder Woman, spinning her around the living room while Donna stretched her arms out, pretending to soar... *If only Mom could see me now.*

Donna looked down and saw Casie, Jay, Chike, and Ryan walking out of the salon. She nodded at Casie, who gave her a disgusted look.

"What are you doing on my sister's broom?" Casie yelled.

Donna leaned forward, causing the broom to move through the air. Her confidence quickly increased, and she picked up speed, smiling and laughing as she flew around the Raceway.

When she finally returned to the ground, her friends ran up to her.

"Curfew!" Noor and Jia said, trying to catch their breath.

"Shoot," Donna said. "How do I turn it back into the tube thingy?"

"Pretty sure there's a button on the bottom of the broom for that," Jia said.

Donna pressed a small, illuminated button on the bottom, and it worked. She looked around for Tamia but didn't see her.

"I have to give Tamia her broom back."

"We don't have time. We have to catch the last bus to Nawlins," Noor said, glancing at her watch.

If they missed curfew without a valid excuse, they would be issued a citation and would also have to spend a week in detention. It could even lead to expulsion. No one wanted that.

The girls ran to the station, but the last bus whizzed off as they turned the corner.

Casie was visible in the back window. She stuck out her tongue at them.

Donna put her hands over her head and sucked in as much air as she could.

"How could they leave without us?" Jia huffed.

"I think Chike may have thought we took a different bus," replied Noor, bending over, gasping for air.

"That's not good boyfriend behavior, leaving your girlfriend behind," Jia said.

"Chill. He didn't know. And I can take care of myself. I have a plan."

Noor pulled out a small skateboard from her backpack. She placed it on the ground, and it transformed into a motorized scooter.

"This is the plan? Uh, how can we all get on that?" Donna asked.

Noor pressed a button on the bottom, and the platform elongated to twice its size. They all got on board.

By the time they reached Nawlins, they were eighteen minutes past curfew. The street by the main entrance was shrouded in darkness, the silence punctuated only by their hurried footsteps.

"If we go through those doors now, we're definitely getting written up. There's always a monitor on duty, ready to snitch," Jia said.

"I can't get written up. My parents are going to kill me," Noor said.

"Hey, girls," Tamia said, walking up to them. "I was looking for you. I knew you were going to miss that bus waiting for Donna to finish up her fun on the broom. You have some good friends, Donna Marie."

"We couldn't leave our girl stranded," Noor added.

"Follow me."

Tamia led them to a small alleyway enclosed by a black chain-link fence.

"Here, chew these," she instructed, handing each girl a stick of gum. "This passageway leads into the college campus, so we'll need to blend in."

"What's this for?" Donna inquired, turning the gum over in her hand.

"It'll make you older. Twenty-one, to be exact."

"Cool," Jia said.

"We have to spit the gum out once we reach the Gardens, so don't swallow it," Tamia explained.

As they began chewing, the transformation was instantaneous. Their expressions mirrored their amazement at the gum's effectiveness.

"Look at us, a bunch of mature college students," Tamia chuckled, donning a tan bucket hat from her bag.

"I look fabulous. I need to hurry up and get to college," Jia said, slinging her new long hair around as she looked in her compact mirror.

"Did I get taller?" Donna asked, stretching her arms in front of her.

"You definitely did, girl," Jia answered, standing next to her and measuring her height.

"Noor, are you okay with removing your hijab?" Tamia asked.

Noor paused, the weight of the decision evident on her face. After a moment of contemplation, she slowly unwrapped her hijab, revealing luscious hair that dropped past her shoulders.

"I am the only high schooler who wears one. You're right, I have to take it off."

"Here, try this on," Tamia offered, handing her the bucket hat. She walked up to the fence and pulled out her wand.

"Wazi!"

The gate unlocked, allowing Tamia to escort the crew into the alley.

An old red streetcar sat abandoned at the alley's end. With another wave of her wand, Tamia opened its door. They hurried inside, and she sealed the entrance behind them. The rear of the streetcar opened, revealing a hidden passage.

They proceeded in silence through a janitor's closet and into the labyrinth of campus hallways. Donna caught her reflection in every mirror and window they passed, intrigued by her altered appearance. She looked sophisticated and mature, reminiscent of her mother.

Finally, they arrived at the Gardens without incident. The girls discarded their gum, and their appearances reverted. Donna felt her hair poof back to its usual volume, and Noor swiftly put on her hijab.

"No. I don't want to be fifteen again," Jia said, pouting in the mirror.

"Bet that was weird, huh?" asked Tamia. "But it worked. My friends and I used these aging gums when we had a curfew."

"Was I a cute adult?" Noor asked.

"Stunning," Tamia replied.

"Thanks for your help, Tamia," Donna said.

"You're welcome. Get back to your dorms before the monitor notices you're gone."

The girls took off running, careful not to draw attention. Something thumped against Donna's leg with each step. She reached into her pocket and froze...

Oh no.

Tamia's broom. She'd forgotten to return it, but there was no time to spare.

There was a knock on room 305. Donna cracked the door open to find a weary-looking monitor in the hallway, clutching a tablet.

"Hey, Monique," Donna said.

"You, Noor, and Jia didn't check in when you got back," Monique said as she put her glasses on.

Donna opened the door to reveal Jia and Noor on the couch with Uno cards in their hands.

"We got back way earlier than expected and didn't see you." Jia waved at Monique.

"What time was this?"

"Around six," Donna quickly answered.

Monique gave her the side-eye.

"I might have been on break," she conceded. "Next time, come back to check in with me. I don't want to have to write any of you up because of a simple mistake. But tonight, I will give you the benefit of the doubt."

As Monique walked away, the tension in the room dissolved into a relieved sigh, fluttering through the space like a gentle draft.

Later, after feeding Mr. Whiskers and settling in for the night, Donna pulled out her journal from her desk drawer. It was the first time she had opened it since arriving at Nawlins. Pen in hand, she began to write.

Hay, Notebook,

It's been a minute. Sorry I have been neglecting you. I think I haven't been writing to you because I have friends now. They are so cool. Noor is from Harlem, and we have so much in common. Jia is from France, and she's different from Noor and me as far as style and attitude, lol, but she's cool and adds some flavor to our clique.

Oh, I think I like boys now. Eww, I know, right? Well, Chad... I admire his strength. And Jay... He's really cute. I've never met a prettier boy, lol. Mr. Whiskers has been keeping me company, too. It's weird, I think he can sometimes understand what I'm saying. He's like my little protector who sleeps on the side of my bed. IDK. I still haven't figured out the mystery of his name tag. There are a few mysteries around here, and I'm looking forward to figuring them out.

I say all this so you know that you don't have to worry about me, Notebook. I'm not lonely anymore. And that's a good thing. But you will always be my first friend.

Chapter Seventeen

Settled into her usual spot in the library, Donna's focus was on the final paragraphs of her English essay. The quiet hum of the library was suddenly interrupted by a notification on her tablet—an envelope had been delivered for her. Curiosity replacing concentration, Donna packed up her things and hurried to the mail room. She arrived breathlessly and scanned the mail bin to find her name on a yellow clasp envelope. With the envelope in hand, she dashed back to her dorm, flung herself onto the couch, and eagerly open it to discover a letter and a photo inside.

Hey, my sha,

I miss you so much. I hope everything is going well. I know it blows that you can't use your phone on campus, but I'm getting used to our emails.

Jacquie was cleaning out her closet and found my old photo album. These pictures are ancient! There were some from college when I was young and hip and hot. Anyway, here's an old Polaroid photo for your dorm room. The photo was taken at your brother's 1st birthday party. Your father was so in love with his Polaroid camera. He didn't want anyone touching it because he was afraid it would break, but he let me use it just this once to take this photo.

Love you,

Mom

In the photo, her father held Link above his head. Link was in a Superman costume and his red cape trailed behind him. Donna traced over her father and brother with her thumb. The tears came. She had new friends, but it wasn't the same as family.

Pull yourself together, Donna. Mom is okay. You are okay.

On the bottom white border of the Polaroid was a hand-drawn heart. Inside the heart was her mother's handwriting.

Cathy, Sammy, Link

Donna tilted her head to the side. She never recalled her mother using the nickname *Cathy*.

She stood and placed the photo on her desk. Mr. Whiskers leaped up right after, giving the picture a curious sniff.

"That's my father and big brother," Donna said softly.

Mr. Whiskers curled up beside the frame, purring loudly.

"Sorry you've got to stay in here while I'm gone. But when I get back, I'll feed you and let you run around the living room." Donna kissed the top of his head. "See you later. I'm heading to the CC."

Donna walked into the CC solo because Jia had a scheduled phone call with her parents, and Noor was having a walk and talk with Chike—most likely about leaving her stranded at the Raceway.

"Yo, Donna," Chad called out from a high table.

"Hey," Donna replied, setting her backpack by him.

"Is everything cool? You seem sad."

"Who? Me? No, no, I'm fine. Still adjusting to this city's pollen. Allergies, you know?" Donna tried to play it off.

Chad squinted at her. "Right... Ah, yo, you are the talk of the Racing Society," he whispered.

"Me? Why?"

"Last night you flew around the track fast as hell and didn't fall off the broom. You know how long it takes for some people to just fly straight without falling off?"

"It felt normal to me. Like I had done it before."

"It took me almost a year of training to fly like that."

"Who taught you?"

Chad looked away. He waited a few seconds before answering. "My grandpa. He's like a father to me. Taught me everything I know."

"If he's anything like you, I know he's a wonderful grandfather," Donna said, touching Chad's hand.

The two looked at each other and then pulled away. Donna felt a flutter in her stomach and her hands were a little sweaty.

Do I have a crush on this boy? No, right?

"Um, yeah... It's kinda hot in here, right?" Chad said, taking off his black hoodie.

"Yeah, it's kind of hot," Donna replied, grabbing her water canister from her bag and sipping.

"Like I was saying, my broom was actually my father's. It's the only thing I have of his."

Donna untucked her necklace from her shirt and rubbed the pendant with her hand.

"This necklace is the only thing I have of my father. Technically he gifted it to my mom, but it still came from him."

"What happened to him? It's cool if you don't want to talk about it," Chad said.

"Car accident."

"Dang. I'm sorry, luv."

Whenever she talked about her father with other people, it often felt like the weight of her words never fully landed. But with Chad, it was different. His silence wasn't dismissive; it was knowing. Donna felt truly heard. Truly understood. They carried the same kind of pain, and in that moment, it felt a little less heavy.

"You know, sometimes I feel kinda angry at kids who have both parents. Well, it's not a bad anger, it's more like a sad anger. And it's not directed at them; it's not their fault my father is absent from my life."

"I get angry too when I see families together. I think that's normal because we're human. Even though we have these magical powers," he said, looking into her eyes.

"What are you two chatting about?" Jia jumped in, sitting down at the table.

"Ah, nothing. Just talking about a lecture. I have to go to class. Peace out," Chad said, grabbing his backpack.

"We don't have class for another forty-five," Jia said.

"Ah, I'm going to grab some pizza," Donna said, waving awkwardly at them as she walked off.

She was in line at the pizza stand when Jay cut in next to her. He looked around and whispered to her as he grabbed a tray.

"That was some flying last night. You've had some training?"

"No, it was my first time."

"Then you're a rare natural... I heard we're skipping a few chapters ahead in Dawas class to start the dream catcher. Want to meet early tomorrow morning to go over it before class?"

"Trying to get a leg up on our competition?" Donna asked.

"We are the number one group in class. We have to maintain our status," he said, smirking.

"Let's do it. I need all the help I can get."

Donna walked back to the high-top table, where Noor had joined Jia, and they trolled her for talking to Jay. Their lighthearted banter halted abruptly as they noticed Zina approaching with a serious demeanor.

"Hey, Donna, the Chancellor wants to speak to you in her office," Zina said.

"Me? Why?"

"I'm not sure, but she says to come now."

With a concerned glance back at her friends, Donna followed Zina. She got more nervous as they reached the main lobby in the Chancellor's quarters.

"She probably just wants to see how you're fitting in. But remember to keep the Raceway a secret, yeah?" Zina whispered.

Donna nodded, her mind racing with possibilities. Was she really in trouble, or was it something else?

They arrived at a dark, narrow hallway that led to the Chancellor's office. Zina gestured towards the imposing double glass doors at the end. Donna's heart pounded as she approached, the doors swinging open automatically, revealing a room that was both gloomy and impeccably styled.

Inside, tall, elegant lamps cast long shadows across the sleek glass desk at the far end of the room. Hanging above a mantelpiece along the wall was a painting of the five original members of the Coven, arms around each other, broad smiles on their faces. They stood in front of the History Villa—the same building Donna had visited over the summer. Just beneath the painting, a black branding iron shaped like a fleur-de-lis hung ominously.

"That painting was done in 1811, the day the first building at Nawlins was completed," Chancellor Decken said, stepping into the doorway. "Back then, the History Villa served as a classroom and cafeteria. Upstairs was a library and the Coven's living quarters. If only our ancestors could see how big and beautiful our campus has become."

"They all look so happy," Donna said.

"I'm sure they were in that moment. They were the best of friends who worked side by side to liberate their people. I bet the feeling was... esoterically beautiful."

"I see the fleur-de-lis symbol all over New Orleans," Donna said, pointing to the branding iron.

"Code noir, do you know what that means?" the Chancellor asked.

Donna shook her head.

"The Black Code," she explained. "It was a set of Louisiana laws designed to control oppressed people of color. Branding runaways with the fleur-de-lis was one of its cruelties. The original Coven members reclaimed that symbol, placing it in Nawlins' crest as a reminder of how far we've come."

The Chancellor spoke about history with so much passion, just like Jia and so many others at Nawlins.

"Anyway, let me stop going on about Nawlins' past before I take up your whole day. Please, Donna, take a seat," she said with a smile.

Donna sat on one of the black leather chairs near the desk. The Chancellor placed her glossy, dark red wand on her desk as she took a seat. She opened a notebook and removed a rose-gold pen from her blazer's pocket.

"A junior, Mya, broke her arm last night. Do you know anything about what happened?" Her expression was soft despite the words.

"I'm still new here, so I don't even know Mya," Donna responded, doing her best to avoid a direct lie.

"Indeed, you are new here; that's why you're the only student I've questioned. I'm hoping your peers haven't tainted your character... There is speculation about underground broom racing. The medical staff thinks Mya broke her arm racing and not by falling from a bicycle, as she claims. Donna, I need to know."

The Chancellor stared at her as if she was looking into her soul. Maybe she knew Donna was lying and was waiting for her to come clean. Donna started to sweat.

She wanted to do right by the Chancellor, who had supported her coming to Nawlins, but at the same time, she couldn't tell on her classmates. It was less about outright loyalty and more about not wanting to be labeled a snitch, which would probably make life here uncomfortable and might even ruin her new friendships.

Besides, the Racing Society was like nothing she'd ever experienced before, and she wanted in.

"I haven't heard anything about underground broom racing, but if I do, I'll let you know, Chancellor," Donna said, trying to sound genuine.

The Chancellor smiled. "Well, if you tell me you don't know, I believe you. But don't let peer pressure turn you into someone you're not, Donna Marie."

As Donna made her way to her dorm, she spotted Tamia sitting on a lounge chair in the Gardens, reading a book. Her long black hair hung from the chair's back as she rested her head on a pillow.

"Thanks for letting me use your broom. It's safe in my dorm. I can get it now if you want," Donna said.

"Keep it," Tamia responded. "It suits you, and you ride it so well. It looked like a part of you. So, I want you to enjoy it. I have another anyway."

"Really? But I can't accept that. It's probably been in your family for a while."

"Nah, I bought it on the black market last year, and I don't use it... You'll need it because I heard the Bandits are looking for another racer. You should try it out."

"I can't race," Donna said.

"I saw you, and you're a natural. You can make the team with proper training," Tamia said confidently.

Donna looked down. "I know Casie is your sister, but do you think she purposely knocked Mya off her broom?"

Tamia sat up and made room for Donna. She looked around the Gardens as if to make sure no one was around. "When I saw it... I thought the same thing. Look, I love my sister, but she can be a real... brat."

Being a brat is one thing. But putting someone's life in danger to win a race is... something else.

"I can't imagine what you had to put up with growing up with her," Donna said.

"Oh, you have no idea," Tamia said, laughing it off.

"Your mom just questioned me about Mya. I felt bad lying to her."

"I'm her daughter, and I always lie to her about the Raceway. So, keep the broom and go to the tryouts on Saturday."

Donna gave Tamia a big hug. No, a huge hug. "You're amazing," Donna said. "Why would Lincoln ever break up with you?" she blurted. "Oh, I'm sorry! That's none of my business."

Tamia looked away. "It's cool. I'm sure your classmates told you about Lincoln and me."

"Yeah, you two are kinda popular."

"We both hate the popularity that comes with our last names... Lincoln and I... He wanted to protect me. That was his reason for breaking up with me."

"Protect you from what?"

"Still trying to figure that out."

Donna felt terrible for bringing up Lincoln. She could tell Tamia was still emotional about the breakup. She seemed lonely. Donna could see why she didn't hang out with her siblings. But why didn't Tamia have other friends? Maybe it was difficult for her to find genuine friends because she was a Decken. Donna was even more curious about why Lincoln broke up with her. What was he trying to protect her from?

Chapter Eighteen

All seniors were privileged to live in spacious studio apartment-styled dorms, something Lincoln had eagerly anticipated since his junior year. He and Nnamdi had been roommates since their first year at Nawlins, so he missed having his friend around, but he enjoyed his newfound independence. His personal space was decked out with shelves brimming with books, and a vibrant contemporary art piece of Tupac adorned the wall beside a large TV.

On school days, Lincoln was usually up at six to work out at the gym in the recreation center before it got too busy. But today, he was wide awake at 4:30 a.m., sitting on the edge of his bed, thinking about Donna and Catherine.

All this time, they were here...

It felt like he had swallowed a cinder block.

I can't tell Donna I'm her brother because it would put her in danger.

How could my parents lie to me like that?

And what if everything Mr. Jenkins said about the Elders is true? What am I supposed to do about these old-ass wizards?

Lincoln rose from his bed and approached the Tupac painting. With careful hands, he lifted the canvas from the wall and set it gently on the floor. He peeled away clear tape covering a Polaroid photo tucked away on the back of the frame.

He was dressed as Superman, and his mother was hugging him. At the bottom of the photo was a drawn heart. Inside the heart was Cathy's handwriting:

Cathy, Sammy, Link

A rush of emotions filled his spirit: anger, pain, and joy.

"Calm yourself, Lincoln," he whispered, steadying his breathing as he headed to the bathroom. "Lock in. You got this. You can solve it all by yourself."

After a rigorous session of bench presses and laps around the indoor track, Lincoln cooled down with a cold shower in the locker room before making his way to the CC.

The morning crowd was sparse, with only a few students scattered around. Lincoln settled into a quiet corner, popped in his earbuds, and sank into the beats and lyrics of Drake's album *Take Care* while savoring his go-to breakfast: an egg white and turkey bacon bagel sandwich.

His moment of solitude was interrupted as Chad approached, breakfast tray in hand. Lincoln pulled out his earbuds, raising an eyebrow.

"Woaaaa. Wassam with ya, ya heard me," Chad said, placing the tray on the table and raising his arms.

"Why are you so loud in the morning? And what are you doing here so early?" Lincoln asked.

"I had a bad dream and couldn't go back to sleep, so now I'm here, ya dig," Chad replied, taking a seat at the table.

"Don't tell me Chad from 17th Hollygrove is scared of a nightmare? If the hood could see you now." Lincoln laughed.

"Chill, woady. I had a dream that the Bandits made it to the championship race, and I blew it for us."

"That is one hell of a nightmare because *when* we make it to the championship, you better not lose us in that race!"

"In the dream, Donna went up to Jay after the race and kissed him. That made it a nightmare," Chad added. "You know her? The new sophomore? I'm tutoring her in Spells."

Lincoln stared at Chad, then looked him up and down. *This lil dude better not have a thing for my sister.*

"Why are you looking at me like that?"

"Why did Jay kissing Donna in a dream make you take a walk?"

"Because that should've been me kissing her... Dawg, she's so hot. I've never liked a girl like I like her. Do you think I have a chance?" Chad asked.

"No. You have no chance."

"Damn. Relax, woa. What's wrong with you? Back off me."

Lincoln realized he had gotten into Chad's face. *What am I doing?*

He looked around to see if anyone else had noticed, but no one was sitting near them. He tapped Chad on the shoulder and started laughing.

"My bad, fam. I'm just playing with you. The last thing I would want is Jay kissing a girl I like. That dude is a dick," Lincoln said.

"Facts! That's what I'm saying."

Lincoln took another bite of his sandwich and sipped his orange juice. He leaned back in his chair and stretched his hands over his head, trying his best to seem normal.

"So, you like Donna, huh?"

Chad's eyes lit up as he chewed a piece of bacon.

"Yeah... She's smart. And she grew up in the Bronx, so she's street-smart like me. We have way too much in common. And she's tall. And she's pretty. And that long curly hair."

"Alright. Alright, I get it," Lincoln said, his stomach turning. "So, how is she doing in class? Is she catching up?"

"Her first week was kinda rough, but now she's catching on fast. Once she learns a spell, she can perform it perfectly. It usually takes other students I tutor at least a few lessons to catch on."

"Seems like y'all have been spending a lot of time together."

"Told you, there is a connection between us," Chad replied.

Lincoln gave him a side-eye.

"Why are you so invested in her? Do you like her too?" Chad asked.

"What? No. I'm too old for that lil girl. My father told me about some of her mess-ups in class. And my mother is the main reason why Donna is at Nawlins. They want me to look out for her."

Chad took a long sip of his orange juice. Lincoln got annoyed by the loud slurping sound he made with the straw.

"That makes sense. Like her big brother or something."

"Yeah, I guess you can say that," Lincoln responded, his body feeling uncomfortably warm now. "Just, um, keep me updated on how she's doing in class."

"I could... but for a price."

"Let me think about that... No."

"Bro, if you want me to spy on Donna, I need you to do something for me."

"It's not spying, just keep an eye on her."

Chad took another sip of his juice, even louder.

"Aight, bra... What do you want?"

"Let me fly in the last leg of the races."

"We got the Vibes in the first series. I won't let you mess that race up."

"Come on, woady, I'm the best racer on the team," Chad said.

Lincoln frowned at him, and he started coughing.

"Sorry, something was stuck in my throat. Like I was saying... I'm the second-best racer on the team, I won't mess it up."

I can't believe I'm agreeing to this. "Okay. You have a deal."

"Bet. I won't let you down, my G."

"Speaking of races, do you think Donna could make it in the Bandits? We need a new racer for Mya," Lincoln said.

"That would be dope. I saw her on a broom at the Raceway. She's fast. But she hasn't had any training."

"Yeah, I saw her too. With training, she could be a great racer."

"I agree." Chad grinned.

"I'll meet you here at lunchtime, and we'll talk to her about it," Lincoln said.

"Aight, bet."

"I'm going to the library before class. I'll see you later," Lincoln said, dapping up Chad.

Ancient Magic was Lincoln's favorite class, drawn in by its unique setting that celebrated the Harlem Renaissance. The room was adorned with vibrant graphic art reflecting Afrocentric perspectives. Besides New Orleans, Lincoln loved New York City—its fast pace, history, art, culture, and Black roots fascinated him. He'd been there only once, on a summer trip with his family, but wanted to return soon.

The students sat in two-person desks that had a glass centerpiece. Between the glass were paper inserts of poetry, song lyrics, speeches, and literature of Black authors, musicians, poets, and iconic leaders of the Harlem Renaissance, such as Langston Hughes, Zora Neale Hurston, and Louis Armstrong.

Lincoln felt a tap on his shoulder.

"Wassam, fam. Aye, you good?" asked Nnamdi, his deskmate. "You've been zoned out since you walked in here."

"Yeah, I'm good. I just got a lot on my mind."

"Fasho. Just checking on you. Never seen you like this before."

"Appreciate you, fam. But don't worry. Everything is cool," Lincoln said, lying through his teeth.

"Since you want to talk during class, Lincoln, why don't you tell us about the force field spell?" Professor Decken said from the front of the room.

Lincoln always paid attention in class, took detailed notes, and never disrespected a professor, but today, he was annoyed.

He bit down on his jaw and rubbed his temples before answering.

"It's a shield that absorbs energy beams and other attacks. They can backfire energy beams toward your opponent if you know what you're doing. Our ancestors used them to block bullets and swords during the revolt."

"Good. Now, come up here and demonstrate how to produce the shield," the professor said.

Lincoln didn't feel like doing it. He really wanted to return to his dorm and look at the photo of Catherine or return to the recreation center and punch the heavy bag for a few rounds.

He got up from his desk, grabbed his wand, and walked toward the front of the classroom. He took a deep breath. He knew his agitation could trigger his anger, and his anger was dangerous. It could cause him to lose control of his powers and go into pure-wizard form.

It hadn't happened in years because he'd learned how to suppress it, but the fear of triggering it still lingered. In pure-wizard form, he had no control over his body or mind. When it passed, he could only remember fragments, like trying to piece together the details of a fading dream.

Lincoln stood still with his wand held tight. Heavy hesitation.

"Do I have to do this?" he blurted out.

The students went quiet and directed their attention to Professor Decken, who walked closer to him.

"I called on you, so yes... Is there a problem?"

Lincoln smacked his lips. "Yeah, there's a problem," he said under his breath.

"What did you say?"

My parents are liars. Apparently, Elders are a thing. And I have to fix all this crap myself. So, this stupid demonstration is a waste of my time. That's the problem!

"I said, no. There is no problem, sir."

"Good. Continue."

His anger was getting the best of him. He felt the coldness creeping up on him—fear taking over his confidence as if his ribcage had just been stuck in a freezer.

Come on, Lincoln. Happy thoughts. Happy thoughts.

He thought of his mom and sister; despite the circumstances, they were still alive, which gave him hope and joy.

He took another deep breath and widened his stance.

"Kulinda," he said, thrusting his right arm in front of him.

A translucent force field with a glowing blue ring expanded from his wand, shielding the front of his body. Waves of blue light rippled across the surface, pulsing steadily like a heartbeat.

Professor Decken approached and tapped the center of the shield with his wand. The border flickered, and the pulsing waves shifted from blue to red, then flared into a bright yellow.

"Good job, Lincoln."

"Can I sit back down now?" he asked, retracting the shield.

"No. You can meet me outside the classroom for a chat," the professor said, walking toward the door.

Lincoln put his head down and followed. Decken closed the door behind them and folded his arms.

"What's going on, Lincoln?"

"I, ah... I... I'm fine, professor."

"You've never smacked your lips and talked back to me before."

"It's just... The pressure of being a senior is getting to me, you know?"

"Or is the breakup with Tamia getting to you?" Decken asked.

Lincoln leaned his back on the wall and placed his hands over his head.

"Look, Lincoln. I was once a young man like you. You have emotions, and it's okay to express them... or else they will burst out eventually, just like what happened in class today."

"You're right. I'm sorry, professor."

"You and my daughter were great friends before you started dating. Don't let this breakup destroy that friendship."

"I understand. Thanks."

Professor Decken was right, but all Lincoln could think about was flying his broom to New York and wrapping his arms around his mom.

Chapter Nineteen

Donna got a whiff of Jay's fresh lemony-scented cologne as he sat next to her in the lounge area in the CC.

"Hey, partner," he said, removing various ingredients in small glass jars from his backpack. "So, the dream-catcher dawa can conjure and broadcast your most vivid dream, good or bad, into a mirror."

"Sounds interesting," Donna said as she opened her textbook.

"I like your hair," Jay said.

Donna blushed and touched her hair.

"I like yours too. It's always wavy." *It's always wavy? Come on, Donna Marie, what was that? God, I don't know how to talk to boys.*

"Try not to drown," he responded.

They shared a laugh and then a long stare.

What do I say? What do I do? Donna thought, repeatedly pressing the clicker of her pen.

"I forgot my book. Do you mind if I sit closer to you to share yours?" Jay asked.

"No, I don't mind..."

Their shoulders touched when he scooted closer to her. Donna had never felt this nervous around a boy. It was like she had lost all her confidence in his presence, and now, being this close to him, her whole body felt warm. It wasn't uncomfortable like her anxiety attacks—this new feeling of crushing over a boy felt good.

"The ingredients are simple: fresh rainwater, owl feathers, lavender flowers, and bat fangs, which I have brought," Jay said, reading from the textbook. "With the perfect wand motion and concentration, a mist will form from the pot and develop into a round mirror-like form."

Jay uncapped the small jars and placed them on the table. Donna carefully emptied the jars into the pot and then stirred the ingredients with her wand.

"Tazama Ndoto Zangu," Jay said, circling the words in the book with a pen. "That's the chant for the dawa to work."

"We have to make a circle movement thingy over the pot with our wands to activate it," Donna added, reading the text.

"A circle movement thingy," Jay said, laughing. "You're funny."

Donna looked away as she blushed.

"Would you like to go first?" he asked.

"I'll give it a try... Tazama Ndoto Zangu."

Donna said the words perfectly but failed to perform the proper wand movement.

A mist from the pot formed a mirror but faded away. She watched in disappointment.

"Almost." Jay gently grabbed her hand and mimicked the correct movement.

Donna stared into his hazel eyes. *He's so handsome...*

She broke her stare to attempt the wand motion on her own again.

"Perfect. Now clear your mind, then think of a dream when you say the chant."

Donna took a deep breath and thought of one of her recent dreams.

"Tazama Ndoto Zangu," she said, moving her wand with the correct motion.

This time, the mist formed a decent-sized mirror and maintained its shape.

A hazy picture started to form in the center of the mirror. After a few seconds, the mirror displayed a vivid dream of Catherine kissing Donna on the forehead and hugging her tightly before she walked into her elementary school.

Donna looked away, trying to disguise the rush of emotions.

Jay patted her back to comfort her.

"Crying 'cause you don't belong here, new girl?" Casie said, walking up with Ryan in tow.

Donna rubbed her eyes. "Something just flew in my eye, and I do belong here. I'm a wizard just like you."

"No, not like me. You're not a Coven member. Never will be."

"Come on, sis, don't be rude," Jay interjected.

"I'm just stating the obvious. She'll never catch up," Casie said, dismissing Donna with a wave as she walked away.

"Yo, Jay! Don't forget we have a team meeting tonight," Ryan called out.

"Aight, bet!" Jay replied.

"What sport do you play?" Donna inquired.

"Football," he replied. "We have a home game on Sunday. You should come."

"I'll try to make it. Thanks for helping me out. I'm sure we'll do great in class today." Donna grabbed her stuff and hurried off without looking back.

Professor Hunt was in the center of the classroom, providing a detailed explanation of the dream-catcher dawa. "For your exam, I will grade you individually, then you and your partner's grade will be averaged together for your overall grade."

Professor Hunt was adamant about teamwork. She was the only professor whose grading system was based on pairs. Donna was a fan of this teaching style because it motivated the students to work together while pushing each other to perform their best.

"Today is strictly practice. You will not be graded, but I want to see your effort. Gather around so I can give you a demonstration."

The students converged around her workstation as she prepped the ingredients.

"One cup of rainwater," Professor Hunt said, pouring a measuring cup into a black pot.

"Two owl feathers." She grabbed the feathers from a glass jar and placed them into the pot.

"Now your lavender," she said, adding a teaspoon.

"And last but not forgotten, bat fangs." She put two fangs into the pot and stirred.

"Tazama Ndoto Zangu," she said as she circled her wand.

A blue vapor hovered around the top of the pot before forming a mirror. A vivid dream appeared of Professor Hunt singing on a stage with thousands of people in the crowd cheering her on. The projection was as clear as if Donna were watching it on a TV screen.

"Would you look at that? Maybe I do need to pursue my solo artist career," Professor Hunt said, smiling.

"You sound amazing," Noor said.

"Thank you. Okay, students. Let's see what you all can do," Professor Hunt said, rubbing her hands together.

Raine went first and maintained a decent-sized mirror for about ten seconds. Donna was up next. She was nervous because she didn't want to bring down Jay's grade. Her first placement test was successful because he helped her with each step, but partner help wasn't allowed now.

This is just practice, she reminded herself. *And you've done it before.*

Her confidence grew as she played out the steps in her head. She closed her eyes and focused on the dream of her mother dropping her off at school.

"Tazama Ndoto Zangu," Donna said.

A large mirror started to form. Professor Hunt stepped closer to the pot.

"Very impressive," she said.

A cloudy mist formed in the mirror's center as a dream began.

"That's it, Donna. Concentrate. You're doing so well."

As the mist cleared, Donna's dream projected into the mirror.

Sammy was driving his red pickup truck through heavy snow.

"Hold on, son!" he yelled into the rearview mirror.

Link cried as he tightly clutched his seatbelt. Sammy steadied the steering wheel with one hand while pointing his wand out the window, shooting energy beams at a red-eyed beast.

"Come on, you ugly monster!" Sammy yelled out the window.

As the beast closed in, Sammy jerked the wheel and veered toward it, slamming the side of the truck into its head. He checked the mirrors frantically. The creature had stumbled, but something else was coming. Two wizards on brooms flanked the truck, one in a burgundy cloak, the other in black, closing in fast. Sammy squinted, trying to get a look at their faces through the windows, but their hoods hung low, masking their identities.

"What do you want from me?!"

"Your blood," the wizard with the burgundy cloak said in a deep raspy voice.

The wizard raised a long wooden wand, its handle bearing a scorched fleur-de-lis symbol. A red energy beam blasted from the tip. Sammy slammed the brakes and yanked the wheel, sending the truck into a wild spin on the slick pavement. The beam struck the road behind them, erupting in a burst of debris.

"Umeme," Sammy said, pointing his wand at the burgundy-cloaked wizard.

A blue beam with static-like pulses fired from his wand. It sounded like a lightning bolt when the beam struck the wizard's body. The wizard dropped to the ground, and a smoky residue hovered around the cloak.

Sammy stomped on the gas pedal as the black-cloaked wizard and the beast headed toward the truck.

Donna woke up as if in a trance, breathing frantically.

"Donna, are you okay?" Professor Hunt hurried to her aid while the other students stood and watched, wide-eyed.

"Yes. I'm fine. It was just a bad dream," Donna said.

But she couldn't escape from this nightmare. Why did it keep coming back? And why did it feel as if she had lived through it when she wasn't even there? Was her father trying to tell her something? Who were these cloaked wizards and the beast that were always chasing them?

After class, Donna went to the call center, which was located in a circular courtyard adjacent to the bookstore. Inside the center were multiple private booths furnished with HD video call tablets and phones. Donna thought they looked like tiny offices but cooler because of the different colored glass that surrounded each booth.

"Hey, Mom."

"Hey, baby. It's so good to see you."

"I see your little curls. You look so good."

"Thanks. Your Auntie Jacquie brought over her curling iron and did it for me. She's here, by the way."

"Hey, hunny," Jacquie said, coming into frame.

"Hey, Auntie."

"I'm glad school is going well. I have to get back to work. I have a showing in an hour and have to catch the train. Love you."

"Bye and love you too."

"I like the background," her mom said. "It almost looks like you're inside of a blue crystal."

"Yeah, this place is pretty cool... Thank you so much for the photo. I love it."

"That was one of my favorites."

"Who's Cathy? I saw that name written inside the heart."

Her mother didn't say anything.

"Mom?" Donna said, getting closer to the screen. "You, okay?"

"Cathy was a nickname I used to go by. Your father loved calling me that. He never called me Catherine, no one really did back then."

"Why did you stop using it?"

"After Link and Sammy died... the name Cathy reminded me of how much I had lost. So, I stopped going by that name."

"I'm so sorry, Mom."

"It's okay. After I had you, I finally had love and joy back in my life. Because of you," Catherine said, whipping her eyes with a tissue. "You know, there was another Polaroid from that party. I think Sammy mailed it to his friend Charles. They were so close."

"Charles? You never mentioned him before."

"After your father passed, he disappeared. No calls, or letters, or anything..."

Donna's ears started to ring.

"What was his last name?"

"DuVernay? Yes. Charles DuVernay."

Professor DuVernay and my dad were friends? Did Rima and the professor know all this time and were hiding it?

Donna didn't want to upset her mom. First, she needed to find out the truth.

"Mom, I have to go. I love you so much," Donna said, trying to keep her voice calm.

"I love you too."

Chapter Twenty

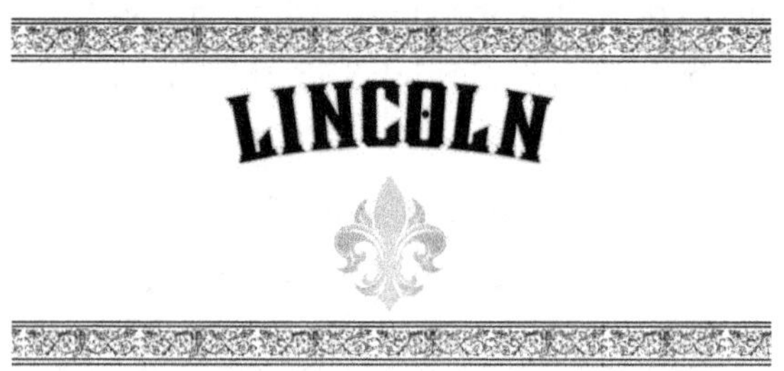

Lincoln rarely went to the CC around lunchtime. He wasn't the chatty type, and other than Nnamdi, he only had a few close friends. He pulled his hat down as he walked through the doors.

Lincoln could've easily found a better candidate for Mya's replacement. Someone who wouldn't need extra training. But if he got Donna to try out for the Bandits, he would be the one to train her. Then he could spend time with his sister. He could monitor how she was adapting to being a wizard. Donna's power was dangerous. If she accidentally activated her pure-wizard form, she could harm someone. And if anyone found out about her true identity, she could be hunted for her blood.

"Hey, you're Lincoln, right?"

A girl tapped Lincoln's shoulder. She was wearing a white shirt with paint stains and black suspenders, her black beret tilted to the side.

"Yeah, what's up?" he replied.

"My pawpaw told me to find you."

"Who's your grandfather?"

"He's more like my great-great-great-grandfather."

"Huh?"

"Pawpaw said you would know him as Mr. Jenkins," Raine replied.

"What?! You're his granddaughter?"

"Like I said, add more GRANDS in there, but yep, I'm Raine. In the flesh. In person. In the CC. That's me," Raine said, pointing at herself.

Yeah, you're definitely related to Mr. Jenkins.

"My grandfather said you could help with the... Elders," Raine whispered. "He said you and I have to be on the lookout on campus for any suspicious behavior. He says nowhere is safe... Me, I think Professor DuVernay is one."

Lincoln frowned.

"Bad joke, huh?"

"Yeah, that wasn't funny."

"Sorry, was trying to lighten up the mood."

"But I think you're right. We have to be on the lookout everywhere."

"A Jenkins is always right. Let's not use our tablets to communicate; the Elders might be monitoring those. You can find me upstairs in the art room at lunchtime or after class."

Raine began to walk away but stopped and turned back. "Um, speaking of Elders, I forgot to tell you... Donna Marie... Do you know her? The new girl?"

Lincoln tensed up a bit. "I think I've heard of her."

"She performed the dream-catcher dawa in class today, and in her dream, a wizard wearing an ugly cloak attacked her. It was an Elder."

"What? Are you sure?"

"Yeah, this wizard had a long wooden wand like the one my pawpaw has," Raine said.

Donna had a dream about an Elder. This is bad. Real bad.

"You, okay?" Raine asked. "Look like you saw a ghost. For real."

"Yeah, I'm cool."

"So... How is a girl who just found out that she's a wizard having dreams about an Elder? Matter of fact, it was an Elder and an original Coven member... And... And... a Rougarou."

"How do you know what a Rougarou looks like?" Lincoln asked.

"My pawpaw showed me drawings. He told me he saw one before," Raine said, getting closer to Lincoln. "So, why was Donna dreaming about one?"

"I don't know."

"Something to think about," Raine said before walking away.

Lincoln was getting irritated as he walked around the CC looking for Chad. Finally, he saw him waving from a high-top table.

"Where is Donna?" Lincoln asked as he approached.

"Dang, woady, hello to you too."

"My bad, you know I don't like coming in here when it's packed," Lincoln said.

"I was just messing with you, ya heard me. Donna should be here with her friends soon. Maybe she's upstairs in the lounge area," Chad said.

When they reached the top of the spiral staircase, Lincoln saw Donna, Noor, and Jia slumped on one of the large couches. They were looking up at the high ceiling where holograms of moons and stars were floating around.

Lincoln stayed by the stairs as Chad went over to Donna. Chad pointed in his direction, and she got up from the couch and walked toward him. Jia stared at him, but Lincoln turned away.

"I want you to try out for the Bandits on Saturday," he said to Donna.

"Why?" she replied.

"I saw you at the last race. You're fast. Like, really fast. And if that was your first time on a broom, imagine how much better you'll be with training," Lincoln said.

"You think I can be ready by Saturday?"

"I will make sure of it," he said. "Zina is your dorm monitor all this week. She'll allow you to sneak out past curfew so I can train you."

"If we get caught sneaking off campus, we could get in serious trouble."

"I've snuck off campus plenty of times and never got caught. If you want to race, this is the only way... You down or what?" Lincoln asked.

Donna leaned on the stair railing and placed her hand on her chin like she was in deep thought.

Even though she was right in front of Lincoln, he felt like she was so far away, so far away from the truth. *My sister has no idea who I really am.*

"Okay, let's do it. I want to race," Donna said.

He handed her a pack of gum.

"I know this trick. It makes you older."

"How do you know that?" he asked.

"Tamia gave us some so we could make it back to our dorm for curfew last weekend."

"Of course she did. She's always saving the day," Lincoln said. "Chew the gum when you reach the Gardens, and I'll come to get you. Nine o'clock. Every night, until Friday."

He walked off down the stairs.

Lincoln hadn't talked to his parents for a few days. But he had to inform them about Donna's dreams.

After the long walk to his father's office, he leaned against the wall by the door for a moment before knocking.

"Come in."

Professor DuVernay sat behind his desk, pausing his lunch as Lincoln entered.

"Hey, son," he greeted, setting aside his napkin. "Have you checked your tablet? We've been trying to contact you."

"I know. I need time to process everything," Lincoln responded.

"I understand."

"We have a bigger problem, though. Donna performed a dream-catcher dawa and dreamed about Elders in front of the entire class. The last thing we need is her drawing attention to her powers," Lincoln said.

His father sank into the chair and rubbed his face. Lincoln could see the exhaustion pulling at him, and beneath it, a flicker of worry he couldn't quite hide.

"Your mom and I are worried that if Donna learns the truth now, she will make a rash decision, like leaving Nawlins without the proper training. And the truth might trigger her anger and unleash powers that she cannot control."

"So, what do we do? Nothing?" Lincoln clapped back.

"Your mother is taking off work for a month to be at Nawlins more. She's going to recommend that Donna try meditation treatments to help prevent her anxiety. When she gets better at controlling her power, we will tell her."

"That's wasting time. If Mr. Jenkins is right, the Elders are planning an attack. We should be doing something now!"

"Do you remember how hard it was for you when you couldn't control it?"

How could he ever forget? His anxiety started in the ninth grade. It was the first time he went into pure-wizard form. Luckily, it happened at home, and his parents helped him get through it—well, Rima had to stun him with an energy beam to stop him. His power was greater than his young body could handle. But meditation helped him a lot.

"Trust me, son. Give her time," Charles said. "And we need to plan. We don't know who the Elders are, where they're hiding, or what positions they hold in the wizard community."

He stood and placed a firm hand on Lincoln's shoulder. "Your mother and I will meet with Mr. Jenkins soon, and when the time is right, we'll take action."

"Yes. We should be fighting back," Lincoln said.

"We?" Charles raised an eyebrow. "You won't be fighting anything. Your mother and I will reach out to our old allies. It's time to reestablish the Rebels."

"More secrets?" Lincoln said, pulling away from his father. "Who are the Rebels?"

Charles walked back to his seat and slowly sat, folding his legs and interlocking his hands.

"When your mom and I were in college, we formed a group with a bunch of friends who wanted to train together in case we had to fight evil wizards."

"Why would you need a group to fight evil wizards?" Lincoln raised his eyebrows.

"Just like there are bad Norms in this world who hurt people and commit crimes, there are bad wizards out there who do the same. We wanted to be able to protect ourselves and others if anything happened. We were a bunch of kids. We thought it was cool."

"Isn't that what the Wizard High Council is for? Why would you all need to be vigilantes?" Lincoln asked.

"At that time, we didn't trust those old wizards. We thought they could be corrupt. And it looks like we can't trust them now. I mean, what better way for the Elders to implement their plans than to have members in our government? Our best bet is to bring back the Rebels and establish our own High Council."

"Was Deedy part of the Rebels?"

Charles unfolded his legs and leaned forward. "Yes, he started the group. He was a smart man, always thinking ahead. He would say, 'It takes only one bad wizard to threaten humanity.'"

"Where were you Rebels when the Elders attacked us and killed my father?"

This was the question he'd been wanting to ask all along—the inevitable confrontation that was heavy on his heart.

Charles slumped in his chair.

"Lincoln, Rima and I flew there as fast as possible, but the damage was already done. We saw a dim light in the water below the bridge. Your father must have put his necklace on you that night, knowing that we would come looking for you. The diamond was shining from inside the protective spell your father cast around you."

Lincoln untucked his necklace and caressed the pendant.

"After we pulled you from the water, we had to make it look like an accident. Deedy would have made the same hard decision."

"When can I meet Catherine?" Lincoln asked, his voice almost cracking.

"During winter break, we'll travel to New York with Donna and tell them both everything. I promise."

"So, until then, I'm supposed to see Donna around campus and lie to her face. And I must live knowing my mother is out there, and I can't reach out to her. Thanks, Dad," Lincoln said, storming out of the office.

Lincoln checked the time on his smartwatch as he sat below the giant magnolia tree in the Gardens. 9:05 p.m. He frowned and exhaled noisily through his pursed lips.

A tall young woman entered the Gardens. She had braided hair and was wearing black sweats and a black hoodie. She was looking around as if she was lost.

"Donna?" Lincoln whispered.

"Yeah, it's me."

Emerging from the shadows, Lincoln stepped onto the concrete path.

"I didn't even recognize you," he admitted.

"I know, this gum is wild. I barely recognized myself in the mirror. Oh, and Noor braided my hair to add to the disguise. That's why I'm late."

"We need all the time we can get for your training. So, don't be late again."

Lincoln unwrapped a piece of gum and began to chew. After a few seconds, he grew an inch, and his body was more muscular.

"You have a beard now," Donna said, laughing.

Lincoln put on his fitted black hat and pulled the brim down low as he led the way through the college campus, expertly cutting corners and avoiding popular chill spots.

Exiting the campus, they walked to a private three-story parking garage across the street. Lincoln retrieved a remote from his black leather jacket and pressed the button. The garage's galvanized steel door folded open, revealing his Scout Bobber parked nearby. He retrieved two helmets from a storage cabinet beside the bike and handed the smaller one to Donna, who hesitated, eyeing the straps.

"What are you doing? Just put it on," Lincoln urged.

"I don't know how. Plus, I just got my hair done, it'll mess it up," Donna protested.

From his jacket, Lincoln retrieved a durag, offering it to her. "Do you know how to put this on?"

"Of course. I'm Black," Donna said, grabbing the durag and placing it over her braids.

"I need that back. I just got a fresh cut."

Donna gently lowered the helmet over her head. Lincoln smirked a little as he helped her buckle the straps. *So, this is what it feels like to be a big brother.*

"Hold on tight and keep your feet up, especially on turns," he instructed as she wrapped her arms around his waist.

The engine roared to life, echoing off the garage walls. "You ready?" he asked, glancing back at her.

"Yes," Donna exclaimed, her excitement palpable as they sped off into the night, the city lights blurring past them.

Chapter Twenty-One

"N ajua Nenosiri," Lincoln said, holding his wand in his right hand as his left gripped the clutch from the handlebar. He could feel his sister holding him tight as an opening started to liquefy from the protective bubble, revealing the Raceway. Lincoln drove through the space and parked on the gravel lot in front of the salon.

"That was fun. Can I drive your motorcycle next time?" Donna asked, smiling from ear to ear.

"Nice try. But, no. You're not wrecking my baby," he said. "Go to the middle of the field below the racetrack. I'll meet you there in a sec."

Lincoln went into the salon, grabbed a duffel bag from his locker, and then headed to the field. He tossed the bag to Donna with a nod. She caught it, unzipped it, and pulled out a pair of black racing boots, brown gloves, and goggles—the essentials.

"Hopefully, these fit. You and Mya seem about the same size," Lincoln said.

Donna took off her Chuck Taylors and slipped on the racing boots.

"These fit perfectly," she said, sitting on the ground, tying up the long laces.

"So... my parents told me your mom is in New York?" Lincoln said.

"Mmhm," Donna replied, lacing her boots quickly. She seemed more interested in getting into the flying lesson than talking.

"How is she doing?" Lincoln asked.

"She's doing better. She started rehab, which should help her walk better."

"Wait... Rehab? What happened to her? Why is she in rehab?"

Donna stopped tying her shoes and finally looked up at him. "Um, she had a stroke a couple of years ago that left her partially paralyzed on her left side. She had to learn how to use her basic motor functions again."

"That must have been devastating. I wish I could have been... I mean, I wish someone could've been there for you two," Lincoln said, dropping his head.

He clenched his fist. *What if I had been there? I could have stopped that stroke.* He could feel his anger building. His arms and neck felt hot and itchy. *Thump, thump, thump*—the pressure around his temples throbbed. He turned his back to Donna and started to walk away, taking deep breaths and massaging the sides of his face.

"Hey, where are you going?" Donna asked.

Lincoln wanted to scream. The throbbing in his head felt so bad he could feel the pain in his eye sockets. Pulling off his jacket, he walked to his motorcycle, knelt near the seat, and took deep breaths.

After a few seconds, he lifted the seat compartment and faked like he had gotten something out. He turned toward Donna and made sure she saw him forcefully putting something in the pocket of his jeans.

"My bad, I forgot my broom," he said, walking back to Donna. He removed his broom orb from his pocket, which was there the whole time.

"Oh, I thought you felt so bad about my mom you had to take a walk or something. I was like, whoa, he's got a lot of empathy for someone he doesn't know," Donna said.

"I am sorry to hear about your mom," Lincoln replied.

"Thanks. It was devastating. I did my best. But sometimes I felt helpless... You know... Like, I was just a kid. What could I do?"

"I feel you... I'm sorry for the loss of your brother, too." Lincoln stopped himself. *Damn, I shouldn't have said that.*

Donna stood up, staring at Lincoln. "How did you know I had a brother?" she asked in a sharp tone.

"Um... my mom told me about what happened," Lincoln said, thinking quickly.

"I never told Rima I had a brother. How does she know?" Donna asked.

"I think she pulled your files from your old school's records and found it there."

Donna folded her arms and looked away.

"Oh, well, um, thanks for the condolence... I bet it would have been nice growing up with a big brother. Maybe he could've been the one to teach me how to race if he were still here."

Lincoln smiled. *I am here.*

His head started to ring with a migraine. He turned away from Donna and massaged his temples with his index and middle fingers. He closed his eyes tightly and took some deep breaths. As the migraine subsided, he opened his eyes.

"Are you okay?" Donna asked.

"Yeah, I'm fine."

"I get anxiety attacks too, and I always do that thing you did with your fingers. The temple massage."

"What are you talking about?" Lincoln asked.

"When I first saw you at the welcome ceremony, you did that same thing with your hands. I know because I was having an anxiety attack at the same time, and I massaged my temples."

"It was just a little headache, not an anxiety attack," Lincoln said.

"If you say so," Donna responded. "Mine started when my mom first got sick. I guess I couldn't handle seeing her like that. At its worst... it feels like my head is going to explode. And recently my hands..." Now Donna looked uncomfortable.

"Your hands, what?" Lincoln asked.

"Ah, nothing. Never mind. It's nothing."

What if she's showing glimpses of her true power? Has she been in pure-wizard form?

"Uh, sorry if I was asking too many questions about your mother," he said. "But it's one of the reasons I want you on the Bandits: we are resilient."

"Thanks," Donna said.

"Let's get to work."

He tossed the black ornament in the air and it transformed into his broomstick.

"Let me see your broom," Lincoln requested.

Donna handed him the compact tube. He pressed the black button, and it morphed into a sleek black broom.

"I recognize this thing," Lincoln remarked.

He flipped the broom, revealing the initials *L & T* intricately carved into its base. He caught Donna looking at him with her arms crossed, giggling.

"What?" Lincoln said, clearing his throat.

He handed the broom back to Donna and got straight to business.

"Straddle the broom."

Donna climbed on, clipped her boot clasps onto the foot pegs, and gripped the handle. Her stance looked awkward—legs jutting out too far, posture too upright.

"Let's start with the proper riding stance and grip," Lincoln said, shaking his head. "Your hands should be about three inches from the tip of the broom. Are you right-handed?"

Donna nodded.

"Then your left hand goes first," he said.

She adjusted her grip.

"Now bring your legs in closer to the frame and lower your body closer to the broom."

He studied her form, then nodded.

"Good. Now you at least look like a racer."

Lincoln pressed a red-glowing button on the side of the broom and a pair of handlebars extended from both sides.

"These grips are for precision turning. But they add resistance which can slow you down."

He pressed the button again and the handlebars folded neatly back into the broom.

From his duffle, Lincoln pulled out a set of orange cones and arranged them in a straight line with a few feet of space between each one. He straddled his broom and demonstrated the cone weave drill, maneuvering through effortlessly. At the last cone, he dismounted and walked back to Donna.

"Racing in a straight line is easy. The turns are where most racers either win or lose the race. So, today we will focus on turns."

This exercise forced Donna to stay low to the ground while maintaining a slow and steady speed. She approached the first cone too fast and hit the second cone, falling off her broom.

Lincoln laughed. "You get an F for effort."

Donna got up, dusted herself off, straddled her broom, and prepared for another attempt at the cones.

She fell off again after clearing the second cone.

"I can't do it," she said, looking frustrated.

"Where is your confidence?" Lincoln asked.

Donna shrugged and put her head down. "There is no way I'm going to learn how to race by Saturday."

Lincoln observed his little sister. She picked a few strands of grass from the ground and angrily tossed them. She sighed and folded her arms.

I couldn't be there for you before... But I'm here now, Lincoln thought.

"Donna... You can do anything. You just have to believe in yourself. You gotta stand on business."

"What do you mean? 'Stand on business'?"

"It means you have to step up to the challenge and prove the doubters wrong. And in your case, you are your biggest doubter."

He walked over to her and offered his hand. She reached for his grip, and he pulled her to her feet.

"You're not maintaining a steady speed and your eyes are focusing on the cones... So, let's fix that," he said.

Lincoln got on his broom and rode alongside Donna, watching her every move. He demonstrated the proper speed for her to maintain perfect balance and control.

"Focus on the path ahead of you. The cones are just markers in your peripheral to use as a guide."

He maneuvered in front of her during the turns so she could mimic his movements. When they reached the last cone, Lincoln looked back, and she was right on his tail.

"Woohooo," Donna yelled as she successfully completed the course.

Lincoln escorted Donna back to the Gardens when they returned to campus.

"You did well today. Same time tomorrow. Don't be late this time," he said.

Donna discarded her gum in a nearby trash can, instantly reverting to her youthful appearance. Lincoln followed suit, pulling off his hat and unzipping his jacket.

"I think our fathers were friends," Donna said.

"Huh?"

She went into her back pocket and removed a Polaroid photo and handed it to him.

"How did you get this?"

"My mom mailed it to me. She said there were two of these and Charles DuVernay had the other. She said they were best friends."

"I don't know. I... Um... Maybe there was another Charles DuVernay in New Orleans that your dad knew."

"Well, my father's name was Sammy. Next time you see your dad, can you ask him?"

"Yeah, sure."

"Thanks. See ya tomorrow," Donna said. "Oh, I forgot to tell you, I saw you let off the gas at the race. You could have beaten Nnamdi by at least two broom lengths."

Lincoln stopped cold. He barely looked at her.

"Why did you do that?" Donna asked.

"I don't know what you're talking about," Lincoln said and walked away.

I know that jasmine scent, Lincoln thought to himself as he paused by the entrance of his dormitory.

"Lincoln."

"Tamia," he responded, turning to face her.

A quiet longing filled him as he noted her presence, too striking to ignore. "It's late. Why are you still up?" he asked.

"You know I enjoy my late-night walks," she responded. "You were training Donna tonight, weren't you?"

Lincoln smirked. *She knows me so well.*

"Why did you give her your broom?"

"Because I can tell she's special."

"Well, she's already faster than you ever were," Lincoln said, smiling.

Tamia playfully shoved him, her touch lingering, charged with an unspoken connection. They fell into silence, Lincoln simply absorbing her company.

"Lincoln, why have you been avoiding me?" Tamia finally said, her voice tinged with a mix of concern and hurt.

Lincoln looked down, the weight of his secrets pressing heavily on him. She stepped closer, tenderly lifting his chin with her warm brown hand to meet her gaze.

"It's not fair, Lincoln. You can't just shut me out like this."

"You don't understand. There's a lot going on right now," Lincoln confessed, his voice low.

"Then help me understand. I want to be here for you."

"I can't tell you. I don't want you to get hurt."

Tamia took his hands firmly in hers. "I can handle myself," she asserted, her eyes glistening with unshed tears.

Feeling the warmth of her hands, Lincoln realized he couldn't bear to keep pushing her away... and the truth was, he wasn't sure he could do this without her.

"If I tell you what's going on, can you promise that you won't tell anyone? No matter how crazy it all sounds."

"I promise. You know me, Lincoln."

"Let's take a walk," he suggested, needing the open space to gather his thoughts.

As they strolled towards the Gardens, Lincoln unfolded his burdens, telling her everything. When they reached a secluded bench, he dropped the bombshell.

"I have a sister."

"Who? Where is she?" Tamia asked.

Lincoln went silent. He put his head down again, then slowly met her gaze.

"Donna Marie," he said.

Tamia gasped. "How?"

"She's the reason we tied all this together. How we found out Catherine was my mother. She was pregnant with Donna when the Elders... when they killed my dad."

"What are your parents going to do about the Elders?" Tamia asked.

"I don't know. I'm not talking to them right now. They lied to me for so long by telling me my mother died... But I need your help to keep an eye on Donna. I'm afraid that she might go into pure-wizard form. If the Elders find out about her, they will come for her."

"I'll always help you," she said, touching his hand.

"I have to ask... Have you heard anything about the Elders from your parents? Do you think Augustin is still alive?"

She shook her head. "I didn't even know Elders existed until now... Augustin is my ancestor. I feel terrible. Lincoln, if they find out who you are... You're not safe here."

"I'm going to be fine, luv. I'm going to figure this out myself."

"You're not by yourself, Lincoln; you have me... And you can't do this alone anyway. No matter if you have the power of Solomon or not. I mean, look what happened to him. Go to your parents and make a plan."

"They don't even know what to do... Look, if anything happens to me, you have to protect Donna. Get her as far away from here as possible."

"Lincoln..."

"Promise me."

"I promise. But nothing is going to happen to you. I won't allow it," Tamia responded.

Lincoln grabbed her hand and kissed it.

"What's next for us?" she asked. "I miss you."

Lincoln had to stop himself from saying how much he missed her. Could he risk putting her in harm's way? What if the Elders found out about him and went after her too?

"What if we got back together... but kept it a secret until the Elders are defeated?" Lincoln asked.

Tamia smiled. "I like that idea."

Lincoln glanced around the Gardens.

"What are you looking for?" Tamia asked.

"Just checking if anyone's around... so I can kiss you."

"Well... I don't see anyone," she said, stepping closer.

"Hey, Tamia..." he said, inching in.

"Yes, Lincoln?" she replied, their lips nearly touching.

"I've missed you so much."

"Prove it."

As their lips met, Lincoln remembered exactly why he had fallen so hard for her.

Chapter Twenty-Two

One more day until the tryouts. It was the only thing Donna could think about all week. Early this morning, while walking to tutoring, she visualized herself on her broom and leaned into every curve on the sidewalk. Chad pointed at the clock when she arrived at the study booth.

"Sorry I'm late. I got home really late last night from broom training. Lincoln had me racing at full speed, and it was so fun."

"Sounds like you're ready for tomorrow," Chad said.

"I hope I make the team. That's all I want."

"You will," Chad assured her, his smile broad. "Not that we get everything we want in life."

Ha. What does he mean by that?

He accompanied his cheeky statement with an equally cheeky grin.

"What?" Chad said, still grinning.

"What?" Donna replied.

"Why are you staring at me?" Chad asked.

"I'm not staring at you."

"Yes, you are."

"Maybe I'm staring at your peanut head," Donna said. "Did you ever consider that? Now, you see... you shouldn't have asked."

It was supposed to be a joke, but Chad stared blankly at Donna, who was worried she must have offended him.

"Oh, God. I'm sorry. You know I'm only—"

Then his lips broke into a broad grin again. "At least I don't have a big juicy fat watermelon head," he said.

They both laughed.

"I can show you what your head looks like right now," Chad said.

He pulled out a tennis ball from his backpack. He placed the ball in the center of the table.

"Kukua," he said, waving his wand in a circular direction.

The tennis ball grew to about the size of a basketball.

"This is the spell we'll be working on today in class. For the spell to work, you must visualize the size of the object you want to grow or shrink."

"Kupungua," Chad said, waving his wand. The ball shrunk back to its standard size.

"Let me show you what your head looks like," Donna said.

She moved her wand in a circular motion.

"Kukua," she said. The ball grew in size until it took up the entire tabletop.

"Is my head really that big?" Chad asked, laughing.

"Sure is." Donna laughed. "Now we're even."

"Great spell. You're improving. Casie better watch out; you might surpass her test scores by the end of the term."

Donna blushed. "You think so?"

"I know so," he said.

"You won't beat my scores, though, watermelon head," Chad said.

Donna gave him a playful shove, and then there was a moment of quietness. They stared into each other's eyes, inching closer. As they got even closer, the school bell rang.

Lincoln parked his motorcycle on the side street, facing what seemed to be nothing more than another house in the area. A black iron fence guarded the exterior of the two-story home.

"What is this place?" Donna asked, getting off the bike.

"We finished your training pretty early, so I want to show you something here at the African American History Museum before returning to campus," Lincoln said. "If you want to."

"Yeah, cool." She nodded enthusiastically.

"This neighborhood is Treme. It's one of the oldest Black communities. And this museum was built in 1828. Inside are African costumes, musical instruments, handmade furniture, artwork, and other stuff," Lincoln said.

"Stuff?"

Lincoln rolled his eyes playfully and then, with a flick of his wand, the front gate creaked open. They walked down a pathway flanked by lush greenery leading to the museum's entrance. Pausing by a garden bed, Lincoln gestured to a set of plants that bloomed velvety black flowers, each with three petals.

"Did you know that the iris plant inspired the fleur-de-lis symbol?"

"I don't even know what an iris plant is?"

"These are iris plants," Lincoln replied, picking a flower from its stem. He handed the flower to Donna.

"Oh, yeah. I've seen these around Nawlins."

"These flowers are usually purple, but at this museum and at school they bloom black. My parents told me when the revolt members were blessed with powers, the iris plants around the area turned black. The wizards dug them up and planted them around campus and here."

"But, why here?"

"I'll show you."

He reached down and picked up a rock from the middle of the iris plants. He peeled off a piece of gray duct tape from the bottom of the rock and revealed a key.

"How did you know that key was there?" Donna asked.

"I volunteer here once a month to host tours. I lost the key once, so I put it here to avoid ever losing it again."

Lincoln opened the door, and they walked to a room at the back of the museum.

"Look around. Do you see anything familiar?" he asked.

Donna's eyes roved over the paintings until she spotted Nawlins' crest in a corner of a painting depicting an African woman in vintage attire cradling a baby.

Lincoln waved his wand at the crest, and a section of the wall near the painting crumbled away, revealing a hidden door.

"It's a wizard sanctuary that houses Nawlins' most ancient books and artifacts."

"In a public museum?" Donna asked, bewildered.

"Few wizards even know about it," Lincoln responded.

"And you keep the key duct-taped on the bottom of a rock?"

"Okay. Okay. Relax," he said.

"Wait... If only a few wizards know about this sanctuary, why are you showing me? You don't even know me. Why are you trusting me with this? Why are you even training me to fly a broom? All of this is too much. I'm not special," Donna said.

Lincoln paused. He tilted his head to the side and didn't break eye contact with her. "You're wrong... You are special. And I guess... I feel bad that you went so long not knowing you had this great power inside of you."

"I don't need you to feel bad for me. I don't want any pity."

"I'm not pitying you. I'm helping you. We all need a helping hand sometimes," Lincoln said. "So, we cool?"

"Yes. We are cool," Donna responded.

She wanted to ask if he had found out more about their fathers' friendship. That would explain a lot, but she didn't want to push him any further right now.

Lincoln pushed the door open as he appeared to have done 100 times before, stepping down into a spiral staircase. The shiny white floor illuminated with every step they took. Floating bookshelves hovered above the ground, and numerous paintings and pictures lined the walls. In the center of the sanctuary was a glass case. Donna gasped as she recognized the wand that floated in the cylinder glass that stretched to the top of the ceiling. The diamond wand glistened as she walked around the enclosure.

"Is this Solomon's real wand or a replica?" asked Donna, as she studied the magnificent object.

"It's real," Lincoln replied. "Wands from all the original revolt members disintegrated after their owners' death, except Solomon's."

"Has anyone else used it after Solomon?"

Lincoln stood still, looking off to the side, like he was deep in thought.

Donna waved her hand over his eyes. "You good?"

"Yeah. I heard some have tried to use Solomon's wand but failed. It only worked for him."

"Maybe someone from his bloodline could use it. I mean, if he had any descendants," Donna said.

Lincoln got quiet again. He looked at the wand and back at Donna.

"I guess we will never know," he replied.

In the center of the room, near Solomon's wand, were *The Book of Giza* and *The Book of Knowledge*. They lay side by side in a square glass enclosure. The books were thick and looked heavy. Two Bronze iron straps covered the black leather of *The Book of Giza*. Black iron straps covered the light brown leather of *The Book of Knowledge*.

"The ancient texts are here? For books that are over two hundred years old, they look in great shape, like new."

"Tampering with ancient texts is against the code of Nawlins," Lincoln said.

"They are so big. And those straps look heavy," said Donna, pressing her face against the glass. "Wait a minute. I think one of the straps on *The Book of Giza* is open."

"That's not possible."

Lincoln got closer to the glass. He looked perplexed. "The strap is undone."

"What does that mean?" Donna asked.

"No one has opened these books in over a century because only a wand of an original Coven member can open them."

"So, how is the strap undone then?" Donna pressed, her gaze following Lincoln's every move.

Lincoln walked around the glass, checking out the book from different angles. "They are planning something," he mumbled.

"Who's planning what?" Donna's question sliced through the thick air of mystery.

"Sorry, it's nothing. The strap probably came loose over time... Come on, let's go."

Donna could tell there was more he wasn't sharing. His sudden urgency to leave and his vague responses raised more questions than answers.

"But I want to check out the rest of this place."

"Um, I have to do some last-minute homework I forgot about," Lincoln said too quickly, clearly evasive.

Donna watched him, her suspicions growing. *What is he hiding? And who is planning something?* Despite his attempts to reassure her, his evident concern hinted at deeper, hidden troubles.

NEW ORLEANS
LOUISIANA

Chapter Twenty-Three

There weren't many people at the Raceway because it was just a tryout. Some of the racers were present, spectating new riders. Other students were there to practice and have a little fun.

Two other students were racing for a spot in the Bandits, a tall boy with an Afro and a standoffish-looking girl wearing a cowboy hat and cowboy boots. Donna was standing against a wall in the racing salon near her competitors, who were sitting on a floating couch.

"You can sit down with us if you want," the boy said, dangling his feet from the floating couch.

"No, thank you. Those things make me sleepy," Donna responded.

"Suit yourself. I'm Jon, by the way."

"I'm Donna."

"The girl next to me is Erica. She doesn't talk much."

"I talk. I just don't want to talk to y'all. Both of y'all are my competition. I'm here to win, not make friends," Erica said in a thick country accent.

"Where are you from? Texas or something?" Jon asked.

"Opelousas, Louisiana," Erica replied with a snappy attitude.

"My bad, luv. I bet you grew up on a farm, huh," Jon said.

"I did. And don't call me luv. I'm not your luv or baby or whatever you New Orleans people say. Now, stop talking to me. I'm trying to focus."

"She's mean," Jon said, turning his face to Donna and whispering.

Erica rolled her eyes at him. Donna placed her hand over her mouth as she giggled. Just then, Lincoln strode into the salon, his presence commanding attention.

"Let's go, racers. It's time to find our new Bandit."

Lincoln held the door open for them. Donna was the last to exit.

As they headed out, Lincoln pulled Donna aside and whispered, "Remember, you're fast, so the straightaway is your best friend."

Lacey took center stage on the racetrack, her voice carrying across the sparse crowd.

"Welcome, racers and spectators! This race is to determine the newest member of the Bandits. In lane two, we have Erica, a senior from Opelousas who is a legacy with the Bandits. Her mom was on the relay team twenty years ago."

The small crowd clapped and cheered.

"In lane three, we have Jon, a freshman track star from New Orleans, East. Can he fly as fast as he can run?"

A couple of dudes, probably his track teammates, cheered for Jon as they made a noise that sounded like a dog barking. *Boys.*

"In lane four, we have Donna Marie, all the way from the Bronx."

Donna was laser-focused as she hovered in her lane, waiting for the signal light to turn green. She broke her focus and smirked as she faintly heard Jia scream her name.

"Racers, are you ready?"

Donna nodded.

"On your marks."

Donna gripped her broom handle.

"Set."

"Never look back and never focus on the competition. Just race," Donna said to herself.

"Go!"

The green flame ignited, and the racers took off.

Jon surged ahead, but Donna was quick on his heels, with Erica not far behind. As the first turn loomed, Donna gauged her entry meticulously, swooping in with precision. She closed in on Jon, the gap narrowing to a single broomstick, but Erica was on her tail.

The straightaway is your best friend. Lincoln's advice echoed in her mind as she approached the second straightaway.

She exited the turn with tremendous breakaway speed, passing Jon as he looked back.

Donna realized she was coming in too hot as the second turn approached.

She pressed the glowing red button on her broom, deploying the handlebars for better control. She managed to stabilize just in time, but Jon seized the opportunity to close the distance.

Determined to recover from her mishap, Donna hugged the arch and picked up speed.

As they entered the last straightaway, Donna glanced over and saw Jon pressing a glowing blue button on the side of his broom. She could hear the sound of a vent channeling air through his broom. He picked up speed, his broom whistling as he started to pull away.

Donna pressed the red button on her broom again, retracting its handlebars, which gave her a little boost in speed. She leaned forward and kept her attention locked on the hologram-checkered finish line floating at the end of the straightaway.

She maintained her speed, flying through the finish line.

"Donna Marie is the Bandits' new racer!"

Donna made her way to Noor and Jia, who were jumping up and down, hugging each other.

"Yay, Donna!" the girls screamed.

"I knew you could do it," Noor said.

"Light work, sis. Congrats," Jia said. "That was amazing."

"Thanks, guys," Donna said.

Chad and Lincoln walked up to Donna.

"Welcome to the Bandits," Chad said, jumping in the air with a big smile on his face.

Donna blushed and bit her lip. Then she joined in.

"I did it. I am a racer!" she said, jumping up and down like a little kid with Chad.

Lincoln threw Donna a black T-shirt with "Bandits" written across it.

"I'll see you at practice tomorrow. We have a week to get you ready for the big relay next weekend," he said.

"Thanks for training me, Lincoln."

"You're welcome... And don't wear that shirt on campus," he said, walking away.

"I told you you'd make the team," Chad said.

"You sure did," Donna replied.

"Tomorrow evening, my grandmother is making her signature red beans and rice. You should pass by. You could come around four or five, and we can take the streetcar back to campus together?"

"I'm down for that," she said.

"Cool... I'll see you tomorrow," Chad said before walking off after Lincoln.

"Donna has a boyfriend. Donna has a boyfriend," Jia and Noor sang.

"We're just friends and study buddies," Donna said.

"Study buddies... Mm-hmm...."

After Donna's victory, the girls went to the CC for milkshakes.

As they reached the top of the staircase leading to their favorite large couch, Donna spotted Raine sitting by herself, drinking a smoothie.

"You can join us on the couch if you like," Donna said.

"Sure. Thanks," Raine replied.

"You have a lot of paint on your clothes," Jia noted as Raine took a seat.

"Yeah, I'm working on something new," Raine said, pointing to a big canvas propped on an easel.

"Are you painting a bat? Eww, they are ugly creatures," Jia said.

"I think they are remarkable animals. Because just like me, they are misunderstood. I know people think I'm weird because I dress differently and what I talk about... but I'm me. And I'm proud of me. Just like this bat I'm painting; he might be ugly, but he owns it."

"You're very talented. And don't mind Jia; she doesn't have an eye for the arts. I'm a creative myself. I make music. It runs in my family. My father is a musician," Noor said.

"Art runs in my family, too. My ancestor from the revolt did some of the original artwork around the school. He actually drew the Coven members' paintings in the entrance hall," said Raine.

"Hey, I do have an eye for the arts! Look at these expensive shoes! These are art!" Jia said, putting her feet on the table.

"Sure," Raine said, raising her eyebrows.

"Does it feel cool every time you walk past those paintings knowing that your ancestor did that?" Donna asked.

"Honestly, the one of Augustin creeps me out. She looks so mean," Raine said.

The girls shared a laugh.

"Your ancestor could have painted her with a smile or something," said Donna.

"I think she's painted perfectly the way she is: PAS BON," Jia said.

"What does that mean in English?"

"Mean, violent, soulless," Jia answered.

Donna shook her head. *That's pretty harsh,* she thought.

"Whoa there, Jia," Noor said.

"What? I don't know how she was in real life... But, Raine, doesn't an artist paint the truth? I'm sure your ancestor painted her the way she acted."

Raine was quiet for a few seconds.

"You know what, Jia? You just might have an eye for the arts because you are right. An artist's real work stems from the truth. I guess my ancestor saw her the way she's painted, which is, yeah, kinda pas bon." Raine shrugged and took a sip of her smoothie.

"Do I hear y'all bashing my ancestor?" Casie said, standing at the door of the game room. "She's an original Coven member, show some respect."

"How about you show us some respect and not butt in on our conversation," Jia said.

"Excuse you! I was leaving the game room. What do you want me to do, cover my ears?" Casie said.

"Maybe," Jia replied, matching her attitude.

What is going on? Jia really hates this girl.

Casie and Jia finally stopped giving each other the death stare when Jay and Chike walked up to the couch in their sweaty football clothes. Chike sat beside Noor at the edge of the couch and kissed her on the cheek.

"Ew, bae, you're all sweaty and stinky," Noor complained, playfully shoving him away.

"My bad, we just got out of practice," Chike replied.

"Aww, you guys are so cute," Jia cooed.

"I heard you made the Bandits. Congratulations," Jay whispered to Donna, taking a seat next to her.

"I guess that makes us rivals now?" Donna teased.

"Looks like it," Jay replied, flashing a playful grin "Are you still coming to the football game tomorrow? We're playing St. Augustine, one of our biggest rivals. It's going to be popping because it's the season's only Sunday game."

"I have race practice in the morning," Donna replied.

"The game's in the afternoon. Swing by after?" Jay suggested.

"Okay, I can't stay long, though. I have plans in the evening."

"You won't make a difference. The Bandits are still trash," Casie said, sitting on the edge of the couch. She rudely rolled her eyes at Donna and Donna rolled her eyes back at her.

"Let's go, brother," Casie said, tugging at Jay's arm as they stood up to join the rest of the Coven.

Chapter Twenty-Four

Nawlins' football arena was packed with fans. Donna, Noor, and Jia were sitting on the first row on the bleachers near the Nawlins players' bench. Donna was on the edge of her seat watching Nawlins battle back and forth with St. Augustine. This was a great contrast to the lackluster performances of Donna's former school's team, which had managed only one winning season in the last decade. The excitement of the closely contested game was something entirely new to her.

The score was 35-34 with five seconds left in the fourth quarter. St. Augustine had just scored a touchdown.

"Nawlins and St. Augustine battle almost every year for the divisional championship, and whoever wins that game usually wins the state championship," Noor said to Donna.

Wizards weren't allowed to use magic in the presence of Norms, so Nawlins' football team would win or lose this game using their athletic talent. St. Augustine were the reigning champs, so they owned the bragging rights—their fans made it known, flashing their purple and gold championship banners and other memorabilia.

"With only five seconds left on the clock, can Nawlins score on the kickoff to win the game?" the announcer said into the microphone.

Chike received the kickoff and ran toward the right side of the field, but the defenders were closing in fast. Jay, who was trailing behind, cut left, and Chike lateraled the ball to him. Jay caught it and sprinted up the left sideline. He was fast. A St. Augustine player lunged for a tackle, but Jay juked right, sending the defender out of bounds.

"No one is in front of him! Jay's about to take it in. The thirty! The twenty! The ten! Touchdown! Nawlins wins with no seconds left on the clock," the announcer yelled.

The crowd went crazy. Nawlins' fans rushed to the field to congratulate their team.

Jay's teammates lifted him in the air as they chanted his name.

"Ja-ay! Ja-ay! Ja-ay!"

"C'mon, we're going to the Raceway to celebrate," Noor told Donna.

Donna and Jay took their brooms out on the track to get away from the loud crowd celebrating in the salon. Other students were flying around, having fun, and practicing tricks.

"Want to see something cool?" Jay asked.

"Sure. Show me what you got," Donna replied.

Jay pulled up on the front of his broom and back-flipped in the air.

"Impressive. I would probably fall off my broom if I tried that," Donna said.

"Yeah, that trick is hard... But I'm sure you have something up your sleeve," Jay said.

Donna attempted to stand on her broom. Jay hovered close to her and held her arm as she stood. She laughed and shook her curly hair as adrenaline filled her body at the warmth of his touch. She wasn't used to a boy's hands on her skin.

Jay got closer, his face just inches from Donna's.

The world around her went quiet as she stared into his eyes.

Her gaze dropped to his lips, then butterflies stampeded her stomach and her knees buckled.

Jay tightened his grip on her arm and gently lowered her back onto her broom.

"Careful," he said.

"Sorry. I lost my train of thought," Donna replied. *You made me lose my train of thought.* That is what she wanted to say.

"That was a neat trick. But I think mine was better," Jay said.

"Maybe I'll try a backflip soon."

"I've never seen a girl do a backflip. Told you, it's hard."

"Wait, so... Just because a trick is hard, a girl can't do it?"

"Nah, nah... I just think girls can't do some stuff that guys do?"

"Like backflips on a broom?"

"Okay, okay. I can see how that sounded pretty bad... What I meant was... I don't want you to hurt yourself. You're too pretty to fall down and scrape up your face."

Donna blushed. *He thinks I'm pretty?*

"Yo, Jay. You owe me a ping-pong rematch before curfew. Let's do this!" Ryan shouted from the salon.

"Aight, bet. I'm coming!" Jay shouted back. "Want to race to the salon?" he grinned at Donna.

"Loser has to do the other's math homework?" Donna replied, tightening her gloves.

"Deal."

As Donna rounded the corner toward Nawlins' main entrance, she spotted Monique checking other students in for curfew on her tablet.

Jay walked up from behind her and wrapped his arm around her shoulder.

"It's 7:50 p.m. We have a couple of minutes to spare," he said.

"You know Monique will count every second we're late. She doesn't play around," Noor said from behind as she and Chike walked side by side, holding hands.

Donna's heart dropped when she noticed Chad approaching alone from another direction—she had completely forgotten to meet him at his grandparents' house as promised. "Hey, I'll catch up with you guys later," she said.

Chad, his gaze down, didn't even glance Donna's way as he reached Monique to check in. He walked through the doorway without a word to her.

Donna caught up to him in the entrance hall, reaching out to stop him with a gentle touch on his arm. "Hey," she called out. "You don't have to walk away like that."

Chad's voice surged with a sharp edge. "Yeah, well you were supposed to be—"

Cutting him off, Donna already knew the grievance. "I forgot. I'm really sorry, Chad. I got caught up and it totally slipped my mind."

"Yeah, it looks like you and Jay had other plans. It's all good," he said.

He left Donna standing in the entrance hall, disappointed in herself for not keeping her word.

What if he doesn't forgive me? Why do I care so much? He's just a boy... No, he's not just a boy; I care about him. He's a good friend. So many thoughts filled her head.

"Boy problems, I see," Monique said.

"No. Chad's just a friend."

"It seems he's more than just a friend, or you wouldn't have that sad puppy look on your face."

"I don't have a sad puppy look on my face," Donna said.

"Ahh, yes you do."

Chapter Twenty-Five

On Sunday evenings, Chad was usually studying in the CC. Donna had it in her mind that she would storm in there and make him forgive her. She critiqued herself in her bathroom mirror, fussing with her freshly diffused curls. She experimented pulling her hair up into a ponytail, then letting it fall again. "Mr. Whiskers?" Donna called.

Mr. Whiskers walked into the bathroom and greeted Donna with a meow.

"Should I wear my hair up or down? I just washed, detangled, and curled it all by myself. Man, I miss Auntie Jacquie's help."

Mr. Whiskers walked out of the bathroom as if he didn't care to talk about the subject.

"Really? I feed you, bathe you, and this is the thanks I get?" Donna huffed, deciding to let her curls hang loose.

Before leaving, she snagged a cannoli from the fridge—a peace offering for Chad, encased in a small plastic container.

If this boy isn't in the CC, I will be pissed. I spent eight whole bucks on this dessert, and it better not go to waste.

As Donna walked down the last step into the dormitory lobby, she spotted Raine standing unusually still in front of the grandfather clock.

"Hey, Raine."

Raine didn't respond, her posture rigid, her usual punky artist attire replaced by a drab gray skirt and an itchy-looking blouse.

"Raine, you okay?" Donna approached, concerned.

Raine continued to stare at the clock, unblinking and eerily still.

"Raine?" Donna waved a hand in front of her face.

The clock struck six, playing a soothing melody. As the last note faded, Raine awkwardly turned and walked past Donna without a word.

Was that some kind of weird wizard trance? Donna pondered, puzzled by Raine's odd behavior.

When she made it to the CC, Donna peeped her head over the railing leading to the lounge area, and sure enough, Chad was sitting on one of the couches with a notebook on his lap.

"Ahem." Donna's failed attempt to clear her throat.

"What is that?" Chad asked, gesturing to the container.

"A gift to apologize for missing red beans night with you and your family. It's a cannoli. I walked around the entire French Quarter looking for a pastry shop that sold one."

"Thanks," Chad said, smiling.

"So, are we cool?" Donna asked.

"Yeah. We're good," he said, reaching out his hand for a shake.

Donna shook his hand, smiling as she looked into his eyes.

"Well, I'll see you in class tomorrow," she said, walking away.

"Wait," Chad said, stopping Donna in her tracks. "Do you want to share it?" he asked, opening the container.

"I would love to."

Good conversation over a tasty treat made an hour and change feel like minutes. It was almost closing time for the CC.

"I must admit, a cannoli might be better than a beignet," Chad said.

"I won't tell anyone you said that, as long as I can get another invite to try your grandmother's cooking."

"I'll see what I can do."

"And for the record, Jay and I are just friends," Donna said.

"It's cool. You and I are just friends too. I shouldn't have reacted the way I did."

The lights began to dim as Mr. Espree appeared around the corner, mop in hand. "Don't you kids have curfew?"

Six other mops dipped themselves into the nearby bucket. Soapy water splashed across the floor as they began to clean.

"Yes, sir. We are leaving now," Chad answered. "Come on, Donna, I'll walk you to your dorm."

They stopped at the dorm entrance. The patio light above the sliding glass door shone into Chad's warm brown eyes, and Donna felt herself getting lost in them.

"There you go with that staring stuff again, lil baabyy," Chad said.

"I think I know the real you," Donna said.

"Oh, yeah? What's the real me?"

"When I first met you, I thought you were this hard boy from the hood," Donna said. "But you have a kind, sensitive heart."

"I'm not sensitive. And I'm proud I'm from the hood. I came from nothing, but it made me work harder than all the kids here," Chad said.

"I mean sensitive in a good way. Like you care about people."

"If you say so," Chad responded.

"What I'm trying to say is, I know how it feels to be alone, like no one understands you because of what you've been through. But you're not alone; you have a friend in me," Donna said.

"Hold on... Did you just quote that famous *Toy Story* song?"

"Boy, if you don't shut up," Donna said, laughing.

"Thank you, Donna Marie. And thanks again for the cannoli," Chad said.

"You're welcome. Your head is still shaped like a peanut, by the way," Donna said. She laughed and playfully grabbed his arm. Chad flashed a smile.

"You should smile more. It's cute," Donna said.

Zina rushed around the corner, her wand casting a frantic beam of light. "Donna, get inside. A Loyal is on the loose. Fang escaped from her enclosure and is roaming around campus," Zina said. "You too, Chad. Report to your dorm now."

Donna hurried inside, but when she opened the door to her room, Mr. Whiskers didn't greet her. She checked under the bed, in the closet, and in the bathroom but couldn't find him. A slight breeze in the room made her realize she'd left the window open again.

Black cat hair covered the white windowsill. Heart pounding, Donna flung the window wide open and peered out into the night. A distant howl pierced the quiet, fueling her urgency.

She dashed out the door, the lobby empty and echoing her quick steps as she slipped through the sliding doors into the uncertain night.

"Mr. Whiskers?" Donna whispered, moving toward the black rosebushes by the luxury suite-style living quarters, which came with a hefty price, way out of her budget.

She was taking an enormous risk being outside. If Fang was hungry, would she go after a small cat or a full-course meal like Donna? Not to mention, their last encounter hadn't gone well. But Donna wasn't worried about herself; her priority was finding her pet.

She stepped into one of the rosebushes in front of a balcony. She shined a light from the tip of her wand onto the ground.

"Mr. Whiskers, where are you?" she whispered.

"Donna?" a voice said.

Donna looked up, and Jay was peeping over the balcony's railing.

"Shhh," she told him.

"What are you doing?" Jay whispered.

"My cat escaped. I have to find him before Fang does."

"You have a cat? On campus? How?"

"Your mom signed off on it."

"Dang, she doesn't let me bring my dog on campus... But I'm down for an adventure, let me help you find it," Jay said before disappearing.

"What? No, I can't ask you to do that," Donna said, trying to stay quiet.

Before she could walk away, Jay jumped over the balcony railing.

"Let's find this cat," Jay said as he freed himself from rose petals and thorns.

Donna and Jay crept toward the outskirts of the school, dodging faculty and staff. Donna was terrified as she recollected Fang's sharp teeth. And she was so big, probably three or four times the size of a regular wolf. *Please don't eat me. Please don't eat me*, she repeated to herself as she timidly flashed the light from her wand on every shadow and sound she encountered.

They crossed a small wooden bridge at the edge of campus, the boards creaking softly beneath their steps. Below, fluorescent water shimmered blue as it curled around the circular land boundary, beyond which stretched a vast green pasture.

"What is this place?" Donna inquired, peering over the bridge railing with wide eyes.

"It is called the Oasis. Come on, this way. Your cat could be by the fountain. There are fish in there," Jay said, grabbing Donna's hand. She felt a tingle from Jay's touch—a brief distraction from the fear.

White lights pointed at the towering trees that formed a privacy barrier around the perimeter, leading to limited visibility in the center of the pasture. Jay led the way down the middle of trimmed grass toward a fountain in the back of the Oasis.

Donna tightly held Jay's hand, trailing behind, head on a swivel. Fang was his family's pet, so maybe she would listen to Jay if she leaped from the darkness.

A pond the size of two swimming pools was in front of the massive rock-fall water fountain.

Donna stepped in front of the pond, admiring the water as its color quickly transitioned to orange, blue, red, and yellow, fiercely flowing down the colossal spillways. Bright goldfish swam her way as she dipped her hand in the water, only to scatter as a deep growl resonated from the dark center of the pasture.

Whirling around, Donna saw Fang advancing from the shadows.

"Fang, heel," Jay commanded, his flashlight beam cutting through the darkness toward the approaching beast.

Fang paused, her large, glowing yellow eyes focusing intently on Donna, then growled, crouching with her tail raised. Drool dripped from her gold fangs as she bared her teeth.

"I am a Decken. My mother is your owner, so you must listen to me," Jay asserted, his voice firm.

Fang snapped her jaws.

"Nidhamu," Jay said.

A blue vapor fired from his wand. Fang juked out of the way of the taming spell. Jay fired another beam at Fang, who juked out of the way again, her claws tearing at the grass as she fixed her gaze on Donna.

Donna took off running, and Fang jumped in her direction, landing squarely in front of her. Jay ran in between them and Fang struck him with her paw, sending him crashing against the fountain's edge.

Donna ran back to the fountain and crouched by Jay.

Fang walked closer, snapping her jaws with every step, drool dripping from her mouth.

"Please don't eat me. I don't even taste good."

Donna's hair moved as something breathed heavily behind her. Whatever it was, it was massive by the way its breath breezed over her.

She covered her head as an enormous black panther leaped from the edge of the fountain behind her, growling.

Donna slid back against the fountain as she watched the stare-down between the two Loyals.

They continued to peer into each other's eyes, growling and snapping. The black panther rose on its hind legs, letting out a roar as it displayed its dominance. Fang crouched down as she transformed back into a puppy.

The panther looked back at Donna and slowly stepped toward her.

She froze, bracing herself, eyes squeezed shut, then flinched as a cold, prickly tongue swept across her cheek.

When she opened her eyes, the panther transformed into a cat and brushed against Donna's legs. Speechless, Donna stared as Mr. Whiskers looked up at her and let out a soft, familiar purr.

All this time, he was a Loyal.

Jay woke up, wincing as he grabbed his head.

"Ow... Am I bleeding?" he asked, showing the crown of his head to Donna.

"No. But it does look lumpy."

Mr. Whiskers pranced back to Fang. The two Loyals licked each other and played around on the grass.

Flashes of light appeared from the entrance of the Oasis. Professor DuVernay and Professor Hunt drew their wands toward Fang.

"Are you two, okay?" Professor DuVernay asked.

"Yes, we are fine," Jay quickly replied. "I just slipped and hit my head on the fountain as I was trying to get Donna's cat."

"Yeah. My cat escaped from my room, and Jay and I went looking for him. He was stuck at the top of the fountain."

Carrying a small cage, Professor Hunt walked slowly toward Fang.

"Careful. Loyals can be unpredictable," Professor DuVernay said, his wand still in hand ready to intervene.

Professor Hunt placed the cage in front of Fang, and the puppy whimpered while walking inside.

Mr. Whiskers ran into Donna's arms, curling himself into a ball. Donna hesitated before petting him.

Chancellor Decken hurried into the medical bay, her presence immediately shifting the atmosphere. Jay, nursing a head wound with an ice pack, was being monitored for a concussion and had to remain overnight for observation. Professor DuVernay moved aside, allowing the Chancellor to approach her son with a stern expression.

"Why were you out of your dorm past curfew?" she asked.

"He was helping me, Chancellor," Donna interjected, holding Mr. Whiskers close. "My cat escaped, and Jay helped me find him."

"Fang could have killed you both."

"She's right," Professor DuVernay confirmed.

"Both of you get detention," the Chancellor said.

"Come on, Ma," Jay complained.

"Mind your language. Remember, I'm not just your mother; I'm also your Chancellor," she reminded him.

Donna clutched Mr. Whiskers tighter.

"And, Donna, if that cat gets out again, you'll force me to send him back to New York."

"I'm sorry, ma'am. It won't happen again," Donna promised quickly.

"Consider the consequences if I had to inform your mother about a tragedy involving Fang. Think about the repercussions for our school and the entire wizard community," the Chancellor said, her voice laden with the gravity of potential disasters.

Donna hung her head. "I'm sorry."

"Come on, Donna, I'll walk you back to your dorm," Professor DuVernay said.

"I shall keep a close eye on you, Donna Marie," the Chancellor concluded.

Donna thought Professor DuVernay would scold her, but he didn't say a peep.

She wanted to ask him about her father, but felt she'd caused enough trouble today.

Mr. Whiskers looked up at Donna with his round black eyes that seemed to disappear into the darkness. He stared at her as if he was trying to tell her, *I was protecting you because you're my owner.*

She brought him closer to her face and kissed him on his tiny head. "Thank you," Donna whispered. "It can be our secret."

"What did you say?" Professor DuVernay asked.

"Oh, nothing. I was just telling Mr. Whiskers he's punished for sneaking out."

"You need to do a better job securing your dorm to make sure he can't escape," Professor DuVernay said as they stopped by the dorm entrance. His expression brightened. "Rima is looking forward to seeing you tomorrow. She asks about you all the time."

"Can't wait to see her. She's done so much for me and my family," Donna said.

Through the sliding glass doors, Donna could see Zina waiting for her by the grandfather clock.

"Oh, I almost forgot," he said, digging in his pockets. "I found his collar on the ground near the fountain. Looks like it ripped. I wonder how that happened?"

"I don't know. Maybe it got caught on the fountain somehow."

"I'm surprised Mr. Whiskers made it through without a scratch in the presence of Fang," Professor DuVernay added, handing the collar to her.

"Maybe it was luck," Donna replied.

"I don't believe in luck or coincidences," he said, giving Mr. Whiskers a pat before walking off.

Does he know? Donna thought as she watched him walk away.

Chapter Twenty-Six

At her old school, detention was held after school; she had never been, but the bad kids in her class constantly talked about it like it was something to brag about. But at Nawlins, detention was early in the morning. "7:30 a.m. detention encourages discipline" was explained in the disciplinary email she received last night. Donna was just happy that the Chancellor didn't contact her mom about her breaking the rules. The last thing she wanted was for her mom to worry that she was misbehaving, which she wasn't; she had to sneak out to save her cat. Well... Being part of a secret racing society could probably get her expelled.

Dang, am I a bad kid now? Donna thought, as she got ready to meet Rima before her detention session. Before leaving her room, she gave Mr. Whiskers a stare, seeing him still sleeping in his bed.

"Please, don't turn into a panther. You won't even fit in this room," Donna said under her breath.

Oh, almost forgot. She stopped herself in the doorway. She grabbed the Polaroid photo from her desk and placed it in the front pocket of her backpack.

Donna yawned as she made her way to the administration building. The only people she saw on her way were some cafeteria staff, janitors, and a few professors. It seemed like she was the only student up and active this morning.

Rima was sitting at her desk, typing on her computer, when Donna entered her office.

"Donna Marie!" Rima said, getting up to greet her. "How are you? How are you liking Nawlins? I'm sorry I've been so busy and out of touch."

"I'm doing great. I'm loving it here."

"That's good to hear. Take a seat... My husband tells me you're improving in your wizard classes."

"Yes. I'm finally getting the hang of this wizard thing," Donna said, sitting down in the chair in front of Rima's desk.

"And your mother and Jacquie? How are they?"

"I think Auntie Jacquie misses me the most," Donna said, giggling. "She told me she always barges in my apartment door thinking I'm still there... And my mom is doing better. Thank you so much for helping her."

"No problem. It brings me joy to help others, that's why I became a doctor. That reminds me, how is the anxiety holding up?"

Donna paused. *Shoot, do I tell her I had an attack when I first saw Lincoln at the welcome ceremony?*

"I haven't had one since I learned that I was a wizard."

"No bad headaches? Abnormal itchy skin? Shortness of breath?"

Yes. I've had all that.

"No. Nothing."

"What about your hands?"

"Huh?" Donna blurted.

"Have you experienced any tingling in your hands or seen any bright colors around them?"

"I don't understand."

"Sometimes you... Well, not you... But I've had one patient tell me when he had real bad anxiety attacks, he sometimes saw things coming from his hands."

"Is that normal?" Donna asked hopefully.

"The shortness of breath can cause a hallucination, which is treatable. So, you should tell me if you've experienced those things."

Donna looked down at her hands, turning them back and forth. She thought really hard about telling Rima about the night she was attacked in New York, when she saw a bright glow radiating from her hands.

It never happened again. So, it's not a big deal. Except the incident with Mr. Walks...

"No. I've never experienced anything like that. But if I do, I'll let you know," Donna said, forcing a smile.

"Great. So, even though you haven't had any recent attacks, meditation is a great method for prevention, and your mom agreed. We want to make sure they don't come back. So, are you ready for your first meditation session?"

"Yeah, let's do it."

Rima sat a mini-Bluetooth speaker on her desk and turned on some calming sounds.

"Can you take a seat on the couch near the fireplace, please?"

"Sure. But those floating couches make me sleepy, and I've been yawning all morning."

"Just do your best to relax. Lay down and cross your arms."

Donna took a seat and stared at the white ceiling. She inhaled deeply as she crossed her arms.

"When your anxiety is at its peak, how are you usually feeling before it happens?"

"Um... It happens when I go see my mom. Or when I'm in danger. Or when I think about my family."

"And what does that make you feel?"

"Angry," Donna replied, her breathing getting louder.

"When you feel that anger, think of something that makes you happy. Like your mother. She loves you. She cares about you. And you're making her proud."

Donna thought about her mom and how she was finally in physical therapy. It gave her hope. Her breathing calmed.

Rima turned off the music.

"Anger is the main trigger. So, next time something upsets you, think of your mother. Let the joy she brings fill you up."

The couch lowered back to the ground and Donna sat up.

"That's it for our first session. Let's meet every week. I'll send you an email with a schedule."

"Okay, thanks again for helping me with this."

"You're welcome. Make sure you let me know if you have another attack."

"Will do... Um, there is something I would like to ask."

"Sure, what is it?"

Donna went into her backpack and carefully removed the picture. Rima's face went blank when she handed it to her.

"My mom sent me that. Said that my father gave another version to his best friend, Charles DuVernay."

Rima didn't say anything, just continued to stare at the Polaroid.

"Did my father go to Nawlins? Was he friends with Professor DuVernay?"

When Rima finally glanced at Donna, she looked sad.

"I don't know anyone in this photo. I'm sorry."

"But, Rima..."

"Sorry, I have a meeting to get to," Rima said, handing the photo back to Donna.

On her walk to detention, Donna couldn't help but think Rima was holding something from her. *Why would she lie about knowing my father?* The detention lab was located on the first floor of the English department. The ambiance in the room reminded her of her old high school. The tarnished white tile floors had various chips and scratches. White cement walls enclosed the square room. Navy-blue, hard plastic desk/chair combo seats were spread throughout the classroom. In front of the desks was a plain green chalkboard covering the entire twenty-five-meter wall. A dry eraser and broken chalk lay on a pallet below the board.

Donna took a seat in the first row. She squirmed as she tried to find a comfortable position in the hard chair. An older boy walked into the room and took a deep sigh. His hair was styled in a slick man bun. His black boots clunked on the ground as he leisurely made his way to an office desk on the opposite side of the room in front of a window.

He retrieved a brown wand from his pocket and pointed it at the window. As he yanked his hand down, a dark window shade swiftly descended, blocking out the sun and robbing half the classroom of its natural light.

"Good morning. I'm Donna Marie."

The boy ignored her as he placed his peacoat on a floating coat hanger levitating by the desk. He removed a red apple from the jacket before taking a seat in the levitating chair. He released an exaggerated yawn as he propped his feet on the desk.

Jay burst through the door out of breath.

"Sorry I'm late, Darius," Jay said.

Darius seemed to ignore him too, taking a bite of the apple. Jay took a seat next to Donna and smiled at her.

"This guy seems like a prick," Donna whispered to Jay.

"That's Darius. He's Ryan's cousin. He's a freshman this year in college so he thinks he's *all that* now," Jay whispered back.

Darius removed small earbuds and finally looked at Donna and Jay.

"You're late, Mr. Decken. Which means you'll be writing more lines today," Darius said.

"I was only one minute late."

"One minute *too* late," Darius replied. "You could just as easily have been one minute early. But, of course, you weren't. So, here we are. And let me remind you there are plenty of activities I could participate in on this beautiful morning, but I'm here babysitting you two juveniles as if I have nothing better to do with my time."

Yeah, this dude is a prick, Donna thought, frowning at him.

"I am supposed to make you two write lines on the board but that's boring... So, how about we have a friendly competition?" Darius said.

"What kind of competition?" Jay asked.

"A friendly game to test the strength of your magic," Darius answered.

He stood and reached inside his bag. He pulled out a glowing oval-shaped object that was translucent, giving the illusion of a dense object no bigger than a basketball.

"This is a Yai. It absorbs energy beams and calculates their strength," Darius explained. "You will produce an energy beam into the Yai. The person with the highest level of power wins."

"But we didn't learn how to produce an energy beam yet," Jay said.

"Looks like you will have a step up from your classmates because I will teach you," Darius said.

"I'm down for that," Donna replied.

"Come on, this isn't a fair game," Jay said.

Donna gave him a look.

"I'm in the Coven. Which means I'm stronger. It's an easy win for me," Jay said to Darius. "It wouldn't be right to play this kind of game against Donna because we already know she will lose."

Donna was surprised by Jay's obnoxious statement. *Now I see why people don't like the Coven.*

"Is that right?" Donna interjected. "So, what are you afraid of then?"

"I'm not scared. Let's play. Don't say I didn't warn you though," Jay said, smirking.

Darius placed the Yai on the ground and retreated a few steps. The device began to levitate, hovering five feet above the ground.

"Energy beams were our ancestors' main line of offense during the revolt. Generally, a red beam is meant for harm, a blue beam for protection," Darius explained. "The most popular stance for a proper energy beam is the weaver position. Your body is angled to the target with your arms bent."

Darius brought his left leg forward, leaned forward, and extended his right arm, which gripped his wand. His supporting arm had a slight bend to it as his left hand wrapped around his right wrist.

"The key to the weaver stance is to push with your dominant arm and pull with your supporting arm."

"Nishati," Darius said.

A bright red beam of energy from his wand struck the Yai.

Its yellow hue glowed as it absorbed the energy beam, pulsing and contracting. A numerical measuring system appeared in a cloudlike square above the Yai. The bright blue numbers rose quickly as the beam's energy calculated, counting to 520 before Darius stopped the spell.

"Easy as pie," he said.

"You had more in you. Why did you stop?" Jay asked.

"This isn't about me, is it? It's about you two," Darius redirected. "You know the chant and the stance. Now it's your turn."

"I'll go first," Jay said, stepping in front of the Yai with a full grin.

Darius shook his head as he watched Jay hold his wand one-handed with his body slouched to the side.

"You don't get any points for trying to look cool, Jay."

"Stop hating on my swag, bro," Jay retorted, taking a deep breath as held his wand steady.

"Nishati," he said.

A red energy beam shot from the tip of his wand, and the Yai's glow expanded as it penetrated its core.

The numbers above the Yai increased quickly. Jay's attack looked powerful, but his stance seemed awkward—he had to push forward to avoid sliding back. He gave a final push, and the Yai glowed bright yellow around its outer layer.

The measuring system reached 509 before stabilizing.

"Not bad. Most sophomores can't reach over five hundred. You probably could have done better with a proper stance," Darius said.

Jay sat back down at his desk with his head held high and a grin on his face.

"Donna, you're up," Darius said.

Donna walked in front of the Yai, put her right foot back into a forty-five-degree angle and slightly bent her knees. Leaning forward, she fully extended her right arm and firmly grasped her wand in her right hand, then placed her left hand around her right with a slight elbow bend.

"Good form," Darius said.

"Nishati."

A blue beam shot from the tip of her wand, striking the Yai with extreme force. The number above the Yai rapidly increased. One hundred. Two hundred. Three-fifty.

The number kept rising as she leaned forward, focusing on the energy she felt rushing through her body and channeling it to her wand.

Four hundred... Five hundred... The numbers picked up pace, breaking through 700, climbing to 800.

"What in the..." Darius blurted.

The Yai started to shake and expand when the counting mechanism reached 999.

"That's enough," Darius's voice rose sharply.

Getting lost in how good her magic felt throughout her body, Donna tuned Darius out.

"I said that's enough," he said louder, walking toward Donna.

Donna continued to ignore him until she noticed a faint blue light permeating from her palms, wrapping around her wand. She tried to stop the energy beam but she couldn't—it felt like her powers had taken over her.

The Yai began to frantically jerk and rattle.

"I said *that's enough!*" Darius yelled.

But it was too late. The outer layer of the Yai exploded, dispersing a bright blue blast of energy around the room. Darius and Jay took cover, shielding themselves behind the desk. Donna was thrown by the force, falling on her back.

The once vibrant Yai was now completely drained of its glow. The only thing left was a smoky residue.

Donna was slow to get up, coughing and wheezing as she regained her breath.

"Is everyone okay?" Darius asked.

"I'm fine," Jay said, brushing off his letterman jacket.

"I'm sorry. I don't know what happened," Donna said.

Darius walked up to the Yai, which was now crumbled on the floor.

"So... Um, who won?" Jay asked.

"Inconclusive," Darius replied, his gaze fixed on Donna.

"Did I break it?" Donna asked.

Darius folded his arms and looked Donna up and down.

"What's your bloodline rank?" he asked.

"Um... I don't know."

Darius walked closer to her and tilted his head.

"Interesting."

"How did that happen?" Jay asked.

"The Yai was faulty," Darius concluded swiftly. "You're both free to go."

Donna and Jay looked at each other in confusion. There were still fifteen minutes left in their detention.

"Go. Before I change my mind," Darius dismissed them abruptly.

They quickly gathered their belongings and hurried out. But for Donna, the mysteries unearthed lingered, swirling in her mind as she stepped into the hallway studying her hands. *How did I just do that? And my hands... The glow, it happened again.*

Chapter Twenty-Seven

*T*hat was no hallucination. Donna was at her desk, fidgeting with her hands as Professor Hunt wrote the ingredients for the resistance dawa, which gave immunity to various poisons, on the board. She was recollecting the times in New York when her hands seemed to glow. *What is wrong with me?*

Jay grabbed her hand and leaned in toward her face. "Hey, are you okay?" he whispered.

"I felt like I couldn't control myself back there. I don't know what happened."

"It wasn't your fault. Darius said the Yai was already broken. There was no way you could have beat my score anyway," Jay reassured her, patting her on the back and giving a light grin.

God, you probably don't even know how condescending that was.

Professor Hunt stopped writing on the board and glanced over the classroom.

"Does anyone know where your missing classmate is?" she asked, gesturing to the empty seat.

The abandoned desk belonged to Raine. Students could only miss class if they were ill or had a family emergency.

They all shook their heads.

After class, Donna, Jia, and Noor assembled in the hall.

"Raine never misses class," Noor said. "I've known her since the sixth grade, and she has even come to school sick sometimes. Professors have had to escort her to the medical bay themselves."

"I'm sure she's fine," Jia said.

On the way to the CC, the girls spotted Raine walking in a single file line with five other students, including Lacey. They were all wearing plain gray clothing.

"Why are they walking like that?" Noor asked.

"Is this some kind of drill or something?" Donna asked.

"Let's find out," Noor said.

"Hey, Raine. Why'd you miss class?" Donna asked.

Raine kept walking, silent and unmoved. Not a glance. Not a word. The whole group ignored her like she wasn't even there.

"Lacey?" Noor tried, stepping onto the sidewalk beside them. "What are y'all doing?"

Still nothing. The group moved in eerie sync, eyes forward, steps matching.

Donna picked up her pace and tapped Raine's shoulder.

Only then did they stop. All at once.

"Raine, what's happening?" Donna pressed.

Raine didn't meet her gaze. Her expression was vacant. After a tense few seconds, the group resumed their march, leaving Donna bewildered.

"What was that all about?" Noor exclaimed.

"Very strange. But you know Raine always keeps to herself. Let's hit the CC. I'm starving," Jia replied.

"But she wasn't by herself, Jia... Did you see how Lacey was acting? We all know how talkative she is. I mean, she's the race announcer for a reason. And she didn't even say a word to us," Noor said.

"I think they are part of the Junior Military Program," Jia said.

"The what?" Noor said.

"Oh, we had that at my old school, it prepares students for the military, right?" said Donna.

"I didn't even know we had that here," Noor said.

"It's new. I got an email about it yesterday."

"I didn't," said Donna.

"Me either. Anyway, I'm sure Raine wants to be an artist when she grows up, not be in the military," said Noor.

"People can change their minds, Noor... So, let's get lunch, I'm starving." Jia said, walking away.

"You guys go ahead. I'll meet you there. Going to stop by the bookstore first," Donna said.

She stopped in the middle of the campus and checked her surroundings before veering off track.

Power walking toward the History Villa, Donna was on a mission. She planned to search the documents on the second floor to see if she could find any information on her father. Maybe she could find something that would explain her glowing hands, and why, when it happened, it felt like her powers were controlling her.

She wiped sweat off her forehead when she reached the villa's gate.

"How are you going to get in there? It's always locked, you know."

Donna turned around and saw Noor standing behind her.

"How did you know I was coming here?"

"Come on now, Donna, I'm your best friend. I knew you weren't going to the bookstore," Noor said, chuckling. "So, I told Jia I was heading back to my dorm, then proceeded to follow you."

Best friend... Donna had never heard anyone call her that before.

"You, okay? Look like you're about to cry?" Noor said.

"Just my allergies, girl," Donna replied, wiping her eyes with her shirt.

"What are you doing here anyway?" Noor asked. "Is this about what happened with Fang?"

Do I tell her the truth or lie to the only best friend I've ever had?

"Honestly... I think Rima is lying about my father. I think she and Professor DuVernay were friends with him and don't want to tell me," Donna said.

"Why would they lie about that?" Noor asked.

"I don't know."

"Welp, I heard there are old yearbooks upstairs. Maybe we can see if they knew him."

"Great minds think alike," Donna replied.

"Let's go around the back so we aren't spotted," Noor said.

They headed around to the back gate.

"This one is locked too," Donna said, pulling on the gate door.

Noor pulled out her wand. "Kufungua," she said.

The gate unlocked and Donna pushed it open.

"How did you know that spell?"

"Chike taught me," Noor replied.

Donna and Noor walked to the side door of the villa.

"Kufungua," Noor said, waving her wand over the door handle.

The door unlocked and Donna walked in first. It was so quiet that Donna gasped when the floorboard creaked as they made their way to the staircase.

Upstairs had less natural light, making it substantially creepier. Noor lifted her wand as if to fend off anything that might leap from the shadows as they moved down the hall.

"Okay, I see you, Superwoman," Donna whispered to her.

The first door on the right was cracked open. Donna peeped through the small crack.

CREEAK! The door swung open, revealing a room filled with shelves stacked with what seemed like thousands of books, all reaching up to the ceiling. There wasn't much light, and the curtains had to stay closed to prevent anyone from spotting them through the large glass panes.

"Where do we start?" Noor asked.

Donna approached the shelf closest to the door and removed a book. Dust covered her fingers as she opened it.

"This is just a poetry book."

"Looks like nothing is in order," Noor said, pulling out another book.

"Let's just see what we can find."

The girls scrambled through manuscripts, novels, biographies, poems, and yearbooks. They made sure to place everything back in its precise location.

Ten minutes passed, and they hadn't found anything significant. They had to leave soon because they only had a few minutes left on their lunch break.

"I think I found my mother's yearbook. She was in the same grade as the DuVernays," Noor called out to Donna.

Donna hurried to Noor, almost slipping in the act.

The yearbook was black with the Nawlins crest on the cover and *Class of '97* on the spine. They flipped the pages.

"That's my mom there," Noor said, pointing to the class president.

Her mom looked similar to her, just with a lighter complexion.

"Slay, queen," Donna said.

Noor turned the page, and Donna's face dropped. In the center of the page was a black-and-white picture of Sammy and Professor DuVernay holding a championship racing trophy along with their Bandits teammates. "Broom racing championships" was the header.

"What's wrong, Donna?"

"That's my father."

"The guy with the Afro?"

"Yes. He was friends with Professor DuVernay. Why are they lying to me?"

"I don't know, but we have to go," Noor said.

Donna put the yearbook back and took another look to make sure the room was in order before closing the door to its cracked position.

Noor was walking farther down the hallway.

"What are you doing? We have to go," Donna said.

"I've never been up here. Want to see what's in these other rooms," Noor replied, sticking her head in an open door. "It's empty," she said.

Donna peeped into another opened door—just an empty room with white walls and white tile floor.

"Check this out. It's the only locked door up here," Noor said, standing in front of the last door.

Donna attempted to twist the cold rusted doorknob, but it didn't budge.

"Kufungua," she said, waving her wand around the doorknob.

The knob clicked, and Donna reached for it. This time, it turned with ease.

"What a spell," Donna said, looking back at Noor.

"All thanks to my baby, Chike."

Another empty room, but something about this one felt... different. The air was colder, and the silence was unsettling. Small cracks split the worn wooden floors, and faint burn marks streaked across the surface.

"There's nothing in here. Waste of time," Noor said, turning to leave.

Donna's eyes caught a narrow wooden door near the back of the room. She stepped forward and eased it open, revealing a small, empty closet.

A single cord hung from the ceiling. She gave it a tug. The bulb flickered, buzzed, and then cast a weak, yellow glow.

Noor popped up behind Donna.

Startled, Donna slipped, landing hard on the rickety floorboards.

"I'm so sorry. I didn't mean to scare you," Noor said, eyes wide.

The girls burst into laughter. As Donna pushed herself up, her right hand pressed against a loose plank. She paused, noticing it shift beneath her weight.

Carefully, Donna peeled the wood back, revealing a hidden square compartment beneath the floor. Nestled inside was a worn, spotted brown leather journal.

Donna turned it over to reveal the cover.

Mary Ann
1811

"Maybe we should put that back... Let's go before we get caught," Noor said, walking away.

Donna ran her thumb across the worn leather, her eyes lingering on the name.

Without a word, she slipped the journal into her bag, gently replaced the floorboard, and pulled the light cord. The bulb flickered once before the room sank into darkness.

Donna hid under a magnolia tree as the humid evening air flowed through the Gardens. Large monarch butterflies gracefully visited the vibrant red rosebushes behind her—two of them had already landed on her shoulder. She was out of her dorm past curfew again, waiting for Lincoln.

After a few minutes, he appeared, sitting on the bench in front of the tree.

"Psst," Donna said.

Lincoln looked around.

"Behind you," Donna whispered.

"Why are you hiding behind a tree?" Lincoln asked.

"I had to talk to you, and I knew you like to come here at night," she said. "I left my bag behind this tree on purpose so I had an excuse to look for it after curfew. Zina let me out, but I have to get back soon."

"I'm so glad I'm a senior because those 8 p.m. curfews were wack."

"Have you noticed people acting strange on campus?" Donna asked, sitting next to Lincoln.

"What do you mean by strange?"

"This girl in my grade, Raine Jenkins, um, she's usually her regular artsy self, but now it's like something has taken over her body. She doesn't even talk or look you in the eyes. I can't explain it."

Lincoln looked uncomfortable. He got up and walked back and forth. "Are you sure she's acting strange?"

"Yes. It's like night and day. She's even dressing funny."

Lincoln paused for a few seconds, and then he looked up as if he was pondering.

Ask him, Donna. Just ask him. Do it!

"Why did you lie to me about your father being friends with my dad? They knew each other. They were in the Bandits together."

Lincoln slowly walked back to the bench and took a seat. He looked Donna in the eye. "I did ask about your father. My dad said they were great friends, pretty much inseparable while they were at Nawlins... But when your father died, he took it hard."

"So, he couldn't even check on my mom from time to time?"

"I understand how you feel, but maybe at the time, he thought the best thing to do was to distance himself. Death can be hard on people, Donna."

She breathed deeply, letting her gaze drift across the landscape.

"How did you find out?" Lincoln asked.

"I snuck into the second level of the History Villa and saw a yearbook photo of them together."

"How did you get into the Villa?"

"I have my ways," Donna replied. "I also found this."

She went into her bag and retrieved the journal of Mary Ann, handing the fragile antique to Lincoln.

"Did you tell anyone else about this?"

"Just you," she assured him.

His gaze lingered on the entries, a storm of emotions playing across his face.

"Donna, I have to tell you something," Lincoln said.

A whistling noise came from the college walkway. There was no time to hide. Swiftly, she snatched the journal from Lincoln's hands and tucked it into her bag.

"Well, what do we have here? A sophomore out past curfew," Darius remarked, his tone dripping with authority.

"She was just retrieving her bag, left here earlier," Lincoln interjected, coming to Donna's defense.

Donna hoisted her bag slightly, offering an awkward smile to Darius as proof.

"Come on, Darius. Leave the girl alone. I remember when you used to sneak out during curfew hours."

"I did. And I found you and Tamia kissing here in the Gardens all the time," Darius replied.

"And you're still jealous?" Lincoln said, standing up.

Darius got closer to Lincoln. "Don't flatter yourself, golden boy. You think you're hot stuff because you're a Three and your father is a professor? You're not good enough for Tamia. You abandoned her, just like you abandoned the Coven," Darius said, stepping even closer to him.

"Get out of my face before I make you get out of my face," Lincoln said.

Donna's eyes opened wide, and her head started to ring when she saw a faint red glow from Lincoln's clenched fist.

"Hey. Knock it off, you two," Zina said, walking around the corner carrying a coffee cup. "Donna, I see you found your bag," she said.

"I did. Thanks for letting me out past curfew to find it," Donna replied.

"First and last time. Now, get back to your room before you get written up," Zina said.

Casting a final glance at Lincoln, Donna hurried back to her dorm. Once safe in her room, she collapsed onto her bed, her temples pounding. She breathed deeply, trying to calm the throbbing in her head. Gradually, the pain eased as Mr. Whiskers hopped onto her lap, as if he knew she needed some comfort.

"Thank you, Mr. Whiskers," she murmured, stroking his fur.

Her gaze then fell on Mary Ann's journal lying beside her. Curiosity piqued, she picked it up and began to turn its fragile pages, eager to uncover the secrets held within.

The Uprising shattered our shackles, reunited broken families, and gave birth to hope. I witnessed the numerous battles at various plantations surrounding New Orleans. The Oppressors were no match for us. They had guns but we had wizards with magical powers and magical beasts called Loyals. Solomon's Loyal is a vicious black panther. I saw him tear a plantation owner's body in half with his sharp teeth. Its hiding form is a cat that I named Mr. Whiskers.

Donna glanced at Mr. Whiskers, who was nestled in her lap. "Dude, is she talking about you?" Donna asked. "I mean, what other cat named Mr. Whiskers would she be describing that turns into a black panther? You ripped a guy's body in half?"

Mr. Whiskers averted his gaze and settled more comfortably into her lap, seemingly indifferent to her rising alarm.

Just great. I have a killer in my lap, Donna thought, before starting to read again.

After each battle, the Oppressors begged for mercy, and the wizards, led by Solomon, spared their lives as they watched their plantations burn to the ground. Some wizards weren't pleased with Solomon's kindness, especially Augustin. But Solomon was against unnecessary bloodshed. To prevent retaliation from the Oppressors, he cast a memory-loss spell, erasing all recollection of wizards and magic from their minds. He also wiped the memories of the people freed from their plantations. He believed the wizards' identities had to remain hidden for their own protection from the world.

The wizards have built a fortress for their safety in the French Quarter. It was Solomon's idea. He named it NAWLINS. As their families grow, this will serve as their haven. Solomon hopes to turn the entire compound into a school for wizards one day. Solomon, Augustin, Philmore, Cane, and Jean Pierre have started to study and break down The Book of Giza and The Book of Knowledge. They call themselves The Coven. Only those born of the original five bloodlines will be allowed entry into this small fellowship. Their powers seem to be stronger than the others. But Solomon's power is unmatched by them all.

I can tell some of the wizards aren't fond of the love Solomon and I share for each other. I overheard Augustin telling him, "You should be with your kind," as if I wasn't good enough because I didn't possess wizard blood in my veins. Augustin has been cold with me and somewhat rude ever since Solomon allowed me to keep my memories. I used to think she resented me for being the only Norm who knew wizards existed, but now, I think she hates me because I married Solomon. It's almost as though she loves him as much as I do. They were born on the same plantation and shared an unbreakable bond long before I ever came into the picture."

Donna flipped a few pages ahead. Mary Ann's handwriting had grown jumbled as if she was writing fast.

They just attacked us in the main house. We were upstairs when they broke through the door. Solomon hid me in the closet and used a spell that kept me hidden. Solomon pleaded with Augustin to stop the ambush, but she had no empathy in her eyes, just a lust for power. Through the cracked door I watched as I fought to hold back my screams and tears.

Solomon's eyes did something I'd never seen before. They turned pitch-black as dark veins protruded around them. I thought he was helpless without his wand, but his powers flowed through his hands as he bravely fought off the wizards.

But there were just too many of them. And there was nothing I could do. It took twenty wizards to restrain Solomon.

I watched Augustin walk up to him, press a kiss to his lips, then drive a knife straight into his heart.

Donna gasped and put the journal down. Tears flowed for someone she didn't know, who watched her husband get murdered before her eyes.

Augustin was evil. She killed her friend. How could anyone do such a thing?

A single page jutted from the back of the journal. Curious, Donna turned to it.

I am leaving this journal behind, hoping the person who needs it the most will find it. I leave you with the knowledge that Solomon's bloodline will not stop with him because I am with child. No one knew besides my husband.

I also leave you with a page from The Book of Giza that has spells only Solomon could perform. One day, you may need these spells to save the world from Augustin.

—*Mary Ann Deslondes*

"Mr. Whiskers, I don't think Mary Ann had many friends so she kept a journal just like me."

Mr. Whiskers started snoring. Donna gave him a rub on the head.

"She was pregnant," Donna whispered. "How many of Solomon's descendants are out there? Oh boy, if I were one, I would be the best wizard in the world. Nobody would mess with me... Wait a minute."

Donna rose from the bed and put her hands on top of her head. She started to pace around the room, recollecting her dream.

She knelt on the side of the bed towards Mr. Whiskers, who looked a bit irritated, probably because Donna slung him off her lap when she frantically got up.

"Mr. Whiskers, my father told my brother that *he was a Deslondes... We are strong and brave...* Hmm... What did my father mean by that?"

Mr. Whiskers stood up and rubbed himself on Donna's cheek.

"There's no way he was a Deslondes... Right? Can't be? That would mean I am a One... I'm so delusional. Let me get these silly notions out of my head."

Donna laughed it off and got back into bed.

Mr. Whiskers climbed on her stomach, cocked his head to the side, and stared at her.

"Dude, what's up with you? You better not be turning into a panther."

Mr. Whiskers glanced down at the journal, then back at Donna. He repeated the motion; his head went down, then back at Donna. And again. And again.

"I wish you could just tell me all the answers."

He finally lay back down in her lap and curled himself into a ball.

Chapter Twenty-Eight

Lincoln was usually the first to arrive at the Raceway on race days. He liked to sit on the grass below the racetrack and visualize how the relay would take place, though it usually never materialized how he played it in his head. Still, the thrill and unpredictability drove him to the sport in the first place. But today, he wasn't the only early one. As he walked through the double doors, Nnamdi and Zina were waiting for him in the salon. "How do you ask us to be here early, and you're late, pretty boy," Nnamdi said.

"I'm not a pretty boy."

"Yes, you are," Zina seconded.

"So, what's up? Why did you want to talk to us?" Nnamdi asked.

Lincoln leaned on the back of the couch at the Bandits section and stared at the mural of Solomon on the wall.

"Something is happening on campus."

"What do you mean?" Nnamdi replied.

"Students are acting strange. You've seen these small groups dressed in all gray, walking together in a line like robots?"

"I was just talking to Nnamdi about that," Zina said. "It's happening on the college campus too. They are calling it some pre-military program."

"Yeah, JMP, but the people who signed up have no business in that program. Like Raine Jenkins, she's an artist. She painted that mural," Lincoln said, gesturing to the anime character on the wall.

"I've seen Lacey in it, too," said Nnamdi. "She wants to be a teacher and always talks about it."

"What does all this mean?" Zina asked.

Lincoln looked at Zina and Nnamdi and then down to his hands. He started to second-guess himself. *Maybe this was a bad idea. What if I get them hurt? What if I can't protect them?*

"Bro, what's up? Talk to us," Nnamdi said.

Lincoln took a deep breath.

"Did you know there was once a war at Nawlins? Wizards vs. wizards?"

"Yeah. My parents told me about it. It's a secret. Only some Coven members know," Nnamdi answered.

"I know, too. He told me," Zina said, nudging Nnamdi on his side.

Lincoln frowned at Nnamdi.

"What, bro? She's my girlfriend. I tell her everything."

"At least it saves me some explanation. Look... Um... Some of the Wizards who attacked Solomon are still alive with the help of a youth dawa. They call themselves Elders."

"No way, bro," Nnamdi said.

"Yes way, bro. My parents and I know one. Well, he's a good one. He's on our side."

"And you think these *Elders* have something to do with the students acting funny?" Zina asked.

"Yes... I will talk to my parents tomorrow about their plan to stop them. They started a group with their old friends called the Rebels. And I'm going to try to get us in on the action."

"The Rebels? Oh, I like the sound of that. I want to whip some Elder tail," Nnamdi said, flashing his wand.

"Sign me up too," Zina added.

"Let's keep our eyes and ears open on campus. Anyone could be an Elder, so we must be aware of our surroundings. We don't know who to trust. Let's regroup after I talk to my parents."

"Cool," said Nnamdi.

"Oh, and can you keep an eye on Donna Marie?" Lincoln asked Zina.

"I always do. She's my favorite of the girls in the dorm."

"But like... Check on her more often. Make sure she's okay."

"What's up with the interest in her?"

"Ah, my mom wants me to look after her. So, keep an eye on her."

"Oh, I was about to pop you in your head if it was like some stalker-type stuff. I know you and my best friend got back together." Zina covered up her mouth with her hands. "Oh, I wasn't supposed to tell you that I know. I take it back. I don't know that y'all are back together."

"You and Tamia are back together?" Nnamdi asked. "Brodie, what's up with the secrets? I thought we were homies."

"We are homies. I was gonna tell you... Tamia and I are just keeping it on the low right now. Well, I thought we were."

"Nah, you keeping secrets, just like when you let up at the relay race and let me catch up to you."

"Damn, you caught that?"

"Yeah, homie, I know you, bro. Just like I've known you and Tamia were back together," Nnamdi said, laughing. "We live on the same floor. I see you sneaking out at night all the time, trying to be slick and stuff."

Lincoln playfully put his arm around Nnamdi's neck. "Say, lil woadie, you lucky we fam. Or I would put my hands on you, ya heard me?"

"Now, Lincoln. I was state champion in wrestling. We both know I could put you on the ground right now crying for mommy," Nnamdi said, flexing his muscles.

"Do it, playboy."

The double doors opened, and a few students started to trickle in.

Lincoln dapped up Nnamdi, went to his locker, and retrieved his duffle bag. Chad was standing next to him when he shut his locker.

"I got an update for you on Donna," he whispered.

"What happened?" Lincoln replied, fully invested.

"Nothing."

"What do you mean nothing?"

"Nothing. She's been the same, ya dig."

"That's it?"

"She's been spending time with Jay. Saw them studying together in the CC the other day. I don't know why she likes that dude."

"Yeah, I don't care about that."

"I do."

Lincoln was starting to get agitated. "Have you seen her having shortness of breath or panic attacks in any classes while using her powers?"

"Um, nah, I don't think so... Why do you ask that?"

"Don't worry about it."

"Hard not to worry about that, but I'll try. So, I get to race the last leg tonight?"

"That wasn't much of an update, but I'm a man of my word... If we lose because of you, you're off the team," Lincoln said, walking away.

"Yo, you're not serious, right?" Chad yelled out.

"Be careful what you wish for, youngin. Pressure breaks pipes. You gonna stand on business or fold?" Lincoln yelled back over the noisy salon.

"Ima stand on business, ya heard me! I'm HIM!"

Lincoln had no intention of cutting Chad from the team if he messed up, but he needed to know if Chad could rise to the occasion. The Bandits would need a new captain next year, and this was the perfect test: closing out the relay match against the Vibes with a spot in the semifinals on the line.

Lincoln dropped a dollar into the donation bucket on the concession stand counter, then flipped open the white ice chest beside it. The ice had melted into a pool of lukewarm water.

"Come on, people, let's keep the ice chest cold!" he said, removing his wand from his pocket and aiming it at the chest. "Barafu."

The water inside the chest began to swirl. As it settled, a thin vapor curled upward, and the liquid rapidly solidified into a single block of ice. Within seconds, the block cracked and splintered into perfectly formed cubes. Lincoln reached in and pulled out a can of fruit punch.

"Can I have one?" Donna asked, walking up.

"Yeah, grab one."

"I don't have any cash."

Lincoln went into the front pocket of his vest and put a dollar in the bucket.

"I got you, rookie... Ready for your first race?"

"More than ready," Donna replied, wiping off the top of the soda can with her shirt.

"Good. I'll see you out there."

"Wait," Donna said, grabbing Lincoln's arm. "I saw a glow from your hands. When I told you about Mary Ann's journal, your fists glowed red when you were about to fight Darius."

"I don't know what you're talking about."

"My hands do it too," Donna said, raising her voice.

"Shh, take it easy," Lincoln said, looking around. "It's not real. It's... It's a hallucination. Yeah, the same thing used to happen to me because of my anxiety."

"Rima said the same thing. But I'm telling you it's real. How else could I see it happening to you? Wait... So, you were the patient she was talking about that had the same symptoms as me?"

"Yeah, I guess so... Look, let's just focus on the race today, okay?" He glanced around the salon to make sure no one was close enough to overhear their conversation.

"You both are hiding something from me. Just like y'all lied about not knowing my father."

"Maybe a lie is better than the truth sometimes."

"I can't believe you just said that."

He sighed. *She knows too much. This is all messed up. What do I do?*

"I understand your frustration, but it's not what it seems," he said.

"It's not what it seems? I'll tell you what it seems. Did you know that Solomon had kids? Mary Ann wrote in her journal that she was pregnant when Solomon's friends killed him."

The intense moment was interrupted by a guy's voice blasting over the speaker. "Hello Racing Society. The name is Owen. I'll be the announcer tonight... This is your five-minute warning. The race will be starting in five minutes."

"Saved by the bell, I guess," Donna said.

"We will talk later. We're up first. Let's go win this race," Lincoln said.

The Vibes' fastest racer was Kirbi, a senior who loved to talk smack before and after the races, regardless of whether her team won or lost. No doubt she probably talked Chad's ear off as they waited in the third-leg exchange zone. Lincoln knew he had to put a decent-sized gap between him and Robin as they battled in the first leg. But Robin wasn't a pushover; she was a mobility expert and caught up to Lincoln in the first turn. He could hear her broom rattling from behind. As they entered the second straightaway, Lincoln picked up speed. He knew he had put some distance between them because the noise of her broom was faint as he entered the final turn.

"Lincoln is pulling away. He's now three broomsticks ahead," Owen said.

The green signal light flared when Lincoln crossed the exchange line, but something was wrong—Donna had lost control of her broom and was veering to the right. Her broom was bouncing up and down.

"You can do it, Donna. Firmly straddle your broom!" Lincoln yelled.

"Oh, no. Donna loses control. Giving the Vibes a chance to catch up!" Owen declared.

Come on, Donna Marie. You can do it.

Donna regained control and leveled out, but she was now about two broomsticks behind Troy, a junior. Donna tried her best to recoup the lead but could only narrow the gap by one broomstick as she and Troy leveled out to the second straightaway.

"The last leg is coming up! Who will take it home?" Owen's voice cracked through the speakers.

"Chad, it's up to you. Let's see if you got that dawg in you," Lincoln said, watching Chad take his mark.

"Troy enters the exchange line first, one broomstick ahead of the Bandits!"

Donna crossed the exchange line, and Chad took off with some pep in his step. He quickly gained on Kirbi.

"Come on! Come on, Chad!" Lincoln shouted.

As they leveled out of the first turn, Chad cut the lead to half a broomstick. But Kirbi was quick. She hunched low over her broom, refusing to give up another inch.

"Take her in the last turn!" Lincoln yelled.

It was clear Chad had an advantage in the turns against Kirbi. He evened the gap as they entered the final straightaway.

"Neck and neck! Who will get the W?" Owen said.

Push! Push! Lincoln shouted.

"The Bandits have won by an inch! Way to go Bandits!" Owen announced.

"Yes!" Lincoln yelled, throwing his hands up.

Filled with joy, Lincoln playfully tackled Chad to the ground when they landed their brooms on the field. Chad put his hands up with a proud look on his face.

"Way to stand on business, boy," Lincoln said, helping him up to his feet and brushing his shoulders off.

"I told you I could do it."

Donna landed her broom next to them with a sad look on her face.

"Sorry I screwed up," she told them.

"We won, what are you talking about?" Chad said.

"Yo, Chad, we'll meet you in the salon. Let me give Donna some pointers." Lincoln said.

"Aight bet," Chad said, walking off. "Yea, what up Kirbi! We smacked y'all slow asses!"

Kirbi ran after him toward the salon.

"What happened, Donna Marie?" Lincoln asked.

"I took off too fast and lost control. I could have lost the race for us."

"But you didn't."

"What if it happens again and I can't recover? I don't want to be the reason we don't win a championship," Donna said, putting her head down.

"You want to know what happened to me during my first race?"

"Something like this happened to you too?" Donna asked.

"No... What happened to me was worse. I entered a turn too fast and clipped a lane post. I spun out and almost fell off my broom. I was literally hanging on for dear life, feet dangling in the air and everything," Lincoln said, laughing at the memory.

"That's pretty embarrassing," Donna said, finally showing a smile.

"And we lost that race because of my mistake. But, look at me now, I'm the captain of the Bandits who led this team to two championships... The only way we get better in life is by trying, failing, and trying again. You could've given up but you didn't. You leveled out and continued the race. That's what matters."

"Thanks, Lincoln."

"It's all good… Let's go check on Chad. Kirbi might have beat my lil woady up, ya heard me," Lincoln said, getting a loud laugh from Donna.

"Y'all say some weird stuff."

"Y'all do too. Like, why do y'all call cold weather, brick?"

"Because it gets cold as a brick in New York, son."

"That doesn't make any sense and did you just son me?" he said.

"My bad, woady."

Lincoln stopped walking and put his hands on his hips.

"It's WOA-DAY."

"WOO-DAY," Donna tried.

"We will work on that."

Chapter Twenty-Nine

T he alley in front of Jenkins Jewelry shop was less creepy during the day—it was still abandoned, but it no longer felt like someone was lurking in the shadows, ready to rob you. Lincoln parked his motorcycle behind his father's truck in front of the shop, where they had agreed to meet.

"Hey, son." Rima rushed to him with her arms extended.

Lincoln embraced her, a surge of sorrow and regret washing over him as he remembered his last harsh words to her: "I'm not your son."

"I'm sorry I acted like a dumbass. I was just angry and confused," he confessed.

"Hey, watch your mouth. And I know you didn't mean it. But we were wrong. We should have told you the truth about your mother when you were younger. We were just trying to protect you, like parents do," Rima said, rubbing his hair. "I'm so sorry."

His father patted him on the back and gripped his shoulder. "We love you, son," he said.

"I know. I love you too. You know, this whole thing made me realize that I can't do this alone. The truth about Deedy, Catherine, Donna, and the Elders, and keeping my friends safe... It's a lot."

"You're not alone, Lincoln. You have us. Always," Charles said, kissing the back of his head.

"Can't you see we closed!" a raspy voice called out from the jewelry store.

"Mr. Jenkins, it's us!" Charles called out.

"Who?"

"The DuVernays."

The loud bolts on the door unlocked.

"What y'all want?" Mr. Jenkins sputtered, wrestling into a long black jacket.

"We talked to you yesterday, and you told us to meet you here," Rima said.

"That was before I found out my granddaughter was in trouble. The Elders have done something to her," he said, pointing his long wooden wand at the door.

The door slammed shut, and the locks bolted. He did his best to hurry down the steps.

"Where are you going?" Rima asked.

"Nawlins, to rescue Raine."

"You can't just storm in there wearing a trench coat thinking you'll save her. We need to strategize like we discussed."

"Let's go inside and talk this over," Charles suggested.

"Fine. But you're not going to change my mind."

The living area of the shotgun house was in much better shape than the store. The hardwood floors looked brand-new and they didn't creak, the walls were bright white, and colorful abstract art brought the space to life. Lincoln's eyes locked on a massive lion painting—its stare seemed to follow his every move.

"It's tracking you," Mr. Jenkins said proudly, sipping his tea. "Who needs an alarm system when your paintings are enchanted? Tea, anyone? Don't worry, I didn't spike it with truth dawa like y'all did mine."

"Excuse me?" Rima blinked with exaggerated confusion.

"You don't have to admit it. I drank it to prove you could trust me."

"I'll take a cup," Charles said from the dining table.

As Jenkins headed to the stove, Lincoln asked, "What happened to Raine?"

"Her mom said she hasn't been home in weeks. Usually, she visits on weekends. We've tried reaching out, but all we get are vague emails."

"Maybe she's just busy," Charles offered.

"I know my granddaughter; she's never too busy for family," Jenkins said, handing Charles his tea. "Yesterday, I used my last age reversal gum and went to the school."

"Please tell me you are joking," Charles said.

"Nope. Felt great being fourteen again; no aching joints, just acne."

"There's age reversal gum, too?" asked Lincoln, trying to imagine a teenage Mr. Jenkins.

"Banned in the 1950s," Charles explained. "A wizard tried to make a permanent version and died testing it.

"Anyway, I saw Raine in the common center. I called her name and she didn't even blink. Her eyes were... empty. That wasn't my granddaughter."

"They say it's some military-prep program," Lincoln said.

"JMP... Faculty and staff were briefed on the program a few weeks ago," Charles added.

"Why would Nawlins need a miliary-preparation-whatever program?" Mr. Jenkins quickly responded.

"You think the Chancellor is involved? She had to sign off on this program, right?" Lincoln asked.

"We've known Nicole forever," Rima said. "We can't assume she's guilty because of her ancestor."

"But what if Augustin groomed her?" Mr. Jenkins countered.

"We were all good friends growing up, but…" Charles hesitated, rubbing his head. "But she did turn her back on us the day after the broom ban."

"I remember that day," Rima said. "We were cheering you and Deedy on at the championship relay."

"What happened?" Lincoln asked. "I've only heard rumors."

Rima looked at Charles, who took over the story.

"A racer lost control and slammed into me. Deedy went into pure-wizard form; his eyes turned pitch-black, and a blue beam shot out from his right hand. He saved me, but the other racer died."

Rima squeezed his shoulder. "After that, Nicole distanced herself. It was like she vanished."

"I was there that day. I saw it," Mr. Jenkins said. "Deedy had no wand… just raw power. That's when I knew he was a Deslondes, a descendant of Solomon."

"Catherine was pregnant with you at that time, Lincoln. He knew wizards would come after him and his family, so he left New Orleans and moved to New York," Rima said.

Lincoln sat with the weight of his father's sacrifices. "So, what's our next move?" he asked.

"Yes, what is our plan?" Mr. Jenkins said, taking a long sip of his tea.

"We've reassembled the Rebels," Rima said. "We're watching for any strange wizard activity."

"A bunch of vigilante wizards planning to save the day. I like it," Mr. Jenkins said.

Lincoln, eager for action, pressed on. "Are there any known spots in Louisiana where the Elders might gather?"

"Yes! The Elder lair deep in the swamps. Not sure if it's even there anymore," Mr. Jenkins replied.

"I say we go there and stand on business," Lincoln said, pushing himself up from his seat.

"What on earth does that mean?" Mr. Jenkins asked. "We go there and F them up."

"Excuse me, son?" Rima said, side-eyeing him.

"What, Ma? I didn't say the actual word."

Charles crossed his arms and gave Lincoln a very stern look.

"My bad, Ma... What I meant to say is, we should go there and put a stop to whatever they are planning. Some of my homies are ready to join the Rebels too, they are ready to fight," Lincoln said.

"This fight is no place for kids. I'm not putting students in danger," Rima insisted.

"Ma, we are already in it. We need to save Raine and whoever else they've taken."

"He's right. If the Elders have infiltrated the school, students on the inside might be just what we need," Mr. Jenkins said. "And the boy is a descendant of Solomon. We might need him in this fight. But your parents are also right, Lincoln. We need to keep you safe."

Lincoln wanted to protest, but he held it in for now. *If they won't let me fight, me and the gang will start our own Rebel group.*

"What do you think the Elders are planning?" Charles asked Mr. Jenkins.

"Augustin used to want revenge," Jenkins said. "Now she wants control. World domination. She thinks wizards should rule Norms."

"And the Elders are okay with that?" Charles asked.

"Some follow her blindly. Others are forced."

"How?" Lincoln asked.

"She'll do whatever it takes," Jenkins said. "And that's why no one can find out who you really are. There is no limit to what Augustin might do with your blood."

"It's not just me," Lincoln said. "I have a sister."

"What?!" Jenkins gasped.

"She's at Nawlins. She doesn't know she's a Deslondes," Rima said quietly.

Jenkins went pale. "This changes everything."

"No, it doesn't," Rima insisted. "She's learning how to control her power. When she's ready, we'll tell her the truth."

"You'd better hope she's ready before the Elders discover who she really is," Jenkins warned.

"Like my wife said, we will handle it," Charles reassured him.

Mr. Jenkins looked skeptical but held back further comment. They agreed to regroup again soon.

Lincoln was last to exit the jewelry store. Mr. Jenkins grabbed his arm before he could take another step.

"Gather your trusted friends, and I will train you all to fight. I think I saw an Elder on campus. Disguised as a janitor."

"Which janitor?"

"He probably isn't using the same name as back then, but he took off his hat and scratched that bald head of his. I'd recognize that dome anywhere."

Lincoln nodded. "Where will we train?"

"Here, once a week. I have a big garage in the backyard with some training equipment. How do you think I stay in such good shape?" Mr. Jenkins asked, flexing his flabby bicep. "Now get out of here. I have to take my nap."

Chapter Thirty

Donna, Noor, and Jia were huddled around a table in the CC lounge, buried in their study guides and class notes. Midterms were looming, which they all voiced their stresses about. Donna felt a particular dread about her upcoming Ancient Magic exam, which demanded she successfully cast an energy beam—a feat she hadn't yet mastered.

Desperate for a break, Donna wandered over to the art studio, which was enclosed in glass and filled with student artwork, showcasing various sculptures and paintings. Raine's paintings were the most captivating, and she always signed her first and last name in yellow paint at the bottom. Her bat painting remained conspicuously unfinished. Resting on a wooden easel, it had looked the same for weeks now: half of the bat had detailed coloring, and the other outlined half had no color at all.

Donna returned to their table. "I haven't seen Raine in the art studio in a while," she remarked.

"I know. It's not like her," Noor replied.

"And when she's in class, she's like a mannequin," Donna said.

Just then, Chike made a grand entrance, striding toward Noor with a bouquet of red roses, his friend Ryan trailing with a rolled-up white poster board.

"Kuonyesha," Chike said, holding his wand in front of the board.

The poster unrolled in mid-air, and stretched about twelve feet. It began to spin, and pieces of the board fell off as if it was reshaping itself. It spun even faster as vibrant colors seeped through the remaining portions. Finally, it stopped spinning, lifted higher in the air, and revealed its final form: a drop-down banner that read, *Will you go to the Winter Formal with me, Noor?*

Noor jumped up in excitement, almost toppling her strawberry slushie over herself.

She raced up to Chike and jumped into his arms, hanging around his neck as he hugged her.

"Of course I'll go to the formal with you, baby," Noor said.

The banner burst into confetti and spilled on the floor.

Donna and Jia looked at each other with sad puppy eyes.

"We are so single," Donna said as they flopped onto their favorite couch.

"The formal is next weekend, and we don't have dates," Jia said, resting her head on Donna's shoulder.

Jia sat up. "How about if no one asks us by the end of the week, we'll go together? Two single baddies on the prowl. It'll be fun."

"I'm down for that. We don't need boys to have a good time," Donna said.

"Oui! Bien!" Jia said in her heavy French accent.

"Hey! Hey! Hey! I'm not cleaning that confetti," Mr. Espree said from the staircase.

The eager students in Ancient Magic bickered back and forth, circling the Yai centered in front of the class.

"I bet I get the highest score."

"This Yai is huge."

"Let me show y'all how it's done."

The six-foot practice Yai was bigger than the one from detention, and it didn't have a power metric system. The students scattered to their desks when they heard Professor Decken talking to someone outside the door. When he entered, he placed his blazer on the floating coat rack behind his desk.

"The passing score for the midterm is two hundred points, which is relatively easy to obtain with about one-third of your power," Professor Decken said. "We've been studying the energy beam, and now it's time for you to practice. Raine, you should go first."

Raine stiffly stood and approached the Yai. Her movements were as gray and uniform as her attire—gray button-up, gray pants, and plain black boots, a total contrast to her once vibrant wardrobe.

She raised her wand, and a red energy beam shot forth, hitting the Yai squarely. Murmurs rippled through the classroom as students craned their necks, their reactions a mix of awe and curiosity.

"Oh."

"Ah."

"Aye, that's tight."

"Excellent job, Raine," Professor Deck praised.

The beam flickered out, and Raine returned to her seat. Donna tried catching her eye, but Raine's gaze was fixed forward, unreachable.

One by one, the students had their turn at the Yai. Professor Decken stood by, observing and giving notes on each performance. He urged each student to perform the energy blast at a low power level so they could get the hang of it. Noor was next up.

A vague blue beam was produced from the tip of her wand.

"That's it. Now let it rip," Professor Decken encouraged.

Noor exhaled, and the blue beam struck the center of the Yai. After a few seconds, she lowered her wand. Professor Decken folded his arms and nodded.

"Good job, Noor. Who's next?"

Jay raised his hand. Just like in detention, he elected not to go with the traditional stance. He fired a red beam, striking the top of the Yai. His arms flexed as he pushed forward.

"That's enough," Professor Decken said.

Still firing the beam, Jay glanced back at his classmates with a proud grin. But the energy veered off course, rising from the Yai and striking the whiteboard. The blast cracked the surface and scorched a black welt into the exposed concrete. Jay's smile vanished as he turned toward his father. Professor Decken snatched the wand from his hand.

"Never take your eyes off the target. Your careless mistake could have hurt someone."

The sound of the bell saved Jay from the scorn of his father.

"For those who couldn't come up and practice, the training rooms are now open in the library. Surrounded by damage-proof and soundproof walls, they are the safest place for young wizards to sharpen their skills. Those renovations took months to complete, so use them."

Donna was disappointed because she wanted to get feedback from the professor, but at least she could practice in the training room before the exam. *What if I break another Yai? I need to nail this test. I can't mess up or I might fail this class!*

Lincoln was in the training room when Donna arrived after dinner. He was standing before a Yai with his wand in hand.

"Are you practicing for your midterms too?" Donna asked.

"Nah, I know I'm going to ace mine. I just wanted to check out these new training rooms," Lincoln replied, striking the Yai with an energy beam. "This is like a stress reliever."

"Oh, I know all about those from my meditation sessions with your mom. She even gave me a squeezy ball to smush in my hand when I was feeling irritated. I wish I had it now because I'm worried about my Ancient Magic midterm. Last time I did an energy beam I broke a Yai."

"What? When did that happen?"

"When I got detention for stepping out of curfew to find Mr. Whiskers."

"And who made you do an energy beam at detention?"

"Darius."

Lincoln let out a slow breath, his expression tinged with concern.

"You good?" Donna asked, noticing his furrowed brow.

"Yeah, it's just... Y'all are doing the energy beam earlier than I expected. When I was a sophomore, we didn't learn that spell until our spring term."

"Yeah, Professor Decken said my class is advancing quicker than the others. He said this was our treat."

Donna scanned the room for another training Yai. Lincoln pointed his wand to the ceiling, and a Yai identical to the one in class descended to the ground.

"Thank you," Donna said.

She stepped in front of the Yai and took a deep breath. She felt her powers twirling in her chest, anxiously awaiting release. As she raised her wand, her heart pounded against her ribcage, her anxiety mounting. She shut her eyes tightly, her temples pulsing with pressure.

With a shout, "Ahh!" Donna unleashed her power. Her eyes snapped open as a thick red beam of energy blasted from her wand, penetrating the Yai and hitting the damage-proof wall behind it. She quickly shoved her right hand into her hoodie pocket, hiding the red glow emanating from her palm.

The Yai crumbled to dust on the floor.

"Let me see your hand," Lincoln approached, his voice calm. "You can trust me. I promise."

Donna hesitated, but then slowly drew her hand from her pocket, extending it to him.

"You saw the glow, didn't you?" she asked, her voice shaky.

Lincoln examined her palm quietly, then glanced at the remains of the Yai on the floor.

"What's wrong with me?"

"Nothing is wrong with you. Next week, you will pass your exam. You should go back to your dorm and don't tell anyone about this," Lincoln said.

"Why can't I tell anyone? What are you hiding from me?" Donna asked.

Lincoln didn't turn around as he headed for the exit.

"Please, Lincoln!"

He stood still with his back to Donna.

"You're my... My... MY..."

"I'm your what?" Donna pressed, her frustration growing.

"My situation was similar, my anxiety... it used to manifest just like this," Lincoln said. "You should keep using the meditation techniques my mom taught you. They really helped me."

"Right," Donna said, unconvinced.

She knew he was lying, but there was nothing she could do about it.

Chapter Thirty-One

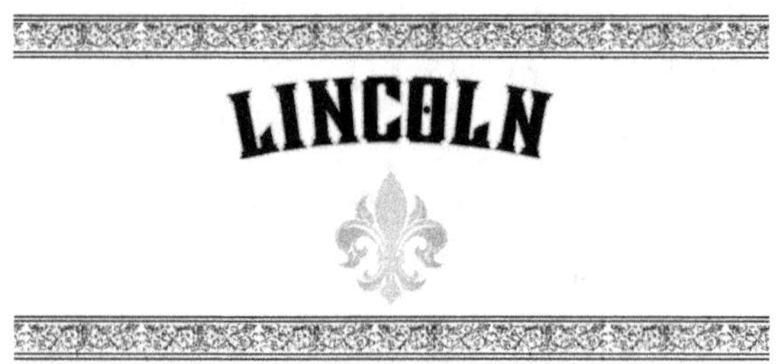

As weeks stretched into a vigilant but uneventful watch, the adult Rebels hadn't spotted any suspicious wizards or any abnormal activity. Meanwhile, the younger contingent, Lincoln, Nnamdi, Zina, and Tamia, found themselves again on the cold concrete floor of Mr. Jenkins's cluttered garage, soaking in the lessons from their teacher. The space was a glaring contrast to the sophisticated training facilities at Nawlins, filled with large rugged tree stumps and logs suspended by ropes, resembling a makeshift dojo.

"Kuua," Mr. Jenkins said.

From his wand erupted a red beam that morphed into a spinning disc, edged with glowing purple spikes. It slowed, hovering in front of Mr. Jenkins. "This is one of the most lethal attacks from *The Book of Giza*. Once it strikes you, it penetrates your body and sends shock waves directly to your heart."

With a flick of his wand, the disc hurtled towards a tree stump, obliterating it into splinters. Lincoln shielded his eyes as debris scattered throughout the garage.

Suddenly, a golden bell above the door chimed.

"What's that?" Lincoln queried.

"Someone is at my front door. It's Saturday morning. My shop is closed!"

The bell rang again.

"Can't these people read the 'closed' sign?" Mr. Jenkins muttered as he walked off.

Lincoln waited until Mr. Jenkins cleared the door before standing and stretching out his legs.

"Yo, this is cool and all, but we've been cooped up in this stank-ass garage for weeks. When are we actually going to fight some Elders?" Nnamdi complained, dropping to the ground to knock out a few push-ups.

"I don't know... It's been quiet, bro," Lincoln said. "But what if he's right, though? What if there are Elders at Nawlins, disguised as janitors or even professors?"

"Then they'll be sorry when they face me," replied Nnamdi.

"Then stop complaining and keep training," Lincoln said.

"But maybe the old man is lying," Nnamdi responded. "He could be a fake Elder with a fake ancient wand. The Elders could really be dead, and he's just stirring stuff up for an adrenaline rush."

"The stuff he's teaching us isn't in our curriculum. I never even heard of half of these spells. He's an Elder," Tamia said.

"What about you, Tamia? Have you heard anything about Augustin? I mean, you are a Decken. If Augustin is alive, why wouldn't your family help her?" Nnamdi asked, folding his arms.

"What do you expect me to do, Nnamdi? Casually ask my parents over dinner if they're hiding a dark family secret about an Elder who wants to take over the world?" Tamia responded, stepping closer to him.

"Hey! Can you two chill out?" Zina intervened, physically placing herself between the two. "We're supposed to be in this together, remember?"

"Zina's right. Let's not take our frustrations out on each other. It's a good thing that we haven't had to fight anyone yet," Lincoln said.

"My bad, Tamia. I wasn't trying to stir up anything. I just feel like we're wasting our time here," Nnamdi said.

"Don't worry about it. We're cool," Tamia replied.

"But what if Nnamdi's right?" Zina said. "What if there aren't any Elders? What if the military program is real? Or what if there are Elders, but they stopped their plans?"

"I know Augustin, she is not stopping anything," Mr. Jenkins interjected, opening the garage door. "Just when we least expect it, she will attack. I'm more worried that you youngsters are the only ones training to fight, while the other Rebels are just standing by."

Mr. Jenkins was carrying a brown box. He set it on a table and pulled away the tape.

"What do you have there?" Lincoln asked.

"They finally came in. Here you go."

Lincoln almost dropped the black phone that Mr. Jenkins tossed to him, bobbling it around before catching it.

"Where did you get these things? I thought they were extinct," said Lincoln, opening and closing the flip phone.

"I ordered them from eBay. The Elders are probably tracking the tablets at Nawlins, so we will use these to   communicate."

"Oh, so these are like trap phones?" Nnamdi said, putting the phone to his ear.

"What's a trap phone?" Mr. Jenkins asked.

"I got two phones! One for my girl and one for the dough!" Chad sang.

"Dawg, you know the song doesn't go like that?" Lincoln said.

"No, but he better sing it like that," Zina added, playfully pushing Nnamdi's head away from her as he tried to kiss her.

"What is a trap phone?" Mr. Jenkins asked again.

"Don't worry about that, Mr. Jenkins, it's just a rap song thing," Lincoln told him.

"Hey, how is that sister of yours?" Mr. Jenkins whispered as they walked over to the corner of the garage.

"She's ah... Yesterday, she um—"

"Come on, boy, spit it out."

"She's good. Yesterday I saw her perform an energy beam."

"Good. Good. Very good."

"Yeah, her meditation work with my mom has been going well... Has Raine been home this week?"

"No, just the same check-in email or a stale video chat. It's taking everything in me not to go into that school and drag her out myself."

"But if she's under Augustin's spell, she'll just go right back."

"Why do you think I haven't done it yet? Hey, like I told you before, I don't mind your girlfriend being here because we need as many Rebels as possible, but it's still a risk. She's Augustin's descendant and if her family has an allegiance with the Elders, they could use Tamia to get to you."

"Tamia wouldn't allow that to happen," Lincoln replied, looking at Tamia as she expertly fired an energy beam at one of the logs.

Lincoln was giving Tamia a piggyback ride after a trip to Café Du Monde for beignets.

"What's wrong?" she asked. "You've been quiet since we left Mr. Jenkins's house."

"Nothing's wrong, bae."

"Hey, wait for us!" yelled Nnamdi, who was carrying Zina on his back a block behind them.

"Lincoln, I know you. Something is on your mind."

Something was heavy on his mind: his sister. He knew she'd need help with her Ancient Magic exam, and to help her, he would have to use a spell he'd never attempted before. If it backfired, it could expose them both.

"It's Donna," he said. "She was in the training room at school, practicing for her midterm, and an energy beam came out of her hand."

"Oh, no. Did you tell your parents?"

"Nah, they would probably freak out. Winter break is around the corner and I don't want them to cancel our plans to go to New York... I need to meet my mom... I mean, Catherine... So, I'll handle this myself."

"Lincoln, baby boy, everyone needs help sometimes," Tamia said, rubbing his chest.

"No. I can't risk it. I'll take care of it. I still remember the spell my parents used to suppress my powers when I was learning the energy beam."

"Hey, do you remember when you first started flying?" Tamia asked.

"How could I forget? I couldn't turn for nothing."

"Because you were relying too much on your speed."

"Until you showed me how to turn like a pro."

Tamia chuckled. "I still remember doing cone drills with you. But what I didn't tell you was that I learned how to race from my father."

"Wait, Professor Decken used to race?"

"Yep. You should see his office at the house, trophies everywhere. When I was a kid, he would take me to the park late at night to practice. My mother and I have our problems, but still, to this day, my dad tells me I'm his favorite child."

"You okay up there? Don't cry on my shoulder," Lincoln joked.

Tamia bit his shoulder and laughed.

"Ow."

"Mmhm, that's what you get."

"I kinda liked that. Bite me again."

"You're so silly, boy," Tamia said. "I say all that to say: we all can use a little bit of help, Lincoln."

"You're right, baby."

"I know I'm right... And don't try to rizz me up; you know I love when you call me 'baby'. That New Orleans accent is something else," Tamia said, kissing him on the cheek. "And give Donna a chance. She might be able to teach you a thing or two about your pure-wizard power."

Tamia climbed off his back when they arrived at Nawlins. After she walked in, he held the door for Nnamdi.

"Zina, get off that boy's back. He looks like he's about to pass out," Lincoln said.

"My baby is strong, he'll be okay," Zina replied.

"Nope, he's right; I'm about to faint."

"Why didn't you say something, big head?" she asked, jumping down.

"I couldn't let Lincoln show me up."

"That's right. When our ladies say their feet hurt, we save the day. No matter the pain," Lincoln said, laughing.

The group got quiet when they spotted Mr. Espree at the end of the hallway on a ladder. He was whistling along to the music that played over his headphones as he dusted the black frame around Solomon's painting.

"Hey, y'all go ahead. I'll meet y'all in the CC," Lincoln said, giving Tamia a kiss on the cheek.

"Do you want me to get you a slice of cheese pizza?" she asked.

"You know me so well. I'll be there in like ten minutes."

Lincoln walked up to the painting, staring at the red beam traveling from Solomon's hand.

"What do you want, kid?" Mr. Espree asked, taking off his headphones.

"How do you think he was?"

"What do you mean?"

"What do you think the rest of the wizards thought of Solomon when he was alive?"

Mr. Espree slowly stepped down from the ladder and stood next to Lincoln. He sighed deeply, resting his hands on his hips.

"I can only speculate, but I would like to think he was a beacon of hope, freedom, and liberation. A true leader."

"I think so too. It's too bad he didn't have any kids to pass his bloodline down," Lincoln said.

"Yes. That is too bad," Mr. Espree replied, squinting at Lincoln.

"I can't imagine what these five friends went through. What all the revolt members went through."

Mr. Espree got quiet. He took off his hat, fiddling with the brim. Lincoln took note of his bald head.

"We went—I mean, they went through things unimaginable; at least that's what I heard."

"If they were alive today, do you think they would want revenge?" Lincoln asked.

Replacing his hat, Mr. Espree met Lincoln's eyes with a piercing look. Lincoln stuck his hand in his pocket and clenched his wand as Mr. Espree took a step closer to him.

"I think they would want more than revenge; they would want power... and not just the magical kind."

"Why would they want power?" Lincoln pressed.

Mr. Espree backed off, inching closer to the painting of Solomon. "To make sure what they've been through never happens again and to protect the future generations of wizards," Mr. Espree explained, dusting off the bottom of the frame with a rag.

"You're an intuitive young man. Have you heard of the new JMP group on campus?" he asked.

"Yeah, I have."

"It's much more than just a military program; they offer mentorships and college preparation. As a proud veteran myself, I'm on the advisory board. We have an important meeting coming up after the winter break."

"I think I'm going to pass," Lincoln said casually, even though his heart was pounding.

"Well, the Chancellor has made attendance mandatory for all students," Mr. Espree informed him. "You're not required to join, of course. The meeting is simply to inform students of this new initiative."

"Right. Thanks for the info."

Mr. Espree put his headphones back on and climbed up the ladder.

Lincoln rushed toward Donna's Ancient Magic class, his mind racing. Over the weekend, he'd uncovered the shocking truth—Mr. Espree was the Elder Mr. Jenkins had warned him about, hiding in plain sight as a janitor.

How many more Elders are on campus?

Why haven't they attacked?

What are they waiting for?

Does he know who I really am?

As those questions swirled in his mind, one urgent thought grounded him: helping Donna pass her midterm without triggering her powers.

Peeping through the narrow glass panel in the door, Lincoln saw Professor Decken call Noor to the front. The Yai scanned her body, then shifted and stretched, adjusting itself to match her height.

She lifted her wand and a bright blue beam struck the Yai in the center. The scoreboard ticked upwards energetically, halting impressively at 380 as she eased off her spell.

"Good job" Professor Decken said. "Bravo."

A grade of ninety-four appeared near her name on the board.

"Donna, you're next."

As Donna approached the Yai, which adjusted slightly to match her height, Lincoln discreetly readied his wand, poised to assist if necessary.

I got you, little sis.

Lincoln held his breath as Donna thrust her hands forward, releasing a powerful red beam that vibrated the Yai. The numbers on the scoreboard climbed rapidly past 300.

As the count soared toward 400, Lincoln softly uttered, "Utulivu," aiming his wand discreetly towards Donna. The score jerked to a stop at 510. Clutching his wand tightly, he exerted himself to temper the surge of Donna's power. A faint red glow began emanating from her palms—a sign of her true strength threatening to reveal itself.

Lincoln glanced around nervously, ensuring his privacy, then intensified his focus. "Utulivu," he repeated, with a more forceful whisper and a firmer stance, channeling his energy to quell the glow that gradually receded and disappeared.

Donna dropped her wand, and the Yai stabilized.

"510! Donna, you just scored in the top ten percentile. Excellent performance," Professor Decken said, picking up Donna's wand and handing it to her. "But next time, keep a firm grip on your wand, young lady."

Lincoln stepped back and leaned against the wall to catch his breath.

"Man, that was close," he mumbled, wiping the sweat off his face.

Chapter Thirty-Two

One thin slice of pizza lay in the box on top of the table where Donna, Noor, and Jia were sitting in the lounge. Donna was in a food coma after celebrating her big win today in Ancient Magic.

She honestly didn't know how she was able to ace the test, given her previous attempts at controlling the energy beam had always spiraled out of control. Yet, in the exam, not only did she top the class, she also thought she could've easily scored even higher, but it felt like something was blocking her powers.

"Aye, Donna, how did you score the highest on the midterm? My energy beam reached only four hundred, and I'm in the Coven," Ryan said, passing by.

"Maybe because the Coven thinks their stuff doesn't stink when it actually does," said Jia, smirking. "We are all wizards. Donna can score high if she studies hard and practices. So can I, and Noor too."

"I know that's right," Noor chimed in, high-fiving Jia.

"I don't know... I just did what the professor taught us," Donna replied.

Jay sat on the edge of the couch by Donna.

"What's up overachiever? You killed it today."

"Thanks, Jay."

"Hey, I don't know if you have plans yet, but how about you be my date for the Winter Formal?" Jay asked, his cheeks coloring slightly with a shy blush.

Donna's eyes widened in surprise. "Sorry, what did you just say?"

"Will you go to the formal with me?" Jay repeated, the blush deepening.

Donna covered her smile with her hand to hide her excitement.

I got asked to the Winter Formal by a boy! A cute boy, even though he's kinda an a-hole sometimes.

Jay chuckled softly, covering his mouth as well, the two sharing a moment of laughter.

She thought about saying yes. The word almost crept out of her mouth. But she wasn't desperate. She knew that Jay wasn't the right boy for her.

"I would love to, but I promised Jia we would go together as single girls," Donna said, not wanting to hurt his feelings.

"That's a relief. I thought someone beat me to the punch. Welp, save me a dance," Jay said, excusing himself.

"What was that about?" Noor asked, scooting closer to Donna.

"He just asked me to the Winter Formal."

"WHAT?" Jia blurted.

"What did you say?" Noor asked.

"I told him I'm going with Jia," Donna replied.

"Girl, you didn't have to do that for me. You should go with a date."

"I just... I don't like him that way," Donna confessed.

"I'm proud of you. He might be good-looking, but he does have a bit of an ego," Noor commented.

"And what's up with boys asking at the last minute? Jia added. "Ryan asked me just yesterday, and the formal is in two days! Like, sir, you had all semester to ask. No thanks."

"Wait, Ryan asked you, and you didn't tell us?" Donna asked.

"Because it wasn't worth mentioning. He probably would've taken longer to get ready than me. That boy is always in the mirror," Jia said, opening her compact and refreshing her lip gloss.

"You're so right about that," Noor replied.

"Hey, Donna, can I talk to you for a second?" Chad called out as the girls neared their dormitory.

"Sure, what's up?" Donna responded.

"Donna, meet us in the living room after. We have an Uno game to play," Noor said, herding Jia through the sliding doors.

Chad lingered awkwardly on the path, scratching his head and avoiding eye contact.

"Are you okay?" she asked.

Chad took a deep breath. "Would you go to the Winter Formal with me?" he blurted out.

For a moment, all she wanted was to say yes.

"Why didn't you ask me earlier?" she asked.

"I was nervous. I didn't want to ruin our friendship by making things awkward," Chad confessed.

Donna nodded, empathizing with his dilemma. "I understand," she said softly. "But I already promised Jia we'd go together as a duo. We decided to just have fun on our own."

Silence hung between them for a moment.

"Yeah, um, it's all good... Well, try to save me a dance," Chad said, walking off.

Upon entering her room, Donna noticed a package wrapped in purple paper on her bed. The accompanying card read:

My beautiful Donna Marie,

Jacquie received a bonus from her job, so she rented a car over the weekend and picked me up. Leaving the nursing home and cruising around the city felt so good! It's the small things we take for granted that I've come to appreciate. We found a Black-owned gown shop in Manhattan, and the owner gave us a really good deal on a dress for your winter formal. Don't worry about the money, it wasn't a lot, I promise. The owner even threw in the shoes for free. I guess telling her about your four-year honor roll streak was the selling point. Make sure you thank Jacquie too. Anyway, enjoy yourself and don't kiss any boys. They have cooties.

Love,

Mom

Donna slid the card back into the envelope and began peeling away the wrapping paper, revealing a sleek white box tied with a black ribbon.

She loosened the ribbon, lifted the lid, and gasped.Inside lay an elegant, one-shouldered, sleeveless light blue satin gown, paired with sleek black heels. Donna lifted the dress from the box and held it against her body, twirling in front of the mirror. She jumped up and down, startling Mr. Whiskers, who darted under the bed.

Come on, Mr. Whiskers! It's just a little jumping." She laughed, kneeling to peer at him. "You're a giant panther and you're afraid of a little excitement?"

As Rihanna's "What's My Name?" filled the room, Donna, Jia, and Noor were in full glam mode, prepping for the Winter Formal in Donna's bathroom. Noor was helping Donna fluff out her curls with a hair pick, occasionally adding holding spray to ensure the curl definition stayed in place.

"Girl, I'm so glad you're my friend because I couldn't have done my curls without you."

"No problem, girl. You're lucky my mother owns a hair salon in Harlem, and she taught me a few things."

Jia, wielding her makeup brush like a pro, chimed in,

"And you'd both be lost without my makeup skills."

"Yes, Jia. Thanks for doing our makeup," Donna said.

"You're welcome, babes. But don't thank me; thank Rihanna for creating a beauty line for Black girls. I mean, look at all these shades."

"Time for the final reveal," Noor declared, stepping back for a full view.

The trio admired their handiwork: Noor was elegance personified in a flowing light purple dress paired with a matching satin hijab, while Jia rocked a sleek black satin dress that highlighted her shoulders and cascaded down in a dramatic floor-length skirt. Her hair was pulled up into a chic bun, showcasing her model-like features. Donna caught her reflection and paused.

I... I... I look... HOT. Donna smiled confidently as she turned to check out the back of the dress.

"Très belle!" Jia said, clapping her hands.

"What does that mean?" Donna asked.

"It means you are very beautiful."

"Belle. I like how that sounds," Noor said.

"That word is special to me," Jia replied.

"Why?" Noor asked.

"I used to know someone by that name."

Jia turned away. It sounded like she was starting to cry.

"Aw, what's wrong, Jia?" Donna asked.

"Nothing. I'm just happy that I'm here right now with both of you. You two are great friends," Jia said, turning back around and fanning her eyes. "Let me stop with these tears; I don't want to mess up my makeup."

"Girl, we've got your back," Donna assured her, gently patting around Jia's eyes with a tissue.

"I'll grab my tablet for a group pic," Noor announced, darting off.

"I left mine in the living room. I want to take a picture, too," Jia followed suit.

Alone for a moment, Donna leaned in toward the mirror, admiring her transformation. She puckered her lips, now painted a bold, confident red, and gave her reflection a playful wink.

Noor and Jia returned, positioning their tablets on the counter.

"Set your timer for ten seconds," Jia instructed.

Linking arms, they posed together, ready for their close-up.

"It's giving... queens," Jia said as the flash captured their radiant smiles.

As Donna entered the auditorium, she paused in awe. The familiar dark, bland interior had transformed into a winter wonderland. Luxurious white velvet drapes covered the walls, and delicate snowflakes drifted down from the ceiling, vanishing just before they touched the ground. The black marble floor had been cleverly converted into the glistening blue surface of a frozen lake.

Standing at the entrance on a circular rubber mat, Donna and Jia took in the scene.

"You two look adorable, my loves," Zina complimented, arriving in a dazzling black sequined gown.

"Thanks, Zina," Donna responded, her eyes scanning the icy floor. "Um, how are you walking on the ice without falling? This is my first time wearing heels, and I'm struggling on solid ground."

"Before you step onto the ice, you have to cover your shoes in these," Zina said, retrieving two small snowballs from a shelf by the door. "They will prevent you from slipping and keep your feet warm."

Zina rolled the balls between her hands and tossed them on the ground next to Donna. They turned into a clear putty material.

"Okay. Step inside them."

Donna cautiously placed her left foot into the putty, feeling it mold and set around her shoe. She repeated the process with her right foot, then gingerly walked over to Jia, who was already waiting on the ice.

Clutching Jia's arm for balance, the two girls ventured onto the icy floor.

A live R&B band was performing on a large platform stage.

"That's The Smooths. They are college students who can sing their asses off," Jia remarked.

Noor and Chike waved at them from one of the multiple gazebos surrounding the dance floor.

"Aww, you guys are too cute," Donna said, admiring how Chike's light purple tuxedo perfectly matched Noor's dress.

Jay entered with Mya, who had fully recovered from her accident at the Raceway. Despite having turned down Jay's invitation, Donna felt a twinge of jealousy watching them; she couldn't help but imagine the allure of entering a room on the arm of a charming date.

Around them, various college chaperones mingled in sleek black tuxedos and dresses, seeming to enjoy the festivities as much as the students.

In a nearby gazebo, Raine, Lacey, and about twenty members of their JMP group sat together, uniformly dressed in gray and black, contributing to their solemn appearance.

Donna walked over to the drink station, grabbed two cups of punch, and offered one to Raine.

"Hey, Raine. I got you something."

Raine looked at Donna for a split second, then looked away.

"No, thank you."

"You look cute by the way," Donna persisted, trying to break through to her.

"Thank you." Raine responded mechanically.

"Um, are you and your friends having fun?"

"Yes, thank you."

"Okay... You know, you can always come chill with us if you want to?"

"No, thank you."

Donna's patience wore thin.

"Hey Raine, what's going on? You've been acting weird for weeks now. You too, Lacey."

"They are just fine, Donna Marie. It's all part of the program," came a calm voice behind her.

Donna turned to see the Chancellor approaching.

"JMP is designed to instill discipline, structure, and teamwork: everything these future leaders need to thrive," the Chancellor said smoothly.

"But Raine wants to be an artist. She talks about it all the time. Why would she want to be in the military now?"

"Maybe she changed her mind like so many young students do. I wanted to be an astronaut before I changed my major to education in college," the Chancellor replied with a smile, placing a firm hand on Donna's back and guiding her away.

"What was that about?" Jia asked, taking a sip of her punch.

"Something isn't right about that JMP thing. I think it's a cover up for something else," Donna said.

"I'm sure it's nothing serious."

"I don't know, Jia. I have a funny feeling about it."

"OMG. Look at Tamia and Lincoln," Jia said, grabbing Donna by her shoulders and turning her around. "They are so freaking cute."

Indeed, under a spotlight, Lincoln and Tamia swayed to a slow tune, their chemistry undeniable. Lincoln spun Tamia gracefully, then pulled her close.

As the song ended, Nnamdi and Lincoln made their way to the drink station. Tamia waved at Donna and began to walk her way.

"You look gorgeous," Tamia said. "Where is your date?"

"I don't have one." Donna shrugged.

"Hey, that's not a bad thing. You don't need a date to have fun."

"Nope, she doesn't need a boy to have fun. Don't they have cooties or something like that?" Lincoln said, putting his hands around Tamia and kissing her on the cheek.

"You two look so perfect together. I really hope you get back together soon," Donna blurted.

She covered her mouth, but Tamia and Lincoln just laughed.

"Have a good time at your first Winter Formal, Donna Marie," Lincoln said, walking off with Tamia.

Donna noticed Chad crossing the transformed icy floor, his appearance strikingly different—dressed to impress with his satin shirt slightly open under a well-fitted tux, revealing a hint of his toned physique.

"Daaaaaaang, Chad looks très bien," Jia said. "He even got a fresh lineup and braids to stunt on 'em. Girl, you should have accepted his invitation."

"Hey ladies," Chad greeted, casually adjusting his gold chain with a confident smirk.

Donna circled him, checking out his style. "You pull the smooth look off very well," she commented.

"You look okay yourself," he replied.

"Aww, you two are blushing at each other," Jia teased, nudging Donna playfully.

"Maybe," Chad replied, his smile broadening.

Caught off-guard by his flirtatious confidence, Donna felt a surprising flutter of attraction. She liked it.

The band started to play a song that flocked the students to the dance floor.

"Donna, do you know how to do the bunny hop?" Jia asked, grabbing her hand and pulling her towards the action.

"What's the bunny hop?" Donna asked, watching the students line up in a coordinated dance formation.

"La da da da da da dah dah. La da da da da da dah dah," the band sang along to a catchy beat.

Donna was swiftly ushered into the middle of the formation by Jia and Noor. Initially out of sync, she soon caught the rhythm, their hips swinging in unison to the infectious beat.

Immersed in the fun, Donna laughed more freely than she had in a long time. Maybe ever.

As the upbeat music transitioned to a slow, romantic tune, the atmosphere shifted. Chike stepped forward, extending his hand to Noor, who joined him gracefully on the dance floor. Ryan, after a playful eye-roll from Jia, took her hand, and they too started to dance.

Jay and Mya, closely intertwined, moved with quiet intimacy across the floor.

Donna felt a gentle touch on her shoulder. Turning around, she met Chad's gaze. His lips parted, invitingly speaking the words she'd been waiting to hear.

"May I have this dance, Donna Marie Guillory?"

Donna grasped his hand and didn't break his gaze as he gently touched her back.

"I don't know how to dance," she shyly admitted. "Not dances like these, anyway."

"It's simple," Chad assured her, drawing her closer. "Just follow my lead."

"Look at you, you're my tutor and dance coach."

"I could be more than that," Chad replied.

His words hung between them, an unspoken question lingering in the air.

"We are good friends... Let's continue to do that until we discover something new," Donna suggested, not ready to define anything just yet.

"I like the sound of that," he agreed, a genuine smile spreading across his face.

"Me too," she said, resting her head on Chad's chest.

He wrapped his hands around her as they swayed. She felt safe in this little cocoon.

They danced in silence for a moment before Donna spotted Rima rushing in through the entrance, her expression tense. Lincoln quickly joined her, concern visible as he grasped her arms. Suddenly, their intense gazes fixed on Donna. Her heart dropped and she hurried over to them.

"What's wrong?"

"It's your mother. She's been rushed to the emergency room," Rima said, reaching out to hold Donna's hand.

"What... What... Did she have another stroke?"

"We don't know yet. We have a red-eye flight ready for you. Pack your bag, and I'll bring you to the airport."

I never should've come here. I never should've left my mother. What have I done?

Chapter Thirty-Three

S till in suit pants and a white tuxedo shirt, Lincoln fell asleep on his parents' couch waiting for an update on Catherine. He woke up to the smell of bacon and eggs, the only food his father was decent at making.

"Any news?" Lincoln asked, rubbing his eyes as he settled at the kitchen table across from his mom.

"Good morning, Lincoln," Rima said, grabbing his hand. "I spoke with Jacquie a few hours ago. Catherine is okay, but she's still in the hospital on an IV for fluids. She was severely dehydrated and exhausted, which put her in a state of hypernatremia, which can mimic stroke symptoms."

Charles set a plate of food and a glass of orange juice in front of him.

"A colleague of mine is looking her over. She should be back at her nursing home by tonight," she added.

"What caused it?" Lincoln asked.

"She pushed herself too hard in rehab, progressing quickly but overdoing it. They're planning to give her a few weeks off, then start rehab again at a much slower pace, maybe just one day a week," Rima explained.

Lincoln covered his face with his hands, overwhelmed.

I have to tell her I'm alive. She needs to know her son is here. I can help her. I can protect her.

"You okay, son?" Charles asked, resting a hand on his shoulder.

"Are we still going to New York? We have to tell her the truth."

Charles and Rima shared a look.

"We talked about it, and that's probably not the best thing to do right now. We should let her recover and tell her sometime early next year. We can go for a weekend," Rima suggested.

"But, Ma, we had a plan. She needs to know I'm here. And Donna needs to know she's my sister."

"We know how you feel, son, but let's not put Catherine under this much stress when she's just coming out of the hospital. We want her to know the truth too, but we also want the best for her. I'm sure you understand that?"

Lincoln sighed deeply and nodded. Though frustrated, he recognized the wisdom in their caution. They were right; showing up to the Bronx and dumping this information on Catherine would probably be too much right now.

"We will tell Donna everything as soon as she's back. I promise," Rima said, kissing him on the forehead. Then she gave an exaggerated grimace. "You should probably take a shower and brush your teeth now."

Lincoln chuckled, appreciating his mother's attempt to lighten the mood.

The day dragged on painfully slowly for Lincoln. He found a temporary escape by the lake, trying to ignore the less than pleasant smell of seaweed and focus instead on the rhythmic sounds of the waves crashing against the concrete steps.

His phone buzzed. Tamia's name lit up the screen, a red heart beside it, then faded as the call went unanswered. He was supposed to meet her at the CC two hours ago to catch a movie in the theater room. But today, he wanted to be alone. Guilt gnawed at him for standing her up, especially knowing her family had left for Africa over the holiday break. She'd stayed behind, counting on his company. Still, if anyone would understand what he was feeling right now, it was her.

That night, exhaustion claimed Lincoln the moment his head hit the pillow in his dorm room. Sleep came quickly, and with it, a vivid dream.

He was three years old again, curled up in Catherine's lap as she gently tended to a scraped elbow from a day spent playing outside.

"Lincoln, I'm so proud of you," she said, looking down at him.

"But I fell off my bike," he mumbled, his voice small.

"I'm proud because you faced your fear and tried anyway."

She kissed the brown bandage on his arm, right over the tiny scrape. Lincoln wrapped his arms around her waist and pressed his cheek to her stomach, listening to the steady rhythm of her heartbeat as the old recliner rocked beside a sunlit window.

He knew it wasn't real, but he didn't care. He let himself linger in the dream, taking in the soft scent of vanilla and soaking in the comfort of his mother's presence.

"I love you, my son. And I would never leave you," Catherine said.

Lincoln awoke with tears streaking his face and his heart racing. He sat on the edge of the bed, taking deep, steadying breaths.

The sun began rising as he made his way to the administration building. He scanned the surroundings to ensure no one was watching before entering. The hallway was immaculately clean. Fresh lemon-scented cleaning products hung in the air, a clear sign of a recent janitorial visit.

He took off his Air Jordan 1s and tiptoed toward the elevator to avoid squeaks.

While waiting for the slow elevator, he noticed Mr. Espree at the end of the hallway, back turned, mopping the floor with music blasting through his headphones.

Lincoln slipped into the elevator, pressing the button for the third floor and repeatedly hitting the door-close button. He let out a deep breath of relief as the doors slid shut.

When the elevator reached the third floor, Lincoln cautiously peeked out. The hallway was deserted. He silently made his way down the corridor, shoes in hand, towards his mother's office.

At the door, he withdrew his wand, waving it in a small circle before the handle. "Kufungua," he murmured. The lock clicked open. He eased the door shut behind him and settled into the chair at the desk. Waking the computer with a tap of the mouse, a password prompt popped up.

Lincoln chuckled to himself, guessing at the password.

"There's no way it's still the same," he muttered, typing in his name.

Access Granted flashed on the screen.

"Come on, Ma, ten years with the same password? It's time to change it."

He navigated to the student database, searched for "Donna Marie," and brought up her file. Scrolling through, he quickly found the information he needed.

New York greeted him with a biting cold.

The full moon hung overhead, its light obscured by a mix of heavy rain and snow.

Standing outside Catherine's nursing home, Lincoln peered through the open window of her ground-floor unit. Donna was asleep on the couch, softly illuminated by a lamp on a nearby dresser, her curly bangs shadowing her face.

Lincoln's eyes filled with tears as he watched his mother for the first time in fifteen years, her face serene in sleep, turned toward the window.

A flash of lightning tore through the sky, followed by rumbling thunder that made Donna stir in her sleep. Lincoln ducked below the window sill, holding his breath. After a tense moment, he slowly peeked over the edge again. Donna lay still.

But Catherine's eyes were open, locked directly on him.

Lincoln froze, paralyzed beneath her unblinking stare.

He waited for her to move, to scream, to say something. But Catherine remained perfectly still.

Then, slowly, she raised her arm toward the window.

Lincoln's breath caught in his throat. Panic surged through him.

He bolted.

He didn't stop running until he was several blocks away, collapsing to his knees on the snowy pavement. Tears streamed down his face as he confronted a torrent of emotions he hadn't expected to feel.

It was midnight when Lincoln arrived back at Nawlins. He dismounted from his broom in front of the college campus entrance.

"Wait until the Chancellor hears about this," Darius said, emerging from behind some shrubs and trailing Lincoln.

Lincoln ignored him and kept walking.

"Hey! You've just put us all in jeopardy by flying where Norms can see you," Darius continued. "And you don't even seem to care."

"Back off. I'm not in the mood," Lincoln warned.

Darius walked in front of him, blocking the entrance.

"Get out of my way, asshole."

"Or what?" Darius challenged, removing his wand from his pocket.

Tamia and Zina rushed over to them. "We can't even enjoy a girls' night without seeing you two go at it. Y'all chill out," Zina said.

Darius pushed Lincoln on his shoulder, and Lincoln lost it. A rush of power erupted from his heart, too fast and too strong for him to control. A red light began to glow from his palms.

"Dude, what's up with your hands?" Darius said, taking a step back.

Lincoln tightly clenched his fist, struggling desperately to suppress his power. His body jerked as he held his breath and squeezed his eyes shut, doing anything he could to fight the feeling that his heart was about to burst. The agony was excruciating. Overcome, he threw his head back and roared into the sky.

"What the hell is happening? Your eyes... What are you?" Darius shouted.

The red glow from Lincoln's hand transformed into an energy beam that wrapped around Darius's neck, hoisting him off the ground and slamming him against a wall.

He gasped for air, clawing at the energy constricting his throat.

"Let him go, Lincoln!" Zina yelled.

"Lincoln, stop. Please! Snap out of it!" Tamia pleaded.

Lincoln's gaze met Tamia's as she grabbed his arm. He relaxed his grip, and the beam dissipated, gently lowering Darius to the ground.

Darius collapsed, his breaths ragged and desperate.

Mr. Espree came running around the corner and checked on Darius.

"I... I didn't mean to... I couldn't stop it." Lincoln said to Tamia.

Tamia brought his head toward hers and hugged him.

"We have to get him to the medical bay," Mr. Espree said.

Realizing the weight of what he'd done, Lincoln stepped back from Tamia. He mounted his broom and soared into the night sky, leaving turmoil in his wake.

Chapter Thirty-Four

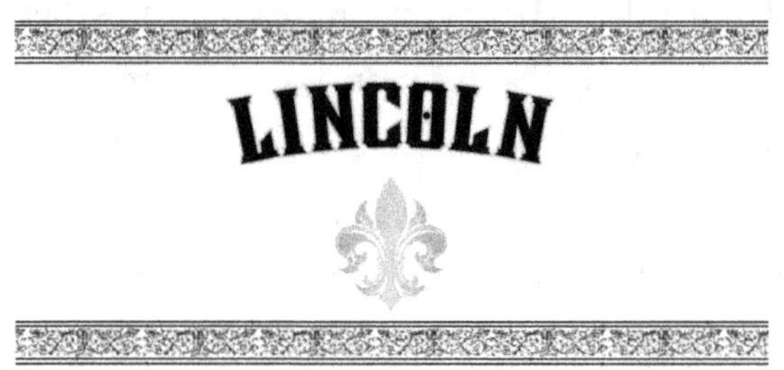

"M om! Dad!" Lincoln shouted, storming through the front door of their home. "Mom! Dad!"

Footsteps came rushing downstairs.

"Son! What's wrong?" Charles said.

"What are you doing up so late?" Rima said, grabbing him. "My God, Lincoln, your body is so cold. What happened?"

Rima sat him down on the couch, draped a throw blanket over his shoulders, and turned on the fireplace.

"I lost control. My powers came out of my hands and I attacked Darius."

"Who else was there?" Charles asked.

"Tamia and Zina, but they're cool. I'm sorry, Dad. It happened so fast, and I couldn't stop it," Lincoln said.

"*They are cool?* You're an anomaly in the entire wizard community, Lincoln. Your blood is worth more than gold. No one can be cool with this information."

"Mr. Espree was there too," Lincoln added, pulling the blanket tightly around him. And I need to tell you—"

Bang! Bang! Bang! Hard knocks pounded on the door.

"Help! Help! Let me in! It's Mr. Jenkins!"

Rima checked the peephole and opened the door.

"Lincoln? Where's Lincoln?" Mr. Jenkins panted.

"Here's right here. He's safe,"

"Oh, thank heavens. They know about your boy. And that's not all," Mr. Jenkins said, taking a seat on the edge of the couch. "There is no military program. The Elders are using a hypnosis dawa to control their minds."

"How do you know that?" Rima asked.

"I got tired of doing nothing so I went to stake out the Elders' lair. I overheard two of them talking about their plans. They want to hypnotize the entire school. An army of over a thousand wizards. Imagine the damage they could do in the world."

"They would do that to kids?" Charles said.

"I told you; Augustin will stop at nothing for power."

The front door exploded inward, sending wood shards flying through the room. A reddish haze, the lingering aftermath of a powerful energy blast, hung in the air as two figures in burgundy cloaks stepped into the house.

Lincoln coughed and wiped his burning eyes with the sleeve of his shirt. Charles pulled a wand from his pajama pocket and stepped in front of Rima.

Rima pushed Lincoln down behind the couch. "Stay down," she whispered, drawing her wand.

Crouching low, Lincoln kept his eyes just above the couch's edge, heart pounding.

"Darlene. Sheldon. Don't do this," Mr. Jenkins pleaded, slowly standing up and lifting his wand.

The two Elders pulled back their hoods. Darlene was tall, dark-skinned, and looked to be in her late fifties. Sheldon appeared younger, his broad frame nearly bursting from his tight cloak.

"Silence, old man. You're no longer one of us. The boy, where is he?" Darlene demanded.

Lincoln edged back, trying to remain unseen, but his movement sent a vase crashing from the ottoman, shattering the tense silence.

Sheldon fired a red energy beam at Rima.

"Kulinda," Rima said, enveloping herself and Lincoln in a shimmering blue shield.

Charles fired an energy beam at Darlene that struck her in the arm, sending her spinning into the wall with a thud.

"Get out of here, Lincoln!" Rima yelled.

"But Mom—"

"You have to go, now!"

Another Elder barged into the room, young with a large Afro, his eyes fixed on Lincoln. Without hesitation, Lincoln vaulted over the couch and dashed towards the garage, the Elder hot on his heels.

"Kamba!" Mr. Jenkins intervened. A crimson beam, like a ropelike tendril, wrapped around the Elder's leg, pulling him backward.

Lincoln grabbed the orb from his pocket and slid under the rising garage door. He tossed the orb into the air and it transformed into his broom. As he soared away, his phone buzzed in his back pocket.

"Tamia!" he said, holding the flip phone in his right hand and steering the broom with his left.

"Lincoln, where are you? I've been calling."

"The Elders are at my house, Tamia. Meet me at the lake."

The headlight of Tamia's scooter shined over Lincoln as she parked in front of the seawall.

"What happened?" she asked, her hands gently cradling his face.

"Darius must've told the Elders about my powers. They are after me."

"You have to leave New Orleans. I'll come with you. Let's go now," Tamia urged, tugging at his arm.

"I'm not running," he said. "Whatever the Elders are planning, we will fight back. I'm sorry to have to ask this again... Do you think your mom has something to do with all of this?"

"She wouldn't hurt people. Why would she help the Elders to attack you? My parents love you. They know you make me happy."

"This isn't about us, Tamia. It's about the entire wizard community, It's about Nawlins. Our friends... Mr. Jenkins said that the Elders are using a hypnosis dawa on the students to build their army... Tamia, she's the Chancellor. She has to know what is going on."

A roar ripped through the night. It didn't sound human or even animal-like; it sounded monstrous.

"What the hell was that?" Lincoln asked, scanning the dark horizon beyond the streetlights.

Tamia jumped when another roar broke the eerie silence. This time, it was even louder.

Red glowing eyes pierced the darkness before them—whatever it was, it was big. White fog from its breath seeped through the air as it snarled.

A flash of lightning rushed through the sky, and finally, Lincoln could see the dirty white fur of the Rougarou. The wolflike beast was tall, ugly, and terrifying.

Side by side, Tamia and Lincoln drew their wands, exchanging a determined nod. As thunder boomed overhead, the beast charged.

Lincoln's energy beam hit the Rougarou's shoulder, causing it to stagger but quickly recover.

Tamia shot an energy beam at its legs, but the beast leaped over the attack, its feet slashing the concrete as it landed.

"Get back!" Lincoln warned Tamia, who quickly retreated down the seawall steps.

The Rougarou lunged, its massive claws aimed at Lincoln, who ducked just in time, the claws missing him by inches. The beast landed heavily, growling fiercely.

"That's enough!" the Chancellor yelled, circling the beast on her broom.

The Rougarou stood still and snarled as it stared at Lincoln.

"Good job tracking my daughter. I knew she would lead me to him," the Chancellor said, dismounting her broom and tapping the beast on the arm.

"Mom, what are you doing here? What is this monster? It could have killed us," Tamia said, rushing to Lincoln's side.

"The Rougarou would never have hurt you, dear," the Chancellor replied. "But it certainly would have torn your boyfriend apart if I hadn't intervened."

"You said it tracked me?"

"Yes, I ordered it to track you using a strand of hair

from your brush."

"Mom, you're scaring me."

Two wizards in burgundy cloaks landed their brooms behind the Chancellor. They removed their hoods and stood next to her, revealing their ancient wooden wands.

"Mr. Espree, I knew you were an Elder," Lincoln said.

"Thank you for exposing your pure-wizard form. I forgot how it looked on Solomon. It was truly fascinating."

"Professor Osborne... You're an Elder? All this time." Tamia gestured to the petite woman.

"Did you really think I was at Nawlins only to teach music? We are destined for greatness, and soon the whole world will understand," Professor Osborne declared.

"Mom, what is this all about?" Tamia asked, stepping closer to the Chancellor.

"Lincoln has the blood of Solomon Deslondes running through his veins, and we need it," Chancellor explained with eerie simplicity.

"I have no idea what you're talking about, ma'am. You know my parents, and Solomon didn't have any children," Lincoln countered.

"Liar! I saw your hands glow bright red," Mr. Espree interjected. "You used your magic without your wand. And your eyes! They were pitch-black. You're a Deslondes, boy."

"The same black eyes I witnessed as Solomon descended to the ground when he was given his powers," the Chancellor said. "The same glow I saw when we fought our oppressors. Solomon was the only wizard with this ability; able to tune out all weakness in his body and surrender fully to his wizard form."

"Mom, you couldn't have been there when Solomon was granted his powers," Tamia said.

"My dear, I am over two centuries old. We made a dawa from Solomon's blood that kept us alive. I was able to make a reverse aging dawa that allowed me to enroll at Nawlins. God, it was awful going back and acting like a child again. But it was a small sacrifice for the greater good."

"Mom, you're making no sense."

The Chancellor snapped her glossy red wand in half and tossed it onto the ground. She pulled a strikingly gold wand from her cloak, engraved with the number 2 at its base.

"The wand of Augustin Decken," Tamia said.

"Onyesha!" the Chancellor chanted.

Her dark brown eyes shifted bright green, and silky black hair cascaded down her back.

"I am Augustin Decken!" she proclaimed.

Lincoln pointed his wand at Augustin.

"Lincoln, I've sacrificed my entire life to make wizards the rulers of this pathetic world," she said. "The Norms don't deserve to rule. We were given these powers for something greater than just to exist."

"We were given these gifts to free ourselves from bondage many years ago. And if we use the same gifts to oppress others, how are we better than our oppressors?" Lincoln argued.

"You echo Solomon's idealism. I tried to convince him to join my uprising, but he refused, so I ended his defiance with a dagger to his heart... So, I'm going to give you the same ultimatum: Join me or die."

"Mom, stop this, please," Tamia cried out.

"Stay out of this, my child," Augustin said.

There was a brief silence. Lincoln glanced at the two Elders and the Rougarou. He then looked to Tamia, who nodded.

"Let's stand on business," she whispered.

Lincoln grinned and shot an energy beam at Augustin, who quickly countered the attack with a translucent shield she produced from her wand.

Tamia fired an energy beam at Professor Osborne, who countered with the same red beam. Their beams clashed mid-air, spiraling into a swirling vortex of energy. Mr. Espree shot a beam at the ground near Tamia's feet, and she fell back.

Using her shield, Augustin deflected the beam toward Lincoln. He leaped aside just in time, the blast hissing past his face before crashing into the lake. Before he could recover, Augustin fired a bright white beam from her wand. It struck his shoulder, sending him spinning through the air before he slammed to the ground. He lay there, immobilized but still conscious.

"That should hold him for a few," Augustin stated.

Tamia positioned herself between her mother and Lincoln, wand raised. "Mom, I won't let you hurt him."

Professor Decken and his father, the president of the High Council, landed their brooms in front of Augustin.

"You're in on this, too? Are you Elders?" Tamia's voice quavered.

"No, grandchild... We are not Elders," President Thibodeaux clarified.

"But we believe that wizards were created to rule, not hide," her father added.

Augustin pointed her wand at Lincoln. "You either choose him or us. Remember, I am still your mother, Tamia. We are your family."

"You've been lying to me my entire life. I won't join you. If you want to harm Lincoln, you'll have to harm me too."

"I am your mother! You dare to defy me? You ungrateful child... I had hoped it wouldn't come to this, but if you won't stand with me willingly—"

President Thibodeaux shot a red beam of energy that wrapped around Tamia's body.

Lincoln tried with all his might to fight against the paralysis that plagued his body, but it was no use. He was rendered a powerless observer, agonizingly forced to watch as Tamia suffered, his heart aching with the urge to speak, to act, to intervene in any way he could.

President Thibodeaux lifted his wand, and Tamia rose in the air and floated closer to Augustin until they were face to face.

"You left me with no other choice, my dear," Augustin said, gently stroking Tamia's hair.

She accepted a glass jar filled with a glowing purple substance from Professor Decken and dipped her wand into it.

"Akili," she said.

The purple vapor penetrated Tamia's airway. After a few seconds, President Thibodeaux lowered his wand, and Tamia descended to the ground.

Tamia mechanically walked over to her mother and gave Lincoln a vacant stare.

Rage surged within Lincoln, his heart pounding as a dark ring blurred his vision. His body shifted into pure-wizard form, breaking him free from the stun beam's hold. As his vision cleared and his heartbeat steadied, he regained full control.

"Stop him," Augustin said to the Rougarou.

The beast charged at Lincoln. He swiftly retrieved his orb, transforming it into his broom just in time to evade the Rougarou's leap.

Mr. Espree and Professor Osborne followed on their brooms.

Sporadic flashes of lightning lit Lincoln's path as the rain blurred his vision.

The two Elders slowly circled him. Lincoln pulled out his wand.

Professor Osborne darted at Lincoln as Mr. Espree shot an energy beam. Lincoln maneuvered upside down to avoid the beam but could not dodge Osborne, who rammed into him. The impact knocked him off his broom.

Free-falling, Lincoln whistled for his broom to return to him as both Elders charged, shooting energy beams. He countered each attack, creating clouds of black smoke where the beams clashed.

Lincoln's broom zipped underneath him, and he quickly straddled it and ripped through the air. Pulling away from the Elders, he glanced back for the perfect timing for a counterattack. He shot a beam in the direction of a dark cloud of smoke and Professor Osborne emerged right into its path, which shattered her broom and sent her spiraling through the air.

Osborne pointed her wand above her as she fell, releasing a reddish substance that unfurled like a parachute, slowing her fall toward the water below.

"One more left," Lincoln declared, pressing down on his broomstick as he dove toward the lake.

Mr. Espree raced behind him.

Lincoln sharply pulled up on his broom, slicing through the air and parting the lake's surface, creating a massive spray. Inches from the water, he leveled out and aimed his wand.

"Maji," he chanted, directing a powerful blast of water upwards.

Mr. Espree, attempting to evade, pulled up on his broom, but it was too late. The water engulfed him before he could divert his course.

Lincoln returned to the lakefront, but there was no trace of Tamia, the Rougarou, or any other wizards. "Tamia!" he called out into the emptiness.

Glass from the shattered windows crunched under Lincoln's feet as he rushed through the front door of his parent's house. Inside resembled the aftermath of a tornado—furniture upturned, his father's cherished television smashed on the floor, lamps toppled. But the Elders who barged in unannounced seemed to have got the brunt of it. Amidst the wreckage, Darlene and Sheldon were sprawled face down on the floor, motionless.

"Lincoln, you're safe," Rima exclaimed, snatching him up in her arms.

"Ma, are they dead?"

"Your mother wouldn't have it, so we stunned them instead," Mr. Jenkins grumbled.

Charles, busy at work nursing Mr. Jenkins' injury, applied healing paste to the open wound on his arm.

"Ouch!" Mr. Jenkins cried out.

"Stop being a baby," Charles responded.

"The High Council is on their way to clean this mess up," Rima said.

"No! The Chancellor is Augustin Decken! She ambushed Tamia and I. President Thibodeaux is on her side too."

"I knew it. We can't trust those bastards," Mr. Jenkins said.

"Where is Tamia?" Charles asked.

"They used the hypnosis dawa on her," Lincoln replied, hanging his head. "Ma, what do I do?"

Rima grabbed his chin and lifted his head. "Hey, you're not alone in this fight. We are DuVernays. We stick together. We will save Tamia, I promise."

"So, what's our next move?" Mr. Jenkins asked.

"Looks like the High Council is compromised, so the Rebels are the only hope left. We need to regroup at the old Rebel base camp. We'll gather our allies and train there." Charles said.

"And what about these two?" Mr. Jenkins nudged Sheldon with his foot.

"Leave them. Let the Elders find them so they know we can fight back," Rima said.

Lincoln couldn't help but admire his mother's

leadership; her strength and determination fueled his hope.

"Where is the Rebel camp?" he asked.

"Your grandparents' house," Charles revealed.

"The ranch house in Opelousas?" Lincoln asked, puzzled.

"No. Their old house in New Orleans," Charles corrected.

"The one we used to live in? I thought y'all sold that house when I was a kid."

"We let everyone think that we got rid of it... but we kept it. We thought it might come in handy one day," Charles explained.

"And it's a Rebel camp? I don't remember seeing anything wizard-related in there. It was just a regular house."

"That's the point, son. Not everything is as it appears," Charles winked.

"Come on, let's get out of here," Rima said.

Chapter Thirty-Five

Lincoln looked younger, around thirteen, as he stood in an empty training room with his parents. Professor DuVernay retrieved a training dummy from a closet and positioned it before Lincoln.

"Do you remember the energy beam we taught you, son? Ready to give it a try?" he asked.

"Why do I have to do this, Ma?"

"Your father and I saw your powers come out of your hands yesterday."

"The pure-wizard thing?"

"Yes. If you don't learn to control this, it will expose your identity. And the bad wizards will come for you. Do you understand?"

"Just like how they killed my birth parents?" Lincoln asked, putting his head down.

Rima tenderly lifted his chin and rubbed his head.

"Hey. We won't let anything happen to you. But you have to do your part and control your powers."

Lincoln hesitated, his hand trembling as he held his wand.

"I'm just... so angry that those wizards killed my family... Ah, ma, my head... It hurts," he said, dropping his wand and covering his ears with his hands.

"It's okay. We can try another day," Rima said.

"Take some deep breaths, son," Charles instructed.

Lincoln's eyes snapped open. An energy beam burst from his hand, shattering the dummy and blasting a hole through the wall.

"Stop!" Charles shouted, grabbing Lincoln's arm.

The beam struck Charles in the shoulder, tossing him back.

"I'm sorry, son," Rima said quickly, casting a white beam that knocked Lincoln to the floor, immobilizing him.

She cradled his head in her lap. "You're okay, Lincoln. You're okay. We will help you control it. I promise." She looked over at Charles. "How's your shoulder?"

Charles, grimacing, peeled off his shirt to inspect a deep gash that was bleeding. "It's not too bad."

"The healing paste will take care of it," Rima said.

"What are we going to do?" Charles said, kneeling next to Lincoln.

"I think meditation will help. Just like Deedy told us it helped him. I can take a course and learn how to do it properly."

Lincoln moved slightly as the stun beam started to wear off.

"I'm sorry, Dad," he murmured.

"Don't worry about me. How are you feeling?"

"I'm scared."

"Hey, don't be scared. We are here. We will protect you."

"Do you remember when we told you about the night we rescued you from the river? How Deedy saved you?" Rima asked.

"Yes."

"You have to be brave like Deedy."

She reached into her pocket and took out a gold necklace with a small bar-shaped diamond pendant. She clipped the chain around his neck.

"This was Deedy's... It's yours now, which means he will always be with you so you can be strong and brave, just like him."

Donna's eyes fluttered open. The dream had felt as vivid and intense as her recurring nightmares about the crash—so real as if she had lived those memories herself. She rose from the couch in her mother's room and drifted to the window.

Lincoln is my brother! Link is alive! Who is Deedy?

"What's wrong, my 'sha?" Catherine asked, sitting up in her bed.

"Mom... I... I had a bad dream," Donna replied, climbing into her mother's bed, and wrapping her arm around her waist.

"I had an interesting dream too," Catherine said, rubbing Donna's shoulder.

"What happened in your dream?"

"Your brother was standing outside the window. He was older, but I recognized him. He was so handsome."

"Did he say anything?"

"No. We just looked at each other until he disappeared."

Donna saw the pain in her mother's eyes.

"I swear the medicine they have me on is too strong because the dream felt so darn real," Catherine said, wiping her tears.

Donna hugged her mother tighter. She wanted to tell her about her dream. Even more, she really wanted to ask her about the DuVernays. But she knew it was probably too much for her mom to handle right now.

How would I even tell her what's going on? Hey, Mom, I think Link is still alive and my professor and my doctor are posing as his parents. Or... Hey, Mom, I'm a wizard. And I might be a descendant of the most powerful wizard who ever lived. Oh, and my pet cat is a panther... I can't bombard her with this. She just got out of the hospital. What if I just stay in New York? She needs me here.

"Mom, I don't want to go back to Nawlins."

"You love that school."

"I do, but—"

"Donna Marie, I know what this is about," Catherine interjected. "Don't you worry about me. I'll be fine... I was pushing myself too hard in rehab because I wanted to surprise you by walking without a cane. My physical therapist told me to slow it down, but I didn't listen. This was my fault and best believe I learned my lesson."

"Breakfast is here!" Jacquie said, barging in the room with two brown bags in her hands.

"Donna, if you don't get your grown behind out of your mother's bed..."

"Aw, hush, Jacquie. She will never be too grown to be my baby girl."

"Okay, but when she squashes you don't call me to help."

"Did you feed Mr. Whiskers?" Donna asked Jacquie.

"I put a can of sardines in his bowl before I left. That cat better not tear up my couch."

"I wish they could let you bring him in here so I can pet him, but some of the other residents are allergic," Catherine said.

"I like those pearl earrings, Auntie," Donna said, getting up.

"Thanks, hunny." Jacquie moved closer so Donna could get a closer look. "Gary bought them for me."

"Who's Gary?" Donna asked, making a stinky face.

"Remember the driver that picked us up from the airport in New Orleans?"

"Yeah..."

"Well, we talk every day and he came to visit me last week."

"So, you have a boyfriend now, Auntie?" Donna asked, putting three plastic plates on the table.

"Let's call him a *man*friend," Jacquie said with a wink. "Catherine, do you want me to set up a tray by your bed so you can eat?"

"No. I'll eat at the table with my daughter and my best friend," Catherine replied, fetching her cane on the side of the bed.

Despite her recent hospital scare, Catherine looked much healthier since the summer. She had lost some weight and was walking without a significant limp. She also had mobility in her left arm.

Donna pulled her chair back, and Catherine sat down with a big smile on her face.

"I'm so proud of you, Mom," Donna said.

"And I'm proud of you too. Shall we say grace?"

"Of course. How about you lead us?" Jacquie said, offering her hand to Catherine.

They all held hands and bowed their heads.

"Dear God, I want to say thank you for bringing my daughter back home safe for winter break. I'm so proud of the young woman she's becoming. Thank you for Jacquie, who's the most selfless person that I know. And thank you for this breakfast that we are about to fellowship over... Last but not least, thank you for my dream last night. Seeing my son's face again was a pleasant surprise. I miss him so much. For this, we thank you," Catherine said.

"Such a good prayer. Now, tell me about this dream of yours," Jacquie said, taking a bite of bacon.

Donna smiled as she stared at her mother. She was grateful for this moment, enjoying breakfast with her family. Life was chaotic and challenging, now more than ever... but as she sat there, she realized what truly made her happy was right there all along: her mother and auntie, whom she loved dearly.

Chapter Thirty-Six

W inter break was over. Donna had just arrived back at Nawlins.

Is Lincoln really my brother? she asked herself, leaving her dorm after dropping her bags off.

Donna had felt that she and Lincoln had a special connection since the first time she saw him. It all made sense to her now, from their matching anxiety attacks to their glowing hands—it was the Deslondes blood running through their veins. *This is what Lincoln has been hiding from me.*

Yesterday, Rima had scheduled this meeting with her, probably to check how her anxiety was holding up. But Donna had a different agenda: make her tell the truth about Lincoln.

It was the first time Donna met Rima at her actual job, which was about a ten-minute taxi ride from Nawlins. A front-desk worker at the fancy hospital escorted Donna to Rima's office. She lifted her hand to knock, but something held her back.

Is this a good idea? Asking someone whether she's been lying about the true identity of her son doesn't seem like a good idea.

With a heavy sigh, Donna turned to leave, but at that moment, the door swung open.

"We've been expecting you. Please, come in," Rima said, standing beside Professor DuVernay.

As Rima shut the door, she waved her wand upwards, casting a spell that created a shimmering bubble around them.

"What is that?" Donna asked.

"It's a privacy bubble," Rima explained.

The closet door opened, and an older gentleman wearing thick eyeglasses and a straw fedora hat stepped out. He spat his gum into the trash, and his elderly body transformed. It was Lincoln.

"Donna... We have something to tell you," Rima said.

"Lincoln... He is my brother."

"How did you know?" Lincoln asked.

Donna untucked her necklace from her sweatshirt.

"You have the same necklace, but a diamond stone... don't you?" she asked, eyes locked on Lincoln.

"You know about my pendant? How?" Lincoln asked, untucking his chain.

"I dreamed about it," Donna said, her eyes getting teary. "Why did you keep the truth from me? Why did you keep the truth from Mom? How could you do this to me?"

"Your father wasn't killed in a car accident; he was murdered by Elders. Lincoln was so young when it happened, and the concussion he suffered that night left his memory blank. So we lied. We told him Catherine died too."

"We did it to protect them both," Rima added softly. "We didn't know that Catherine was pregnant with you. I'm so sorry."

"What's an Elder?" Donna asked.

"Wizards from the revolt of 1811. They used a dawa to stay alive all these years. Augustin Decken is their leader," Professor DuVernay explained.

"And last night, we discovered that the Chancellor is Augustin Decken," Rima added.

Donna absorbed their words, the gravity of the revelations making her dizzy. She collapsed into a chair, silent for a long moment before lifting her gaze to Lincoln.

"But you still knew you were my brother all this time and didn't say a word? How could you look at me and not feel guilty? How could you not feel anything?" Donna said, her voice rising. She clenched her fists and fell to her knees. Her breathing got heavy, and her body felt hot.

"She's going into pure-wizard form," Rima said, lifting her wand at Donna.

Donna's vision was starting to blur. She squeezed her eyes shut.

"Mom, wait. Don't stun her. I can help her through it," Lincoln said.

Donna rocked back and forth on her knees with her fists pressed against her eyelids.

"Take a deep breath through your nose and slowly let it out through your mouth, Donna," Lincoln said, sitting on the floor in front of her and gently holding her shoulders.

Donna met Lincoln's eyes, inhaled through her nose, and exhaled slowly through her mouth.

"That's it. Take another breath," Lincoln said, placing his fingers over her temples and massaging them.

After a few moments, Donna's anxiety subsided. The tears flowed as she embraced Lincoln.

"I'm sorry... I'm sorry, I thought you were dead," Donna said, sobbing.

Rima, who was crying too, brought Donna some tissues and rubbed her on her back.

"I want you to know that I've felt everything," Lincoln said. "Pain, heartbreak, love, deception, and anger. All these years I didn't even know you existed. It's been so hard. No one can know who we really are. I kept the secret for so long. My best friend, Nnamdi, doesn't even know."

"Does Tamia know?" Donna asked.

"Tamia—" His voice broke. "The Elders got her. They are using a hypnosis dawa to build their army. It's why Raine and those other students have been acting so weird."

"The Rebels will get Tamia back. We will save them all," Rima said.

"Who are the Rebels?" Donna asked.

"We are," Lincoln said with a smile.

Donna was sitting in the back of the DuVernays' SUV as they drove through a suburban neighborhood in New Orleans. The highway signs suggested that this area was considered the East. Lincoln was sitting next to her. Apparently he was exhausted, because he had fallen asleep leaning on the door panel. Professor DuVernay and Rima remained quiet as old-school R&B played through the speakers. Donna could tell the Range Rover was new because of the temporary tags and the new-car smell. *It must've been nice growing up with money while I struggled in NYC*, she thought, glancing over to Lincoln.

The SUV entered a side street with a small green sign that read *Asphodel Dr.* The neighborhood was picturesque, lined with elegant two-story brick houses, each bordered by neat picket fences. Front yards were spacious, equipped with basketball hoops, soccer goals, or volleyball nets—emblems of suburban leisure. It was the kind of setting often depicted in movies, where perfect families with pets, parents, and honor roll children lived seemingly flawless lives.

They pulled into a driveway where an older gentleman in brown overalls was standing in front of the house. Donna had to nudge Lincoln a few times to get him awake. He didn't look too happy about it.

"Donna, this was my childhood home. It was one of the first houses built in this predominantly Black community. My grandparents passed it down to me my first year in college after they bought a ranch house in Opelousas," Rima said.

"And we turned it into the Rebel camp... And then it became more like an off-campus dormitory. We were all living here in college at some point. Me, Rima, Deedy, some of the other Rebels," Professor DuVernay said as they got out of the vehicle.

"Deedy? Was that my father's real name?" Donna asked.

"That's how the Deslondes family hid themselves all these years—using fake names and bloodlines," Rima explained.

"You two are the last descendants of Solomon. The family did what they had to do to survive," Charles added.

"Is this her? The princess of the royal Deslondes throne?" the old man said, twisting his long mustache.

"Donna, that's Mr. Jenkins. Raine's grandfather," Lincoln said.

"Aw, come on... tell her the truth... I'm an Elder," Mr. Jenkins said with a grin, extending his hand to Donna.

She hesitated for a moment, then took a step back.

"You're really an Elder?" she asked.

"Why does everyone ask that? Yes. I'm an Elder. Over two centuries old. I'm an ancient old fart."

"Don't worry, he's on our side," Rima said.

"Raine is my friend. She's a very talented artist," Donna said, shaking his hard, dry hand.

"Where do you think she got it from, little girl?" Mr. Jenkins said.

"Wait, are you the one that did the paintings in the entrance hall?"

"That would be me. Mr. Jenkins in the flesh. Not the bones."

"Seems like I was right about Augustin; she looked mean in your painting."

"Oh, yes. As an artist, I paint the truth. And you have no idea how mean she really is."

Donna had only been inside a few beautiful homes like this one. Her entire building in the Bronx was probably the size of this home. In the summers, Jacquie sometimes took her along to preview properties, where Donna would wander through lavish brownstones in Harlem, dreaming of one day owning enough space to comfortably house herself and her mother. This house surpassed those dreams.

When she walked in, an open foyer greeted her, anchored by two sweeping curved staircases that gave the space a bold, luxurious feel.

"This way," Rima directed, leading them toward the living room dominated by a large rectangular mirror against one wall.

"Onyesha," she said, pointing her wand in the center of the mirror.

Donna watched her puzzled reflection ripple as the glass transformed into a liquid portal. Rima stepped through, then reached through the mirror's surface and pulled Donna in.

Donna emerged into the vast training facility of the Rebel camp. The room was lined with black padded walls that cushioned Donna's touch like plush pillows. Training dummies of various sizes filled the space alongside a fully equipped gym and a combat arena. There, a tall, muscular man was energetically blasting an energy beam at a dummy, shouting triumphantly in a robust African accent, "Take that, you Elder. You can't beat me!"

Donna chuckled at his animated battle with the inanimate dummy.

"Donna Marie!" Chike's voice called from across the room, descending the stairs with Nnamdi.

"You're joining the Rebels too, huh?" Chike asked, giving Donna a fist pump.

"Yeah, I am," she replied, her gaze shifting to Lincoln.

"How does that feel, Elder!" the man by the dummy yelled.

"That's my father. His name is Superb," Chike said. "And the woman next to him is my mom, Annette." Annette wore a fitted vest that showed off her toned arms. *Glad they are on our side*, Donna thought.

"Rima and I called on our old friends from college to rejoin the group; most of them are parents of the students whose lives are in jeopardy," Professor DuVernay said.

"We have a plan to sneak into the school tomorrow to confront Augustin. You're a Rebel now—you're going to fight with us," Mr. Jenkins said.

"Again, are we sure we want kids fighting Elders?" Professor DuVernay asked.

"We probably have no other choice," Rima replied.

"Donna and I can recruit more friends we trust," Lincoln said.

"And I know some college students who would make excellent Rebels too," Zina said, coming down the stairs.

"Donna. Lincoln. There is something we want to show you upstairs," Professor Duvernay said, placing his hand on Rima's shoulder.

The second floor of the Rebel camp housed a meeting area, a fully-equipped kitchen, and sleeping quarters with multiple bedrooms. On the third floor, a large open space was filled with food and supplies neatly stacked against the walls. Rima led them down a corridor to a room distinguished by a carving of Deedy's name above the doorframe. Donna and Lincoln gazed up at the carving for a moment before they went inside.

Inside, the sparse furnishings included only a wooden bed frame holding a mattress dressed in a crisp white sheet, and a small, dark brown rectangular box tucked into the corner.

"What's that?" Donna asked, pointing to the mysterious box.

"Deedy left that here the day he took off for New York."

Lincoln picked up the box. Donna laughed as his muscles flexed, struggling to open it.

"It's not budging," Lincoln said, placing the box back on the floor.

Suddenly, the box vibrated and tipped onto its side. Donna stepped back, her eyes wide. "Um, what is it doing?"

With another shudder, the box expanded upward and outward, transforming into a tall, dark wooden armoire.

Professor DuVernay opened the double-hinged doors where three shelves hosted deep drawers. He slid open one of the drawers; a round golden ornament and a plain, grayish wand rolled forward.

"The wand. Pick it up, Lincoln," he said.

Lincoln picked up the wand and held it in front of him.

"Now say 'Onyesha'."

"Onyesha," Lincoln echoed.

The wand shifted in appearance; its shaft darkened to a deep black, and the handle morphed into a shimmering crystal.

"That's our dad's wand," Donna stated.

"How did you know?" Professor DuVernay asked.

"I've seen him in my dreams. Well, it's always this one particular dream when he's driving this red truck and... And you're always there too, Lincoln."

"Interesting," Rima said.

"That was indeed his wand," Professor DuVernay confirmed. He then tossed the orb into the air, which transformed into a gold broom. "And this was his broom."

"We found both by the Hudson River the night we rescued you, Lincoln."

The same river from my dreams? Were my dreams trying to tell me something?

"The Chancellor... Augustin... She killed my father, didn't she?" Donna said.

The room filled with a heavy silence before Lincoln solemnly nodded.

"I've seen her in my dreams, too. She was wearing a black cloak and had a golden wand. She pushed my father's truck off the bridge. But... Dad saved you, Lincoln. He wrapped your body in some kind of barrier. And there was this creature chasing us. A monster with a hairy, humanlike body and a wolf's head."

"That monster is called the Rougarou," said Mr. Jenkins, stepping into the room. "It appears you've inherited the gift as well."

"What gift?" Donna asked, puzzled.

"Solomon had the gift of prophecy. I can't explain it, but these visions allowed us to locate some of the folks we freed during the revolt because he would see their locations in his dreams. Donna, those dreams of yours weren't just dreams; they were windows to the past and perhaps insights into your future," Mr. Jenkins explained. "Your dreams were trying to reveal your true heritage. The Deslondes lineage is indeed extraordinary."

"Seems more like a curse, having to watch my father die over and over again."

"A gift. A curse. We are wizards. It's all subjective. The big difference is what you do with it," Mr. Jenkins stated philosophically.

The broom gently drifted towards Donna.

"It looks like the broom already chose its new owner," Rima said.

The large broom felt surprisingly light as Donna held it in her hands. She pressed a glowing button on its side, and foot pegs expanded from the bottom while handlebars expanded from the sides.

"Man, that's not fair. That broom is mad lit, ya heard me," Lincoln complained.

"What does mad lit mean?" Mr. Jenkins asked.

"Let's just say it means very cool," Rima interjected, giving Lincoln a serious look.

"Seems like the wand found its new owner, too," Professor DuVernay said, gesturing to the crystal handle which brightly glistened in Lincoln's hand.

"Yeah, this wand is even better. Besides, I'm already too fast on my broom. Any more help would be wrong," he joked.

Donna smiled at him.

"This wand is special. The handle is made of raw diamonds," Rima explained.

"Solomon made it himself using a piece of his wand," Professor DuVernay added.

Mr. Jenkins cleared his raspy throat, drawing attention.

"The rest of the Rebels are gathering for the meeting," he announced.

Donna stood next to Lincoln in the meeting room on the second floor, surrounded by other Rebel members who listened quietly, awaiting orders. The Rebel High Council, consisting of fifteen wizards, was deep in discussion around a long rectangular table. At the head of the table sat Rima, the newly elected president, leading the strategic plan to invade Nawlins.

"What do we know about the hypnosis dawa?" Professor Hunt asked.

The room fell silent, punctuated only by Mr. Jenkins eating a muffin.

After wiping his mouth with a handkerchief, he stood.

"I so slightly remember the hypnosis dawa from my early wizard days," he said, grinning as he stuffed the handkerchief into his pocket. "It was in *The Book of Giza*. The main ingredient is blood from the person controlling the hypnosis, and Deslondes blood. There is one more key ingredient I can't seem to remember, but that doesn't matter because the Elders obviously have all three if they tricked y'all into thinking there was a new military program on campus!"

Donna gasped, covering her mouth as Mr. Jenkins scrutinized the Council.

"Thank you for that, Mr. Jenkins. You may sit down now," Rima said.

"Is there a spell or a dawa to reverse it?" asked a woman with short red hair, who was sitting next to Zina.

"Who's that?" Donna whispered to Lincoln.

"That's Zina's mom. The bald-head dude on the other side of Zina is her dad."

Mr. Jenkins stood again and loudly blew his nose into the handkerchief. "I don't remember if there is one," he replied.

"Thank you again, Mr. Jenkins. But you don't need to stand up when talking," Rima said. "*The Book of Giza* and *The Book of Knowledge* were tampered with in the wizard sanctuary. The Elders probably knew we would look for the reversal spell."

"So, realistically, what are our options here?" Annette asked.

"We need to stop Augustin before she uses the dawa on the rest of the students," Rima stated firmly.

"I say we do more than just stop her. We need to put an end to her," Mr. Jenkins said, rising once more.

"We will not resort to killing," Rima countered firmly.

"I agree. I say we capture her and make her stop the hypnosis," Monique added, fixing her glasses.

"You look like a child. How old are you?" Mr. Jenkins asked, raising his voice at her.

"I'm twenty-two, thank you," Monique replied, standing her ground.

"See! She's a child!"

"We will have order, Mr. Jenkins. Monique is a senior in college. She has valuable input at this High Council," Rima said.

Donna was impressed by how Monique stood up for herself despite her and Zina probably being the youngest at the table.

"But why does Augustin deserve so much mercy? After all she has done? The lives she took?" Mr. Jenkins said, glancing over to Lincoln and Donna.

"Because we follow in the footsteps of Solomon. Just as he advocated for peace after the revolt, we must do the same," Professor DuVernay said.

Mr. Jenkins took a seat and shook his head slightly.

"Let's see if the Elders show us the same mercy if our plan fails. I know those people. They are ruthless."

"What is our plan?" Professor Hunt asked.

"Mr. Espree told Lincoln that there is a mandatory JMP meeting after winter break. We need to get to Augustin before that meeting takes place. We will invade the school early in the morning and set a trap in the Oasis to lure Augustin and her crew there," Rima explained.

"What kind of trap?" Annette asked.

"We are going to set one of the oak trees ablaze. Once Augustin arrives, will we face her and put an end to this."

"Yes. I'm ready to fight," Lincoln declared.

"No. No high school students will be part of this battle. We are not putting you all at risk," Professor DuVernay said.

"But Dad, we want to fight!" Lincoln said again, stronger.

"Yeah, we want to fight," Chike insisted.

"You will not!" Superb interjected, rising to his feet and staring down both of his sons as Nnamdi also stepped forward in solidarity.

"Let's all take a moment to relax," Rima said soothingly. "Young wizards, your eagerness to help is appreciated, and rest assured, each of you will have a role in what's to come. The trap also serves as a diversion."

"In case of hazards such as fires or natural disasters, the safety plan for students and staff is to meet in the auditorium where a mass protection spell can be cast,"

Professor DuVernay said. "During this time, you all will collect your friends and meet Zina in the Gardens. She will escort you to a secret passageway out of campus. This way if something goes wrong you can come back to the Rebel camp."

"Ah, you know the old secret passageway in the janitor's closet, aye?" Mr. Jenkins said, grinning.

"Oh, yeah, we use it to sneak back into school from the Raceway sometimes," Chike said.

Professor DuVernay's eyes narrowed. "So it's true; there *is* a secret broom racing league at Nawlins?"

Silence fell. Every student turned to Chike like he'd just sold them out.

"Bruh..." Nnamdi muttered, smacking him upside the head.

"I guess it's not a secret anymore," Mr. Jenkins remarked.

"Do all Elders know of this secret passageway?" Rima asked.

"Not sure. But just to be safe, we should think of something else," Mr. Jenkins replied.

"There is another secret passageway," Superb said. "Only my wife and I know about it."

"That's right," Annette said.

"My ancestor, Cane Hargis, helped with the construction of Nawlins. He built a secret passageway that leads into one of my businesses."

"What? Which one?" Nnamdi asked.

"The barbershop in the French Quarter," Annette revealed.

"Great, so we will get the coordinates and Zina can lead them there," Rima said.

"So, y'all get to fight and we do nothing?" Lincoln complained, crossing his arms.

"The most important thing is that you stay safe... that all of you stay safe," Rima said, glancing at Donna.

Donna nodded, but she shared Lincoln's frustration. How could she do nothing when she and Lincoln might have the power to save them all?

Chapter Thirty-Seven

As the morning sun climbed over New Orleans, Donna and Noor sat in their dorm's living room, their backpacks filled with clothes and personal items in their laps, eyes fixed on the clock.

"We should hear the signal any minute now," Donna said.

"Jia still isn't here. She was supposed to meet us in our room thirty minutes ago," Noor replied.

"She's probably just finishing up packing," Donna reassured her, tossing a treat to Mr. Whiskers, who lounged in his mesh carrier at her feet.

Suddenly, Donna noticed a cloud of black smoke from the window.

"It's coming from the Oasis. They did it," she said.

The fire alarm blared, disrupting the dormitory's calm as students scrambled outside in a panic.

"Hey, girls," Chad said, waving his hands at Donna and Noor as they gathered on the sidewalk.

Chike hustled over, still wrestling with his backpack straps, accompanied by three guys and two girls.

"These are some of my homies and cheerleaders from the football team," he introduced.

"Dang, you didn't bring Ryan?" Chad said.

"I don't trust Ryan or the rest of the Coven members," Chike responded.

"I had you all wrong this entire time, lil woady," Chad said, dapping him up. "I thought you were just like them."

"Nah, bro. I don't care about that bloodline stuff."

"We can't find Jia," Noor said.

"She's probably already at the Gardens. Let's head there," Chike suggested.

They veered away from the crowd, taking a secluded route. After a few minutes, Donna spotted Lacey walking with her hypnotized crew.

"Let's cut through here," Chike said, leading them to the Spells building. As they made their way through the empty main hallway, Raine appeared abruptly around a corner. She stood silent, blocking the double doors.

"Raine, we know what happened to you. We can help you," Donna said, taking a step forward.

"Auditorium. Now!" Raine demanded, her wand raised.

"We're actually on our way there now," Chike said, digging in his pocket.

He quickly pulled out his wand and fired a white beam at Raine. The beam struck her in the arm and she fell to the ground, motionless.

"It's a stun beam. My dad taught me that," Chike said, blowing the tip of his wand.

"Chike, I know you didn't just blow on your wand like it was smoking," Noor said.

"What can I say, I'm on fire." He grinned, walking with a confident bounce.

"Oh, no, now you're doing a pimp walk," Noor groaned, playfully tugging at his arm.

The campus was much quieter now. A gentle breeze whispered through the Gardens, rustling the flowers and trees.

"Psst."

Donna heard the call coming from a cluster of tall magnolia trees.

"Who's there?" Chad asked, lifting his wand.

Lincoln, Nnamdi, and a group of older students stepped out from hiding.

"Did you see Jia anywhere?" Donna asked Lincoln.

"No. Have you seen Zina? She was supposed to meet us here."

"She's over here," came a familiar voice from across the Gardens. Darius stepped into view, wand raised high, as Zina, entwined in tree roots, floated above him. She winced in pain.

"Let her go!" Lincoln said.

"Or what, you freak?" Darius snapped.

Lincoln lifted his wand.

"Oh, look who's here," Darius mocked, nodding toward an approaching figure. Tamia entered the scene, wearing a Coven letterman jacket, her expression unreadable.

"Tamia, are you okay?" Lincoln said, lowering his wand.

"Ryan! You too?" Chike said as Ryan stepped behind Darius.

"What did you expect? He's my cousin. We are in the Coven, bro. We have an obligation to help Augustin."

"Not me," Chike said.

"Yeah, our family don't rock like that. We make our own choices. We don't follow some power-hungry old woman who killed her own friend," Nnamdi chimed in, standing beside his brother.

"Damn, dawg, looks like you were right about Ryan," Chad said, glancing at Chike.

"Darius, put Zina down and stop this," Lincoln said, taking a step forward.

"Did you tell your friends you have Deslondes blood running through your veins?" Darius said.

"What?" Nnamdi asked.

"What is he talking about, Lincoln?" Chad asked.

Donna watched the unfolding drama, torn between jumping in and staying out of it. Inside her carrying bag, Mr. Whiskers remained quiet.

"It's true. He's a ONE," Darius gloated. "What a waste of power. You're weak, Lincoln. You should want to show the world how superior we are. No more hiding. Wizards are supposed to rule the world. Not the Norms."

"I'm going to ask you one more time. Put Zina down," Lincoln said.

"You know she led me right to you. I saw her running in the wrong direction when the fire alarm went off. A little truth dawa got her to spill the beans. Call yourselves *Rebels*, huh?" Darius laughed. "Oh, and I warned Augustin about the attack at the Oasis too. She and the Elders should be done finishing up with your parents now."

"Tamia. I know you're in there. Please, stop this," Lincoln pleaded.

Tamia fired an energy blast at him. Lincoln dove to the ground.

Nnamdi fired a beam at Darius. He dropped Zina and shot a counterattack. Zina fell to the ground, and the tree roots binding her broke apart. She tried to rise to her feet, but she stumbled and grasped her leg.

"Take everyone to the secret passageway. Lincoln and I will hold them off and meet you there. Go, now!" Nnamdi said to his brother.

"Let's go, Rebels," Chike said.

Donna crept toward a nearby bush as the group followed Chike to the college campus. Chad reached for her hand to join the others, but she shook her head. She was not leaving Lincoln behind. Chad hesitated but followed her behind the tall bush.

"Your friends have nowhere to go. The Elders have secured all the exits, including the secret passageway in the janitor's closet," Darius announced, smugly confident.

"Who says there's only one secret passageway?" Nnamdi replied.

Darius shot an energy beam at Nnamdi, who countered with a beam of his own. The beams collided, creating a massive ball.

Lincoln fired a beam from his left palm, which struck the giant energy ball, sending it skyrocketing into the air where it burst into a spectacle of flames. Simultaneously, Lincoln fired a white beam at Darius with his wand. It struck him in the neck, and he fell to the ground.

"He really is a Deslondes," Chad whispered to Donna.

"Take Zina out of here and meet the others," Lincoln said to Nnamdi.

Nnamdi picked Zina up in his arms and carried her towards the college campus. Chad and Donna moved closer to the bushes to avoid Nnamdi and Zina spotting them.

Lincoln dropped to his knees, clutching his head as if in excruciating pain.

"What's happening to him?" Chad whispered.

"It's his pure-wizard form," Donna said. "I don't think he can control it."

She started to rise, but Chad grabbed her arm. "There's too many of them," he pleaded. "I'm sorry, Donna. I won't let you get hurt."

Lincoln rose to his feet as Tamia slowly approached. He lowered his father's wand and took a few steps toward her. "Tamia, it's me."

"Aw, look at the lovebirds," Casie mocked as she and Jay emerged into the Gardens.

"My mom knew you would come back for Tamia, and you fell right into her trap," Jay said.

"Lincoln, just stop it. You're being so pathetic. My sister is on our side now," Casie added.

Tamia stood her ground, keeping her wand pointed at Lincoln.

"Tamia, this isn't you. Listen to my voice. Remember me," Lincoln said.

Tamia's expression remained bland as Lincoln stepped closer to her. A red beam started to form from her wand.

"I love you, and you love me. Remember?"

Lincoln took another step closer, and her wand touched his chest as he reached his hand toward her face.

Suddenly, an energy beam struck Lincoln, tossing him into the air. His wand flung from his hand and landed near the bush where Donna was hiding. She gasped as Augustin walked into the clearing with her gold wand raised.

Augustin stepped up to Tamia and glided her thumb on her daughter's cheek. "Good job being a distraction, my child," she praised coldly.

"A few students escaped," Darius reported, rising to his feet.

"Let them go. We will have an entire army soon. And thanks to the Rebels and that fire alarm buffoonery, the students have already gathered in the auditorium," Augustin said.

"We will be unstoppable," Darius added.

"Take Lincoln to the Elders' lair," Augustin instructed.

Donna carefully reached for Lincoln's wand, which was in front of the bush.

"We have to go," Chad whispered.

With the wand securely in her grip, Donna nodded and together, they quietly retreated to the college campus.

"Where were you? We almost left you behind," Nnamdi exclaimed, his relief evident despite his stern tone.

They got Lincoln," Donna sobbed, tears welling up in her eyes.

Zina immediately grasped Donna's hand, offering silent support as they entered one of the college buildings. At the end of the hall, Chike signaled to them from an open door.

The room they entered had brown leather study booths at the front and a large brick fireplace at the back. Nnamdi removed his wand from his pocket.

"Nija ya siri," he said, tracing a sharp circle in the air in front of the fireplace. The bricks crumbled away, revealing a dark, narrow passageway.

Illuminated by small candles that flickered to life along their path, the group ventured through the tunnel. Donna squinted at the light growing brighter toward the end of the passage, where Mr. Jenkins awaited, his wand casting a light to guide them to safety.

"Glad to see some of you made it," he said, his gaze falling on the carrier bag. "What are you doing with a cat?"

"He's my pet," replied Donna.

Mr. Jenkins leaned in closer to the bag. "This *pet* of yours... I like its name tag."

They stepped through a door into a dimly lit basement. Donna placed Mr. Whiskers' bag down and used her hoodie to dab at her tears. Around her, the room was grim yet filled with familiar faces. Annette and Superb sat on the ground, while Rima applied healing paste to Professor Hunt's arm. There was still no sign of Jia.

"Mom... Dad, what happened?" Chike's voice broke the silence.

"We were ambushed by the Elders at the Oasis," Annette said.

"Where is everyone else?" Zina asked, her voice shaky, her leg injured. "Where are my parents?"

"Some of our group stayed behind so the rest could have a chance to make it out," Professor DuVernay said.

"This is my fault. They used a truth dawa on me. My parents are gone because of me," Zina confessed, her voice breaking with guilt.

"It's not your fault, Zina," Rima consoled her, rubbing her back gently.

"More kids got out than I expected. Good job, students," Professor DuVernay said. "Wait, where's Lincoln?"

"That was the last one," Mr. Jenkins said, flashing his light back into the tunnel.

"Augustin captured him. She said they are taking him to the Elders' lair," Donna murmured, holding her head low.

Rima sank to her knees. Professor DuVernay crouched beside her, offering a supportive shoulder.

"What do we do now?" Nnamdi asked.

Rima rose to her feet and looked around the room. "We will regroup at the Rebel camp. We will tell the rest of the parents what just happened. Hopefully, they will now see the severity of what's going on and join the Rebels. We will call on all of our friends, associates, peers, and any wizards we know who might join us. We will increase our numbers and train to fight to save the students and stop Augustin before she starts a war with the Norms. *This* is what we will do."

Donna admired Rima's courage. Despite her son being taken by the Elders, her leadership never wavered. But Donna didn't need a pep talk. She was ready to fight for her brother, no matter what.

I lost Lincoln once... I will not lose him again.

A few hours later, Donna stood laser-focused in the crowded circle around Mr. Jenkins, who had his wand raised toward one of the training dummies near the wall. She was locked in, determined to learn everything she could to save her brother.

A glowing blue beam shot from Mr. Jenkins' wand as he pushed forward, striking the training dummy in the center of its chest plate and pierced through to the padded wall behind it.

"Oops. Forgot how strong I was." Mr. Jenkins chuckled. "As the only Elder among the Rebels, my strength is substantial, but remember, the Elders we'll face are younger and even stronger than I am. To stand a chance against them, mastering your energy beam is crucial."

Rima stepped forward, her voice clear in the crowded room. "The energy beam can be defensive or offensive," she explained.

"For the energy beam to work, you must have a strong intention. The blast can generate multiple forces, such as a stun attack that temporarily paralyzes your opponent, a beam that causes pain, or a beam that can cause death," Mr. Jenkins said.

"Our mission is to get the Elders to surrender. Stunning them and inflicting some pain will complete that task. Our goal is not to kill," Professor DuVernay added.

"But aren't they going to aim to kill?" asked Chad, standing beside Donna.

"That's why we have to master defense," Mr. Jenkins responded. He positioned himself in front of the dummy and signaled to Professor DuVernay.

Professor DuVernay lifted his wand and shot an energy beam at him.

Mr. Jenkins widened his stance.

"Kulinda," he said, pointing his wand at the beam.

A purple translucent force field expanded from his wand, shielding the front of his body. The beam deflected off the shield and ricocheted toward the professor, who jumped out of the way. Donna gasped as the beam landed near his feet, scorching the cement floor.

"This shield can deflect or absorb a beam," Mr. Jenkins explained. "Remember, the Elders' powers are formidable. It might take teamwork to bring one down: one providing defense, the other offense."

He then scanned the crowd, his eyes finally resting on Donna. "How about a little challenge?" he proposed. "Donna Marie, come show us what you've got. Bring that young man with you, the one with the nappy braids."

Donna gave Chad a fist pump as they walked toward the center of the training area.

"Come on. We don't have all day. I'm an old fart, and I walk faster than that," Mr. Jenkins said.

Donna could feel everyone's eyes on them.

"We got this," Chad whispered as they stood side by side.

Mr. Jenkins, with a playful wag of his fingers, beckoned them to begin.

"Kulinda," Donna said, expanding a purple force field in front of her.

She kneeled, and Chad jumped on top of the shield. Donna pushed Chad in the direction of Mr. Jenkins. Chad catapulted into the air, shooting a stun beam at Mr. Jenkins, who dodged the attack and countered with a stun beam. The white beam struck Chad in his shoulder, and he twisted in the air before landing on the ground.

Mr. Jenkins shot a beam at Donna, who blocked the attack with her shield.

He stepped forward, channeling more power, but Donna held her ground and pushed her shield forward.

The Rebels started to clap and cheer for Donna as she faced off with the Elder.

Mr. Jenkins took another step forward, and Donna started to lose her footing and then slipped backward. In a split second, an energy beam fired from her left hand toward Mr. Jenkins, who produced a shield that absorbed the attack.

The facility went quiet as Donna rose to her feet.

She looked down at her hands and then around the room at the wide-eyed Rebels. Some gasped. Others took a step back.

"How did she do that?" someone shouted.

"She produced an energy beam from her hand!"

"I saw it too!"

Mr. Jenkins, cutting through the noise with his laughter, confessed, "I forgot how puny my power is compared to the Deslondes bloodline."

His admission sparked a flurry of questions.

"She's a Deslondes?" Professor Hunt asked, stepping forward.

"How is that possible?" Nnamdi asked.

The Rebels started to whisper and shout out more questions.

"Solomon didn't have any children!" an older Rebel shouted.

The training facility became bombarded with voices.

"Quiet!" Rima commanded, her voice echoing as she joined Donna in the center. "Yes, Donna is a ONE. A descendant of Solomon Deslondes. And so is her brother, Lincoln. Their father, Deedy, was a dear friend of ours. The Elders killed him, and my husband and I raised Lincoln as our own."

"To protect him from the same Elders who've taken over our school," Professor DuVernay added, standing near Rima.

"Just like Solomon, who hid the truth that his wife, Mary Ann, was pregnant to keep his family safe. Sometimes, we must make hard decisions to protect those we love," Rima continued.

Donna, surrounded by stunned faces, felt an unexpected calm. *A wizard's heart is the source of our power*, she reminded herself. All those years, not knowing who she really was had kept her powers trapped in the locked cage of her heart. Maybe now she could finally be free.

"Lincoln is my brother, and I must save him," she said. "We must save all of our friends at Nawlins."

"She's more powerful than me. I want her fighting on my side," Mr. Jenkins said, winking at Donna.

"Same," Rima said, walking to Donna and touching her shoulder.

"Same," said Professor DuVernay.

"Yeah, me too," Chad said, struggling to his feet.

Noor initiated a slow clap, and Chad followed. Other Rebels began to get on board, and the place erupted with praise.

Donna felt embarrassed but she stood tall.

"Now, let's get back to work. We have a world to save," Rima said, nodding at Donna.

Chapter Thirty-Eight

*A*lone.

The word rang in Lincoln's head as he fell in and out of consciousness. His hands and feet were tightly bound to a stiff wooden platform inside this gloomy, hot, circular chamber. Candles floated around his body, enough for him to see the massive leeches feasting on his skin—otherwise, darkness. He tried desperately to move, but his powers and energy were too weak.

The chamber door creaked open, flooding the space with a harsh sliver of light that traced over Lincoln's body. Augustin approached and levitated the bloodsuckers away from his flesh. Lincoln grimaced as the leeches' teeth dislodged from his skin with a sickening tear.

"Beautiful creatures, aren't they?" Augustin said, her voice echoing slightly in the cramped space. "They are precise in their task, drawing just enough blood to keep you teetering at the edge of life. They were created by the vampires... Oh, you didn't know we truly had vampires in New Orleans? They came from France many years ago, just like the stories say."

She paused, a twisted smile playing on her lips. "I once killed a vampire myself, tore her teeth out as a souvenir."

She held up a leech as though she was examining the creature. "Vampire blood is the other key ingredient to the hypnosis dawa. But your blood, Lincoln, is far more important. With your blood... Oh, child... I can do unimaginable things."

Augustin's cold fingers caressed Lincoln's cheek before forcefully guiding his gaze towards the flickering candles.

"You know... I only had enough dawa to use on the students, but now, because of you, I can have the entire wizard community on my side. I should have known you were a Deslondes. I can see the resemblance... I loved him so much, but Solomon couldn't see that wizards were destined to do more than just survive in this world. Why else would we be blessed with these gifts, if not to rule?"

She sighed, her expression softening.

"Then he met Mary Ann at a plantation that we freed, and I lost him forever... but I'll do whatever I have to do to make sure the Norms see just how fierce, powerful, and resilient we are."

With a final, lingering look of sorrow mixed with resolve, Augustin left the chamber, the door shutting with a definitive thud.

Lincoln shut his eyes and drifted off into a dream.

He was sitting on the familiar steps by the lake. The sounds of the waves hitting the pavement and the strong scent of the saltwater enveloping him.

Deedy took a seat next to him.

"Pop. I'm scared," Lincoln confessed, his voice breaking.

"I'm sorry you had to do this alone, son."

"You should never have left me. You should've fought harder when the Elders attacked us. You should still be here!"

"You're right, son. I should have been there for you, and I should be there now."

As tears streamed down Lincoln's face, Deedy's arm wrapped around him, a gesture filled with the warmth and safety long missed. Lincoln sank into his father's chest.

"But you're not alone, son. Your sister will come to save you soon. And I have something for you... Solomon tore it out and burned it because he knew this spell would create chaos in the wrong hands. He memorized it before he set fire to it. My parents told me the spell. Sorry I wasn't there to tell you in person... You will need the wand of Solomon for it to work. You will chant: K I N Y U M E... The spell will drain Augustin of all her powers."

"The youth dawa kept her alive all these years. Once her magic is gone, how will that affect her?" Lincoln asked.

"She will perish," Deedy responded. "But I am more concerned about how this spell will affect you. It could drain the powers of the wizard who performs the spell, which means you won't be a wizard anymore, Lincoln."

"If it comes to it, I will do anything to protect my family," Lincoln said.

"I know."

"I love you, Pop."

"I love you too, son. Good luck. I'll be watching from above. And one more thing: the DuVernays were my best friends. They did what they had to do to protect you and your mother. Tell them how thankful I am for how they raised you. I'm very proud of the young man you've become... and tell Donna Marie that I love her so much and I'm so proud of her too."

Chapter Thirty-Nine

The Rebels were close to one hundred members now. They were spread out on the training floor, practicing their combat moves and strategies. Donna looked on from the steps leading to the second floor. Chad, Chike, and Noor sat beside her.

"I heard that Augustin has more than twice as many wizards in her squad," Noor said. "And the Elders have been training for this battle for centuries. We've been here for two days."

"I don't know how we can compete with that," Chad replied.

"I just don't understand how people could follow her. A war with the Norms? It doesn't make sense," Chike said.

"Our friends have been hypnotized while we do nothing," Donna added.

"We need your brother. You two are the only ones more powerful than Augustin," Chad said.

"You're right. We do need Lincoln."

"We don't even know where he is," Chike argued.

"We know they took him to the Elders' lair," Donna said.

"Yeah, but where is that?"

"I don't know, but I'll look everywhere until I find him."

"I agree with Donna. We have to do something," Chad said.

"We wait until Rima says it's time to attack," Monique said, walking down the steps, followed by Zina.

"Break up this little confab and get back to training," Zina added.

As they followed Monique and Zina down the steps, Donna tugged on Chad's arm.

"I have a plan," she whispered.

Later, under the cover of night, Donna slipped from her bed, Mary Ann's diary tucked securely in her hoodie. She gently nudged Mr. Whiskers awake, who mewed softly beneath her bunk. The large room, lined with bunk beds housing both high school and college girls, was still filled with the gentle sound of slumber. Notably, Zina's bed lay perilously close to the exit.

Foot by foot, Donna navigated through the maze of beds. Her heart skipped as Mr. Whiskers stretched and yawned loudly in her arms, the sound piercing the silence.

She paused, scanning the room. Fortunately, no one stirred.

Reaching the door, she carefully turned the metal handle, easing it open just enough to let a sliver of hallway light spill in. Her eyes darted nervously, half-expecting Zina to wake. With a silent breath of relief, she slipped through the door, gently closing it behind her without a sound.

She heard a whisper as she crept up the stairs, the dim light casting long shadows. From the darkness, Chad approached, his voice low and cautious.

"Took you long enough," Chad said.

"I had to make sure not to wake anyone. Did you bring your broom?" Donna asked, her voice barely above a whisper.

"Yeah. Why are we on the third floor? It's cold up here."

"Because Mr. Jenkins doesn't like sleeping in the bunk beds, so he sleeps in the common area up here."

Chad paused, eyeing Mr. Whiskers. "Wait, why did you bring the cat?"

"Oh, he's not just a cat, he's a Loyal. We might need him."

"Did you just say your cat is a *Loyal*?"

"Mm-hmm."

"And you didn't tell anyone?"

"I didn't want to freak anyone out."

"Well, I'm freaked out. What does it turn into?"

"Mr. Whiskers turns into a black panther. A big one."

"Actually, that's kinda tight, ya heard me. Good call, we might need him."

Together, they tiptoed toward the brown leather sofa where Mr. Jenkins snored loudly. His thick mustache flapped up and down as he breathed through his mouth.

"Mr. Jenkins," Donna whispered, trying not to startle the old man.

He didn't wake up; instead, his snoring became louder.

"Mr. Jenkins," Chad tried, a bit louder this time.

Unresponsive, Donna resorted to a gentle kick to the sofa. Mr. Jenkins jolted awake, his wand instantly in hand, casting a glaring light over the two young Rebels.

"What do you troublemakers want? I was having a lovely dream about pancakes."

"We are going to free my brother," Donna said.

"Ah, you want me to tell you where the Elders' lair is," Mr. Jenkins replied. "You got some guts, kid. That place is dangerous... but you and your brother might be the key to saving us all. The lair is in the deep swamplands of Jean Lafitte."

"Jean Lafitte? Isn't that on the West Bank?" Chad asked.

"Yep. Deep in Marrero. Fly south until you see those swamps. There's a barrier disguising the lair, but you'll see a light pole surrounded by a patch of dry land and a cave. That's where the back entrance is."

"Will the place be swarming with Elders?" Chad asked.

"Most of them are probably at the school by now," Mr. Jenkins said. "But I'm afraid something more dangerous lurks in the swamps... the Rougarou."

"A werewolf? Like from the folklore?" Chad asked.

"Yes. But Donna, you're a Deslondes. You can defeat the Rougarou. I believe in you," Mr. Jenkins said.

"Thanks," Donna said.

"And watch out for Loyals, as well."

"This is just great... Swamp creatures and Loyals. What did I get myself into?" Chad said.

"You'll be fine. You have a Loyal too," Mr. Jenkins said, pointing to Mr. Whiskers.

"How did you know?" asked Donna.

"That's Solomon's old cat. I recognized his name tag because I'm the jeweler who made it. Good to see you're still alive, old friend."

Mr. Whiskers purred as Mr. Jenkins petted his head.

"Make sure you take that collar off before he changes into a panther. Don't want to lose that tag, that's fourteen- karat gold."

Donna unclipped his collar and stuffed it into her pocket.

"There is one more thing that you might need. Donna, do you know where Solomon's wand is?" asked Mr. Jenkins.

"Yes. In the wizard sanctuary, but it's locked up in a glass case."

"You're a Coven member. Say 'Onyesha' near the case and it'll open up for you," Mr. Jenkins advised, settling back into his makeshift bed. "Now, let me be. I need my beauty sleep."

Chapter Forty

Donna and Chad landed their brooms outside of the African American History Museum.

Mr. Whiskers stuck his head out of the big front pocket of Donna's hoodie. She took him out and he sat down on the sidewalk and started licking his paws, making it clear he wasn't going inside.

"Your dad's broom is fast," Chad said.

"So fast. And it rides smoothly. We are definitely going to beat the Coven in the championships now," Donna said.

"If there still is a Raceway when this mess is all over with."

"Hey, we will stop the Elders, save our friends, and be back to racing in no time."

"Do you really believe that?" he asked.

"I have to."

Donna picked up the lone rock by the iris flowers and grabbed the key.

"You have got to be kidding me. The wizard sanctuary is hidden away in a public museum, and the key to the entrance is taped under a rock?" Chad said.

"Yep," Donna replied.

She led Chad to the room with the crest and waved her wand across it just as she had seen Lincoln do.

Chad's eyes lit up. "This place is fiya, ya heard me."

They went through the hidden door and down the spiral stairs.

"Yo, the books of *Giza* and *Knowledge* are just chilling right here?! All this time?!" he asked, pointing.

Donna nodded as she walked over to the circular glass enclosure where Solomon's wand was floating in the center.

"That thang is sick," Chad said, pushing on the glass, which didn't budge.

"Onyesha," Donna said, pointing her wand to the glass.

The glass dissolved into a liquid state. A chill ran down Donna's arm when she grabbed the wand. Its diamond base was cold and heavy in her hand.

Suddenly, her peripheral vision dimmed, shadows creeping in from the edges. She turned to Chad, who took a step back.

"Donna... are you okay?" he asked, his voice edged with concern.

For a moment, Donna couldn't answer. Her body refused to move, frozen in place like something had seized control.

"Donna?" Chad asked, grabbing her arm.

"I... I'm fine," she finally stammered, regaining control and blinking away the blackness clouding her sight. "For a moment, it felt like I couldn't control my body. Lincoln told me this would happen. It's called pure-wizard form. It's when my powers are at their peak."

"Glad you're okay," Chad responded.

Donna wasn't okay; she was terrified. She took a deep breath as Chad patted her on the back.

She raised the wand, its weight still unfamiliar in her hand.

"Yeah, you definitely couldn't walk through the hood with that," Chad said, chuckling. "I know some goons who'd flip it for a couple racks."

Donna gave him the side-eye.

"Come on. It was a good joke," Chad said.

"Oh, there are secret spells I found in Mary Ann's journal that I want to try," Donna said, unzipping her pocket. She removed the journal and opened it to the handwritten spells and dawas toward the back.

"'This spell makes Solomon invisible: Kutoweka. You must circle the wand around your body for it to work,'" Donna read.

"Kutoweka," she said, moving the wand around her body.

She felt a slight tingle throughout her body. She lifted her hand in front of her face and couldn't see it.

"Yo, where did you go?" Chad asked.

"Right here," Donna replied.

"Come on, Donna. This isn't funny," he said, looking up and down.

Donna tapped on his shoulder, and he turned around and scratched his head.

"Donna? Come on, stop playing."

"Kutoweka," she repeated, reversing the spell.

"Yeah, don't do that again," Chad said.

"Let's go save my brother."

Jean Lafitte, located a few miles south of the French Quarter, was dominated by vast stretches of swampland and plagued by an uncanny silence except for the natural chorus of wildlife. Finally, Donna spotted the tall light pole that Mr. Jenkins had told them to look for.

Landing on a dry patch under a moss-draped tree, they dismounted. Donna lit the path with her wand, the dim light cutting through the darkness. The swampy ground squelched under their feet as they navigated through the terrain, Donna clutching Mr. Whiskers tightly.

Chad abruptly stopped. Donna walked beside him, stepping into a large footprint, about three times the size of her own. The print appeared to have claws at the end of each toe.

She pointed her light around the trees as a slight wind blew the leaves, creating an unsettling symphony. They picked up the pace, splashing mud on their clothes as they ran toward the cave.

They both stopped to catch their breath as they entered the cave. The reek of feces filled Donna's nasal passage as they maneuvered through the dark and narrow opening.

The cave led to a rusted door at the far end, light seeping from beneath it. They pushed against the metal, its hinges squealing in protest.

Stepping into the lair, Donna was taken aback. Expecting a dilapidated shelter, she instead found an expansive, elegant space that bore a striking resemblance to the architecture of Nawlins itself.

Donna and Chad advanced cautiously down the corridors, their wands at the ready, with Mr. Whiskers darting between their steps. They halted as the sound of footsteps approached from around the corner. Peering around, Donna spotted two cloaked Elders.

"It's only two of them. Let's stun them and keep moving," Donna whispered.

Chad nodded.

"One. Two. Three..." she said.

With swift coordination, they rounded the corner and discharged their stun beams, knocking the Elders to the ground.

They navigated through the halls until they rounded another corner where a circular chamber stretched up to the ceiling.

Darius stood with his wand at the entrance. Mr. Espree emerged from the chamber and closed the door before standing next to him.

"Well, well. Look who it is. Donna Marie and... who are you?" Darius asked.

"Backup," Chad retorted sharply.

"Yeah, whatever... how did you find this place?"

"Mr. Jenkins is on their side. Augustin should've killed him a long time ago," Mr. Espree said.

"Ain't it a shame the Rebels sent kids to save Lincoln? Are they that desperate?" Darius mocked, exchanging a glance with Mr. Espree.

"I'm sure we can handle you. I heard you're the one that Lincoln sent to the medical bay," Chad said.

"Oh, you think you're funny?" Darius said, pointing his wand at Chad.

"No. I'm just stating the truth, ya heard me."

"Look at you two juveniles trying to be heroes. Bad news, only a wand of a Coven member can open this door, you peasants," Mr. Espree said, laughing.

"We will find a way," Donna said.

Darius charged at Donna, throwing red energy beams from his wand. She countered and the blasts collided, absorbing each other's energy.

Mr. Espree shot a beam at Chad, who back-flipped out of the way. The Elder shot at him again, and Chad activated his shield that absorbed the attack. Chad held his ground, pushing the purple translucent shield forward with his shoulder.

"You were always the meanest janitor at school. No wonder you're an Elder," Chad said.

"You think I enjoyed cleaning up after you little hooligans?" Mr. Espree replied.

Darius fired another beam at Donna. She jumped out of the way but dropped her wand in the act.

Mr. Whiskers jumped and bit Darius on the hand. He shrieked and threw the cat to the ground. Mr. Whiskers landed on his feet and hissed at him.

Donna unzipped the front pocket of her hoodie and grabbed Solomon's wand.

"Kutoweka," she said, moving the wand around her body.

Darius looked around in confusion.

"Where are you?" he said, spinning around.

Donna blasted him with a stun beam, and he fell to the floor.

"Kutoweka," she said, becoming visible again.

She shot another stun beam at Mr. Espree and he fell to the floor.

"That should hold them for a few hours," she said, picking up her wand and turning to Chad.

"Hey, I had him right where I wanted him," Chad said.

"Sure you did."

They approached the chamber's steel door.

"Kufungua," Donna said, moving her wand around the handle.

The door detached from its base. They pulled on the handle, and the door smoothly glided open.

Two candles floated above Lincoln as he lay bound on a square platform. Donna rushed over to him. He struggled to open his eyes. Chad walked over and gestured to the open wounds on his body.

"He's weak. They probably drained his body of blood, left just enough to keep him alive. We have to get him to Rima," Chad said.

They untied the restraints on his arms and legs, then carefully picked him up by his shoulders.

As they exited the chamber, Jay appeared, blocking their path. Chad and Donna raised their wands. However, Jay slowly placed his wand into his pocket and raised his hands.

"What do you want?" Chad asked.

"I didn't know they were hypnotizing our friends. I swear," Jay said.

"I don't believe you," Chad said.

"Donna, I promise. My mother told me she had big plans for the wizard community, but I didn't know she would do this. The Rebels have to stop her. She has enough of Lincoln's blood to control all the wizards."

For a moment, Donna saw a glimmer of sincerity in Jay's eyes, portraying him not as an enemy but as a conflicted soul caught in his mother's shenanigans.

He reached into his pocket and withdrew a crumpled piece of paper, offering it to Donna. Their fingers brushed as she took it from him.

"I'm sorry, Donna Marie," he murmured before turning away.

Donna and Chad held Lincoln over their shoulders as Mr. Whiskers led the way out of the cave. Murky fog and brooding silence had overtaken the terrain.

Thump.

Donna and Chad exchanged a wary glance. Mr. Whiskers jumped onto a rock and stuck his head up as he sniffed the air. He growled as the head of a giant reptile seeped through the fog ahead. Chad and Donna stumbled back and landed in the mud, their bodies breaking Lincoln's fall.

"It's an alligator," Donna said.

"Nah, alligators aren't that big. That gator is a Loyal," Chad replied.

As they propped Lincoln against a sturdy rock, the massive beast roared menacingly. Donna unleashed an energy beam at the alligator, but it deflected the attack with its thick, scaled tail.

Mr. Whiskers jumped over Donna and transformed into a black panther as he landed in front of her. Donna covered her ears as he roared.

The two Loyals circled each other.

The alligator lunged, jaws snapping viciously, but Mr. Whiskers agilely dodged and countered with a powerful swipe of his colossal paw.

As Chad helped Donna to her feet, they cautiously retreated from the skirmish, only to freeze as a chilling howl cut through the fog.

When Donna recognized the Rougarou's glowing red eyes that pierced through the fog, her heart raced, her anxiety manifesting as a sharp pain that thudded within her skull. Collapsing to the ground, she gasped for breath, clutching her temples in a futile attempt to quell the overwhelming sensation. Chad wrapped his arms around her, but his comfort did little to ease her torment. She would have killed for her anxiety medication right now.

The Rougarou charged full speed at Mr. Whiskers, its massive head colliding with the panther's side, sending him rolling across the muddy terrain.

Chad raised his wand to fight, but he was no match for a Rougarou and Loyal.

Donna jumped as another sharp howl ripped through the swamp. The fog coiled and slithered across the land, restless and alive, hiding whatever might be lurking within.

Two glowing yellow eyes emerged from the fog as Fang approached Mr. Whiskers. The Gator hissed, and the Rougarou flexed its chest as Fang licked Mr. Whiskers on the head.

Mr. Whiskers regained his footing, shook off the mud, and let out a defiant roar, drool dripping from his jaws.

"Come on, we have to get away from this battle," Chad urged, pulling Donna to her feet.

"I have to make sure Mr. Whiskers is okay," Donna insisted.

"You should be worried about yourself; you're having some kinda panic attack."

"I'm fine."

"I know you, Donna. You're not fine, luv."

Chad grabbed Lincoln by the shoulders and dragged him away from the action.

The Rougarou lifted its long claw toward Mr. Whiskers, who slowly circled the creature, snarling. The Rougarou jumped at Mr. Whiskers, but Mr. Whiskers juked out of the way and jumped into a tree. The tree leaned as the heavy panther used it as a slingshot, catapulting himself toward the beast. With a fierce growl, he opened his large mouth and bit the Rougarou on its shoulder. His teeth latched onto its flesh as he yanked the Rougarou down into the mud.

The gator swung its tail at Fang. Fang grabbed the tail with her mouth and dragged the Gator toward the cave. However, the gator twisted free from Fang's grip, lunging again with its tail. This time, Fang leapt over the gator and delivered a fatal bite to its head, crushing its skull. The gator hung lifelessly in Fang's mouth.

"Yes, Fang!" Chad cheered.

Blood seeped through the Rougarou's bite marks on its shoulder as it stood up.

Fang dropped the gator and ran toward the beast. Mr. Whiskers charged from the opposite direction. The Rougarou stood still in the middle of the swamp. Its bright red eyes looked back and forth to the two Loyals approaching quickly. The Rougarou leaped up in the air, and the other Loyals collided, knocking skulls. The beast expanded its claws as it descended toward Fang. Before Fang could move, the Rougarou thrust its long claws into her body.

"No!" Donna screamed.

Blood leaked into the muddy water as Fang cried for help. Mr. Whiskers lay in the swamp, struggling to breathe as the water started to cover his snout.

The Rougarou stuck its claws deeper into Fang, picking her body up as it stood tall, bringing her face inches away from its disgusting mouth. Fang squealed for the last time as the beast retracted its claws, dropping her body into the swamp.

Donna wept as she hunched over. Her heart was pulsating vigorously, as if her powers were trying to escape from their prison. She tried her best to suppress it, dreading losing control of her body again.

The Rougarou ran toward Chad, who had Lincoln wrapped in his arms.

I can do this. I can do this. I am the master of my powers. They don't control me. I control them.

Donna stopped fighting against her anxiety attack and allowed her powers to flow freely throughout her body. She screamed as she transitioned into pure-wizard form. But this time, she had total control of her mind and body. The feeling was invigorating. Her body felt lighter and stronger. Her senses were heightened; her vision was sharper, and she could hear the ground thump with every step the Rougarou took. A bright red light covered her hands.

She brought her hands together, and the red circles of energy combined and expanded. She yelled as she pushed forward. The energy beam erupted from her hands and pierced through the Rougarou's chest.

The beast stopped in his tracks. Its eyes rolled back as it collapsed into the swamp.

Wow... I guess I am special after all.

Chad caught Donna before she could fall to the ground. Exhausted, she rested her head on his chest.

"Hey... That was pretty amazing," Chad murmured.

Mr. Whiskers limped toward them, gently carrying Fang's body in his mouth.

"Mr. Whiskers, I'm so sorry about your friend," Donna said.

Mr. Whiskers transformed back into a cat and curled up in Donna's arms. He licked her on the cheek as she caressed him.

Chad knelt beside a tree, using a rock to dig a hole. He carefully placed Fang's small body inside the grave and tenderly covered it with earth.

"Thank you for your help, Fang," Donna said softly, placing a rock over the grave.

Chapter Forty-One

L incoln began to open his heavy eyes, his gaze hazy.

"Lincoln, can you hear me?"

He knew that voice.

He mustered a faint smile. "Hey, Ma," he rasped. "Where am I?"

Rima clasped his hand gently. "Hey, handsome. You're back at the Rebel camp. Don't try to get up. You're on an IV to help stabilize your body temperature. How are you feeling?" she said, adjusting a cool, damp cloth on his forehead.

"Better now. Hey, Dad," Lincoln greeted, extending his other hand toward his father.

Professor DuVernay took his son's hand, pressing a kiss to the side of his head.

"We thought we lost you, son," he said, his eyes watery.

"I think I had some saviors," Lincoln said.

He glanced over to Donna and Chad, who sat on wooden chairs next to his bed. The rising sun cast warm rays through the cracked blinds, filling the room with a soft glow.

"What those two did was careless and dangerous, but they also saved your life," Rima said.

"Mr. Whiskers helped too," Donna chimed in, lifting the cat onto her lap from the floor.

"Guess what, Lincoln? Turns out Mr. Whiskers was the cat I told you about this summer. The one that led me to find Donna. I knew I recognized him!" Rima said.

"He's a Loyal," Lincoln noted, memories beginning to piece together. "I remember seeing a panther. He was huge."

"Your father and I planned to rescue you tonight while the rest of the Rebels headed back to Nawlins. But I'm afraid another day in that chamber, and you would have died of blood loss and dehydration."

"The Rebels are going back to Nawlins?" Lincoln asked.

"Jay gave us the reversal for the hypnosis dawa," Donna said.

"We attack tonight," Rima added.

"Hey, Ma, I had a vision about Deedy. He told me to tell you and Dad, thanks for raising me into the young man I am. And Donna?" Lincoln asked, looking over to her.

"Yes?"

"Our father said that he loves you so much and he's proud of you."

Donna smiled as her eyes watered. She put her head down, and Chad patted her on the back.

"Deedy also told me of a spell," Lincoln said.

Mr. Jenkins stuck his head into the room. "Lincoln. It's good to see you awake." He turned to the others. "We're ready for the meeting."

"We will talk more when you get your energy back," Rima said, rubbing his head.

Lincoln hated needles, so he looked away as he pulled out the one in his arm. His mouth was dry, and he felt weak, as if bags of bricks were lying on top of him. He swung his right leg out of the bed with his hands and sat up. The wounds from the leeches had healed, with help of the healing paste, but a tingling sensation lingered uncomfortably. He brought his other leg around and steadied himself on his feet. Each step felt monumental as he shuffled out of the medical bay.

When he reached the meeting area, the Rebel High Council was in full session, strategizing their next move. Lincoln, sweating and out of breath, leaned against the back wall for support, listening as Rima delineated the plan.

"You all know your groups," Rima said. "Using the invisibility spell, Donna and I will secure the main entrance, then the rest of our group will follow when the coast is clear."

"My crew and I will secure the entrance in the janitor's closet," Mr. Jenkins said.

"Professor Hunt and I will lead our group of Rebels through the secret passage from the basement of Superb's barbershop," Professor DuVernay said.

"And Annette and I will lead our group as we secure the college entrance," Superb finished.

"Some of you have been tasked with keeping the hypnotized students at bay in their dorms using the containment spell," Rima said.

"Rima and I will lure Augustin and the Elders to us in the Gardens. The key ingredient to the reversal is a drop of blood from the wizard who initially conjured the dawa. Rima and I have the job of taking Augustin down to get her blood," Professor DuVernay said.

Mr. Whiskers let out a loud meow. Donna gave him a few pets on his head in the front pocket of her hoodie.

"I didn't forget about you, Mr. Whiskers. The Loyal will be fighting in the Gardens with us. And lastly, we will administer the reversal dawa through the ventilation system of the dorms, ridding the students of their trance," Rima said.

"Mom. I can help," Lincoln said.

The Rebels made a pathway for him as he limped to the table.

"What are you doing here? You should be resting," Rima said, rising to her feet.

"When I was at the Elders' lair, Deedy came to me in a vision and gave me a spell that will strip Augustin of her powers," Lincoln said.

Rima shook her head.

"I can do this, Ma. It might be the only thing that works."

"You should be resting. You can barely stand. How are you going to fight Augustin?"

"Your mother is right, Lincoln. You must stay here," Professor DuVernay agreed.

"I want to fight. We can take Augustin down together," Lincoln said.

"That's enough. You're too weak. I will not allow you to put yourself in danger. We don't even know if that spell works," Rima said.

"It will work," Lincoln said, stumbling.

Professor DuVernay caught him before he could fall to the ground.

"I'm just a little lightheaded," Lincoln reassured, managing to stand upright again.

"Let's get you back on the IV. Your body needs to heal. We can win this fight without you. I promise," Rima said.

Chapter Forty-Two

A fireplace burned in the common area on the third floor, where Lincoln was sitting on the sofa, staring at the blazing fire and muttering a word over and over. Donna watched him from the corner as the crackling noise of dying wood filled the room.

"You've been watching me for over five minutes now. Are you going to sit?" Lincoln said.

"How did you know I was there?" Donna asked, taking a seat next to Lincoln.

"Your shadow on the wall. I could tell it was you from the outline of your puffy hair."

"Do you think it will work?" Donna asked. "The spell Deedy gave you?"

"I do," Lincoln replied confidently.

"How are you feeling?" she inquired.

"Much better," Lincoln grinned, patting his stomach. "I think the red beans that Chad's grandmother cooked for us refueled my energy."

"Yeah, I think everyone is in a food coma now," Donna said, giggling.

"You know, when I was in that chamber, I thought a lot about our father. I don't remember much of him, but he used to always tell me that being a Deslondes meant we were strong and brave... and now I see that he was right, because it took a lot of strength and bravery to do what you did. Thank you for saving me, sis."

"You're welcome, Link," Donna replied.

"Link... no one has called me that in a long time. It feels good hearing it again."

Donna wished she had a memory of her father. Or a scent. Pretty much anything to remember him by.

"Can I ask you a hard question?" Donna asked.

"You can ask me anything you want, little sis."

"How was it growing up with a father? I mean, I know Professor DuVernay isn't your real dad, but he was still your father. Sometimes I wonder what it's like to have one."

"Let's see—"

"It's kinda weird, you know? I've never called a man 'Father' or 'Dad.' I don't know how the words should properly feel when they roll off my tongue. Father sounds colder, and Dad sounds warmer, doesn't it? Oh, sorry for cutting you off."

"It's all good... Let's see..." Lincoln said, putting his hands on his head and slumping more onto the couch. "It felt like I always had someone by my side. A protector. A provider. He's a good man, who made me into the young man I am today. He was a leader, and I humbly followed. And you are wrong about something; he is my real dad."

Donna wanted to ask Lincoln so many other questions: what was his favorite color, what did he like to do for fun, how did he feel about having a sister now, how was it growing up rich... But she just sank deeper into the couch, humming "By Your Side" by Sade.

Donna was caught off guard when Lincoln began to hum the same song.

"What do you know about that?" he asked.

"It's our mother's favorite song."

Lincoln puts his head down. There was another brief silence.

"Your mom… Do you think she's going to remember me?" he asked.

"She's your mom too."

"It doesn't feel like it. I don't know her and she doesn't know me," Lincoln replied.

"How could she ever forget her son?" Donna said, smiling.

Lincoln took a deep breath and sighed. A gigantic smile filled his face.

"How did your parents hide you? I mean, how did they get away with adopting you without anyone finding out?" Donna inquired.

She thought she might have asked a sensitive question, judging by the way Lincoln's demeanor changed. He shifted on the couch and looked away for a few seconds.

"After my mom and dad graduated college, they got married and tried to have kids. But they couldn't. My mom was devastated."

"That's very sad," Donna said.

"Ma needed a break from New Orleans and took the opportunity to do her residency in Georgia. My dad supported her and went back to college in Atlanta to get his PhD at Morehouse… Then they rescued me from the river the night the Elders attacked us. The wizard community thought that I was a miracle baby that my mom had while they were in Georgia. So, when we moved back to New Orleans when I was six, no one questioned it."

Even though they grew up in different worlds, Donna could tell he had troubles too. They both experienced loss and heartbreak. They shared a bond even after being so far apart all these years. Those same troubles brought them back together.

"Am I tripping or did I see you defeat a Rougarou?" Lincoln asked.

"Yeah, I did. I went into pure-wizard form. I think I know how to control it now. Instead of fighting to suppress it, I just let my powers flow freely throughout my body. It felt unbelievable," she said. "I had no fear, no doubt. I finally believed that *I am the master of my powers.*"

Lincoln placed his hands on his knees and looked away. "I don't think I can control it," he said. "It always takes over me."

"Hey, where is your confidence? My big brother once told me, 'You can do anything. You just have to believe in yourself.'"

"I'll keep that in mind," Lincoln said, grinning.

"You better. You gotta stand on business."

"Hey, don't steal my line," he said, playfully bumping on her side.

They both lay back and put their feet on top of the small table in front of the couch.

I really have a brother. This is so cool. I wonder if he likes cheese pizza like me. Is he allergic to peanuts too? Donna stuck her hands in her hoodie and looked over at him. She was so grateful that he was there.

"You and I could take Augustin together," she said.

"We are definitely brother and sister because you just read my mind. We're the only ones who can match her power."

"Rima is putting guards outside your door tonight, so you can't wander off. I think one of them will be Monique; it will be kinda hard fooling her."

"I figured that. And I don't have a wand. I lost our father's wand in the Gardens and my parents have my old one," Lincoln replied.

"You didn't lose our father's wand," Donna said, pulling Deedy's wand from her pocket.

"What? You saved it? No way! Thank you," Lincoln said as she handed it over.

"I could teach you the spell from Mary Ann's journal that makes you disappear?" she offered. "You could use that to escape later."

"Good plan." He nodded with approval.

"You have to circle the wand around your body and chant KUTOWEKA."

Lincoln, clearly excited, swirled the wand rapidly around himself. "Kutoweka," he said and vanished. "This is a game changer!"

"I know," Donna said, looking around the room.

"Kutoweka," Lincoln repeated, turning himself visible again. "Let's do our family proud tonight, little sister."

"We will," Donna replied, getting up and walking toward the door.

"Wait," Lincoln said. "I know you heard me practicing the spell that can strip Augustin of her magic. If it comes to it, I am the one who has to use it on her."

"Why does it have to be you?" Donna asked.

"There is a chance the spell can drain both parties of their powers. You just found out you are a wizard. I won't let you lose that."

"I'll do anything to protect my family. In the end, I'll have my brother and mother. That's all the power I need," Donna said.

Lincoln exhaled. "I was afraid you were going to say that."

Mr. Jenkins shuffled into the room. "Can y'all leave? I have to take a nap before we attack the Elders," he said, flopping onto the couch.

Chapter Forty-Three

Donna and Rima peeked around the corner at Nawlins' main entrance. Three Elders wearing red cloaks stood guard by the door. Donna moved in closer to Rima and circled her wand around them.

"Kutoweka," she whispered.

She held Rima's hand as they crept toward the entrance, conscious of their footsteps as the spell kept them hidden. Donna and Rima stunned the Elders, and they fell to the ground. Donna looked on as Rima cracked open the door and fired three white stun beams through the gap.

"Nice shooting," Donna said as Rima opened the door, revealing three Elders on the floor.

"Signal the others," Rima said.

Using her wand, Donna flashed a light toward the side street. Zina and a group of Rebels started to run toward the entrance.

"Hey, Rima. I can't see you. Can you follow my voice and hug me so I can make us visible again?"

Donna felt Rima's arm touch her, and then she wrapped Donna up in a tight hug.

"Kutoweka," Donna said, restoring their visibility.

Donna wasn't scared or nervous as her Rebel group made their way to the Gardens; she felt invigorated—she was a teenager with wizard powers fighting Elders to save the world. *If my mama could see me now! I am strong like her*, she thought as she stunned an Elder patrolling the grounds.

In the Gardens, Professor DuVernay, Mr. Jenkins, and other Rebels were waiting.

"What took you so long?" Mr. Jenkins said.

Joining hands, Rima and Professor DuVernay aimed their wands skyward, unleashing a beacon of white light as a signal to all Rebels.

Mr. Espree and Professor Osborne entered the clearing, lifting their wands at the Rebels.

"If it isn't my old friends," Mr. Jenkins said.

"If it isn't the traitor Jenkins. You look horrible. Age has finally caught up to you, I see," Mr. Espree said.

"It's so fitting that you would disguise yourself as a janitor; you always cleaned up Augustin's mess. She killed our friend Solomon, and you justified it as the greater good for our people. You are pitiful. There isn't a day that I don't blame myself because I was there and could have stopped it," Mr. Jenkins replied.

As Augustin and an ensemble of fifty Elders in burgundy cloaks flooded into the Gardens, Rima called out, "We don't want to hurt you. Lower your wands."

"You can't stop us," Augustin declared, launching an energy beam at Rima, who jumped out of the way and countered with a stun beam. With a flick of her wrist, Augustin diverted the beam into the ground.

The Gardens turned into a battleground as the Elders and the Rebels traded attacks, the air crackling with exchanged spells.

"Enough of this foolishness. You want a war? Watch me wake my army!" Augustin shouted. "Kushambulia," she said into the tip of her wand.

The battle halted and tense silence in the Gardens followed.

"She's trying to summon the hypnotized students," Donna murmured to Rima.

"Let's hope the containment spell holds," Rima replied, her eyes scanning the quiet Gardens.

Frustrated, Augustin barked orders at her followers. "Go check the dorms!"

At her command, the Elders whisked out orbs and mounted their brooms, soaring towards the student quarters. Mr. Jenkins and the Rebels gave chase, the sky illuminated with energy beams.

Donna took cover behind a magnolia tree, watching as the DuVernays continued their fierce duel with Augustin.

"Kamba," Professor DuVernay said.

A glowing blue ropelike vapor expanded from his wand. Augustin smirked and braced herself. Professor DuVernay whipped the rope in her direction as Rima fired a stun beam at her. Augustin summoned her shield, absorbing the stun beam and deflecting the ropelike vapor, which recoiled towards Professor DuVernay.

In a swift counter, Augustin launched another energy beam, striking Rima in the arm. Rima dropped to the ground, crying out in pain.

Without hesitation, Augustin fired again, but Professor DuVernay threw himself in its path, raising his shield to intercept the attack. He grunted, the impact knocking him to the ground.

A roar shattered the air as Mr. Whiskers, transformed into a massive black panther, charged at Augustin.

"Come on, you filthy animal!" Augustin taunted, directing her wand towards the surrounding trees.

The trees seemed to come alive, expanding their branches and wrapping around Mr. Whiskers. He toppled to the ground. He clawed and bit at the trees, but as soon as his sharp claws broke through the branches, another branch wrapped around his body. Roots burst through the ground and wrapped him up in a cocoon, leaving only his snout free.

Seeing her Loyal in danger, Donna's palms radiated a fiery red glow. "Leave him alone!" she demanded, advancing towards Augustin with determination.

"Ah, Donna Marie... After I found out who Lincoln truly was, I did some research, and what do you know? Cathy is your mother, too. I should have known you were a Deslondes when Fang tried to attack you. I originally sent her to track your father, but when she failed, I sent the Rougarou."

Donna, unfazed, aimed Solomon's wand at Augustin. "You will have to kill me before I let you hurt innocent people."

Augustin's laughter filled the air, cold and menacing. "I'm not going to kill you. With your blood, I can hypnotize the most influential Norms worldwide, from presidents to corporate giants. And with them under my control, the world will be mine."

Augustin shot an energy beam at the giant magnolia tree next to Donna. The tree sliced at its base and toppled toward her. Reacting quickly, Donna shot a beam above her, shredding the tree in pieces.

As the debris settled, Augustin mounted her broom and soared away. Donna followed suit, throwing the gold orb into the air that transformed into her father's broom. As Augustin hurled shots at her, Donna maneuvered out of the way, twisting and spinning. She returned fire, but Augustin deflected the attacks with her shield, sending them whizzing back towards her. Donna backflipped in the air and the beam hit one of the buildings, ripping apart its roof.

"Nishati," Donna said, holding her wand steady toward Augustin.

A red beam blasted from her wand. She clenched the front of the broom tight with her left hand as the force pushed her back.

Augustin countered, her wand emitting a smoky red beam that met Donna's in a clash of power, creating a swirling dark red mist. Donna coughed as she flew through the dissipating haze, but when it cleared, Augustin was nowhere in sight. Below, the auditorium lights dimmed as the double doors began to close. Donna dove toward the auditorium and slipped through the closing doors just in time.

Donna walked into the middle of the auditorium, tightly gripping her wand as she scanned the dimly lit space. The sound of footsteps echoed from the rear of the room. Casie and Tamia emerged from the shadows.

"How does it feel being in the Coven?" Casie asked, drawing her wand.

"The Coven is trash," Donna retorted, the wand of Solomon gleaming in her grip.

"I've been waiting for this." Casie smirked, launching a red energy beam at Donna.

The beam struck the ground, blasting Donna into the air. She landed hard on her side, pain shooting through her.

"Get up, you waste of Coven's blood," Casie sneered.

Donna quickly rolled aside as another blast from Casie scorched the wall, leaving behind streaks of burn marks. Casie, fueled by rage, unleashed a flurry of beams.

"Kulinda," Donna said, projecting a purple translucent shield around her.

The shield held firm, absorbing the energy assaults with a hum.

"That's all you got?" Donna challenged.

Casie bombarded Donna with more beams. Donna, kneeling behind her shield, braced as the impacts ricocheted off, gouging the floor around her and filling the air with smoke.

"Kutoweka," Donna whispered, circling her wand around her body, vanishing as the smoke thinned.

"Where are you?" Casie growled, scanning the clearing smoke.

Donna, barely containing her laughter, enjoyed Casie's bewildered expression.

"I'm right here," she taunted, darting away unseen.

"Show yourself, you Bronx lowlife!" Casie yelled, frustration mounting as she fired a beam at the wall.

Creeping up behind Casie, Donna whispered in her ear, "Someone's big mad."

"Where are you!" Casie screamed, blasting aimlessly.

Seizing the moment, Donna reappeared, firing a stun beam that knocked Casie to the ground.

Donna turned to see Tamia approaching, her wand raised menacingly.

Chapter Forty-Four

Two Rebel guards, Monique and Rima's college friend Gary, were stationed outside Lincoln's door. Although confident in his abilities against them, Lincoln chose stealth over confrontation. He stood up and pulled his wand from his pocket.

"Kutoweka." Gazing into the mirror, he smirked at the empty space where his reflection should have been. "Swaggy." He chuckled.

He knocked on the door.

"Yes, Lincoln," Monique answered.

"I need to use the bathroom."

"Alright. But no funny business. You hear me?" she cautioned.

"Yep."

Monique and Gary had confused looks on their faces as they opened the door.

"Where is he?" Gary said.

They entered the room, and Lincoln reappeared in the middle of the doorway.

"Did you guys know there were spells that only Solomon could perform?" he asked.

They looked shocked, clearly baffled by how he'd appeared out of nowhere.

"Yeah, me neither. But good thing he's my ancestor," Lincoln said, swiftly sealing the door behind him with a flick of his wand.

Lincoln emerged through the secret passage into the college's study hall. Professor DuVernay was tending to Rima, who sat propped against the wall, grimacing as he wrapped his shirt around her bleeding arm. Lincoln hurried over.

"What are you doing here, Lincoln?" Rima asked.

"I came to help. Are you okay, Ma?" he asked, kneeling beside her.

"My arm is a little busted, but I'll be fine when I get some healing paste."

"Go back now, son. Augustin and the Elders... they're too strong," Professor DuVernay urged.

"Charles, we are DuVernays. We don't back down; we keep faith. And right now, Lincoln and Donna might just be the hope we need," Rima countered, wincing as he tightened the knot around her arm.

"You're right. Lincoln, go strip Augustin's powers. We believe in you," his dad said, placing his hand on Lincoln's shoulder.

"Last time we saw her, she was near the Gardens. Go kick some ass," his mom said.

"Bet! Say less... Love you," Lincoln said, darting out.

Running as fast as he could, Lincoln reached the living quarters where the Rebels were holding steady with their containment spells around the dorms. The hypnotized students were shooting beams from inside, creating red and blue flashes of lights against the cloudy shield.

Mr. Espree attacked Annette from behind, while she was administering the containment spell. Lincoln quickly intervened, blocking the energy beam with his shield and countering with a stun that sent Mr. Espree sprawling.

Two Elders dismounted from their brooms, firing multiple beams at Superb, who was defenseless. Nnamdi leapt from his broom, absorbing the beams with his shield.

"Lincoln, good to see you, fam," Nnamdi said.

"I couldn't let my best homie get beat up by Elders," Lincoln joked, joining the fray with a stun beam of his own.

The skirmish escalated as more Elders swooped in. Suddenly, an Elder's body plummeted from the sky, landing with a thud near them.

"It was him or me," Mr. Jenkins declared, landing beside Lincoln. "Go find Augustin. Not sure how much longer we can hold them off."

"I can't just leave y'all here."

"We will be fine," Nnamdi said, shooting a stun beam at another Elder.

"I saw Donna flying toward the auditorium. You and your sister are our last hope. Go, now!" Mr. Jenkins urged.

With a determined nod, Lincoln mounted his broom and soared away. Suddenly, he was blindsided and knocked off his broom by Darius, who cackled as he zoomed past. Lincoln whistled sharply, summoning his broom back to him. He caught it and swiftly regained his footing just inches from the ground.

"Careful. You almost died, and we need your blood," Darius said, smirking.

Darius rammed into him again. Lincoln extended his leg and kicked Darius away. As Darius tried another time, Lincoln pulled up on the handle of his broom, flipped backward, and avoided the attack. Darius lost his balance and fell through the air.

"Kukamata!" Lincoln shouted, firing a red beam at an enormous magnolia tree. A branch stretched out, wrapping around Darius and breaking his fall gently.

"Careful. You almost died," Lincoln called out mockingly. "And you're welcome!"

Lincoln quickly dismounted his broom upon reaching the auditorium and dashed inside, where he found Tamia aiming her wand at Donna, who held up her shield.

"Tamia, don't do this!" Lincoln said as he sprinted towards them.

Tamia turned to him and shot multiple beams that Lincoln blocked without firing back. She grabbed an orb from her pocket, mounted her broom, and soared towards the roof. Lincoln chased after her, flying agilely. As she turned to attack, Lincoln redirected her beam to the front of her broom, causing her to hurtle towards the ground.

In a swift motion, Lincoln spun his broom, caught Tamia by the arm, and saved her from a deadly fall.

"I got you," he said.

Tamia tried to pry herself free. Lincoln hurried to the ground, but she kept pulling away, slipping out of his grasp. Lincoln jumped off his broom and grabbed her. He positioned his body toward the ground, absorbing most of the impact.

"Lincoln, are you okay?" Donna asked.

"Yeah. The fall wasn't that bad," he grunted, rubbing his shoulder.

Tamia stood over him with her wand pointed to his face. She suddenly fell to the ground, immobilized. Donna stood by with her wand drawn.

"What did you do that for? I had her," Lincoln protested.

"No, she had you wrapped around her finger," Donna replied, helping him to his feet.

Click... Click... Click... Click... Click... The distinctive sound echoed from the dark rear of the auditorium.

Lincoln knew the sound of those heels. He readied his wand.

"There's no point. While my daughters kept you two occupied, my Elders captured all your Rebel friends. It's over. Join me," Augustin declared as she stepped into the light.

"Never," Donna said.

"Yeah, it's gonna be a NO for me," Lincoln added.

"I only need one of you alive. If you don't join me, one of you will die. So, what will it be?" Augustin challenged.

Lincoln glanced at his sister, her wand raised and ready. Donna gave him a firm nod.

"Let's stand on business, big bro," Donna murmured.

"We got this," Lincoln affirmed, returning her nod.

Facing Augustin again, Lincoln lifted his wand with determination. "We said no. You old witch."

In unison, Lincoln and Donna unleashed stun beams at Augustin, who swiftly countered. The beams met in midair, mingling and whirling into a vortex of profound colors.

Augustin pushed forward, funneling more power into the growing ball of energy between the three wizards.

"Mom, stop. Please," Jay said, entering the auditorium.

Augustin pushed the ball of energy upward. It quickly blasted through the ceiling, tearing the building's roof apart.

They all lifted their shields as debris fell to the ground.

"My son disobeys me too? I guess Casie is the only one who can have her free will. She's my favorite anyway," Augustin said, firing a stun beam at Jay. He fell to the floor.

Augustin pointed her wand to a door at the rear of the auditorium.

"This has gone far enough," she said.

The closet door swung open, revealing Catherine bound to a chair. A red ropelike substance was wrapped around her neck.

"Zaidi," Augustin chanted.

The substance flared bright red and tightened around Catherine's neck. She struggled to breathe, gasping for air.

"Mama!" Donna cried.

"Drop your wands," Augustin ordered.

Lincoln and Donna slowly lowered their wands.

"Please, don't hurt her," Donna pleaded, tears welling up.

"I said drop your wands!"

They both dropped their wands. The sight of his sister's defeated expression and the harrowing sound of Catherine's labored breathing fueled Lincoln's rising anger. His skin grew hot, his heart raced, and an intense throb pounded at his temples.

"You will surrender and join my quest, or I will kill her," Augustin threatened.

Despite Lincoln's warning headshake, Donna's gaze shifted toward the wand of Solomon on the floor. She made a move to grab it, but Lincoln acted swiftly, stunning her with his wand before she could reach it.

"Sorry, lil sis. I can't let you do the spell. It's my burden to bear," he said gently, easing her to the ground.

Lincoln glanced at his mother, and his heart rate began to increase, his body became prickly, and his lungs began to compress. He placed his hand over his heart—it felt as if it were beating out of his chest.

"Good job, Lincoln. I knew you were smart enough to join me," Augustin said.

Lincoln closed his eyes. *I am the master of my powers.*

"I will never join you."

Grabbing Solomon's wand, he let his power surge freely through his body. Suddenly, his senses sharpened, bringing the world into a hyper-clear focus. His body felt lighter, almost ethereal. Lincoln was now in pure-wizard form, but this time, entirely in control.

"Kinyume!"

He blasted Augustin with the power-stripping spell. Black smoke enveloped her, then began to encircle him, lifting them both off the ground.

The force of the spell shattered the auditorium's windows, flinging doors wide open. Elders rushed in, firing energy beams, but using his left hand, Lincoln deflected each attack with stun beams, knocking them to the ground.

More Elders and hypnotized students flooded the auditorium, shooting beams at the swirling black cloud of smoke, but Lincoln enclosed himself and Augustin in a translucent shield that absorbed the attacks.

Lincoln's body pulsed as the black smoke wove through his body. Clutching the diamond wand firmly with both hands, he pushed forward, channeling a final, mighty surge of energy. The black smoke completely enveloped Augustin, sealing her in her fate.

The winds began to ease, and slowly, both Lincoln and Augustin descended to the ground amidst settling debris.

Lincoln dropped the wand and stared at his hands. He couldn't feel the power that once ran through his body. He felt nothing.

Weak and disoriented, he collapsed to his knees beside the now still figure of Augustin. Her once formidable presence rapidly decayed before his eyes—hair graying, skin wrinkling, and body shrinking until she was nothing more than a fragile shell of her former self. Moments later, she disintegrated into ash, swept away by a gentle breeze, leaving nothing behind but the echo of her lust for power.

Chapter Forty-Five

Still weak and disoriented from the stun beam, Donna crawled to Lincoln and placed her hand on his back.

"I'm fine. I'm just exhausted. Go check on Catherine," he said.

Donna rose shakily to her feet and rushed to Catherine, quickly undoing her bindings. "Mama," she gasped.

"I'm okay," Catherine reassured her, her eyes wide as they fixed on Lincoln, who was now standing. "I know that face... Link."

"Yes, Mom. It's me," Lincoln replied.

Catherine gripped the arms of her chair as she attempted to stand. "I can do this, baby girl. Let me walk to my son," Catherine insisted, gently refusing Donna's offered help.

Taking small steps, she moved toward Lincoln, who quickly closed the distance and took her hand in his.

"I had forgotten how much you resemble your father," she said softly, caressing his cheek before pulling him into a tight embrace.

"Your touch is just like I remembered, warm and safe," Lincoln said.

Donna walked up and wrapped her arms around them.

"It was you, wasn't it? In New York, outside my window. That wasn't just a dream," Catherine said.

Lincoln nodded, his eyes moist.

Catherine tenderly wiped away his tears. "How? What is all this?" she asked, gesturing around them. "I saw magic coming from your hands. I saw wands, flying brooms, and all sorts of things..."

"We have a lot to tell you, Ma," Donna said, gently squeezing her mother's hand.

"Thank God they're okay," Rima said, walking into the auditorium. Professor DuVernay was close by her side.

"I knew they would save the day," Mr. Jenkins chimed in, his voice trailing behind them.

A group of students entered the auditorium from a different entrance. Leading the way was Raine.

"Pawpaw!"

"Raine. Raine. You're okay," Mr. Jenkins said, taking off running like a much younger man.

They met in the middle of the auditorium, where Mr. Jenkins lifted her in a joyous spin, his laughter filling the space.

"What happened?" Raine asked. "The last thing I remember is when Augustin requested I come to her office for a meeting."

"I'll tell you everything, just let me look at you first," Mr. Jenkins said, taking a step back. "Ah, yes. You're still the best looking in the family. Besides me," he jested, laughter warming his words.

The mood shifted as Elders began to file into the auditorium. Rima, Professor DuVernay, and Mr. Jenkins raised their wands defensively.

"Augustin is dead," Rima announced. "You Elders can surrender, and the wizard community will hold a trial to determine your guilt. Or meet the same fate as Augustin. You are outnumbered and have no leader. Make the wise decision and drop your wands."

More Rebels entered with their wands pointed at the Elders. Donna smiled, seeing Chad walking with Nnamdi and Chike.

After a tense silence, the Elders dropped their wands.

Jay, Tamia, and Casie stood solemnly around the spot where Augustin had fallen. Tamia sank to her knees, her sobs echoing in the auditorium. Jay comforted her, while Casie remained still with a vacant stare on her face. Tamia crawled over to Casie and grabbed her arm. Finally, Casie fell into her sister's arms and cried in her chest.

"Do you really remember me?" Lincoln asked, looking at Catherine.

"Of course I do... You still look like that three-year-old boy I kissed on the forehead when Sammy took you on that camping trip. Wait... Is he still alive too... your father?" Catherine said, her face lighting up with joy.

"No," Lincoln said, dropping his head. "He was murdered by Augustin, the wizard that captured you."

"Hey, it's okay, son. I have you. That's more than enough... Both of you," she added, turning to Donna and brushing her cheek tenderly. "Donna, I saw how you defended me. You were so strong, so confident."

"I learned it from you, Mama," Donna replied, embracing her mother tightly.

"Cathy, do you remember us?" Rima asked, stepping forward with Professor DuVernay.

"No one has called me that in a long time."

"We are Sammy's old friends from college," Professor DuVernay said.

"My Lord. Yes! I remember you two. We met once at dinner at your grandmother's home."

"We sure did," Rima confirmed with a smile.

"Charles, Sammy had so much love for you. He thought of you like a brother," Catherine said.

Charles looked away, rubbing his eye. Rima wrapped her arms around him.

"We are so sorry, Cathy. This is our fault," Rima said.

"When that lady captured me last night, she told me what happened," Catherine said. "That you saved my son and raised him as your own. She thought I would be upset, but I was grateful that he had you to look out for him. I am no wizard. I couldn't keep him safe, not after what I just witnessed."

Professor Decken and his father walked into the auditorium, disrupting the tender reunion.

"What is the meaning of this?" President Thibodeaux demanded. "You have violated the laws of the Wizard High Council."

Rima and Professor DuVernay raised their wands at them.

"Nice of you to join us, Mr. President. We want to report that your Council has been compromised," Rima said.

"Compromised by who?" he countered sharply.

"You and the rest of the wizards and Elders who took part in Augustin's plan," Rima replied.

"How dare you accuse me of such a thing! I will have you tried for treason."

"Only if the truth dawa doesn't reveal your involvement first, Mr. President," Rima retorted. "You and the rest of the Council, wizards, and Elders who conspired against the bylaws and constitution set by the original members of the Uprising will pay for your crimes, including the murder of Solomon."

President Thibodeaux drew his wand, his face a mask of fury.

"Kuua!" he yelled.

His wand fired off a red spinning disc with a spiked outer rim.

Professor DuVernay stepped in front of Rima, casting a shimmering purple shield just in time. The disc collided with it and ricocheted back, striking President Thibodeaux in the chest and sending him crashing to the ground.

"Father!" Professor Decken rushed to his side, kneeling beside him.

Professor Decken frantically checked for signs of life, then drew his wand. "He's gone!" he cried out, pointing his wand at Rima with trembling hands.

"Dean, don't do this. It's over," Professor DuVernay urged, his wand ready.

"What do I have left? I'll lose everything," Professor Decken said, his voice breaking.

"You will face a fair trial, as will all who sided with Augustin. Don't make it worse, Dean. Think of your family," Rima said gently.

"Dad, put your wand down, please," Tamia pleaded.

"Put it down, Daddy," Casie echoed, slowly walking to him. "You're all we have left."

Casie continued to walk to her father, taking small steps. "Daddy, we love you. We need you. Put the wand down."

Professor Decken slowly lowered his wand. Casie stepped forward, gently taking it from his hand before letting it fall to the floor. Then, without a word, she wrapped her arms around her father.

As students and faculty poured into the auditorium, confusion spread among those who couldn't recall recent events. The Rebels, along with Rima, Professor DuVernay, and Mr. Jenkins, gathered to explain the situation and began collecting the wands from the Elders and their allies.

"Donna! You're okay," Noor said, maneuvering through the crowd.

"We did it. It's finally over," Donna replied, hugging her best friend.

"I stunned about a hundred Elders," Chike boasted as he approached.

"No, you did not, knucklehead," Nnamdi said beside him.

"I'm just glad you all are safe," Zina added.

"Have any of you seen Jia?" Donna asked.

"No, I couldn't find her," Noor said.

The others shook their heads.

"I'm sure she's fine. She's probably on her way here now," Chike said.

Donna felt a tap on her arm. When she turned around, Chad had a big smile on his face.

"You and Lincoln did it. I knew you would."

"Thanks... Glad to see you're safe too," she said, suddenly feeling awkward under the watchful eyes of the group.

"I had to stay safe because I still owe you dinner at my grandparents' house." he said, offering his hand.

Taking his hand, they stepped slightly away from the crowd.

"I'm looking forward to this date," Donna said, blushing.

"It's a date?"

"Yeah. You asked me to dinner and I said yes."

"I've never been on a date before," Chad confessed.

"Neither have I," Donna admitted, her voice softening.

"I'll bring my A game then."

"Just be you. I like you how you are."

"Yo, Chad, how many Elders did you stun?" Chike called out.

"I lost count, ya heard me."

Donna glanced over at Lincoln, who was conversing with Tamia. Despite the conversation, there was a hint of sadness in his posture. He stared down at his hands, shaking his head slightly. Tamia gently grabbed his hands and caressed them. He looked over to Donna and they locked eyes. And then she knew.

My brother has lost his powers.

Chapter Forty-Six

*H*ey, *Notebook,*

It's been a while. It's pretty late right now, but I can't sleep. Maybe because I'm too happy? It's cold in New Orleans, not as cold as New York, but it's still cold enough for a cozy fire in the fireplace. This couch isn't comfortable, though. I don't see how Mr. Jenkins slept on this thing.

You know, I started writing to you because I was in complete shambles after Mom got sick, and I needed someone by my side. I think I loved writing to you because I was really talking to myself, encouraging myself, lifting myself up, and doing everything I could to help find my confidence. And guess what???? I finally found it. I am strong. I am resilient. I am beautiful. I am courageous. I am confident.

I want you to know that I have a real family now. I have a mother AND a brother, soooo cool, right??? Mom is doing great, by the way. She's been in New Orleans for two weeks and decided we are moving here permanently. The DuVernays are letting us live at their second home until we find our own house, which is especially cool because I like using the training facility. I've been working on mastering pure-wizard form. Jacquie moves in next week. She found an opening at a real estate firm here. I know Norms aren't supposed to know about wizards, but I'm sure she can keep a secret, especially now that she's dating one, LOL. Gary is going to break the news to her soon.

Nawlins has reopened, and since we didn't have a Chancellor, the students and faculty elected a new one. Professor DuVernay won by a landslide. It's been hard calling him Chancellor DuVernay, but I'm getting used to it. His first action was to terminate the wizard ranking system and any group on campus that discriminates by bloodline. No more ugly lettermen jackets. Speaking of the Coven, Casie doesn't say much in class and always looks like she's in low spirits. At least she, Jay, and Tamia have each other. Oh, and Jia moved back to France. She emailed me and Noor and told us Nawlins feels too dangerous now. I've been trying to call and text her, but she doesn't answer... It really feels like I lost a friend.

The Rebels' High Council took over as the leaders of the wizard community with Rima as president. They charged the Elders with major crimes against magic and stripped them of their ancient wands. They are in some kind of probation period to see how they are adjusting to living a life outside of the wizard community. How are they going to fit in with the Norms? They were once these mighty old wizards planning to take over the world until they were stopped by a teenage girl and her big brother. Haha! Serves them right! Good should always prevail in this world.

Notebook, I feel so bad for Lincoln. He's always smiling and joyful at home with our mom, but when he's at school, it's like he's not himself anymore. It's like being around wizards sucks the joy out of him. I would feel the same if my powers were gone. I can't imagine what it feels like walking the halls of Nawlins and thinking you don't belong there anymore. He even talked to my mom about transferring to another school, but it's too late because he's graduating this term. Sometimes I wonder if he blames me. He always says he's okay, but I can see the pain in his eyes. I know that pain. It's the pain of losing something that you love so much. It kills me that I can't help get his powers back. I hope having Mom and I back in his life will replace what he lost. I'm sure Tamia is helping him too. So happy that they are together. He also has his special spot by the lake. I think he's still there right now because I haven't heard his motorcycle pull up. It's really late. I should fly over there to check on him, but I wouldn't want to intrude on his alone time.

Well, I love you, Notebook, but this may be my last entry. I'm happy now, and I know that's what you wanted for me from the beginning. And most importantly, I finally feel special. I was so scared to be vulnerable because I felt like no one would be there to save me if I failed. But the only person I truly needed was myself. It turns out that self-love was the key to confidence all along... I mean, not to brag or anything, but I did kinda save the world, LOL... I promise I'll always keep you safe, just like Mary Ann kept her journal safe. You never know... maybe you will help one of my descendants someday.

Epilogue

The humid air clings to my skin as I sit on the hard steps by the lake, staring at my father's wand in my hand. Once, I could feel the magic coursing through me, a power so alive, so uniquely mine. Now... there's nothing. The wand feels like a relic from a life I no longer belong to. I used to be a Deslondes—a ONE. Now, I'm just a Norm, a damn nobody.

Still, I have no regrets. Stripping Augustin of her powers had to be done. She was too dangerous; her vision of a war between wizards and Norms was too catastrophic to allow. Even knowing it would cost me my own magic, I wouldn't hesitate to make the same choice again.

"Lincoln."

I freeze. The voice came out of nowhere, soft and almost melodic.

"Lincoln."

There it is again. A woman's voice, soft and distant, cutting through the night. I scan the darkness, but there's no one around, just the lone streetlight above me casting a faint glow. I know I'm not tripping; someone called my name. I can feel my heart beating out of my chest as I continue looking for the culprit.

Then, out of nowhere, Jia steps into the light.

"What the..." I mutter, scrambling to my feet.

It's her, but not her. Jia looks... different. Older. Taller. There's something eerie about her presence, like she doesn't quite belong in this moment. Her white dress clings to her frame, which appears to be slimmer, and her skin slightly greyish, almost sickly.

"Jia? What are you doing here?" My voice wavers.

"Lincoln, Lincoln, Lincoln," she says, smiling as she steps closer. "It's good to see you again."

"Where have you been? I thought you moved back to France. My sister has been worried about you."

"Ah, yes. I heard the news about you two. Descendants of Solomon... Isn't that something? But there was always something different about you, Lincoln. I could never figure it out, but I was right," she says, stepping closer to me.

I narrow my eyes, trying to make sense of her words. "How did you find me here?"

She takes another step closer, her voice soft and hypnotic. "I smelled your blood... all the way from the French Quarter."

My stomach drops. "What?"

"There's so much you don't know, Lincoln. About me. About yourself. About what's coming."

"Jia, you're not making any sense," I say, taking a step back.

"You know, I'm supposed to be graduating this year with you. I'm really eighteen in human years. But sixty in vampire years," she says.

"Huh?"

"You see, just like wizards... oh, right. I forgot you're not a wizard anymore. What a shame. But just like wizards, vampires have some unique abilities too. We age slowly. Like, really, really slow. We're strong. We can see into the past. And our blood can be used for hypnosis... A very long time ago, Augustin put me into a deep sleep, along with others of my kind. Then, just a couple years ago, she woke me. At that time, I was about fourteen in human years. But the sleeping spell preserved my youth because in truth, I'm supposed to be three hundred years old."

"What are you talking about, Jia?"

"Can you please stop calling me that? My name is Belle... When she woke me up and took my blood, I used the energy I had left to bite her neck. I saw all of her memories and discovered everything I needed to know about Nawlins and the wizards and why she needed my blood, which was for her stupid hypnosis dawa. Then, Augustin struck me with an energy beam and left me for dead. But I was actually turning into the creature I despised most: a wizard."

"Um, Jia... I mean, Belle. I have to go," I say, walking away.

She lunges forward, grabbing my arm with a grip so cold it feels like ice against my skin. Her strength is terrifyingly inhuman.

I try to yank my arm free but it's no use. She pulls me closer, her eyes glowing like amber crystals.

"Don't be rude, Lincoln. I'm not done talking."

She lets me go and I rub my arm. Damn, that hurt.

"Anyway, I didn't know I would turn into a wizard because a vampire had never bitten one before. But I could feel that same power I had seen in Augustin's memories. After that, I broke out of my coffin and laid eyes on the other fifty coffins at the Ursuline Convent. I tried to wake my family, but I didn't know how. So, I found a wizard family in France to adopt me. It worked out perfectly because they didn't want kids, just money. So, I became their twelve-year-old daughter entering her first year at Nawlins. I only wanted to find a way to wake my sisters and seek revenge on Augustin. Every time I saw the Chancellor, I wanted to kill her and her daughter. Not your precious Tamia; Casie, I couldn't stand that little witch. You know, Lincoln, being a wizard felt good, but being a vampire feels so much better."

She opens her mouth, licking her lips. And now I see her long sharp teeth.

"Oh, hell nah," I mutter, turning to run, but this girl is fast—really, really fast. What would I do for my powers right now? For a broom? But I'm just a Norm. I'm helpless.

She appears in front of me in a blur, blocking my path with ease.

"Stop running," she says, her voice calm, almost amused.

My legs tremble, and I stumble back. She's toying with me, circling like a predator.

"Belle... please," I stammer, my voice barely a whisper.

"You're so cute. I wonder how Donna will feel once you belong to me. I did enjoy her company... Aw, she can be my sister-in-law," she says.

Her cold hands grip my shoulders like iron. She tilts her head, her lips brushing against my neck as she inhales deeply.

"The veins in your neck," she whispers, her voice trembling with delight. "Très beau."

I twist and pull, desperate to get away, but her strength is overwhelming.

"Don't fight it," she says, her voice soft but commanding. "This is your destiny."

With all the might I have left, I pull away again. My shirt tears completely, freeing me from her grasp.

"Help! Help!" I yell. But no one is out here. I'm alone, like I always am when I come here this late at night.

I run toward the steps of the lake. I could jump in. I don't think vampires can swim, can they? I don't care; it's worth the try. I'd rather risk my life being swept away by the currents than die being drained of blood by a vampire. I'm almost in... one more step...

Bam!

I don't think I've experienced pain like this. Her punch must have tossed me back twenty feet. I grab my ribs; yeah, they're broken, and I can tell I have a collapsed lung by the way I'm gasping.

"The bad boy tried to run again... tsk, tsk, tsk," she says, prancing my way.

I'm too tired to fight and too hurt to move. I just lie on the grass, looking up at the stars.

I'm not scared. I'm sad. I'm sad because I'll never see my mother again, my little sister, or my parents.

I smile as I think of Tamia's soft lips touching mine. If I die here, I'll die happy knowing I loved her with all my heart.

"Tamia," I cry out as a tear slips from my eye.

Belle climbs on top of me.

"Don't worry, you will only love me now."

She starts to laugh hysterically.

"Funny isn't it, how things work out? Augustin killed my sister and yanked her teeth out of her mouth, all because Colette fell in love with a wizard. And now, you're about to fall in love with me. Think of this gift I'm about to give you as a thank-you for killing her. Once Augustin died, her sleeping spell was lifted off my sisters, and I turned back into a vampire. My body was so weak then, I had to quench my thirst from a Norm boy. Don't worry, I didn't turn him because I didn't feed him any of my blood, and I let him live after I wiped his little memory of me. But I have far bigger plans for you... Speaking of my sisters, here they come."

A white girl with pale skin, freckles, and red hair stands above me.

"Bonjour. Je m'appelle Juliette."

Another girl slowly walks closer. She has the longest hair I've ever seen. She kneels down and gets closer to my face. Her brown skin is almost translucent, just like her sister's.

"He's beautiful," she says.

"Back off, Eloise. He's mine," Belle snaps.

The last girl looks older. She has short hair and sharp features. She sniffs at me, then looks me up and down with a disgusted face.

"He's human, how can he help us?" she asks, pulling out a bag of blood from her purse.

She pierces the bag with her teeth. After she takes a few gulps, she hands the bag to her sister.

"Thanks, Gertrude," Eloise says, taking a sip.

Gertrude wipes her mouth with her hands, then licks her fingers.

"That's it, eat up. In a few more days we will be back to full strength. And relax, big sister. Lincoln is the key to our dynasty in this city. He comes from the strongest wizard lineage. His mom is now the president of the council and his father is the new chancellor of Nawlins."

"He should die. All of the wizards should die! I will tear them apart!"

Gertrude opens her mouth and launches at me. Belle grabs her by the neck and pushes her away.

"Enough! We will get our revenge. But times have changed. There are thousands of wizards now. We can't go on a killing rampage. We have to follow laws and rules. We can't bring unwanted attention to our plan before we are ready."

"Who made you the leader? You are the youngest!" Gertrude says.

"Those years I spent as a wizard aged me. I am more than capable of leading. Challenge me if you want that title."

Gertrude flashes her fangs but Belle doesn't flinch. After a tense few seconds, Gertrude frowns and walks away.

"Did the other families wake yet?" Belle asks.

"We just checked the convent," Eloise answers. "They are awake but weak, barely moving their eyes."

"Good. The lack of blood should slow them down for a while. Which gives us some time to reclaim our territory in the city."

"I'm still hungry," Eloise whines.

"Moi aussi," Juliette says. "Hospital bags aren't as tasty as fresh blood."

"Get used to it. Like I said, times have changed. We can't just go around feeding on townsfolk like we used to."

"Belle, please let me go," I plead.

"Oh, mon amour, it will be over soon."

Belle opens her mouth, and with her fangs, slits her tongue. Blood trickles down her chin as she methodically coats her fangs with it, each movement deliberate and almost ritualistic.

And then I feel it. Her fangs sink into my neck, and pain explodes through me. My body jerks violently, and my vision blurs. Memories flood my mind—hers, not mine.

It's 1729, and she's been brought to New Orleans from France, and forced to be married off to a local boy. But it's not just her: it's her three sisters and many other girls. They are dragging caskets from their ship. Men of all ages are waiting for them by the dock. I want to tell the men to run, but I can't. I'm in a purgatory state where I can't move or talk—I can only watch. The girls flash their teeth and bite the necks of the men, draining their blood until they die.

The vision skips many years ahead, but Belle doesn't age. She's at the Ursuline Convent in the French Quarter. The front door bursts open. My God, it's Solomon and Augustin.

"You killed a wizard. Now we will kill you all," Augustin says.

A fight breaks out between the wizards and the vampires. The vampires scatter, trying to escape, but Solomon casts a cloudy containment spell around the perimeter. The vampires run to the third floor and hide in their caskets. Solomon and Augustin burst through the door.

"Wait!" Augustin says as Solomon points his wand at the caskets. "What if more of their kind come and find them dead? We will have a war on our hands."

"What do you suggest we do?" Solomon asks.

"I found an eternal sleeping spell from *The Book of Giza*. They will stay alive until I undo the spell."

"I agree, we do not want a war. But I am afraid this will come to haunt us, Augustin."

"Kulala," Augustin says, pointing her wand over the caskets.

A red energy beam shoots from her wand, then quickly turns into a smoky substance. The smoke seeps into the cracks of the coffins.

The portal is closing. I want to cry out to Solomon, but I can't.

Belle yanks her teeth from my flesh and the visions fade. I'm desperately gasping for air. My chest feels like it's on fire, my veins burning with something dark and powerful.

"Lincoln," Belle says, kneeling beside me. "It's over now. You're one of us."

My body contorts. My heart feels like it's being crushed from the inside. I roll on the ground to try to ease the pain, but it is no use. I can see my chest inflating and deflating as my veins protrude from my skin. With each breath, it feels like my lungs are getting smaller. I keep thinking about my mother, sister, and Tamia, but my body wants me to forget them. As I fight to keep their memories in my head, my heart crushes more and more, as if my love for them is sucking my life away. I have to hold on! I can't give up! Their love is all I have left.

"Mama! Donna! I'm sorry I can't hold on," I say, straining every word.

I bury my hands in the ground, doing everything I can to fight the pain.

"Donna! Bring me back!" I yell with my last breath.

Complete darkness. It's the only thing I see. The pain is gone... but its replacement is thirst. My mouth feels so dry and bitter. It's like I can taste the salt in the air. My vision is starting to come back. The light pole far away is overbearingly bright. I put my hand up to my eyes as I continue to blink.

My vision is... so clear... so sharp. I can see so far away; the outlines of the stars above look like I could almost grab them.

My eardrums pound as I take in the sounds. The waves crashing into the steps sound like I am right by the water.

Oh, I smell her. I smell Belle. She smells so sweet. As I look into her eyes, I can feel our connection.

And then I feel it. My teeth ache, and I realize what's happening. My hands tremble as I reach for my mouth, feeling the sharp edges of fangs cutting through my gums.

"Drink," Belle says, offering her wrist.

I try to resist, but the hunger is too strong. I bite down, her blood flooding into me like fire and lightning.

It feels... Incredible.

I feel... Powerful... Invincible... Alive.

I'm not Lincoln Deslondes anymore.

I'm something else.

Something monstrous.

Something unstoppable.

About the Author

DERIC AUGUSTINE is a New Orleans native who has carved a unique path through the arts, blossoming from a theater performer into an acclaimed actor, writer, and producer. His artistic journey began in the vibrant theater scene of New Orleans, leading him to pursue Theatre and Drama at the University of New Orleans. After graduating, Deric honed his craft in New York City, studying at the prestigious Negro Ensemble Company and William Esper Studio. Deric's acting credits span a variety of significant roles in television and film, including appearances in "The Rookie," "All American," "Cloak and Dagger," "Swagger," "Shameless," "Queen Sugar," "Godfather of Harlem," and many more.

Follow him : @DericAugustine

Nawlins.net

Socials: Nawlins_Series